PROOF
OF
LIFE

PROOF
OF
LIFE

R.J. ELLORY

ORION

First published in Great Britain in 2021 by Orion Fiction,
an imprint of The Orion Publishing Group Ltd.,
Carmelite House, 50 Victoria Embankment
London EC4Y 0DZ

An Hachette UK company

1 3 5 7 9 10 8 6 4 2

A CIP catalogue record for this book
is available from the British Library.

ISBN (Hardback) 978 1 4091 9856 7
ISBN (Trade Paperback) 978 1 3987 0395 7
ISBN (eBook) 978 1 4091 9858 1

Typeset at The Spartan Press Ltd,
Lymington, Hants

Printed and bound in Great Britain by Clays Ltd,
Elcograf S.p.A.

MIX
Paper from
responsible sources
FSC® C104740

www.orionbooks.co.uk

Acknowledgements

This book was born out of an abiding fascination for the political and social upheavals that filled the newspapers, magazines and television screens of my childhood. Researching the events I remembered was both nostalgic and unsettling, if only because it highlighted the fact that so very little has changed in the last five decades.

I also have to acknowledge writers such as Fleming, Forsyth, Ludlum, Deighton and MacLean, whose works and adaptations were so thoroughly addictive, entertaining and transporting for a lonely, introverted kid.

My thanks go to Emad Akhtar and Tom Witcomb at Orion for letting me write a very different book, and for their wisdom and utterly invaluable support during the editing process.

Last of all, my heartfelt gratitude goes out to my readers, without whose unfailing loyalty I would be dead, in jail or on the run.

LIVE
BORDERS

I

Airports, like crowded cities, seemed a perfect contradiction to Stroud.

People escaping, people returning, the swollen hearts of tearful separations and long-awaited reunions, emotions exaggerated inside an endless wave of anonymity: at once both the crossroads of humanity and yet somehow the loneliest places on earth.

From a bench in Schiphol Airport, Stroud watched faces and eyes and body language. A girl alone, beautifully fragile. A small man, muscle-bound and furious, patience tested in every direction as he hurried his wife and children along the concourse. An elderly luggage attendant, carrying not only the world-weariness of someone to whom things just happened, but also the knowledge that he was powerless to change them.

Stroud wanted a drink, badly. He wanted another cigarette but had smoked too many already. He had decided to go back to London and face the music. If he knew one thing, it would not be a melody he wished to hear.

In truth, Stroud's primary motivation for leaving Amsterdam was money. The flight, the hotel, the promise of a further two hundred pounds just for showing up. 'No obligation, no expectation,' he'd been told. Marcus Haig, subeditor at the foreign department of *The Times*. Long ago, they'd been compatriots.

Despite the time, the distance, the memories they both wished to forget but perhaps never would, they'd remained friends.

'Just come and talk to me, Stroud. Let me tell you what's happened, and you can decide if you want to get involved.'

Involved didn't sound like something he wished to become.

'Two hundred pounds. Cash.'

'No promises, right?'

'Christ almighty, Stroud, just get on the sodding plane, will you?'

No matter where he went, Stroud carried the same things. His cleanest dirty shirt, his ever-faithful camera, his notebooks, his pens. He carried shadows and awkward memories, moments of his life that seemed hollow and unrelated to anyone or anything else.

Behind him were a number of failed relationships, none so significant or burdensome as his marriage, the bitter divorce that followed, the daughter he'd left behind. Eva. A girl he'd not seen in a decade. As had been said, it would all be okay in the end. If it wasn't okay, it just wasn't the end.

Stroud wanted to believe this. He *needed* to believe it.

The flight out of Schiphol was delayed. Stroud found a bar, drank two doubles, smoked three more cigarettes. The news played on TV in the background. The Israeli Defense Forces had pulled off a rescue mission at Entebbe Airport in Uganda. Two hundred and forty-six passengers and twelve flight crew had originally departed from Tel Aviv. A layover in Athens saw a further fifty-six passengers and four hijackers board the aircraft. The hijackers took control, diverting the plane to Benghazi for refuelling, and then continuing to Entebbe. Once there, a number of hostages were released – the elderly, the sick, mothers with children. They were flown to Paris, and it was from these people that Mossad had secured their intelligence. Full details were not known and would not be known for some time. Regardless, an Israeli mission had been initiated, and the hostages had been rescued with negligible collateral damage. Prime Minister Rabin and Defence Minister Peres were outwardly resolute, inwardly jubilant.

Stroud was thirty-seven, looked at least forty-five. He had covered everything from Khrushchev in the US, the Belgian Congo, the OAS insurrection in Algeria, the Paris riots of '68, Biafra, Yom Kippur and Palestine to the Black September hostage crisis at the Munich Olympics. Between March of '65 and February of '68, he'd been into Vietnam nine times. In March of '75, just a little more than a year ago, he'd been asked to cover the fall of Da Nang. He'd refused. By that time, too many seams had come undone.

For the last year he had drifted without anchor. Prague, Paris, a couple of weeks back in London, back again to Paris and then south for warmth and wine. In Montpellier he had met a girl. Elise Durand. She was from Marseilles, so there was fire and violence in her blood. Stroud was English: stubborn, prone to bouts of harsh self-criticism, so quick to find blame elsewhere. Hard now to say which of them was more damaged. Their relationship had been a car crash of personalities. Drunken sex, hangover arguments, often unnecessarily recriminatory and bitter. With hindsight, even though it was only three months in the rear-view, Stroud knew that neither and both of them were to blame. Their union had been one of strangers, to one another and to themselves. The person he'd been with Elise was now someone he would not recognise. As was the case with so many love affairs, people tried so very hard to be that which was desired, forgetting who they really were in the process.

Leaving Montpellier, Stroud had headed for Amsterdam. Despite its supposedly libertarian and free-thinking reputation, he found the city self-absorbed and unengaging. He had stayed in a series of shabby hotels, money running out fast, and when Marcus Haig had called him, he had been down to his last few hundred guilder. He had considered fleeing the hotel, but they'd checked his passport on arrival. Haig – one-time foreign correspondent, a man who'd dodged bullets and venereal disease on three continents – was settled in London, holding down a nine-to-five, married, a family, and yet requiring of help for some unspecified task. If he had called Stroud, then whatever he had in mind was foolhardy and potentially fatal, and he had run out of options.

Stroud had worked with Haig on the Sharpeville massacre in March of 1960. They'd covered the Elisabethville killings in the Congo, the Greek–Cypriot war just four years later, and together they'd watched the horrors of Biafra unfold. The last time they'd shared column inches was in Dacca. In an attempt to subvert Bangladesh's hopes for independence, Pakistan had resorted to genocide of the Bengalis. For Haig, it had been the last in a long line of horrors. 'If I stay, I will lose my mind or my life,' he'd said, and left the next day.

Haig was a good man – tough, uncompromising, yet somehow forgiving of others where he would not forgive himself. He was a professional, through and through, and Stroud didn't resent the man his Chelsea flat, nor his weekend place in St Albans. Of course, the wife had money. She came from a long line of money. Haig had been seduced and tamed by it.

It was through Haig that Stroud had met his wife. His ex-wife, to be exact. Marcus Haig and Julia Montgomery were cousins, and Haig had been the inadvertent catalyst that brought them together.

For Stroud, Julia Montgomery had represented everything he had once believed unreachable.

For Julia, Stroud had been a challenge, perhaps more of a challenge than she'd anticipated. Each promised the other a life they could never have otherwise had.

What he'd imagined he would find in her he didn't know, and still didn't understand. Perhaps some kind of peace, some sense that not everyone in the world was hell-bent on self-destruction. What she had found in him was the absence of routine and predictability, at first exciting, after a while merely exhausting and fraught with worry.

'You have a death wish,' she said. 'It's not normal.'

'You didn't marry me for normal.'

'Sometimes I wonder what I did marry you for.'

'Because you thought you could make me into the husband you really wanted.'

'You weren't this cynical when we met.'

'You weren't this complicated.'

'I can't talk to you. And frankly, I have lost the will to listen.'

And Stroud – weary, a little battered, feeling like a stranger in his own life – would smile and say no more.

They'd met in 1960. Between coverage of Berliners escaping the east in April and Belgians fleeing across the Congo River, Stroud had been back in London. A private art exhibition in Kensington, his attendance secured by Haig's promise of infinite free booze and good-looking, unattached rich girls. He had gone, was immediately out of place in leather jacket and shabby boots, spent much of the time haunting the open bar, glass of Scotch in his hand, listening to people he didn't understand talk about pictures that made no sense.

'You don't belong here.'

That was Julia Montgomery's opening line.

'There are very few places I do belong.'

She smiled and introduced herself, said she was Marcus's cousin.

'I'm Stroud.'

'What's your first name?'

'I'm just Stroud. Have always been called Stroud. I don't answer to anything else.'

'Why are you here?'

'Honestly? Haig told me there'd be an infinite supply of free booze and good-looking single rich girls.'

Julia smiled. 'I might be one of those good-looking single rich girls he promised.'

'How rich are you?'

She laughed suddenly, sprayed Stroud's sleeve with champagne. She grabbed a serviette. 'Shit, I'm sorry,' she said. 'That's pretty disgusting.'

'If having pretty rich girls spray you with champagne is disgusting, then all I can say is that you've led a very sheltered life.'

'You're one of Marcus's war junkies, aren't you?'

'Is that how we're known?'

'Isn't that what you are? I mean, seriously, why would you want to risk life and limb in some godforsaken hellhole on the other side of the world that no one even knows about?'

'So that people *do* know about it.'

She looked at him wilfully, held his stare. She was beautiful, no doubt, but there was something cold and aloof and altogether disconnected about her.

'And you really think what you do makes a difference?'

'I don't want that discussion with you,' Stroud said. 'You have your own thing. Your wine-tasting and your art galleries and whatever. We're just different people who are interested in very different things.' He nodded towards a gaggle of suited business types on the other side of the room. 'And to be honest, I'm not really into the sort of conversations you have with trust-fund wankers.'

Julia didn't flinch.

'Why are you still here?' Stroud asked.

'I'm waiting for you to get a pen.'

'A pen? Why do I need a pen?'

'So you can write down my phone number, you belligerent arsehole.'

Stroud smiled. 'Just tell me. I'll remember.'

She told him. He remembered. He called her the next day. He took a taxi, paid for on arrival, and he went up to her Knightsbridge flat where they smoked weed and fucked like teenagers.

Stroud married Julia in August of 1961. Her family disapproved. She didn't care. At least not at first. But when his lifestyle and habits gave her cause for aggravation, she never missed an opportunity to remind him of how she really should have taken her parents' advice.

'I should have listened,' she said.

'You don't listen to anyone but yourself,' he countered.

And so it went on. It was not a bad marriage. Not at all. It was just a marriage that perhaps should never have happened. They didn't hate one another. Even their fights were strangely half-hearted. They could have been great friends, and had it stayed that way they probably would have been great friends for the rest of their lives.

Ultimately, the only truly good and worthwhile thing to come out of the marriage – aside from memories of those first wild, passionate months – was Eva, born in May of '62. Their divorce was finalised in September of 1966.

The judge decided that Stroud was 'neither capable nor equipped to provide a stable domestic environment in which the nurturing of a child could be accomplished'.

Stroud couldn't disagree. Besides, his legal counsel was no match for Montgomery money. Julia got sole custody.

Haig stayed out of it, taking neither one side nor the other.

Eva was now fourteen. A while ago Stroud had waited outside her school and watched her leave. She was tall and beautiful like her mother, but she seemed to possess more substance. Delusion it might have been, but he knew that there was something of himself in his daughter, something that would soften and temper the harder facets that Julia wore for the world. If he could only have talked to his daughter – *really* talked to her – he knew he would have been able to make her understand. He had not left her; he had been excommunicated. He had not abandoned her; he had been cast out into the wilderness for various crimes, some revealed, others not. He appreciated one thing, however: she was Eva Stroud, not Eva Montgomery. Understanding Julia as he did, that must have been Eva's choice. He had been there for the first four years of his daughter's life. They had been inseparable. Perhaps there was still a true connection, despite the distance, despite the silence. Stroud so desperately wanted Eva back in his life. He had convinced himself that the sentiment was reciprocated.

On the plane, he drank more. More than he should have, but when did he not? If it was there, he would drink it. If it wasn't, he would find a way to make it there. The blunt fist of alcohol facilitated selective amnesia. He remembered things the way he wanted to, leaving out those moments when he had been the architect of his own undoing. It was a pretence, and he knew it. A lie that he just kept on telling.

One day he would stop drinking, or perhaps it would stop him.

It was gone seven in the evening when Stroud landed. He found a phone kiosk on the airport concourse and called Haig.

'Where are you?'

'Outside the airport,' Stroud said. 'The flight was delayed. Do you want me to come over to the office?'

8

'I have something to do. Let's meet in the morning.'

'I don't have anywhere to stay.'

'But you have money? You must have enough to get a hotel room.'

'I've got about thirty quid, but it's in guilders.'

'Jesus Christ, Stroud.'

Stroud said nothing.

'Do you know the Grange in Covent Garden?'

'I can find it.'

'I'll call them, get you a room.'

'Thanks, Marcus.'

'Bloody hell, Stroud, you really need to pull yourself together.'

'I've been busy. I'll get to it.'

Marcus hung up.

Stroud changed his guilders for sterling and took the Underground into London. The city was suffering a record-setting heatwave. Stepping out into the street, Stroud was sideswiped by the humidity. It didn't serve to improve the place, nor heal the psychic bruises it had left him with. Though it had been his home for more years than anywhere else on the globe, he didn't like it. To Stroud, London represented more loss and grief than any other place in the world. It was here that his life had unravelled. It was here that demons awaited his return from whichever far-flung corner of the world he had last tried to escape from them.

Stroud walked streets that had forgotten what it was like to be rained on, the sky between the too-high buildings a feature-less gunmetal grey. He found the hotel. Haig had been as good as his word and there was a room for him, though he guessed it was the cheapest in the place. Breakfast was not included.

'Would sir like a wake-up call?' the receptionist asked.

'Thank you, no,' Stroud replied. 'Sir would not.'

For a while, Stroud lay awake. The window open or closed, it made no difference. His head hurt. Everything hurt, and the heat just served to exaggerate it. The only reason for being here was because he wanted to know what was worth two hundred pounds to Marcus Haig. It was going to be trouble. Of that he was sure. But what was the worst that could happen? No wife, no family, no house, no money, no job, no prospects. Maybe he was just one step away from having nothing left to lose.

It was with this thought that he fell asleep.

2

'You look bloody awful.'

'That's the welcome I get?'

'Did you run up some horrendous bar tab at the Grange?'

'No, Marcus, I went to bed.'

'Alone?'

'No, Marcus, with your mother.'

Marcus smiled. 'What the hell were you doing in Amsterdam?'

'Looking for the meaning of life.'

'And you thought it might be prostitutes and grass?'

Stroud looked surprised. 'It isn't?'

Haig got up and walked to the window. The view of the city was the same through so many other windows in so many other offices. The view came with the salary, the agreement, the compromise. Stroud doubted he would ever want such a view.

'So, why am I here?'

'I'll get to that,' Haig said. 'First, tell me how you've been?'

'Eating badly, sleeping badly, drinking a bit too much.' Stroud paused. 'Or maybe too little, depending on your perspective. Single, lonely, broke. Don't see Eva, not much hope of seeing Eva. Aside from that, there's been some bad stuff as well.' He restrained himself from asking Haig about Julia. He didn't want to find out that she no longer even mentioned him.

'Whatever else you may have lost, your sense of humour remains,' Haig said.

'When that goes, it will herald the End of Days.'

'And work?'

'Usual things. Freelance bits and pieces, a couple of editorials. I even did a piece for your magazine.'

'You did. It was good. Not great, but good.'

'I am overawed by the generosity of your compliment.'

Haig was quiet for a little while. To Stroud it seemed that he was weighing his words before he voiced them.

'Are you in trouble, Marcus?'

Haig smiled, then laughed. 'I gave up getting into trouble when I stopped hanging out with people like you.'

'But you miss it, right? The rush, the uncertainty, the feeling that everything pulls at you and nothing holds you back.'

Haig didn't reply. He was still pensive, his attention on his motive for summoning Stroud from Amsterdam.

'Seriously,' Stroud said. 'You're all right?'

Haig waved the question aside.

'How's Cathy? The kids?'

'Cathy is fine. The kids?' Haig smiled. 'Noisy. Expensive.'

He returned to his desk, opened the drawer, took from it a bundle of tenners. He flicked through it, then slid it across to Stroud.

'Two hundred. Get a haircut, some decent clothes, for God's sake. You really do look like the rough end of a bad party.'

Stroud pocketed the money. He lit a cigarette and waited.

'Okay,' Haig said. 'In at the deep end. Vincent Raphael.'

Stroud looked up suddenly. Of all the names he'd imagined he would hear, Raphael's was the last.

'What about him?' A strange sense of disorientation invaded Stroud. He felt on edge, uncomfortable.

'He saved your life.'

Stroud nodded. 'More than once.'

'When did you first meet him?'

He shook his head. 'Why? What does it matter? Why are you asking me about Raphael?'

'Humour me, Stroud. If for no other reason than the two hundred quid.'

'I met him here,' Stroud said. '*The Times* employed him. You know this. You were with us. We did the Transvaal and Brazzaville together. And Cyprus. You were there in Cyprus with us too.'

'But I didn't cover Jordan in 1970.'

'No. So what?'

'So I wasn't there when he died.'

Stroud frowned. 'Why are you asking me questions that you already know the answers to?'

'I know you were close. You worked together, did all those trips to Vietnam, then Stanleyville, then the Paris riots. But *how* close?'

'I don't know what you're asking, Marcus. The man was my mentor, my best friend. He saved my fucking life more times than I can recall. Anything I ever did that was worth something in this lousy business was because of what he taught me.'

'Right,' Haig said. 'Right.'

'Tell me what the hell is going on, Marcus. Tell me why I'm here, or I'm leaving.'

Haig looked up. There was something in his expression – a toughness, a sense of resolute determination – that Stroud had not seen for a long time.

'No one really knows what happened to him, do they?'

'Yes, they do. He was killed. Some say murdered. A grenade went through the window of his Land Rover and that was that.'

'And he had half a dozen jerry cans full of petrol in there. According to reports, there was nothing left, not only of Raphael but of the car as well.' Haig paused. 'Right?'

Stroud closed his eyes. He didn't like where this was going.

'You and I both know that there was no body for them to send home. They buried an empty coffin in a small graveyard in Hereford and that was that. He was like you in the end. No wife, no parents, no one who really gave a damn except us, and we were too stunned and grief-stricken to consider any possibility but what we were told.'

'Are you telling me that what happened and what we were told were not the same thing, Marcus?'

'There have been rumours.'

'There were always rumours. It was nothing *but* rumours for months after he died. But that was six years ago. Six years.'

'I know how long ago it was.'

'So what makes whatever rumour you've heard now any different from the rumours back then?'

Haig opened the desk drawer again. From it he took a single photograph. He looked at it for a moment, and then passed it to Stroud.

A street. Somewhere in the Balkans, perhaps. The image was small and blurred, but there appeared to be two men on the corner.

'This is where? Macedonia? Greece?'

'Turkey,' Haig said. 'Istanbul.'

'You're saying that one of these men is Raphael?'

'I'm saying that the person who took the picture says that one of those men is Raphael.'

'And who took the picture?'

'I can't tell you. Let's just say it's someone who would be in the business of being more sure than I am about something like this.'

'And the other man?'

'Institute for Intelligence and Special Operations.'

'You mean Mossad.' Stroud paused. 'So if whoever took this picture would be in the business of knowing the identity of a

British newspaperman, and he was also interested in a Mossad presence in Turkey, we're talking Special Intelligence Service.'

Haig remained silent.

'So, someone from MI6 tipped you off that Raphael was in Istanbul talking to someone from Mossad?'

'Not exactly, no.'

'Then how did you get the picture, Marcus?'

'Look, there may be nothing in it, okay? People get interested, jump to conclusions. Sometimes people have to jump to conclusions so those conclusions can be verified one way or the other.'

'So what are you asking me to do? Go to Istanbul and find out if Raphael is still alive?'

For a few moments there was silence.

Haig didn't need to speak for Stroud to get his answer.

'You are out of your mind.'

'I am well aware that that may be how it appears.'

Stroud turned the picture towards Haig. 'This could be you and me. This could be anyone. This is complete crap, Marcus. Raphael is dead. He died outside Karameh, near the Allenby Bridge. His fucking car blew up and there was nothing left of him.'

'You saw it happen.'

'Fuck off, Marcus. You know I didn't see it happen.'

'Don't you wonder? Even now? Not even a fleeting thought?'

Stroud sighed audibly. He got up from the chair. He patted his pocket. 'Thanks for the contribution to the Stroud salvation fund. I'm going to use some of it to buy a plane ticket, if that's okay with you, but it sure as hell won't be to Istanbul.'

'Before you go, there's something else.'

Stroud shook his head. 'I don't want to know, Marcus.'

'I think maybe you do.'

Stroud sat down again. He lit another cigarette.

'The French are after him.'

'What? All of them?'

Haig smiled wryly. 'How much do you know about French intelligence?'

'Aside from the fact that that opens up another line of wise-cracks entirely, I'd say very little.'

'Direction Générale de la Sécurité Extérieure. That is... *was* France's external intelligence agency. They go all the way back to the late forties. Before that they have a history through the Free French spy network in the Second World War and the Deuxième Bureau. Anyway, back in the autumn of 1965, a Moroccan politician by the name of Mehdi Ben Barka went missing in Paris. He was the head of the National Union of Popular Forces. Anti-monarchists, nationalists, far more extreme than the more established republicans. The guy vanished. Not a trace. French intelligence was implicated. There were rumours that Barka had been kidnapped and murdered by the DGSE. And so the DGSE and its overall administrative senior office were placed under the jurisdiction of the French Ministry of Defence. In essence, the Ministry of Defence *is* now French external intelligence.'

'And these are the people who are looking for Raphael?'

'Strenuously.'

'Why? And what gives them any reason to believe that he's still alive? Surely more than a grainy picture of two people who could be just about anyone.'

'We don't know.'

'We? Who's *we*, Marcus? I feel like I'm in the middle of something written by Fleming or Le Carré.'

'It's just an expression, Stroud. *I* don't know, okay?'

Stroud looked at Haig. He didn't know what to think, didn't know what to feel. The whole thing was sufficiently ridiculous for him to give it no credence. He and Raphael had been joined at the hip. There was only one man who had carried a wilder

16

reputation than Stroud himself, and that had been Raphael. He had been the catalyst for so much in Stroud's career. That he could still be alive was beyond belief. They had lived together, travelled together, almost died together a hundred times. There was no way that Raphael would not have contacted him in the last six years.

Stroud couldn't afford to invest any emotion in the idea that Vincent Raphael was alive. He was dead, plain and simple.

'MI6, Mossad, French Ministry of Defence,' Haig said. 'And *The Times*, of course.'

'And Uncle Tom Cobley and all,' Stroud added, doing nothing to mask his cynicism. 'I'm not interested, Marcus. I don't care who wants to know. I am not buying the possibility that Raphael is alive.'

Haig paused before speaking. He looked towards the window, the view beyond, and then he cleared his throat. 'Okay, for argument's sake, let's just say he was alive. What would that mean?'

'I have no idea, Marcus.'

'It would mean something to you, right? That he hadn't contacted you? After everything you experienced together, I mean.'

'You have no idea what we experienced together.'

'But you do, and so does he. Aren't you curious ... *beyond* curious to know what could have been so important as to make him vanish like that, to contact no one?'

Stroud paused for just a moment, and then he got up.

'I'm not even slightly convinced, Marcus.'

'That's exactly why I am asking you. You're not caught up in the myth of Vincent Raphael ...'

Stroud shook his head and smiled. Haig fell silent.

'It's been good to see you, Marcus. I think you did the right thing, getting out of this ridiculous game. Maybe we'll catch up another time, eh?'

'Two thousand pounds.'

Stroud couldn't conceal his surprise.

'You heard me. That's over and above the two hundred I just gave you. Flights, hotels, expenses all covered, and a flat fee of two thousand pounds to find Vincent Raphael. Either find him, or prove beyond any shadow of a doubt that he really is dead.'

'You are actually serious.'

'As serious as it's possible to be.'

'Why, Marcus? Why are you even giving this your attention?'

'Because I want to know, Stroud. I want to know what happened. I want to know what he knows. If he did survive Jordan and has been playing dead all these years, what has he been hiding from? You have any idea how big a story that could be? Maybe not as big as finding Lucan, but it would sure as hell sell some papers. The mere fact that MI6 say he's talking to Mossad, and then we get word that the French are looking for him but won't say why... Just that alone is enough to get me very, very interested.'

Stroud stood in silence. He knew that Haig could hear his thoughts – loud as church bells.

'Two thousand pounds.'

'Two thousand pounds,' Haig repeated.

'Flights, hotels, expenses.'

'Everything except bar tabs.'

Stroud smiled.

'Not a joke, Stroud. No bar tabs.'

Stroud didn't reply. A million thoughts went through his head. He was feeling things he hadn't felt in years.

'So?'

He looked up. 'Okay,' he said. 'But I'm doing it to prove, once and for all, that he really is dead.'

'What do you need?'

'Photos of him. Clean-shaven, bearded, short hair, long hair. Just give me whatever you've got. I'll need a couple of lenses.

Telephotos. I need another two hundred in cash, an agreement on how I get the rest of the money, whatever visas I need for Turkey. I need a day to pack. I'll leave tomorrow. Get someone to book me a flight. One-way. Cheapest seat. I don't want it known that I'm going, and I don't want to draw attention to my reason for being there.'

'Your passport is up to date?'

Stroud smiled. 'You know me, Marcus. That's pretty much the only up-to-date thing in my life.'

3

It all came back. The heat, the smell, the atmosphere. Byzantium, Constantinople, Istanbul. By whichever name it went, it would always be far beyond anything that could be expressed in words alone. Some said that it was impossible to see this place and remain a disbeliever.

The Grand Bazaar, the Sultan's Palace, Divan Yolu Street. The Lale Restaurant in Sultanahmet, christened 'the Pudding Shop' during the great hippie migration. Once upon a time they congregated for *tavuk göğsü*, *şöbiyet* and *baklava*, to buy hash and hitch rides and convince one another that free love and good acid was the only way to save the world. Booths and couches, books everywhere, an entire wall composed of glass, and from the garden you could see the Blue Mosque and the Hagia Sophia. For a while, the Pudding Shop was the only place to get good information about reliable routes into Asia. They came in their thousands, following the Beatles and Donovan and Mia Farrow, looking for something *out there* that could only be found within. Stroud understood it, sure, but he didn't buy the hype.

Istanbul sat between Europe and Asia. It straddled the Bosporus, and that river connected the Black Sea with the Sea of Marmara and thus the Dardanelles. It was a strategic point on the Silk Road, and though it was not the capital, it was a city far greater in history and significance than Ankara. Here were Turks, Greeks, Kurds, Armenians and Arabs; here you could hear a dozen languages, and a dozen more dialects within, as you merely crossed the concourse at Yeşilköy. The entire breadth of the Anatolian peninsula between the Black Sea and the Mediterranean had left its footprints and fingerprints here – from the Gulf of Alexandretta to the Armenian Highlands, and beyond that, from neighbouring Georgia, Soviet Azerbaijan, Iran, Iraq and Syria.

The city itself was just as Stroud remembered. Nothing would really change it but the passing of centuries.

Stroud took a cab from the airport to the Sultanahmet district. He found a small hotel off Atmeydani. He wanted to be within walking distance of Divan Yolu, the park, the local government and newspaper offices, but in a place that was sufficiently shabby and nondescript to attract no attention. He paid in cash, said very little, and refrained from making eye contact with anyone but the desk clerk.

In Istanbul, all Westerners looked and sounded the same. Despite his dirty blond hair and stubble, Stroud hoped that his face would be as unremarkable and forgettable as everyone else's.

By mid afternoon, the heat was close to unbearable. Stroud wished he'd been a little more selective. He opened the windows and got the smell of the river, beneath that the faint stench of spoiled meat and rotting vegetables. He took a walk, found a place that sold a half-decent bourbon. He bought two bottles, two dozen packs of Turkish cigarettes and a box of assorted *baklava*. With his bag of provisions, he sat outside a small café facing the Arkeolojik Park. He ordered a medium-sweet coffee, smoked a cigarette, watched the world for a while.

As with all such things – finding local contacts, beginning to establish a network of reliable informants, locating a bolthole in case things got rough – he had to merely select a point at which to begin. It was the same with any new job, any new location. Journalism was investigation. It was asking questions in such a way as to get required information without becoming the subject of investigation oneself. He was no stranger to this, but now the motivation was very different.

As was the case with those who lived extraordinary lives, Vincent Raphael was even more a myth in death than he had been in life. It had to be said that it didn't take a great deal of exaggeration to make his exploits utterly implausible. He had stretched the bounds of life and living as a matter of course. To an observer, he had been fearless in everything he did. He very rarely gave his word, but when he did, it was never broken. His rationale was simple.

'I don't know if I will be alive this afternoon, let alone to-morrow,' he would say. 'I am not going to promise something I can't deliver.'

Raphael's charm was his frankness, his bravura, his almost reckless disregard for conformity, expectation and the obvi-ous. Well read, of staggering intellect, possessed of a wealth of knowledge concerning the most impressive array of subjects and issues, he could nevertheless be one of the most impossibly stupid people. He didn't appear to think beyond the minute, the hour, the day. He didn't see the future as something inevitable. His own incurable strain of madness didn't often allow for the sensitivities and necessities of others.

But then, with time, Stroud had discovered a different Raphael. Here was the flawed man, the insecure man, but – as was the case with all those left behind – memory granted him forgiveness for his faults.

As far as relationships were concerned, Raphael could love someone for three months, love them with a fury and passion that was all-consuming and obsessive. And then suddenly, without warning, he was gone. He would seemingly forget them in hours, their name and face blurring into one mass of memories that contained all the women he'd ever loved. But in truth, he was as fragile as everyone else.

Stroud remembered one girl specifically. She was American, Californian as far as he could recall. Alice Gerritty. She worked for American Express. Raphael met her, got drunk with her, moved into her company-funded apartment in the centre of Rome and stayed there for nine weeks. Stroud, at first, thought that she meant nothing to him. But then, one night, some situation demanding his attention on the other side of the world, Raphael threw what little he possessed into a canvas bag and vanished. Time and again – much to Stroud's surprise – he spoke of Alice Gerritty and that handful of weeks in Rome. He spoke of her as if some great rend had been torn from his heart, and Stroud saw a side of Raphael that he had never before witnessed. When it came right down to it, others could create just as much as an effect on Raphael as he did on them.

Ironically, Stroud saw Alice again. She asked after Raphael, but Stroud didn't have the heart to tell her he was dead. He just said he didn't know, hadn't heard from him. Alice opened up to him a little.

'You don't think I knew what I was getting into?' she said. 'Hell, whoever thinks they could control that man is deluded. I knew something like that would happen. I'm surprised he was able to stay as long as he did, for Christ's sake.'

'So why?' Stroud had asked her. 'Why get into it if you knew it would end like that?'

'You've never driven way too fast? Drunk far too much? Taken a pill without knowing what it was just to see what the hell happened?'

'Sure I have.'

'That's why. There aren't many people like Raphael. They don't live like anyone else. Hook up to that, it's like sitting on the back of a firework. You appreciate that you might get burned, and sometimes badly, but you're never gonna forget it.'

'And you're not sorry?'

'Look,' she said. 'I know what we had. I know what it meant to both of us. I know how much it hurt afterwards. But if you're asking me if I'd change anything, then no. Even with what I know now, I would do it all again.'

Stroud understood completely. Inviting Raphael into your personal life was like opening the door to a hurricane. When he was there, there was nothing else. When he was gone, there was nothing left.

That he could have survived Jordan, that he could still be alive, seemed surreal. To the Palestinians, to the Israelis, to the Viet Cong, both Raphael and Stroud had been nothing more than journalists, no more significant or insignificant than the rest. That day had been no different from so many others. And then someone threw a hand grenade through the open window of the Land Rover. Had it been intended for Raphael's vehicle? Even if it had, was it an act of impulse, a response to some other factor in which Raphael had played no part? That was a simple fact you very quickly appreciated: in war, there were no favourites. There was no way Raphael could have escaped in time. The force of the blast was heard for a half a mile; it blew the vehicle apart, sent people flying.

It was the Palestine Liberation Army who confirmed Raphael's death. There was no body to send home because there was no body to recover from the wreckage. Raphael's funeral had been a memorial and a homage to a man who had not known how to live his life any other way. The small church in Hereford had been crowded with colleagues, associates, acquaintances, former employers, even a couple of SAS men who had been able to keep up with him on his drinking binges. There were no family members. In truth, it was hard to even imagine that someone like Raphael could have had parents at all. More than likely, he'd been launched into being fully grown and fierce from the barrel of a cannon.

That was Raphael, and that was everything he was.

Stroud intended to approach this undertaking in as impersonal a manner as possible. Whether or not he would manage that had yet to be seen, but that was the plan.

The first thing to do was look up anyone he might know at the *Hürriyet Daily News*. An inside line would give him access to newspaper archives, additional contacts, research facilities and the like. Failing that, there could be someone who had known Raphael and might be willing to help.

He dropped off his bourbon and cigarettes at the hotel and took a cab out to Güneşli. The traffic was heavy and it took more than an hour. It gave him time to think of all he'd tried so hard to forget about his friendship with Vincent Raphael.

They'd met in London in the autumn of '59. Stroud was twenty, and had been freelancing for a while already, seen a little of Europe, spent a hair-raising couple of weeks in Haiti. Raphael was six years his senior.

Stroud just happened to be at the reception desk of *The Times* when Raphael came bursting through the doors.

'Stephanie!' he'd shouted, and the receptionist had left her chair and come around the desk to meet him. He tossed her a paper bag. She caught it.

'Tell Hunter there's a gold mine in that lot and not to fuck it up.'

And then he was gone.

The bag was full of rolls of undeveloped film.

'You're taking stuff up to Barry, right?' Stephanie asked. She handed Stroud the bag. 'Take that for me, would you?'

Barry Hunter was deputy commissioning editor for *The Times* Sunday magazine.

'Raphael was here?' was Hunter's first question.

'That's what Stephanie said. He dropped these off, asked for them to be delivered to you.'

'Bugger,' Hunter said. He sat down heavily.

'You needed to see him?'

Hunter looked up. 'Who are you again?'

'I brought some stuff over from the Central Press Agency.'

'You work for Simon Broome?'

'I do, yes.'

'He still as much of a self-absorbed wanker as he always was?'

Stroud laughed.

'I'll take that as a yes, then.'

Stroud started for the door.

'Can you develop film?'

'Sure.'

'What's Broome paying you?'

'Twenty-one quid a week.'

'Jesus, my wife spends more than that getting her hair done. You've done overseas stuff?'

'Some, yes.'

'Okay. I can use another snapper. Stay here, develop this lot, do whatever else is needed in the picture department and I'll give you twenty-five.'

They shook hands.

That was where his career with *The Times* had begun. His next meeting with Raphael would be in Berlin a year later. By that time, he had seen action in the Belgian Congo, covered the French Riviera flooding, and as he turned twenty-one, he was in the Transvaal with Marcus Haig reporting on the Sharpeville massacre.

*

At the *Hürriyet Daily News* office, Stroud was referred to a man called Murat Kaya at the foreign desk. He was heavy-set, short, immediately suspicious.

'You are English?' he asked.

'I am, yes.'

'From which paper?'

'Freelance.'

'And you want the Turks to help you find another Englishman.' It was a rhetorical statement.

'His name is Vincent Raphael,' Stroud said.

'What makes you think we know anything about him?'

'Nothing.'

'Then why come here?'

'Professional camaraderie.'

Kaya stared at Stroud for a good fifteen seconds, his expression serious, almost intimidating, and then he burst into laughter.

Stroud started laughing too.

'Show me a picture of this Englishman,' Kaya said.

Stroud passed one across the desk.

Kaya's reaction was immediate. There was no disguising his surprise.

'I know this man,' he said. 'Or at least I knew him. That was many years ago. Eight, perhaps ten.' He started to shake his head. 'This man is dead. He was killed.'

'Yes,' Stroud said. 'That was the report.'

'I think the report was correct, no? He has been dead for some years now.'

'There are rumours that he may not have died.'

'Rumours from where?'

'I don't know,' Stroud said. 'My understanding is that the French are looking for him.'

Kaya seemed lost in thought for some time. He stared at the

photograph of Raphael. Every once in a while his eyes flickered as if in recognition of something.

'This man was destined to die young,' he eventually said.

'What makes you say that?'

Kaya looked up. 'You knew him?'

Stroud nodded.

'Then you do not need to ask the question.'

'So you've not heard or seen anything of him for several years.'

'No, I have not.'

Stroud took back the picture and gave Kaya the name of his hotel.

'If you think of anything—'

'Of course,' Kaya said.

Stroud got up.

'We have an expression in Turkey, Mr Stroud. Perhaps you have heard it.'

'An expression?'

'He who looks for the dead must wish to join them.'

4

The following morning there was a message from Kaya at the hotel desk. It simply read: *Ask for a man called Aydin Bekarys. Perhaps he can help you*, and gave a telephone number.

Stroud asked the girl at the desk about the area code.

'That's an Ankara number,' she said.

His first thought concerned Kaya. Why was he helping him? There was no advantage, no money, nothing. If Stroud knew one thing, people – most people – didn't do anything unless there was a specific motivation. Personal benefit, financial gain, even guilt. Very rarely did they do anything from some deep-seated philanthropic impulse.

He asked for an outside line and was directed to a small hooded phone kiosk at the far end of the lobby. The call would be billed to his room. He restrained himself from calling Kaya. Instead he called the number given.

The all-too-familiar click and hum of a recording system could be audibly discerned as the call connected.

'Millî İstihbarat Teşkilatı,' a voice said.

Stroud's heart stopped for a second. MİT. Turkish National Intelligence.

'Hello,' he said.

The voice at the other end – a man – switched effortlessly from Turkish to English.

'Yes, sir. How may I help you?'

'I was looking for someone,' Stroud said. 'Aydin Bekarys.'

'And what is the nature of your business, sir?'

'I'm a journalist. I was referred to Mr Bekarys for a comment on an article.'

'Very good, sir. Please hold.'

Stroud wished he was somewhere less public than the foyer of the hotel. The girl behind the desk paid him no attention. The door to the street was mere feet away but someone could enter at any moment.

'Yes, hello. Who is this?'

'My name is Stroud. I was given your name by a mutual acquaintance.'

'Who?'

'Murat Kaya.'

There was a moment's hesitation.

'From the *Hürriyet Daily News*—'

'I know Kaya,' Bekarys said. 'Who are you?'

'I'm a journalist.'

'And why did Kaya give you my name and number?'

'He thought you might be able to help me.'

'With what?'

'I'm looking for someone.'

Again a moment's pause, and then, 'Turkish National Intelligence is not the lost-and-found department, Mr Stroud.'

'No, of course not. I understand that, but—'

'Who is it you are looking for?'

'An English journalist. Vincent Raphael.'

'Who do you work for?'

'I work for myself. I am freelance.'

'You paid your own expenses to come here and look for this man?'

'Well, no, not exactly.'

'Then who do you work for, Mr Stroud?'

'It's not as formal as that. I am not under contract to anyone. I came here as a favour to someone.'

Bekarys didn't respond. His silence was an invitation to elucidate further; more than that, it was a condition.

'I have an old friend at *The Times* newspaper.'

'*The Times* newspaper,' Bekarys echoed.

'Yes.'

'And what makes Murat Kaya think that I can help *The Times* of London find this Vincent Raphael?'

Stroud didn't reply. He was on the back foot. He felt as if he was being interrogated, every answer queried, every question challenged.

'Might I ask who *you* work for, Mr Bekarys?'

'You know who I work for, Mr Stroud. I work for Undersecretary Gürgüç.'

'Everyone at MİT works for Undersecretary Gürgüç. I meant which department, which office…'

Again Bekarys paused, and then he said, almost as if it was of no consequence at all, 'I work in counter-intelligence liaison for the National Security Council.'

Stroud's thoughts unravelled quickly. Bekarys was a spymaster.

'Have you ever heard the name Vincent Raphael, Mr Bekarys?'

'I have heard a lot of names, Mr Stroud. I cannot be expected to remember every one.'

'This is just one name, Mr Bekarys. An English name. Do you ever recall hearing that name?'

'Are you conducting an investigation into this matter for the London *Times* newspaper?'

'No, Mr Bekarys. I am trying to find someone for a friend. That is all.'

'When did you arrive in Istanbul, Mr Stroud?'

Stroud wondered how Bekarys knew he was in Istanbul. Perhaps because of Kaya. The newspaper offices were here.

'I arrived yesterday.'

'And you spoke to Mr Kaya in person?'

'Yes, I did.'

'I do not believe that I can help you, Mr Stroud,' Bekarys said. 'I do not remember anyone of this name, and I am uncertain why Mr Kaya felt that I might be able to assist you.'

'Perhaps because you are the national intelligence organisation. I can imagine there is very little that happens in Turkey that you don't know about.'

'Oh, I think you overestimate our resources, Mr Stroud. Now, if there is nothing else...'

'One more question, if I may?'

'Please.'

'Do you have any idea why the French Ministry of Defence might be interested in Raphael? Why they might have someone stationed here taking photographs of a man they suspect might be Raphael? Do you have any notion of why such a thing might be, Mr Bekarys?'

Bekarys laughed. 'I have no notion whatsoever, Mr Stroud. It sounds as if you Englishmen have concocted a *Boy's Own* adventure for yourselves.'

The line went dead.

The woman at the desk registered nothing as Stroud crossed the lobby and headed for the lift.

The fact that Kaya had given him up to Bekarys was troubling. Stroud was in no doubt that that was what had just happened. But there was something more than that. It was Bekarys' manner, the apparent humour in his final comment. That tone had been intentional. Bekarys had just warned him off in the most indirect way possible.

By the time Stroud reached his room, he was already experiencing a very significant degree of unease.

5

The world in which Stroud lived was one of confidences and contradictions, promises and blatant perjury. There were no laws, only agreements, and yet such agreements were broken with the same significance as superstitious men broke spent matches: it happened without thought, a matter of routine.

The feeling of ever-alertness, a cat on hot coals, was all too familiar. Stroud had not felt it for a long time, and yet it returned like some old friend from years past, the conversation picked up as if it had paused only the day before.

He was a newsman, a photographer. This, above all, had been his life, his calling. He had neglected a wife, a child, and lost them both. He had sacrificed heart and soul to this, and yet somehow had allowed himself to slide into self-pity and a sense of entitlement. Anything worth having had to be fought for; that much he knew from experience. So how had he slid so far from his own motives and ideals? How had he allowed himself to become this pathetic?

He stood at the window of his hotel room and looked at the Istanbul skyline. Changing hotels would be nothing but a delaying tactic. Wherever he went he would be required to show his passport. If they wanted to speak to him, the National Intelligence Organisation would find him, no matter what evasive action he took.

The urge to call Kaya was strong. It would come as no surprise if Kaya was also MİT, a plant within the news network, capable of accessing all manner of newspaper records, an entire research staff at his disposal, but also there to suppress, propagandise, exaggerate and run the disinformation lines so vital in times of political upheaval, civil turmoil and social unrest. And then there were the electoral campaigns, both local and national, and the degree to which the news outlets could influence public opinion. *The Wall Street Journal* had its share of CIA, *The Times* and the *Telegraph* had their people from MI5 and MI6. Turkey would be no different. And if Kaya wasn't MİT, then why had he directed Stroud to Bekarys? Why would he want government intelligence to know of Stroud's interest in Raphael? To mislead him? To derail his efforts? Why would a newsman – if Kaya really was nothing but a newsman – want to stop a freelance journalist from England looking for a man believed to be dead for the past six years?

Questions without answers.

Stroud took a drink and sat on the edge of the bed.

He remembered a South African expression he'd heard: if you want to go quickly, go alone; if you want to go far, go together. Speed was of no real concern. Haig would fund this thing until it was done, or until he sufficiently tired of it. Stroud was working alone in this country, now potentially hostile. He knew no one, possessed no real resources or contacts. He needed help, preferably an insider, someone who knew the ropes, could speak the language, had some degree of familiarity with the kind of tradecraft that might be applied by those intent on stopping any further search for information about Raphael.

He understood then that he was thinking of Raphael as alive. It was ridiculous. Nothing had happened to suggest he was anything other than dead.

But if that was the case, then why did Stroud's existence here in Istanbul warrant any attention at all?

He shrugged off the impending sense of paranoia. He needed to eat, to sleep. He would review it in the morning, perhaps there finding a more rational frame of mind with which to consider his situation.

Downstairs, he asked the woman at the desk for a good restaurant within walking distance.

'Meyve Bahçesi,' she said, looking up from a book. 'From here to the left, left again. There are many lights outside. You cannot miss it.'

'What does it mean?'

The girl shrugged. 'I don't know. Fruit garden, maybe. Like an orchard, I think.'

'Your English is very good.'

She half smiled. 'I try. I watch the television. American television. You are English, yes?'

'I am, yes.'

'I think it is raining all the time there.'

'Most of the time, yes.'

'I would like to go to London. And Paris and Rome and Vienna. I would like to travel in Europe.'

'What is your name?'

'Nadire.'

'A beautiful name.'

The girl's expression didn't change. Perhaps she feared that Stroud was embarking on some ill-fated attempt at seduction.

'Enjoy your dinner,' she said, and went back to whatever she was reading.

Stroud followed her directions. The restaurant was busy, but there were one or two empty tables near the kitchen. The menu was simple and traditional. He ordered *köfte* with sides of bulgur *pilavi* and fried aubergine. He accepted the waiter's recommendation of a bottle of Boğazkere despite the price. It came, it was good, and he drank two glasses before his food arrived.

His thoughts turned to his parents. He'd not seen them since Christmas. Dinner had been stilted, his mother making comments about how nice it would have been to have Julia and Eva with them, 'like a proper family'. His father just diverted the conversation to his standard track of banality with a single 'Now, Kathleen...' The conversation turned to the weather, the expected chill, the fact that the neighbours three doors down were now the owners of some sort of terrier that yapped and howled all hours of the day and night.

'I've a good mind to write a letter to the RSPCA,' Desmond had said, but both Stroud and his mother knew he would never do any such thing.

Stroud cared for his father, of course, but he seemed such a caricature of small-mindedness and lack of ambition. Desmond had been a quantity surveyor. He'd taken an apprenticeship right out of grammar school and stayed with the same firm for the entirety of his working life. At thirty years of age he'd been called up, served five years in the Army Pay Corps, the closest he'd ever come to action being the obligatory field exercises, assault courses and shooting ranges. He'd been demobbed, gone back to work, and never said a word about it.

Stroud's mother, Kathleen, was different. Even when he was a child, Stroud had seen something in her eyes that told of a deep-seated frustration, even anger, that she had been dealt a life so dull and monotonous. She had encouraged her son's adventurous streak, and Stroud believed that she was somehow urging him to live the life that she herself had always desired. If she couldn't do it, then he would do it for her. A life by proxy.

And so, as Desmond remonstrated about Stroud's lack of security, the fact that he hadn't even established a good pension plan, Kathleen remained wordless. Stroud took this as a silent protest against normality, an unspoken vindication of her son.

Stroud's food came. He hadn't realised how hungry he was,

and he ate quickly, ravenously. He had consumed half a bottle of wine when he became aware that someone was standing beside his table looking down at him.

'Mr Stroud,' the man said.

Stroud looked up, stopped chewing. He frowned.

'You are Mr Stroud, are you not?'

Stroud nodded. He swallowed. 'I am. Who are you?'

The man smiled. The expression was one of practised calm, but it still appeared supercilious. 'May I join you?'

'Who are you?' Stroud asked again, an immediate uneasiness invading his lower gut. He looked back towards the door. There were two other men there, in dark suits and topcoats. They didn't look directly at him, but there was no doubt in his mind that the three had arrived together.

'My name is Orhan Yilmaz,' the man said in impeccable English. He drew out a chair and sat across from Stroud.

Without asking, he lifted the bottle of wine and looked at the label. 'A good choice, Mr Stroud. This comes from the Diyarbakir province in the south-east. Near the Tigris. Excellent with Anatolian cheese.'

Again without asking, he took a glass from an adjoining table and poured some wine from the bottle. He drank it down.

Stroud set down his cutlery. He leaned back and folded his arms.

'Behaviour like that would see you thrown out of most restaurants in London.'

Yilmaz smiled. 'But we are not in London, Mr Stroud. We are in Istanbul.'

'I can't imagine that manners and courtesy have not made the journey, Mr Yilmaz, especially when I am talking to a man who has been educated in England.'

Yilmaz refilled Stroud's glass, then held the bottle up.

'This is a dead soldier,' he said. 'I believe that this is the term employed.'

He gave an almost indiscernible nod of his head, and within moments a waiter appeared with another bottle. He filled Yilmaz's glass and stepped away discreetly.

Stroud glanced around the room. There was only one couple remaining, and they seemed to be readying themselves to leave.

'Please, Mr Stroud,' Yilmaz said, 'don't let me stop your finishing your meal.'

Stroud pushed the plate away. 'All of a sudden I've lost my appetite.' He lit a cigarette. He didn't offer one to Yilmaz.

'Does anyone refer to you by your first name, Mr Stroud?'

'My parents.'

'Your wife, no?'

'My ex-wife, you mean. No, she calls me Stroud as well.'

Yilmaz took a silver case from his jacket pocket. The cigarettes within were dark, hand-rolled, more than likely custom-made. His suit was tailored, cut in a style that was somewhat old-fashioned, but it was a silk-wool blend that hung beautifully. Yilmaz was no ordinary government bully.

'So, to what do I owe the pleasure of your company, Mr Yilmaz?' Stroud asked.

'Polite even under pressure. So very English.'

'Am I under pressure?'

'Perhaps a little.'

'Because of my telephone call to Mr Bekarys?'

Yilmaz waved the question aside. He drank his wine, refilled the glass once again.

'So who are you? Who do you work for?' Stroud asked.

'I work for the Turkish people. I work for the common good.'

Stroud laughed. It was an immediate and reflexive reaction. 'You are National Intelligence.'

38

'Are we not all part of our respective national intelligences, Mr Stroud?'

'I have no idea why you are here. How did you even find me?'

Yilmaz leaned forward, elbows on the table, his fingers steepled together. The smoke rose from his cigarette and hung between them until he spoke.

'It is my business to know things, just as it is yours, my friend. I know who you are. I know of your career. I know where you have been. Let us say that I am familiar with the apple carts you have upset.'

'I am a journalist,' Stroud said, 'and Turkey signed up for the Universal Declaration of Human Rights along with forty-odd other countries right after the Second World War, Mr Yilmaz. That declaration includes article number nineteen.'

'Freedom of speech, freedom of thought, freedom of the press. I know, Mr Stroud, I know.'

'Then why do I get the very definite impression that you are here to tell me that my presence in Istanbul is not welcome?'

'Did I say such a thing? Have I even implied that I am here for such a reason?'

'Not directly, but then when are you people ever direct?'

Yilmaz feigned both mild surprise and insult. 'Saying such a thing is not mannerly, Mr Stroud.'

'Be straight with me, and I'll be straight with you,' Stroud said, aware that the wine was giving him nerve that he would not otherwise have possessed.

'We know who you are, Mr Stroud. We know where you have been – South Africa, the Congo, Cuba, Cyprus, Palestine, Lebanon, Syria, Pakistan. We know who you know, and we know who knows of you. You are – what shall we say? – a man who does not slip under the radar so easily. You are a trouble-maker, as was the friend you are looking for. If that is indeed the reason for your presence in Istanbul.'

Stroud didn't respond. Yilmaz had raised the dead, and it had been without prompt or invitation.

Yilmaz moved the ashtray aside. He placed his hands flat on the table. His demeanour was quietly intimidating.

'Turkey is a country at peace, Mr Stroud. We have our troubles, of course. All nations have their troubles, but the resolution of those troubles has never, as far as I can see, been aided or expedited by interference from the press. You are a representative of the press, the English media behemoth, and... how shall I put this? Let us just say that I am not of a mind to encourage your continued presence in Istanbul.'

'Are you telling me I have to leave?'

Yilmaz laughed, almost to himself. 'No, Mr Stroud, I am not telling you to leave. You have done nothing that would warrant extradition from our borders.'

'Then tell me what's going on. I came here of my own accord. Yes, I was asked by a friend, and yes, that friend works for the British press, but Vincent Raphael was first and foremost a friend of mine, and certain information has become available that suggests some doubt that he was killed—'

'Mr Raphael is dead, I assure you,' Yilmaz said.

'I am not doubting that fact, nor have I come across anything that would suggest he is alive, aside from the strange sense that I am being discouraged from looking into this matter any further.'

'Politics is a delicate matter,' Yilmaz said. 'The creation, stabilisation and management of a government is addressed not with bombast and marching bands, but with diligence, due care, patience and attention to detail. You, perhaps more than most, understand the nature of what we have endured as a nation, as have so many nations in this part of the world. There are European interests, American too, and perhaps – in time – there will be interest from South-East Asia and the Orient. It is my job, amongst and alongside many others, to see that those interests that serve us are maintained, and those that do not are carefully extricated and removed. Do you understand what I am saying, Mr Stroud?'

'Bluntly, you think that if I continue asking questions about the death of Vincent Raphael, then people you don't want to piss off are going to get pissed off.'

Yilmaz smiled. 'Sometimes forthrightness is so much more effective in making a point.'

'So let me ask you a question.'

'Please.'

'Why would my interest in this matter cause difficulty for the French? And what are the French doing in Turkey?'

'Who says we are talking about the French?'

'Let's just say I made a wild stab at it.'

Yilmaz leaned back. He went through a slow routine of selecting another cigarette from the case, lighting it, even breaking the match. He smoked a third of it, leaning his head back and blowing smoke towards the ceiling, before he finally looked at Stroud.

'If the French are here, though I am not saying they are, and if Turkey has some mutual interest with the French, which could be nothing more than hearsay, then the fact that you have mentioned them tells me all I need to know about the source of this information.'

Yilmaz took a sip of wine.

'Vincent Raphael was not a good man, Mr Stroud. That is, and remains, my personal opinion. He didn't care for the lives he ruined with his inflammatory headlines and unfounded news articles. He met his deadlines, he took his photographs, he made his money... or perhaps he was driven by nothing more than some addiction for danger and mayhem. Regardless, and as is the case with so many of your ilk, he took what he wanted and then left with no sense of conscience or responsibility for the lives that were truly and profoundly affected by whatever war or civil conflict he was reporting on. Yours is not a noble profession, Mr Stroud. Not a noble profession at all. It is a profession for scavengers and vultures. You do not build or create, you do not uplift, you do not assist or support anything. You see what you want to see, you hear what you want to hear, and if it does not suit your editorial brief then you twist it accordingly.'

'You seem to forget that I am not here as a newsman, Mr Yilmaz.'

Yilmaz waved aside the interruption.

'I forget nothing, Mr Stroud.' He extinguished his half-smoked cigarette in the ashtray and swallowed the last inch of wine from his glass. He rose from the chair and looked down at Stroud.

'You have been here twenty-four hours,' he said. 'It has taken only this long for me to find you, to speak to you, to invite you to leave. Whether or not you do is your prerogative. I am not going to force you. That is not my way. What I will advise is that you do nothing that might generate ill-will from those with whom we share common interests.'

Stroud didn't reply. He was angry, his head now clear despite the wine he'd drunk. Yilmaz was telling him to back off, and that was now the very last thing he intended to do. If Raphael was dead, and of this he had little doubt, then someone somewhere was interested in ensuring that something about his death didn't come to light, and Yilmaz – by all appearances – was telling Stroud not to upset them. The photograph in Haig's possession had come from the French. MI6 must have secured it, seemingly without agreement or collaboration. Something was very definitely not right, and Stroud was damned if he was going to let a Turkish spook chase him off.

'I give you my word that I have no intention of upsetting

anyone, Mr Yilmaz,' Stroud said. Even to his own ears he sounded sincere.

'Very good,' Yilmaz said.

Stroud stood up too. He nodded to the waiter for the bill.

'Allow me,' Yilmaz said, and motioned for one of his goons to pay.

'You really are too kind,' Stroud said.

'Not at all.'

Yilmaz extended his hand. Stroud took it. Yilmaz's grip was firm, and he looked unflinchingly at Stroud. His lips smiled but his eyes did not.

'It has been a pleasure,' he said. 'It is refreshing to speak English with an Englishman. I miss it.'

'Oxford?' Stroud asked.

'Cambridge,' Yilmaz replied. 'Most fortunate, you may think. And yet, in this business, it can be both a blessing and a curse to come from a moneyed family.'

He turned and walked to the door. The two goons followed him, their eyes on Stroud until they reached the street.

It was late, but Marcus picked up almost immediately.

'Something is definitely not right, Marcus.'

Stroud tried to pull the kiosk door tight to lessen the sound of traffic. He was close to shouting, and had to strain to hear what Haig was saying in response.

'I need you to check out some names for me... Some names. People I've spoken to.'

'Okay, got it. Go ahead.'

'Murat Kaya. Aydin Bekarys. Orhan Yilmaz.' Stroud spelled them in turn. 'Kaya is a journalist at *Hürriyet*. I think the other two are Turkish National Intelligence.'

Haig didn't respond.

'Marcus, are you still there?'

'Bloody hell,' Haig said.

'One of them found me at dinner. He was fairly straight-forward. In so many words, he told me to get out of the country.'

'Bloody hell,' Haig repeated. 'That's a bit worrying.'

'Yes, I would say it was a bit worrying.'

'What do you think?'

'I don't know what to think.'

'What's the name of your hotel?'

Stroud told him.

'Okay. I'll call you there. There's a fellow I went to school with who works at GCHQ. I'll get hold of him in the morning.'

'Can you send me some more money? I might need to get a flight out of here at any moment.'

'Yes, of course. I'll send another hundred pounds with Western Union. If there isn't a more local office, there'll be a place at the airport you can pick it up. What are you thinking of doing? Do you want to come home or keep digging?'

'Keep digging,' Stroud said.

'Right,' Haig said. 'But take care, okay?'

'Of course, yes.'

'Well, if nothing else,' Haig added, 'we can be sure that someone somewhere doesn't want you knowing what happened to Vincent.'

6

'The shot that kills you is not the one you hear.'

Raphael had told him that. They were drunk, lying low in some shelled ruin on the wrong side of the Bar Lev Line; Raphael had opened up and said things that Stroud had never imagined he would hear. They had just got word that Larry Murtaugh from Associated Press had been blown in two by a landmine. What could be found of him was shipped back to Philadelphia. Apparently his life insurance had lapsed. Perhaps an oversight, perhaps a cost-cutting exercise; regardless, his widow got nothing but some broken cameras and three dozen rolls of Kodachrome.

Raphael was stoic, uncomplaining. Some said cold, unsympathetic, but that was not the truth. As was the case with so many in his line of work, he had merely learned to block out what he felt. That night he confessed terrors and paranoia, and it was then that Stroud saw him not as an icon, but as a contemporary, subject to the same irrational phobias and good-luck routines. Always lace your left boot before your right. Light one cigarette from the last, but only once; a third cigarette gets a match. Quirks and obsessions calculated to appease the name-less deity that governed who would die and when.

'People spend their entire lives trying to make sense of it, and then die ignorant and exhausted,' Raphael said. He smiled wryly. His face was dirty and old. His eyes were polished stones in some river of long-spent tears. 'There is no sense to life, just as there is no sense to death.'

Stroud held his gaze for an eternity, and then Raphael shook his head as if finally reconciling himself to something unspoken.

'You could be dead in an hour, Stroud,' he said. 'Less, even. Or you could live to a hundred. You don't know, and there's no way to find out.'

'Would you want to know?' Stroud asked. 'If you could know the moment of your death, would you want that knowledge?'

Raphael laughed. 'Christ, no! That would be a hideous burden to carry.'

'You would never waste time, though.'

'You don't know what you would do. You could waste even more. Who's to say that knowing you had only ten years left wouldn't make you apathetic? What's the point? Why try and accomplish anything?'

Stroud didn't reply.

'No, my friend, there is no sense to any of it. Unless there is something beyond your three score and ten, then I don't even know what the point of any of this is.'

'People asked me why I chose this life,' Stroud said.

'Same here,' Raphael replied. 'And we all give them the same answer. Where did they get the idea it was a choice?'

7

The sound of the phone was shrill and invasive.

Stroud had been dreaming of a time in Stanleyville when he, Raphael and Haig were laid up in a makeshift medical facility, all of them vying for the attention of one overworked Swiss-French nurse called Veronique. As he and Haig dozed feverishly, he remembered Raphael reading *Les Fleurs du Mal* to Veronique as she fell asleep.

Fighting to hold onto the sound of Raphael's distant voice, he turned over and reached for the receiver.

'Stroud?'

'Marcus. What did you find out?'

'Not a great deal, unfortunately. Seems that your man Kaya is who he says he is. Bekarys is National Security Council, but low-level. A desk guy, a functionary. This Yilmaz character, however, is a different kettle of fish. He's National Intelligence, like you said, but according to the info we have, he retired three years ago, apparently on medical grounds.'

'Where's that come from?'

'My source here.'

'Well, he's making home visits with a couple of goons.'

'Did he say he was National Intelligence?'

'Not directly, no. I said he was and he didn't deny it.'

'That doesn't really give us anything, does it?'

'Whatever he is or whoever he works for, he doesn't like the fact that I'm here.'

'What do you want to do?'

'What I want to do and what I need to do are two different things.'

'You think there's anything further to follow up in Istanbul?'

'This is where your photo was taken. This is where your apparition presented itself. That photo came from the French, and Yilmaz is trying to keep the French sweet for some reason.'

'If you think you're in danger and you want to get out, I will understand, Stroud.'

'I can't leave here until I have somewhere else to go that promises to be more fruitful.'

Haig was silent.

'I suppose I need to speak to the French,' Stroud said.

'You think that's wise?'

'You can't let fear stop you getting to the truth.'

'Raphael used to say that, didn't he?'

'He did, yes.'

'You know, it wouldn't seem right if you wound up dead as well,' Haig said. 'I never believed I'd be the last one of us to go.'

'No one's going to wind up dead,' Stroud said, disbelieving of his own words even as he uttered them.

Stroud went to the same restaurant, ordered the same food. He didn't care whether Yilmaz's goons were watching him or not.

He drank wine and thought about Eva. More than ever, she was on his mind.

What a fucking mess.

He remembered an incident when the truth of what he had married into had really hit home.

It was Eva's second birthday. Everyone from Julia's side of the family was present, no one from Stroud's. That had been

48

intentional. Bitter experience had demonstrated that Donald Montgomery took any opportunity he could to belittle anyone who wasn't blood. Stroud's parents had come under scrutiny on two occasions – once at the wedding, once at Eva's christening party – and on both occasions had been found sorely wanting in all aspects. Stroud's father, a man of relatively few words and never one to curse, had called Montgomery 'a boorish bloody pig of a man'.

That second birthday had been a catastrophe of insinuations and snide remarks. Everything from Eva's clothes to the colour of her bedroom rug had been criticised.

'When Julia was two, we felt it was important that she had...' seemed to be the precursor for every scathing belittlement that Donald levelled at Stroud. That was his true skill: to say the most unapologetically vicious things as if he was merely pointing out the obvious. While recommending ways in which he felt things could be improved, he was actually eviscerating you with a filleting knife.

That day, of all days, things came to a head between Stroud and Julia's father.

Montgomery had taken him aside, literally taken him by the arm and led him away from the throng.

'So, how are things?' he asked. The smile was there, always there – that sly, supercilious expression that spoke of how much he was looking forward to this next fusillade of defamatory comments.

'Things are good,' Stroud replied.

'They're good,' Montgomery repeated. *You may think that*, he was saying, *but it certainly doesn't appear to be the case from where I'm standing.*

'What do you want, Donald?' Stroud had asked, already tiring of the game.

Montgomery closed his eyes for just a moment. Was he counting to ten?

'What I always want,' he replied. 'The best for Julia and Eva ... and you, of course.'

'Of course, yes.'

'Is everything okay between you and Julia?'

'Yes, Donald.'

'And is Eva happy? Does she seem happy to you?'

Stroud willed himself to be patient. 'Look, Donald, it's Eva's birthday party. We are here for her, not for anyone else. If there's something you need to say, just say it. I have to be completely honest and tell you that I am growing weary of this bullshit game you seem to endlessly play.'

'I think that's a little uncalled for,' Montgomery said.

'I don't think it's uncalled for at all,' Stroud replied before Montgomery had a chance to go on. 'I understand that you don't like me. I understand that your wife doesn't like me, but I actually believe that she would be perfectly content to get to know me and give me a chance if it wasn't for you. You have soured her opinion of me. I can only imagine it's a matter of time before you start to sour Julia's opinion of me. I know you think I'm a good-for-nothing, unreliable, hopeless hack, but there's a fundamental difference between you and me, Donald. You want to know what that is? Well, I'll tell you. I may very well be a good-for-nothing, unreliable, hopeless hack, but what you see is what you get. I am who I am. I know who I am. People who take the time to get to know me quickly find out that I am exactly who I appear to be. If I say I'm going to do something, I'll move heaven and earth to see that it's done. If I make a promise, I'd die rather than break it. I don't wear different faces for the world, and I don't pretend to be something I'm not.'

'I think this sort of thing is completely unaccept—'

'Just shut up for once in your life, would you? I'm not finished.

I may not be even remotely like the sort of husband you had in mind for Julia, but I am the one she chose. You didn't choose me, Donald, she did. The mere fact that you are trying to undermine me and get her to leave me tells me that not only do you have no respect for me, you also have no respect for her. You won't even grant your own daughter the right to live her life the way she wants to live it.'

'I've never been spoken to like this in my life!'

'Well it's about fucking time you *were* spoken to like this. You back everyone off with your bravado and your ignorant fucking opinions, and yet I see right through you, Donald. I see you for the bigoted, unsophisticated, loud-mouthed bully you really are. This isn't the schoolyard any more. This isn't some teen-age pissing contest. We're adults. We have responsibilities and loyalties and we say what we mean and we mean what we say, and we don't fuck around talking this kind of shit. If you have a problem, say so. If you don't, then fuck off and leave us to live our lives the way we choose to.'

Montgomery was stunned, wide-eyed, the apoplectic rage somehow held in check by the fragment of truth that had perhaps managed to inveigle its way through the self-important veneer he'd built around everything he was.

He glared at Stroud.

Stroud knew he'd blown it. At that point, he didn't care. It was only later – as he bore the brunt of Julia's anger – that he understood that challenging Donald Montgomery had not been a smart move at all.

He'd known from the outset that Julia's family loyalty would always take precedence, but he'd believed it to be her choice. He now appreciated that there was no choice in the matter. Julia was owned and controlled by her father. Donald Montgomery had succeeded in manipulating his daughter into subjugation because he'd begun that process even as she took her first breath.

51

Ultimately, the fact that she couldn't operate independently of her family was the death knell for their marriage. That knell had been sounding somewhere in the far distance for a long time, but after Eva turned two, it grew ever closer and ever louder.

Stroud had never forgotten what Julia said to him that night – after her parents and siblings had departed, after Eva had been put to bed.

'You think you understand how people work. You understand nothing. You think that behaving this way makes you tough. You want to know something? It's exactly the opposite. The things my father would do to help you if only you took the time to make him an ally, but no. Oh no, not you. You have to assert yourself and be right and have your opinion, even when that opinion is just worthless bullshit. Well, you're the one who's going to lose here. You do realise that, don't you?'

Stroud was drunk; he'd had enough; he didn't want to fight any more.

Julia had got up from the kitchen chair where she'd been sitting. She walked to the door, and then turned on him with a sneer.

'The only thing you're proving is that you're not strong enough to bend without breaking.'

He'd sat there alone in the kitchen. He knew that relationships were tough. He understood perfectly well that they didn't make sense. Was it really possible to spend your entire life with one person and always love them? Did that actually happen?

But kids were different. They were so, so different. That was another kind of love altogether.

He'd thought of when Eva was born. He thought of Julia's rat-tail hair and sweat-drenched hospital gown, the expression on her face like someone had just flown a helicopter through the middle of her body. But so happy. Both of them so happy.

And then the nurse gave Stroud his daughter. She weighed nothing. Less than nothing.

He held her, looked down at her, and when she opened her eyes and looked right back at him, he knew that was it. She would be the one and only constant love of his life.

It had now been a decade. Stroud didn't believe that Julia would have turned Eva against him. She was not that kind of person. But to love someone you had to understand them, and Stroud had just not been there.

Perhaps men such as himself, Raphael too, would never be understood, and thus could never be loved. Not completely. Not without reservation. Despite all they had seen and experienced, they were still too human to subject those close to them to the truth, and thus there would always be some part of themselves that remained hidden.

It was the perfect irony. They were – and always would be – the architects of their own loneliness.

8

Stroud woke to the sound of *ezan* being called from the minarets across the city. The muezzins echoed in triplicate; it was both ghostly and uplifting.

He stood at the window and smoked a cigarette. He didn't have a hangover, at least not noticeably so. That was a bad sign. Maybe he was becoming inured to the effects of alcohol. He guessed his liver possessed the same texture and consistency as a pumice stone. It had to stop. But when? Tomorrow. Same as always.

The French embassy was easy enough to find. Stroud sat across the street and drank a medium-sweet coffee. The building was discreet. Ahead of it was a neat garden behind a high fence, in the centre of which was a single gate with an intercom. A tricolour atop a twelve-foot mast hung limp in the breezeless air.

Stroud braced himself and walked over there. He didn't know who to ask for, even what he would say. He knew he was doing it simply to do something. Anything was better than nothing. Aside from proving Marcus wrong about Raphael, he really needed the two grand.

It seemed that a specific appointment or order of business was not required to get through the outer gate. However, once at the front door, he was questioned more closely. Name, reason for visit, for whom did he work. Stroud lied. He said he was there on behalf of the London *Times*. He wanted to speak to someone about recent intelligence reports.

The door was opened by a security guard. Despite the tailored suit, the mirror-shined shoes, there was no doubting the substantial physique, the telltale bulge beneath the right armpit, the way he presented himself as a very real obstacle.

Stroud was shown into a reception lobby, asked to please wait. A chair against the left-hand wall was indicated. He sat. He waited. The guard returned to the other side of the room and played the role of inscrutable sentinel. Stroud went on waiting, a good twenty minutes, in fact, and then a door to his right opened and a second man came through.

'This way, Mr Stroud.' The accent was strong.

Stroud got up, did as he was asked, and then followed the man down a hallway.

'If you would wait here, please,' the man said, opening the door to an office on the right.

Stroud entered the room. The door was locked behind him.

There was a single window, but it was close to the ceiling, no more than three by two, and the glass was thick and patterned. It permitted a good deal of light, but even if one could look through, there was no way to see much of anything.

Beneath the window were three plain wooden chairs. In the centre of the room was a table, a fourth chair, and it was here that he sat. He wanted to smoke but there was no ashtray. He wished he'd brought something to read.

It was a holding room, designed for exactly the scenario in which he now found himself. An unknown, an unwanted visitor, a potential troublemaker.

Forty minutes went by. On numerous occasions he heard footsteps along the corridor, the murmur of voices, the opening and closing of other doors. He didn't feel nervous. What could they do? Ask him to leave? Physically manhandle him from the building? If they did, so be it.

Another fifteen minutes passed by and he became irritated. He got up and tried the door even though he knew it was locked. He thumped on it a couple of times.

'Hey!' he called out. 'If someone isn't going to talk to me, then at least let me the hell out of here!'

Nothing.

He waited another ten minutes, and then a door opened somewhere, footsteps approached, paused, and the door was unlocked.

An older man entered. He carried a dossier, perhaps half an inch thick. He looked at Stroud, nodded, and then took another step into the room.

No sooner had he set the dossier down on the table than a second man entered the room. Orhan Yilmaz.

Stroud smiled, but behind that smile was a profound and sudden sense of real fear.

'Mr Stroud,' Yilmaz said.

'Mr Yilmaz.'

The first man brought a chair to the table, then a second. He sat down. Yilmaz sat beside him.

'This,' Yilmaz said, indicating the man beside him, 'is Monsieur Jean-Michel Fournier. He is assistant to the deputy ambassador. He deals with all matters of security relating to the embassy itself, French officials, visiting dignitaries and the like. He also manages press relations from his office in Paris.'

'Monsieur Fournier,' Stroud said.

Fournier didn't acknowledge him. He merely looked at him with practised disdain.

'You have entered the building under false pretences, Mr Stroud,' Yilmaz said.

Stroud smiled knowingly.

'Unless the information you provided in our first conversation was misleading, then you are not officially employed by *The Times* of London, nor are you here as an accredited representative of *The Times* of London. Either way, one of the stories you have given us is false.'

Stroud looked at Yilmaz. He looked at Fournier. He looked down at the dossier. He wanted to know what was in it.

'And so, given this duplicity, you have placed me in a position where I have no choice but to ask you to leave.'

With that, Yilmaz put his hand inside his jacket and withdrew Stroud's passport.

'The rest of your possessions are ready for you to collect. A car will take you to the airport. You will be leaving Turkey this afternoon.'

'You have got to be kidding me,' Stroud said. He feigned shock. He knew very well that a man like Yilmaz was not in the business of kidding.

'You step on toes, Mr Stroud, and people no longer want to dance with you.'

Stroud laughed to mask how anxious he truly felt.

'I am happy that you find some amusement in this situation,' Yilmaz said. 'I asked you not to embarrass us, and you have embarrassed us. I asked you not to make trouble, and here you are making trouble.'

'Making trouble? I am doing nothing of the sort. I came here to look for my friend.'

'Your friend is dead, Mr Stroud.'

Stroud looked at Fournier. 'Vincent Raphael,' he said, matter-of-factly. 'Why are the French interested in him? What is really going on here?'

Yilmaz leaned forward. 'Mr Stroud—'

'Tell me why French intelligence is interested in a man who's been dead for six years, Monsieur Fournier. Just tell me that much.'

'Stroud—' Yilmaz started.

Fournier raised his hand. Yilmaz fell silent.

'Mr Stroud,' Fournier said. 'I am not in the business of discussing anything that might relate to French intelligence except with those who possess the authority to have such discussions.'

'You know the name, though? You have heard of Vincent Raphael?'

Fournier looked at Yilmaz.

'Don't look at him,' Stroud said. 'I am asking you, assistant to the deputy ambassador, not some agent from the Turkish security services.'

Fournier smiled. 'You are not very adept at making friends, are you, Mr Stroud?'

'No disrespect, but I don't care whether we're friends or not. And if you are running press relations from an office in Paris, then what the hell are you even doing here? Why are you so interested in what I'm doing?'

'It is not uncommon for ambassadorial staff and representatives to spend considerable amounts of time in the countries they represent. The fact that you are here, that you have entered this building under false pretences with this imaginative story, is of concern to me. You are, after all, on French soil.'

'I want you to tell me whether you have ever heard of Vincent Raphael.'

'I have not.'

'You're lying.'

Fournier smiled. 'Enough.' He started to get up from the chair.

Stroud grabbed the dossier. Both Fournier and Yilmaz instinctively reached to seize it back. Documents spilled across the table and onto the floor.

Stroud saw pictures of himself. There was one of him in the restaurant, even one of him speaking with Nadire in the lobby of the hotel.

Suddenly Vincent's face caught his attention. A small picture affixed to the top of a sheet of paper. He snatched it before Fournier could retrieve it.

Yilmaz pushed him back into his chair and took the paper, but not before Stroud saw the name that was clearly typed beneath Raphael's picture. *Hendrik Dekker*. Alarm bells rang loud and clear.

He held up his hands. 'I am sorry. That was stupid.'

Yilmaz said nothing. Fournier commented angrily in French, bundled the papers back into the dossier and left the room.

'Now you are aggravating me, Mr Stroud,' Yilmaz said. 'I have nothing further to say to you. You are leaving for Yeşilköy now. You will be on the first available flight back to London.'

Stroud didn't reply. He had what he came for. A thread.

'Let me make it clear that returning to Turkey would not be advised,' Yilmaz said, and with that he left the room.

Stroud, much to his surprise, wasn't surreptitiously spirited out of Istanbul. Yilmaz had him in first class, had the goons walk him right onto the plane and ensure he was buckled up. It was a nice touch. He was demonstrating that he was in charge, that he could swing whatever he wanted.

On board, Stroud took advantage of Yilmaz's hospitality. Now more angry than afraid, he ordered one drink after another. By the time the flight landed in London, he was three sheets to the wind.

He took a taxi, stopped at the first hotel he saw. He paid for a room. Once inside, he pushed a chair against the door, and then fell onto the bed in his clothes.

9

The following morning, Stroud had nothing but two cups of black coffee for breakfast.

He made his way across to *The Times*. Marcus was at his desk and asked him to go up right away.

After a brief summary of what had happened, he said, 'I called the French embassy in Istanbul this morning. I asked for the assistant to the deputy ambassador. The girl told me there was no such office.'

'Why does that surprise you?' Haig asked. 'I mean, seriously, if I was French Ministry of Defence or whoever the hell he was, then I wouldn't go announcing it.'

'I know, Marcus, I know. Anyway, Vincent's picture was in that dossier, and the name underneath that picture was Hendrik Dekker.'

'Dutch?'

'Maybe. Or South African. The question that begs an answer is whether this was an alias, and if it was, then how did neither of us know about it?'

'We might not have done,' Haig said, 'but someone did.' He leaned back in his chair, swivelled it slightly to the left and looked out across the London skyline. 'You've upset the Turkish, upset the French. Now what?'

'Find out whether there is any such person as Hendrik

Dekker and chase it. I figured I could start with the archives here. I wanted to see if you had anyone who could help me.'

'Sure, sure,' Haig said. 'Sounds like a needle in a haystack, though. If it's just an alias, then it's very unlikely that the name will appear in a newspaper article.'

'I know that, but I have to start somewhere, and this is as good a place as any until I think of something better.'

Haig leaned forward and picked up the phone. 'Carole, call down to Archives, would you? Tell them Stroud is on his way. And find someone we can send down to give him a hand for a couple of hours.'

The someone sent by Haig was Nina Benson. Nina wasn't an abbreviation of anything; her parents were just Simone fans, it seemed.

'We're looking at Franco–Turkish relations. Conferences, meetings, trade agreements, all that kind of thing,' Stroud told her. 'And these names.' He handed her the list he'd made. *Jean-Michel Fournier. Orhan Yilmaz. Aydin Bekarys. Murat Kaya.*

'The first one, supposedly, is a French embassy official in Istanbul, but that's more than likely a cover for the French Ministry of Defence. Number two and three are Millî İstihbarat Teşkilatı, which is—'

'Turkish National Intelligence.'

'You know of it?'

'Foreign affairs desk, three years,' Nina said.

'Bravo,' Stroud replied, without a hint of sarcasm.

'Murat Kaya is *Hürriyet Daily News.*'

'Okay. Anything else?'

'The names Vincent Raphael and Hendrik Dekker. Hendrik with a K, Dekker with two.'

'So what are we actually looking for?' Nina asked.

'Last five or six years, those subjects, those names. It's

ludicrous to think we can scroll through microfiche for the entire paper, so stick with intelligence-related issues, civil and national conflict, elections, that kind of thing, but only in overseas news for now.'

'That's still a huge amount of material, Mr Stroud.'

'Drop the Mister. I'm just Stroud.'

'You don't have a first name?'

'Stroud is fine. And yes, I know it's a huge amount of material, and that is why I am going to help you.'

'Carole told me you might be challenging.'

Stroud laughed. 'Challenging?'

'That's what she said.'

'I think that's polite English for difficult bastard.'

'Well, what you want is not difficult; it's just very dull, time-consuming and more than likely fruitless.'

'I think that's perhaps the way my ex-wife would describe me, too.'

'Oh, I don't think you could be classed as dull,' Nina said. 'Not from the reputation that precedes you.'

'I have a reputation?'

Nina smiled. 'I am not going to inflate your fragile ego, Stroud. I know who you are, and I know who Vincent Raphael is. I also know why Marcus is having you do this.'

'How do you know about Vincent?' Stroud asked.

'I worked on Syria, Lebanon, Israel, Jordan, the Middle East. I was familiar with all those regions: who was out there, who came back, who didn't. I remember when he was killed—'

'*If* he was killed.'

'You think he wasn't?'

Stroud checked himself. He was talking out of turn. 'I have absolutely no doubt he's dead. However, I am more interested in the circumstances of his death. Whether it was random, whether it was intentional. Too many seemingly unrelated people seem entirely too interested in me snooping around for there to be nothing of interest.'

'You got booted out of Turkey.'

'I did.'

'I think you and Raphael are cut from the same cloth.'

'I'll take that as a compliment.'

'It wasn't meant that way.'

'I know,' Stroud said.

There was a few seconds' silence between them, but it was neither stilted nor awkward. What needed to be said had been said; now there was just the task at hand ahead of them.

'You cover '70 to '73,' Stroud said. 'I'll take '73 onwards.'

'Carole said we could use one of the annexe offices. It's poky, but there's a window.'

'Good enough,' Stroud said, and let Nina show him the way.

They called it a day a little after seven.

Nina looked at him askance, a flicker of suspicion in her expression, when he invited her to dinner.

'Really?' he asked. 'You think every one of us is the same?'

'Frankly, yes.'

'Maybe I am the exception that proves the rule.'

'I doubt that very much.'

'It won't be fancy. I don't really do fancy. A pub dinner. Lots of people. A smoky bar. Witnesses, right? You want plenty of witnesses.'

Nina laughed. She fluttered her eyes mock-coquettishly. 'You surely do have the most charming manner, Mr Stroud.'

'To hell with you, then.'

'I'll come and have dinner with you,' Nina said, 'but just so we understand one another, I have absolutely no interest in anything other than a purely professional relationship. I want that out there in the open right from the start.'

'You think I'm someone I'm not. Or someone's told you that. This is just dinner. And a cheap dinner at that.'

Nina lived near Camberwell. She suggested they head out that way. She knew a couple of decent places that weren't expensive.

'I was kidding about cheap,' Stroud said. 'Anyway, whatever we spend is going on Marcus's tab.'

'A pub is fine,' she said. 'I'm actually a pint-and-a-pie kind of girl, to be honest.'

They wound up at the Bricklayers Arms. The landlord knew Nina by name, got them a table in the saloon. Stroud ordered food, two pints of Guinness, and they sat for a while in silence.

'Tired,' he said.

'Me too. There's something about trawling through that stuff that just wipes me out.'

'I really appreciate your help.'

'I do get paid for working there, you know. If I wasn't doing that, I would be doing something else equally riveting, I'm sure.'

'What's your job? Officially.'

'I am – officially – the assistant copy-editor for the City desk. I cover crime, too.'

'And how did you wind up in the newspaper business?'

'Read English and journalism at university.'

'How old are you?'

Nina frowned. 'And this is relevant because ...?'

'Because I am interested.'

'I'm twenty-nine. You?'

'Thirty-seven.'

'How did *you* end up in this racket?'

'Born in Birmingham, moved here in '47. Interested in

pictures. Took a job as a darkroom assistant at the *Standard* when I was sixteen. The rest is history.'

'Your mother?'

'Still around, as is my father. He's a retired quantity surveyor. And now it's my turn to be curious about the questions.'

'I can be interested too,' Nina said. 'I'm trying to figure out what kind of background people like you must have to wind up doing what you do.'

'People like me?'

'You, Raphael, others of your clan. The wild ones. The crazy ones. Those who run towards the things that everyone else is running away from. War junkies.'

'That was one of the first things my ex-wife called me. First time we met, actually. She asked if I was one of Marcus's war junkies.'

'How long were you married?'

'Five years.'

'Kids?'

'One. A daughter. Eva. I don't see her. Ironically, Marcus probably sees more of her than I do. Julia is his cousin.' Stroud reached for his beer. 'Can we talk about something else?'

'Later. I'm not done with my questions.'

Stroud laughed inadvertently.

'Why did you get divorced?'

Stroud looked at her. She was beginning to irritate him.

'I'm beginning to irritate you,' Nina said, reading his expression accurately.

'My ex-wife, Julia, came from a very wealthy family. She was a rich girl. Home Counties. Pony for her fifth birthday and all that. We had a great relationship, but it wasn't built on anything substantial enough for it to last. I think we were each an answer to a question, but the wrong answer. I used to think I was a protest against the norm, a statement of rebelliousness against the life that had already been mapped out for her.'

'That is such a cliché.'

Stroud was bemused. 'Do you just say whatever comes into your mind?'

'Mostly, yes. Otherwise we're wasting a lot of time, right? So, now you can ask me some more questions.'

'I don't have any more questions for you,' Stroud said.

'That's disappointing. Do I not engender even the slightest degree of curiosity, Mr Stroud?'

'Okay. Why are you single?'

'Because the last man I slept with told me he loved me and then slept with my flatmate.'

'And that was how long ago?'

'Christmas Eve last year.'

'And you moved out?'

'The hell I did. I made her move out. That night. Threw the pair of them out onto the street.'

'Harsh. But fair.'

'Did you ever fuck anyone else while you were married?'

'Jesus, Nina, you really are no-holds-barred, aren't you?'

The food arrived. Stroud asked for two more pints; Nina ordered a Scotch for them both.

They ate in silence for a little while.

'So?' Nina prompted.

'Let it go, will you? I was enjoying a respite from the interrogation. You could do freelance for the Stasi.'

The Scotch came and Stroud sipped it reluctantly. 'I prefer bourbon.'

Nina turned her mouth down at the corners and nodded. 'Okay. I can drink bourbon too.'

She pushed her plate to one side and lit a cigarette. 'So, where were we?'

'You asked me if I had ever had an affair.'

'I actually asked you if you had fucked anyone else while you were married. That's not the same thing.'

'You're right. It's not. Anyway, even if I had, why would I tell you?'

'Because it doesn't matter. It's just conversation. I'm not going to judge you. Whether you did or not is of no importance to me.'

'Okay,' Stroud said. 'Yes, I did. Twice. Two different girls. One in Berlin in 1963, one in Cyprus in '64.'

'Did you ever tell your wife about them?'

'No, and nor do I think I should have done. In fact, I'm fairly certain she cheated on me as well.'

'How old is your daughter?'

'Fourteen.'

'Is she yours?'

'Fuck off, Nina.'

'It's a valid question. A woman always knows who the father is. A guy doesn't. You think she might have cheated on you, there's always the possibility that the kid is someone else's, right?'

'No, there's no possibility of that.'

'How are you so sure?'

'Because she looks like me. Because she has mannerisms like me. Because I look at her and I would stake my life on the fact that that girl is my daughter, not only physically, biologically, but also beyond that. I know she's my daughter. I *know* it.'

Nina nodded. 'Then I think she is too.'

Stroud looked down at his half-eaten meal. He turned to look at Nina. 'What the fuck is this? What the fuck are you trying to do?'

'Sounding you out, I guess.'

'Sounding me out?'

'Sure. I'm just curious about what kind of guy you are. You

and Raphael were like this.' She crossed her fingers. 'Close, right?'

'Yes, we were close.'

'Is it true he saved your life?'

'Yes, it is.'

'Instinct tells me that you are very, very definitely not the sort of person I would want to get involved with.'

'Well, we dealt with that right at the outset, didn't we?'

'We did,' Nina said. There was something in her tone.

Stroud looked at her and she smiled.

'What?'

'Where are you staying tonight?' she asked.

'Hotel. Why?'

'Do you want to come back with me?'

Stroud didn't reply. He didn't know what to say.

'Better than sitting alone in a hotel room, right?'

'Yes, it would be better than that.'

'So what the hell, eh? We're liberated adults. We're not tied to anyone else. We won't be breaking any rules or hiding from anyone. I live alone. I could use some intelligent company.'

'But nothing beyond that, right?'

Nina shook her head. 'See what you did there? You are so predictable. Now you've gone and spoiled the moment.'

Stroud reached for his glass. 'Story of my life.'

'Get your jacket,' Nina said, smiling. 'We can pick up a bottle of something dangerous up the road.'

IO

Stroud woke to the smell of cigarettes and frying bacon. He could hear the radio. He lay there as news of the execution of three British mercenaries in Angola and the publication of the Drought Bill blurred seamlessly into Candi Staton declaring that 'Young Hearts Run Free'.

He opened his eyes and saw a different ceiling. Around him, twisted in a sweaty knot, were chocolate-coloured sheets. He was on a five-foot-long sofa and his neck hurt like hell.

He leaned up on one elbow and looked around the room. Nothing about it was familiar. It was a good thirty seconds before he remembered where he was and how he'd got there. The night before. Drunk as a lord. Nina Benson.

No sooner had he thought her name than she entered the room. She had on a vest and denim shorts. It was early – a little past eight – but already the temperature was intolerable.

'Morning,' she said. 'How's your head?'

'Blunt-force trauma. Yours?'

'Multiple vehicle pile-up. Slim chance of survivors.'

Stroud grimaced. 'This is your flat.'

'Yes, I know,' she said, and there was that sly and disarming smile again.

'How much did we drink?'

'More than enough going on way too much.'

'Jesus, I know I must look bad, but I feel ten times worse.'

'I made you a bacon sandwich and a pint of industrial-strength coffee. Then we need to go back to work.'

It was close to ten by the time they reached *The Times*. They made their way as inconspicuously as possible to Archives. Stroud felt like a kid who'd skipped a school lesson.

'Was Raphael really as extraordinary as the myth suggests?' Nina asked at one point, perhaps to break the boredom, perhaps because she was genuinely interested.

He thought for a moment, and then he said, 'The myth is what people want to believe. Like Kennedy, James Dean, Marilyn Monroe. In truth, Kennedy was a drug-dependent, egomaniac sex addict. Dean was a nervous, introspected narcissist. And Marilyn ... well, Marilyn was perhaps smarter than she could ever have let people believe, because that would have broken the spell she created. Smart women are intimidating, and that was not the game she chose to play.'

'So what was Raphael really like?'

'He blew hot and cold. He made enemies far more easily than he made friends. He pissed me off no end. I've lost count of the number of times I swore never to have anything to do with him again.' Stroud smiled nostalgically. 'But then he could turn everything on its head in a second and you would love him all over again despite yourself. One of the smartest people I have ever known, and yet capable of some of the most spectacular stupidity.'

'Brave?'

'More like reckless.'

'I heard he was shot twice and carried on taking pictures.'

Stroud laughed. 'That never happened.'

'And he was a drunk?'

'Sometimes. Other times, stone-cold sober for weeks, months

on end. I guess the real thing about Raphael was that he was never predictable. He never did what you thought he was going to do. That was the most disarming thing, the thing that made you uncomfortable. However, you also knew that if you just went after him blindly and without caution, you would wind up with the best pictures, the stories that were the closest to the truth.'

'I think you've lived more life in the last twenty years than most people live in fifty or sixty.'

'Depends how you define living.'

Nina hesitated – as if she intended to say something, and then changed her mind. Stroud didn't pursue it. They went back to the laborious task of scanning old newspaper records.

After lunch – Stroud had gone out, returned with sandwiches and more strong coffee – they once again pored over microfiche files and cutting binders, committed to the thankless and potentially futile search for anything that might help Stroud understand a little more of what had really happened in Istanbul.

It was Nina who found something. It was merely a thread, but it was something.

'H. Dekker,' she said. 'NATO summit on Palestinian terrorist activities, September 1970. According to this, someone called H. Dekker worked with the British authorities for the release of Leila Khaled.'

'And she would be…?'

'There was an attempted hijacking of an El Al 707. The crew overpowered two hijackers, killed one, and then landed at Heathrow. Leila Khaled was the surviving terrorist. She represented herself as acting on behalf of the Popular Front for the Liberation of Palestine. She was held in the UK, and then released on the first of October in exchange for hostages taken in another hijacking.'

'When in September was the summit?' Stroud asked.

'Looks to be around the middle of the month. Three other airliners were hijacked, flown to Dawson's Field in the Jordanian desert: a TWA 707, a Pan Am jumbo and a Swissair DC-8. Looks to be all part of the same operation.'

'Well, the name can't be anything but a coincidence, because Raphael was killed on the fourth.'

Nina didn't reply. She was staring intently at something in front of her.

'What have you got?'

She indicated the microfiche reader with a nod of her head.

The image was small, little more than a postage stamp, but the face that looked back at Stroud from the screen bore an almost unmistakable resemblance to Vincent Raphael.

II

Stroud couldn't reach Haig. He'd left early; no one seemed to know where he'd gone.

Nina suggested they keep on working, pursue this NATO line, but Stroud wanted to talk to Marcus before he went any further.

'If that's Raphael, then there is a whole world of things going on that make no sense. He's not Dutch, he's English. He's not negotiating the release of terrorists here in London, he was blown apart in Jordan two weeks earlier.'

'Maybe, maybe, maybe,' Nina said. 'We don't know. That's the whole point of doing this, right?'

'But that name was right there on the picture in Istanbul, and yes, people can have the same name, but those people then looking almost identical? Really? Don't you think this is stretching coincidence just a little too far?'

'I do, yes,' Nina said, 'but a single unsubstantiated report is not sufficient foundation for action.'

'Get a source, confirm it twice,' Stroud said.

'Exactly. So what now?'

'We talk to Haig.'

'If that's what you feel is best,' Nina replied. 'You're the one who's running this. I'm just the help.'

'So tell me what you know about the Palestine thing.'

'What I know? Aside from Black September, the Munich

Olympics massacre, the hijackings, the hostages, the assassination of the Jordanian prime minister, the PLO and Yasser Arafat? You know as much about all of this as I do, Stroud. Christ, you were out there.'

'Not generally. I mean this specific incident.'

'Airliners were hijacked, blown up, the Pan Am plane was taken to Cairo, the crew and passengers were released, and then that plane was blown up too. The El Al hijacking was part of the same wave of actions, as far as I understand, but it didn't go according to plan. Hence the Khaled girl wound up here and became a bargaining chip for other hostages.'

'And NATO was involved in the negotiation?'

'I have no idea, Stroud. Who people are and who they say they are . . .'

'Are never the same thing.'

'Right.'

'But ostensibly NATO *was* involved, and they assigned a negotiator called H. Dekker to get some other hostages back from some other hijacking, presumably also a Palestinian operation.'

'Presumably, yes.'

Stroud fell silent. He looked toward the window. It was mid afternoon, the heat was brutal, and he would have preferred to be in any one of a million other places.

'What are you thinking?' Nina asked.

'That we are looking at a very remarkable coincidence, or that Vincent Raphael, the Vincent Raphael I knew anyway, was not the man I thought he was at all.'

'You think his death was faked?'

Stroud smiled and shook his head. 'This is insane. It can't be true. This is just too much to take on board.'

'If this is what happened – and I know that's a big *if* – then it wouldn't have been the first time.'

'I appreciate that, Nina, but we're talking about a man I knew for over ten years, and when I say *knew*, I mean we lived out of one another's pockets in half the hellholes of the world. You'd think those kind of situations would be very telling, right? The very scenarios where people would show their true colours.'

'Depends on the people.'

Stroud looked at Nina for some considerable time. His gaze was unerring, almost as if she was in his line of vision but he was seeing something or someone else entirely.

'Stroud?'

He came back to the moment, but in slow motion.

'Tell me,' she said.

'What's to tell? If it's true, then it's like finding out... Christ, I don't know... that your daughter actually isn't your daughter at all. That you were adopted and your parents never told you.'

'It's that big a deal for you?'

'The guy saved my life, Nina. More than once. He taught me pretty much everything I know about this crazy business. I did the eulogy at his funeral... a eulogy over an empty coffin for a man who wasn't dead?'

'We don't know that. We have a name and the face of someone who might just look like how you remember Raphael. You also have to take into consideration the possibility that you're projecting something into this that isn't there.'

'Like I want him to still be alive?'

Nina shook her head. 'Don't ask me, Stroud. I didn't know him the way you did. I just heard the rumours and listened to the stories. Raphael was always a myth to me. He was never flesh and blood.'

'I need to get out of here,' Stroud said. 'This fucking heat...' He left the sentence incomplete.

'You want some company?'

'Not right now,' he said. 'But—'

'I understand,' Nina interjected. 'I really do.'

75

'I was going to say that maybe we could meet up later.'

'Yes,' she said. 'You know where I live. Come over around dinner time if you like. We'll go out. Or stay in. Whatever you feel like.'

'Okay,' Stroud said. 'I'll do that. Yes, I'll probably do that.'

Nina watched him leave the room and head down the glass-walled corridor towards the lift. He didn't look back.

Once he was out of sight, she closed the office door and picked up the phone.

12

Stroud walked until the heat became too much. Even without his jacket on, his shirt was glued to his back. His mind reeled. If Raphael's death was faked, then why? And if he wasn't a free-lance photojournalist, who was he working for, and what was he doing? Was Vincent Raphael even his real name? If not, then what was it? Hendrik Dekker? And if this wasn't true, then what else wasn't true?

He stopped walking. He was going nowhere, and for no reason. He took the Tube back to *The Times*. Before he went into the building, he stopped in a supermarket and bought two bottles of cold orange Corona.

Back inside the annexe office, he wrote down what he could remember about Raphael.

Born Hereford, 20 June 1933. Father's name David. Mother's name?

No siblings.

Places where we worked together: DC, Belgian Congo, France, South Africa, Cuba, Berlin, Cyprus, Greece, Vietnam, Biafra, Palestine, Syria, Pakistan, Bangladesh, Munich.

He leaned back in his chair, trying his best to remember any personal details at all. As far as he knew – and this because Raphael had told him – Raphael had never been married, had no kids, owned no property, rarely saw his parents, never seemed to have been in any kind of long-term relationship.

He'd been slated for the army, had gone in another direction entirely. Lifelong disappointment to his father. There were girls, of course, but mostly one-night stands and prostitutes. Perhaps there were others like Alice Gerritty. If so, Stroud didn't know of them.

'If it stops you running, don't take it on,' Raphael would say. 'If you get involved with someone who could influence your judgement, then don't get involved. Emotions make everything complicated. Better to be alive and feel nothing than be in love and dead, right?'

It was now no longer a viewpoint to which Stroud ascribed, but back then – back at the beginning of his career – Raphael, a mere six years older, had seemed profoundly wise. With hindsight, knowing what he did of the man, Stroud suspected that Raphael didn't always subscribe to his own philosophy. There was the person he was for the world. Perhaps things were said simply because he believed they were expected of that person.

Then again, a year in this business was a year at war, a year behind walls, in bunkers, running from burning cars and collapsing buildings. It aged you, it soured you against humanity, it made you cynical and bitter and suspicious, and yet you kept coming back and coming back. Adrenaline – even when born out of fear – was more addictive than heroin. His own view of the world had changed. Raphael's would have changed too. The man he'd met back in '59 was not the same man a decade later.

Stroud drank the orangeade he had bought. It was too sweet and did little to quench his thirst. He looked at the scrap of paper in front of him, the even scrappier facts about Vincent Raphael, and he wondered if they were facts at all.

He understood that his unwillingness to accept that Raphael was alive was founded in his unwillingness to accept that he'd been duped. He'd believed in the man, trusted him with his life, and that trust had been reciprocated, or so he'd thought. To now accept that it was all a lie – that Vincent Raphael and Hendrik Dekker were one and the same person – was to also accept his own naïvety, his gullibility, the ease with which he'd assumed that what he was being told was in fact the truth.

Fool me once, shame on you; fool me twice...

Raphael had carried a passport, had been issued visas, press credentials. Work had been published under his name, and he'd even won photographic awards. It was almost inconceivable that the entire thing had been a facade and a sham.

But as Nina had said, faking your own death had been done before, and would be done again. Christ, they were still looking for Lord Lucan, the assumption being that he'd gone to ground in some corner of the Empire and would eventually surface.

'You're back.'

Stroud looked up. Nina stood in the doorway.

'Yes, sorry. I was just wrestling with this thing. I was going to come and find you.'

'Marcus is in his office,' she said. 'He got back about half an hour ago.'

'Never heard of him,' Haig said.

'Could be a remarkable coincidence,' Stroud said, 'but that was the name on the picture in that dossier in Istanbul. And here we have a man who looks remarkably like Raphael under the name Dekker, and he's in London negotiating the exchange of a terrorist for hostages a month after he's been blown to pieces in Jordan.'

Haig shook his head. He leaned back and looked up at the ceiling. 'To me that's no clearer than the picture from Istanbul.'

'For God's sake, Marcus, look at it again. That really could be Raphael.'

'You think we should drop it?'

'What?'

Haig looked at Stroud. His expression manifested worry. 'It was a rhetorical question.' He paused. 'Or maybe it wasn't.'

'I'm going to the General Register Office in the morning,' Stroud said. 'I want to know if Vincent Raphael was even a real person.'

Haig laughed nervously. 'Of course he was a real person. Hell, we went all over the world together, the three of us.'

'You know what I mean, Marcus.'

'Fuck. What the hell is happening here?'

'Maybe nothing,' Stroud said. 'There have been stranger coincidences than this.'

'How did you even find it?'

'Nina, the girl Carole sent down to help me, she found it. We were covering the six years since 1970. Franco–Turkish politics, intelligence, anything to do with Istanbul, and then the names of the French guy and the three Turks that kicked me out of the country.'

'But how the hell did that lead you to Palestine and hostage release negotiations in London?'

'It didn't. Not exactly. The only connection is this name, Hendrik Dekker.'

'So it really could be nothing more than one hell of a co-incidence.'

'Yes, it could.'

'But unlikely.'

'Very unlikely.'

'So go. Go to the Register Office. Check it out. And if Vincent Raphael never existed, then ...' Haig shook his head. 'Christ only knows, Stroud. I guess we'll be asking ourselves a great deal more questions.'

*

Stroud stopped by and explained what he was planning to Nina.

'It was in Somerset House, right? Then it moved.'

'To St Catherine's, on Kingsway.'

'You want me to come with you?'

'Because...?'

'Because it's a lot more interesting than sitting here copy-editing the monthly round-up of Chamber of Commerce squibs.'

'Sure thing.'

'And tonight?'

'I think I should take a hotel room,' Stroud said. 'Don't get me wrong. I appreciate the invitation, but I really think I need to stay sober.'

'We don't have to get drunk, Stroud.'

He looked at her and said nothing.

She got the message. He needed a little breathing space. She didn't take it personally.

'What time do they open?' she asked.

'Nine, I'd imagine.'

'See you on the front steps.'

13

The next morning, Stroud took the Tube to High Holborn and walked the rest of the way. The heat was ugly. Every conversation he overheard seemed to wish the summer gone. The British were never satisfied unless they had something about which to complain.

Nina was already there.

Once inside, she produced her press credentials and charmed her way around the fact that they didn't have an appointment. Nevertheless, they were asked to wait, and wait they did. It was the better part of an hour before a man came to assist them.

'I am the assistant to the deputy registrar,' he said. 'Paul Curtis.'

'Nina Benson, and this is Mr Stroud.'

'I do apologise for the delay, but we really are considerably understaffed. Surprising the number of people stricken with head colds and the like, what with the weather being so terribly warm.' Curtis gave a polite smile.

Brief pleasantries dispensed with, Curtis asked how he could help.

'Just a registration of birth,' Stroud explained. 'Hereford, as far as we know.'

'Well, let's see what we can do for you,' Curtis said.

*

The General Register Office had been moved a few years earlier. Stroud couldn't even begin to imagine the manpower that had been required. How many years' records they held, and how they managed to protect those records from natural deterioration – damp, mould, the fading of ink – he didn't ask, but it couldn't have been anything but an ongoing Herculean endeavour.

'If you're right, and it is Hereford, then it shouldn't take too long,' Curtis said, his tone one of optimism. 'Registrations of births, deaths and marriages, also changes of name and suchlike, come in from the various city or county registry offices. We hold them also by postal area, and they are – of course – in date order.'

He took off into a network of narrow corridors at a brisk pace.

'Herefordshire,' he said, indicating a towering column of wooden filing drawers. 'This is where it gets a little time-consuming. The registrations come in by date, and we have to generate a code for that date, that time, that individual registration. Registration of birth within the city limits of Hereford will have one code, outside will have another.'

'So can you tell us what we're looking for exactly?' Nina asked.

Curtis took a pen and paper and made some notes as he spoke.

'Hereford city limits is HFDC. Outside is HFDXC. Then we have B for birth, the date ...'

'As far as I know, it was June the twentieth, 1933,' Stroud said.

'That would be 20061933, and then we will have added either SH for Somerset House or SC for St Catherine's. Once you have those cards, you go through them for the name.'

'Makes sense,' Nina said, and took the paper from Curtis.

'Pre-war is up there and to the right,' Curtis said, nodding to a row of cabinets a good fifteen feet above them. 'Access to the walkways is via stairs there and there,' he added, indicating a pair of wrought-iron spirals at each end of the section. 'And that, as they say, is that,' he added with a smile. 'I shall leave you to it, and if you require any assistance, do make yourselves known at the front desk. Notes only, no cards to be removed or placed elsewhere, of course.'

'Of course,' Stroud said.

'These are Her Majesty's government records, you understand. Their misappropriation, misuse or maltreatment carries a considerable financial penalty, even imprisonment.'

'That goes without saying,' Nina replied, her tone one of re-assurance.

'Indeed,' Curtis said. 'You might very well be surprised, Miss Benson, at the disregard with which these documents are sometimes treated.'

He nodded his head, gave one more perfunctory smile, and then left them to it.

By lunchtime they had gone through the relevant sections three times. There were only two or three possibilities: the official document registering the birth of Vincent Raphael had been either removed or mislaid, or it had never existed.

Stroud and Nina sat on the floor, their backs against the filing cabinets. Neither spoke for some time.

'Could be the wrong date, wrong city, wrong county, anything,' Stroud said eventually. 'Not finding it where we thought we might doesn't help us one way or the other.'

'There is something else we could look at,' Nina said. 'His death.'

Stroud was up on his feet, his interest renewed. 'September the fourth, 1970,' he said. 'There's no way that won't be recorded here.'

Nina didn't reply. She didn't wish to disillusion Stroud before he embarked upon another potentially fruitless task.

Working with the code that Curtis had given them, they found the county and the date with no difficulty. Once again, however, they came up empty-handed.

Back in reception, they asked for Curtis.

'Success?' he asked as he came through the door.

Their expressions gave him the answer to his question.

'Oh dear. What a shame.'

'Okay,' Stroud said. 'My understanding is that the man we are looking for was born somewhere in the county of Herefordshire. Of course, that could be incorrect, as could the date of his birth, but there is one other question.'

He looked at Nina. Nina indicated for him to go on.

'This man was killed, as far as we know, in Jordan.'

'In the Middle East?' Curtis asked.

'Exactly. He was a British citizen, killed in the line of duty, so to speak. Even though he died abroad, would his death still have to be registered here?'

'He was serving in the armed forces?'

'No, he was a journalist.'

'Irrespective of where he died, if he was a citizen of the British Isles, the record of his death would be here.'

'And it would be under the date of death, rather than the date his body arrived back in the UK or the date of the funeral, yes?'

'Yes, the date of death,' Curtis replied, 'unless an error was made in the paperwork overseas and we received incorrect information. I am sorry to say that such things have happened, and unless someone goes looking for the registration and demands that the record be changed, it will forever remain incorrect.'

'It's a needle in a haystack,' Nina said.

'Could I perhaps ask what it is you're trying to accomplish here?' Curtis said.

'I had a colleague,' Stroud explained. 'A very dear friend. He was killed in Jordan six years ago. His body was never recovered, but a funeral service was held in Hereford, the county where I believed he was born—'

'I'm sorry,' Curtis interjected. 'Where you *believed* he was born?'

'Where he told me he was born.'

'Quite the conundrum,' Curtis said. 'I assume he drove a car while he was resident in the United Kingdom? Moreover, I assume he had a passport?'

'Yes, he did.'

'Well, as you know, one cannot—'

'Obtain a passport without a birth certificate,' Nina said.

'Exactly.'

'The passport office it is, then,' she added.

'Splendid,' Curtis said, a note of triumph in his voice. 'I am happy to have been of assistance.'

14

Stroud and Nina Benson took a break for lunch. London's Office of Passport Services was not far, a stone's throw from Victoria Station. They took a table in a café near the recently closed Apollo Victoria cinema. Stroud ate half a sandwich, drank two cups of coffee, smoked three cigarettes. He was frustrated, his head ached, and the last thing he wanted to do was trawl through more dusty files and endless paperwork.

'You do realise that this could very easily turn out to be nothing, don't you?' he said. 'I had the wrong birth date or the wrong county, he did exist, he did die in Jordan, and we've wasted an awful lot of time and effort for nothing.'

'You're not getting paid for this?'

'Yes, I am,' Stroud said. 'There is that.'

'How much?'

'Two grand.'

Nina raised her eyebrows, impressed. 'Well, it seems to me that if we wind up proving that Raphael died back in 1970, it will be the fastest and easiest two grand anyone ever earned.'

'Good point, well made, Miss Benson.'

'Which begs the question, why would *The Times* be prepared to pay so much for this?'

'Just in case it turns out to be a year-long odyssey fraught with personal danger and I wind up getting myself killed. Then it would be the best two grand they ever spent.'

'You actually do have a sense of humour. I know that you pretend to be all moody and intense, but I'm not buying it.'

'So I don't come across as deep and complex?'

Nina laughed. 'I am beginning to wonder whether this tortured conscience thing you guys do is just a front. You can't stay still, can you? It must be a rush. It's gotta have something to do with that. Always trying to find some other place where there's gunfire and decimated bodies. War junkies is too narrow because you lot fly into famines and droughts and political coups and insurrections. Trauma junkie, maybe, but on a global level. I mean, I have to ask you, don't I? What on earth makes you want to do this with your life?'

'The fact that if we didn't do it, we wouldn't have a life, I guess.'

'What kind of answer is that, for Christ's sake?'

'Only one you're going to get,' Stroud said. 'I don't know why I do this. I mean, why I *did* it. I haven't done it for a while.'

'Burned out.'

'Maybe. I don't know.'

'Because you can't see it making any real difference?'

'Perhaps. One thing I do know is that other people analyse what I do an awful lot more than me. Sometimes you do things because you have to, not because you actually believe they're a good idea.'

'Don't I know it.'

Stroud lit another cigarette. 'So what's your deal? You're not planning on copy-editing Chamber of Commerce articles for the rest of your life, are you?'

'God, no. Jesus, can you imagine?'

'So what are you waiting for?'

'An epiphany.'

'Mark Twain. The most important days in your life are the day you're born ...'

'…and the day you find out why.'

'And when that day comes is anyone's guess.'

'We just have to hope it isn't the day before you croak,' Nina said. 'The realisation that you've wasted your entire life doing the wrong thing precipitates the heart attack that kills you.'

Stroud laughed. Black humour. It was a genuinely disturbing thought.

'So, what's *your* background, family-wise?' he asked.

'Middle class, middle England, nothing noteworthy. I had a great-grandfather who did something interesting as a missionary in Africa, so the story goes, but aside from that the Bensons are memorable only for their ordinariness.'

'What does your father do?'

'Accountant. Mother was a schoolteacher, but she's quit now.'

'Brothers and sisters?'

'One of each. She's a nurse, he's studying to be a barrister.'

'Neither of them married? Any nephews and nieces?'

Nina shook her head.

'And you? You want kids?'

Nina looked away towards the window. She seemed pensive. 'Uncertain,' she said. 'I'm in that limbo where I don't know which career path I should pursue, and yet I don't want to commit to marriage and kids in case it prevents me from pursuing my career path.'

Stroud leaned back in his chair. 'Right.'

'It's fucked up, isn't it?'

'I think that's a bit strong. You're young. You have time.'

'It's Christmas in five months, Stroud.' She looked at him deadpan. 'And that will be here before we know it, and then we'll make New Year's resolutions that we won't keep, and then another year will fly by and 1978 will be here and I'll be past thirty and if I haven't got myself together by then, well…'

'You might as well kill yourself.'

'Right. I might as well kill myself.'

'It's a very sorry state of affairs, Miss Benson.'

'Thank you for your understanding, Mr Stroud.'

'I don't see any way to avert this dreadful inevitability.'

'Really? And I was going to hang all my future hopes on you and your equally desperate and inadequate life.'

'Shall we go and wallow in the pathetic wretchedness of our respective lives at the passport office?'

'I thought you'd never ask.'

The Office of Passport Services, at least the designated official who represented it, was singularly unhelpful. Appointments were mandatory, no exceptions, no special circumstances, and when Nina flashed her press credentials she might as well have been showing them her Tube ticket.

'Driving licence?' Stroud suggested.

'But the DVLC's in bloody Swansea,' Nina said.

'There must be some sort of administrative office in London, for Christ's sake.'

'I have an idea,' she said. 'The police.'

'The police?'

'Speeding tickets, fines, traffic violations, all that stuff. I bet you there's a central records department in London for such things. If Raphael ever got fined or ticketed, then there would be a record here, and alongside that—'

'Would be a record of his licence.'

'It's worth a shot, right?'

'Right now, I'll try anything. We just need to get an accurate birth date and then we can go back to Curtis at the GRO.'

'I know someone in the Met,' Nina said. 'He's not traffic, but he might know someone who is.'

*

Nina's contact paid off. She was given a number for the National Police Administrative Department, Vehicular Division.

Two phone calls and they had someone who was willing to assist. He took the number of the phone box from which Nina was calling and said he'd call her back.

He was as good as his word. Fifteen minutes later, Stroud having had to get rid of four different people who wanted to use the phone, Nina was writing down details from Vincent Raphael's driving licence.

'Gloucestershire,' she said when she hung up. 'We were looking in the wrong county.'

Caught up in the intrigue of the situation, Paul Curtis was all too willing to help them again. It was perhaps the most exciting thing that had happened at St Catherine's House since the GRO had moved in.

Using the newly amended code, Stroud and Nina went through the filing drawers as conscientiously as possible. The registration had to be there. It just *had* to be ...

'Nina?'

Nina turned and looked along the walkway. In his hand, Stroud held a small white postcard.

'Really?'

'Really,' he said. 'Vincent Thomas Raphael, born on the twentieth of June, 1933 in Lydney, Gloucestershire.'

'Thank Christ for that,' Nina said.

They found Curtis down below. He had come through to let them know that the building would soon be closing.

'Success,' Stroud said. He held up the card. 'I'll put it back exactly where I got it from, I promise.'

'Wonderful,' Curtis said.

He looked at the card and a furrow creased his brow.

'Oh my,' he said.

'What?'

'Here,' Curtis said, and indicated a small red circular sticker on the back of the card. Alongside it was a date: 24 June 1933.

'What does that mean?' Nina asked.

'It means, Miss Benson, that we have in our system a record of the death of this individual. Whoever this Vincent Raphael was, he died just four days after he was born.'

15

'Not the first time,' Nina said, 'and not the last. It's an old, old method.'

'Marcus—' Stroud said, but Haig raised his hand and silenced him. He walked to the window of his study and looked out across the lawn behind his house.

His wife, Cathy, and two kids, Justin and Emily, were out in their swimming costumes. A paddling pool, brimful of water, was the focus of attention. The kids were young – five and seven respectively – and Cathy was keeping them entertained while her husband dealt with the unexpected visitors.

'We'd have left it until Monday,' Stroud said, 'but... well, you can see why we felt you should know.'

Nina had driven from London to St Albans. They'd called at Haig's Chelsea flat but there was no answer. Stroud knew his country address but had no number. Haig was ex-directory, which was perfectly understandable considering his line of work. They'd had no choice but to pay a visit. He had been out in the garden too, had put a bathrobe on over his swimming trunks. Now he stood in the bay of his study considering the ramifications of this latest bombshell.

A man both he and Stroud had known and worked with for over twenty years, a man reported to have died in Jordan in September of 1970, had never in fact made it out of the hospital where he'd been born. Vincent Raphael was a fabricated identity.

There was also the possibility – as yet supported by nothing more than a photo in a dossier in Istanbul and a second image in the newspaper – that Raphael had gone under the name of Hendrik Dekker.

'What do you want me to do?' Stroud asked.

Haig turned and looked at him. His mind was elsewhere, his gaze unfocused, and it was some time before he spoke.

'Keep on going?' he asked, but it was more a question for himself. 'Christ, I don't know, Stroud. I don't know what the hell to make of this.'

'We spent time in Archives last night, also checked the official register for all current NATO employees this morning,' Nina said. 'No one called Hendrik Dekker. However, Dutch telephone directories gave us three of them: one in Amsterdam, another in Hilversum, a third in Leiden.'

'So, what? You want to go chasing some other unknown person all over the Netherlands?'

'You asked me to do something, and I'm doing it,' Stroud said. 'This is what we have right now. This is all we have. However, I don't think phoning them up is going to hack it. I think if Raphael really is one of these Dekker characters, then showing up unexpectedly is the only way we're going to find out. Tip him off, and he's gone. So no, I don't have to go to the Netherlands, but if you want me to keep at this, I think it's my only option.'

Haig sat down at his desk. 'You think there's a chance one of them is him?'

'I have no idea, Marcus. Maybe Vincent's real name was Hendrik Dekker. Maybe it was something else. Whoever the hell he was, there is also the possibility that he really did get blown to kingdom come in that Land Rover. This NATO guy could just be someone who looks like him.'

Haig looked at Nina. 'What do you think?'

94

'Me? What does it matter what I think? Monday morning I'm back at my desk, right?'

'Not necessarily.'

'Meaning what? You want me to go to Holland with Stroud?'

'Which department did Carole get you from?'

'I copy-edit for City and the crime desk,' Nina said.

'I'm sure they can manage without you for a while,' Haig said. He looked away again. The machinery in his head was almost audible.

Stroud could hear the kids squealing with laughter in the garden. Cathy was chasing them with a bucket of water. This was a life he didn't know, and believed he never would.

'You know Holland, don't you?' Haig asked him.

'I wouldn't say I know it. Not well, anyway. I spent some time in Amsterdam, sure, but I can't honestly say I remember a great deal about it.'

'Do you have a cigarette?' Haig asked.

Stroud frowned. 'I thought you'd quit.'

'Bollocks to that. Give me a bloody cigarette, will you?'

Stroud passed one across the desk, his lighter too.

Haig smoked half of it before he spoke again.

'Whoever we knew as Raphael was a real person. I don't care what name he had at the time or how many names he had before, he was a real person. He was my friend.' He looked at Stroud. 'Yours too. He was more than a friend.' He turned to Nina. 'I've been chased and shot at and got very, very drunk in more places with those two than anyone else I've known. Nearly a quarter of a century in this ridiculous bloody business and who do I remember most? Vincent sodding Raphael and this clown here.' He indicated Stroud with a thrust of his chin. 'Telling me that Raphael was not really Raphael is like telling me... Christ, I can't even think of a comparison.' He shook his head disconsolately. 'No matter what kind of life you've led, there are certain events and certain people you will never forget. For me, it's events and people at the same time. Raphael in South Africa, in Cyprus, in Biafra, in Bangladesh.' He closed his eyes. 'You remember when they bayoneted those kids in Dacca? A dozen of them. Called them insurgents, militia, rebels, whatever. Didn't matter. They fucking bayoneted them in public.'

'Listen, Marcus,' Stroud said. 'You want me to go to Amsterdam, to Hilversum, to wherever, I will. You want me to go back to Istanbul and find out why that name was written on Raphael's picture, I'll do it. It's not the money, okay? I'm going to take your money, sure, but that's not the motive any longer. There's too much about this that makes no bloody sense at all. I want to find out. I *need* to find out—'

Stroud stopped talking and turned as the door opened behind him.

'Marcus...' Cathy said, and then she frowned. 'You're smoking? Oh Marcus...'

'Cathy, I have to sort something out. I won't be long.'

'The children are—'

'Cathy, really. This is not the time. I'm sorry, but something really serious is happening and I need to just deal with it.'

Cathy looked around the edge of the door. 'Tell him, Stroud.'

Stroud shrugged his shoulders, held up his hands in defence. 'You're the boss around here, Cathy.'

'Marcus, what's going on? You're in your study, Stroud's here, you're smoking.' She looked at Nina. 'And who's this?'

Nina smiled as sincerely as she could. 'Nina Benson, Mrs Haig. I'm a copy-editor from the paper.'

Cathy didn't acknowledge her. She looked at Stroud once more, then back at her husband.

'It's Saturday, Marcus. The weekend. That's all we get of you.'

'Cathy, sweetheart—'

'Well, all I can say is that it better be bloody well important.

Someone really, really bloody important better have died or Callaghan's announced he's a bloody communist or something. And you promised you wouldn't start smoking again.'

With that she closed the door behind her with a slam.

Haig sighed. 'Do you ever wonder if people would be happier if you weren't around?'

Stroud didn't reply.

'Give me another cigarette,' Haig said. 'And fetch that bottle of Scotch over there. Might as well be hung for a sheep as a lamb, right?'

16

As the attention of the nation was consumed by the Montreal Olympics and the lurid details of the Nielsen trial, Stroud and Nina Benson flew into Schiphol.

Asked why he wanted Nina to accompany him, Haig had said, 'So she can keep a bloody eye on you, Stroud. I can imagine that the last time you were in Amsterdam you nearly drank a hole through your liver.'

That return from Schiphol to London had only been twelve days earlier, Stroud still smarting from a sour break-up, drawn back to England with the promise of easy money. Not so easy, it seemed, and that initial motivation now buried beneath the weight of further confused revelation.

'Are you okay with me coming?' Nina had asked as they took their seats.

'A little late to be asking that,' Stroud had said, but without the slightest hint of resentment. He was pleased that she was along.

A stewardess appeared. Stroud asked for a Scotch, double, no ice. Nina ordered the same.

For a while they sat and smoked, Nina gazing out of the window as they headed towards the coast.

Eventually she looked back at Stroud and said, 'Just for argument's sake, let's say that Vincent Raphael did fake his own death. Maybe planned, maybe just opportunist, but let's say he actually did it.'

Stroud didn't respond.

'I think he wanted to disappear, don't you?'

'I don't know what he wanted, Nina. Most of the time I don't think Raphael himself knew what he wanted.'

'But if he did, it begs the question why.'

'Seems to me that the only reason would be something life-threatening. Once you're dead, people stop looking for you.'

'Except people like us. We're looking for him.'

'And French intelligence. *The Times*. And then there's the Turks.'

Stroud downed the last of his Scotch and tried to catch the attention of the stewardess.

'So where do you want to start?' Nina asked.

'First things first, I can't think of him as anything but Raphael. Considering we have to call him something, it might as well be that. Anyway, that aside, I think someone wanting to remain hidden would choose somewhere less accessible and well known than Amsterdam. However, the smaller the place, the more likely you'll get noticed. Big city, lot of commuters and tourists, I guess people can just vanish. I don't know either Leiden or Hilversum. We'll start in Amsterdam simply because that's where we're landing. These places are ten, twenty, thirty miles from one another, so we're not exactly crossing the country.'

'When I said where do you want to start, I meant more from the viewpoint of how we approach this when we're there. You know, actually finding out if Dekker in Amsterdam is really Raphael.'

'That's the easy part, isn't it? Get an address, concoct some reason for you to knock on the door.'

'Me?'

Stroud looked at her.

Realisation dawned. 'Because he doesn't know me.'

'Precisely,' Stroud said.

The stewardess arrived, refilled Stroud's glass. Nina declined.

'A person often meets his destiny on the road he took to avoid it,' Stroud said.

Nina smiled. 'That's a little deep.'

'Generally, or for me?'

'Are you speaking of Raphael or yourself?'

'Myself,' Stroud replied, 'but I think it applies to most people. It can be significant or inconsequential. I have found, quite routinely, that trying to avoid the inevitable makes the inevitable happen that much faster and that much more uncomfortably.'

'You ought to copyright that.'

'I didn't come up with it. Jean de La Fontaine. Seventeenth-century French poet.'

'Is that so?'

'It is.' Stroud caught Nina's expression. 'What? You thought I couldn't read, right?'

She laughed. 'I guess I didn't expect seventeenth-century poetry from a man like you.'

'You don't know anything about a man like me, Nina.'

The co-pilot announced the beginning of their descent into Schiphol. Apparently it was a mere twenty-three degrees Celsius in Amsterdam.

'Thank God for that,' Nina said. 'Maybe I'll actually get some sleep tonight.'

'Don't bank on it,' Stroud said. 'Let's see what kind of truck drivers' hostel Haig has arranged for us, eh?'

17

Haig surprised both Stroud and Nina. He'd booked double rooms for them at one of the better airport hotels. The restaurant and bar exceeded their expectations; they went to bed well fed and pleasantly drunk.

In the morning they took a taxi to Amsterdam Centraal. Stroud didn't want there to be any record of their final destination, so they took a local train to De Pijp. At the station, they used a phone kiosk to confirm the address of H. Dekker. It was in an apartment building above a bakery on Van Ostadestraat. Another short taxi journey and they were there.

'Keep it simple,' Stroud said. 'Ring the buzzer and tell Mr Dekker that he needs to come down to the street and sign for a parcel. Tell him you have a bicycle and other deliveries and you can't leave them unattended.'

'You do realise that I don't speak Dutch?'

'Everyone speaks English here. And it's such a diverse city no one will even think twice about it. Just say "*Goedemorgen*" and go from there.'

'You're sure about this?' Nina asked hesitantly.

'What's the worst that could happen? Whoever's there comes down and it's not Raphael. Or there's no one in.'

'And where will you be?'

'I figured I'd take the train back to the airport and leave the country without you.'

'I think I'm going to stop asking stupid questions.'

'Good plan,' Stroud said. 'Now go.'

Nina crossed the street and headed for the apartment building. She located the buzzer for H. Dekker, and glanced back to see Stroud stepping into a shop doorway.

She pressed the buzzer. There was almost no delay.

'*Ja. Wie is daar?*'

'Dekker?' Nina asked. 'Hendrik Dekker?'

'*Ja.* Hendrik Dekker.'

'I have a parcel for you here. I need a signature.'

'Yes. Come in. Third floor.'

'I have my bicycle here. I have a lot of deliveries. I cannot leave them.'

'Okay. I come now.'

Nina stepped away, paused for just a moment and then hurried back across the street to where Stroud was waiting.

'He's coming down now.'

'Definitely Dekker?'

'That's what he said. I told him he had to sign for it.'

'Okay. Go over by that bookshop. Wait for me there.'

Stroud backed up. He watched the entrance to the building intently, his heart racing. What if it was Raphael? What the hell would he do if it really was Raphael?

The ramifications were endless, both personally and publicly.

He looked back towards the bookshop. Nina was out of sight. Not that it mattered – she and Raphael were unknown to one another.

Stroud turned his attention back to the apartment building; he felt a strange sense of disquiet and anticipation. Surely Dekker should have been down by now. What floor was he on? The third? The fourth?

The door started to open.

Stroud held his breath.

He watched closely. Raphael would have aged, just as he himself had done, but only by a handful of years. There would be no mistaking him. There was only one Vincent Raphael.

Stroud exhaled audibly, only then realising that he'd been holding his breath.

The man looked left and right down the street. He scratched his head, appeared understandably irritated, and gave it a further ten or fifteen seconds before he turned and went back into the building. He slammed the door behind him.

Stroud exited the kiosk, met Nina halfway to the bookshop.

'Not him,' he said. 'Leiden it is.'

They were back at Centraal by eleven. The first train out to Leiden left in twenty-five minutes. They sat in a café and drank coffee. Stroud was silent. Nina could see he was both relieved and disappointed.

'What if it had been him?' she asked. 'What would you have done?'

'I was just thinking that exact thought.'

She didn't prompt him to speak further. She stayed quiet and waited.

Finishing his coffee and lighting a cigarette before he went on, Stroud seemed somehow different to her. Withdrawn was the wrong word. He seemed in limbo.

'Have you ever nearly died, Nina?'

She smiled, almost nonchalantly, but it was reflexive, born out of anxiety. It was certainly not a question she could have anticipated. 'No,' she said. 'I can't say that I have.'

'Did anything ever happen where you thought you might get badly hurt?'

'I fell out of a tree once,' she said. 'I was nine years old. I broke my ankle. I remember falling. It seemed like a long time. I wondered what would happen if I turned upside-down somehow. I don't know why I thought that, but I did. If I had turned upside-down I would have landed on my head and I would have been killed. More than likely, anyway.'

'Do you remember what you felt?'

Nina felt uncomfortable. Where Stroud was going with this, she had no idea.

She shook her head. 'No,' she replied. 'I was just a child. It was a long time ago.'

Stroud put out his cigarette. 'Ever heard of a place called Elisabethville?'

'I know of it, but can't say I know anything about it.'

'It was a Belgian colony. Strong nationalist movement. They wanted freedom from colonial rule, and they got it in June 1960. It was a mess. No one knew what the hell was going on. Tribal uprisings, ethnic divisions, those who wanted a federal republic, others who wanted independent regional governments.' Stroud waved his hand dismissively. 'The Belgians gave them what they wanted but they hadn't made any real preparations. You also had opposing factions, some supported by the US, others by the Soviets. It became a Cold War pissing contest, basically.

'So there it was. June of 1960. Raphael, Haig and I went out there in the first week of July. There was mutiny in the army. People were battling in the streets. Belgium sent troops to protect the white communities. Patrice Lumumba, the head of the largest faction in the country, asked for help from Russia. It went from bad to worse. There had been riots in Léopoldville the year before. Dozens had been killed. Now there were riots all over the country. We got there just as people were fleeing the capital, but before the UN sent in the peacekeepers. We didn't hang about. We went down to Elisabethville and holed up in a hotel near the cathedral.'

Stroud paused. He looked away, looked back at Nina, but she knew he wasn't seeing her.

'I was twenty-one years old, for Christ's sake. I'd been in the Congo in '59, but only briefly, and it wasn't up close and personal like this. I was in the Transvaal too, but I arrived long after the massacre was done and dusted. This was the first time I was really in the line of fire. The three of us charging around with cameras and notebooks like we were bulletproof. Haig and I were so fucking naïve, but Raphael...' He shook his head and sighed. 'As far as we were concerned, Raphael could walk on water. He could do no wrong. Stand in his shadow and you were not only bulletproof, you were invisible.'

He leaned forward and took another cigarette from the packet on the table.

'We left the hotel. It was dusk. There had been running gun battles all day, but it seemed to have calmed down. We actually went out to find some booze, believe it or not.' He smiled, recalling the moment. 'Idiots.'

Nina leaned forward with the lighter for his cigarette.

'So, we were heading down the street, staying low and close to the walls. As we turned a corner, there was a gang of people ahead of us. Raphael goes on, and before I know it we're ten yards away and they see us. I turned to say something to Marcus, but he was halfway up the street. First sign of trouble and he just ran straight back to the hotel. It wasn't cowardice, it was instinct. Self-preservation. Hell, if we'd been as smart as him we would have done the same. But we just blundered on into that situation like a couple of lunatics. Before I knew it, one of these guys had his hand around my throat. I was up against the wall with the barrel of a revolver pressed against my forehead.'

He looked at Nina. 'And do you know what I remember most?'

'What?'

'How cold it felt. That's what I remember. How cold that muzzle was against my skin.'

'And what did Raphael do?'

'He bluffed us out of there.'

'*Bluffed* you out of there? How?'

'He had a camera with him. Be bold, stick a camera in someone's face, smile a lot and you'd be amazed. Within minutes he had them all lined up with their weapons. He was snapping one picture after another, running it like a fucking wedding shoot. You stand there, you stand over there, shorter guys at the front. Hold your gun up higher, he said to the one who was going to shoot me. Hold it up higher, you know? Let's show the world how big and brave and powerful you are.'

Stroud laughed. 'Jesus. I still think about it even now, how brazen and nonchalant he was.'

'And then?'

'He promised them he'd get them all prints by noon the next day. He told them not to worry, he'd find them. Then he asked for directions to the nearest bar.'

Nina smiled. 'Incredible.'

'That was Raphael. And you know what? He never spoke about it. He never said a word. He didn't even tell Haig when we got back to the hotel. I was the one who told him. Raphael had nothing to prove. He was who he was, and he wasn't being that person for anyone else but himself. And that, in truth, was both a blessing and a curse.'

'Seems to me that you could just as easily have wound up getting killed.'

'Sure. Of course. But he was like that with everything. No half-measures. The Norwegians have an expression. *Å få blod på tannen.* Literally, to have blood on the tooth. Like an animal. It gets a scent, or it gets a taste of blood. It goes crazy, and will stop at nothing until it has hunted and killed the prey. Something like that.'

'Driven.'

'Unstoppable.'

'Until Jordan.'

'Maybe,' Stroud said. 'Maybe not. That's what we're here to find out.'

'So why did you ask me if I'd ever experienced anything like that?'

'To see if you felt the same thing as me.'

'And what is that?'

Stroud leaned forward. 'Nothing. Nothing at all. Like your life is meaningless, without reason. Like you're there and then you're gone in the blink of an eye. Nothing that you've said or done and nothing that has ever happened to you really means anything at all. Not in the grand scheme.'

'So if that's the case, what the hell is the point of any of it?'

'I don't know, Nina. Maybe we get the answer when we die.'

18

Leiden was not the kind of place Stroud would have expected to find Raphael. It was moderate in size, the population approaching a hundred thousand or so.

Nina had picked up a guidebook in the station, and from this she'd read a few lines as they sat waiting on the train.

'Suburbs of Oegstgeest, Leiderdorp, Voorshoten and Zoeterwoude. Sits on the Oude Rijn.' She looked up from the page. 'That's a river. The Hague is about twelve miles south, Amsterdam is twenty-five miles north. Known as the City of Discoveries, it's had a university since 1575, and has a host of Nobel prize-winners. Birthplace of Lucas van Leyden, Jan van Goyen, Jan Steen and Rembrandt. Also, Marinus van der Lubbe, the guy the Nazis claimed set fire to the Reichstag. Twinned with Oxford, England, Buffalo City, South Africa and Nagasaki, Japan.'

'Nagasaki?'

'That's what it says here.'

'I appreciate the guided tour.'

'You're most welcome.'

Upon their arrival, the city's academic heritage was evident not only in the architecture, but also in the sheer number of residents in their late teens and early twenties. The fact that it was so busy was good news. Two more unfamiliar faces were of no consequence.

Again Stroud confirmed the Dekker address in a city phone book. It was on a street off Schuttersveld, near the Valkbrug bridge, and not far from the train station. He and Nina walked. They smoked, said very little, conscious of remaining inconspicuous.

The Dekker residence was a relatively modern affair, suited – by appearance – far more to student accommodation than to that of a man in his forties. Again Stroud hung back across the street as Nina approached the building.

'Just say you're going to be lecturing at the university next year and you need a place to rent. Ask about noise, late-night parties, that kind of thing.'

Nina seemed relaxed and confident, and if she wasn't, she played it well.

She buzzed for Dekker on the intercom. She waited a good twenty seconds and then buzzed again. Nothing.

Back across the street, she asked Stroud if they should wait.

'No. We'll buzz one of the other residents and see what they know about him. Maybe we can find out where he works, at least.'

Stroud crossed the street with Nina. Knowing that there'd been no response from the Dekker apartment, he was unconcerned about being seen.

The second of the three remaining residents answered.

'Hi! Who's that?' a bright and cheery voice answered.

'Hi there,' Stroud said. 'Sorry to bother you, but I'm looking for Hendrik.'

'Who?'

'Hendrik Dekker.'

'I don't know anyone called Dekker. Oh, wait a minute, is that the guy in number three?'

'That's right, yes. Hendrik Dekker in number three.'

'I don't know, man. I've seen him maybe five times in the last year. He's never here. You'd have to ask the landlord.'

Stroud looked at the name on the intercom. *Paul Timmerman.*

'Is this Paul?'

'Yeah, this is Paul.'

'Do you have any idea where Mr Dekker works, Paul?'

'No, I don't.' Paul hesitated. 'Hang on, let me ask Livia.'

Stroud looked at Nina. Nina tried to look hopeful.

'Hey, you still there?'

'I'm here,' Stroud said.

'Livia thinks maybe he's a cop or something. She thinks he works in Wassenaar.'

'Wassenaar?'

'Yeah, man. That government place over there.'

'Okay. Thanks for your help, Paul. I really appreciate it.'

'Hey, who is this anyway?'

'I'm his cousin.'

Stroud released the buzzer and walked away.

'Quick,' he said, grabbing Nina's hand.

They were across the street and out of line-of-sight when an upstairs curtain moved and a face appeared. A young man, fair-haired, a close-cropped beard. Evidently Paul Timmerman trying to see what Hendrik Dekker's cousin looked like.

Stroud waited until Timmerman had given up looking, and then he and Nina headed back to the train station.

'Wassenaar,' Nina said. 'Why have I heard that name before?'

'Because it's where the IDB is headquartered.'

'IDB?'

'Inlichtingendienst Buitenland,' Stroud replied. 'Dutch foreign intelligence service.'

'Dekker is foreign intelligence?'

'I have no idea, Nina. Right now, I'm beginning to wonder if

Raphael, Dekker, whoever the hell else we might uncover, are all aliases for the same person, and that person is actually none of them.'

'Meaning what?'

Stroud just stopped walking right there on the pavement and looked up at the sky. He closed his eyes and breathed deeply.

'Stroud?'

'Have you ever had one of those moments when something you thought was true turns out to be a lie? And then everything else becomes uncertain, and you just don't know what to think or who to trust or how the fuck you're going to make sense of things. That's what this is, Nina. Like you woke up one morning and the room is empty, and you realise you've slept right through someone stealing everything you own.'

Nina didn't reply.

'We have to go to Wassenaar,' Stroud said.

'You really think that's a good idea?'

'Do you have a better one?'

'Maybe there's a way we can find out what this Hendrik Dekker looks like before Dutch foreign intelligence gets curious as to why we're looking for him. I mean, it could be someone else entirely. That doesn't even take into consideration that the girl in the apartment could be wrong. All she said was that she thought he worked in Wassenaar. And then there's still the other Dekker in Hilversum.'

'Yes,' Stroud said. 'Yes, you're right. I need to think about this. I can't react. I'm jumping to conclusions here.'

'So let's go somewhere nearby and get something to eat and just look at our options, okay?'

'Okay,' Stroud replied. He started walking again, looking straight ahead, doing all he could to focus his attention on what he knew, not what he was assuming. The truth was that he was certain of nothing; from London to Istanbul to the Netherlands, he really was none the wiser about the nature of Raphael's death, nor whether Raphael was someone other than the person he'd believed him to be. That sense of uncertainty was not a good feeling, and it was that feeling he needed to get rid of.

19

March of 1964, Stroud was pretty much reconciled to dying.

After the Bay of Pigs, the Algerian insurrection in '62, after JFK's *Ich bin ein Berliner* speech at Rathaus Schöneberg in June of the following year, Stroud, Raphael and Haig had flown into the middle of the Greek–Cypriot war. Where they were precisely, which side of an ever-moving front line of battle, Stroud didn't know and couldn't recall.

He had taken a wrong turn out of a shelled building, found himself caught in crossfire. Nothing serious, a deep graze along the middle of his right thigh, but – inadequately dressed and treated – it had turned septic. Within a day he had dropped into shock and fever, his blood pressure had plummeted, and he was delirious. Raphael had recognised the symptoms, and in the absence of antibiotics had done all he could to raise Stroud's blood pressure – making him drink water, giving him endless salt tablets, doing his best to keep the wound as cold as possible – until the battle had abated sufficiently for him and Haig to get Stroud into a Land Rover and to a field surgical facility.

Raphael didn't tell him what had happened. Stroud remembered nothing. It was Haig who told him how and why he'd wound up in a makeshift hospital with IV drips in his arms.

A day before he was released, Raphael showed up. He brought a bottle of ouzo.

'I'm not sure alcohol is such a bright idea,' Stroud said.

Raphael laughed. 'Nothing that we do is a bright idea, for fuck's sake.'

Stroud took the proffered paper cup and drank. 'So why do we do it?'

'I have no goddamned idea,' Raphael said.

'You couldn't walk away from this?'

'And do what?'

'Stay in London. Write. Travel, but not into war zones.'

Raphael smiled wryly. 'My life is hotel rooms, aeroplanes, bars, dirty clothes, and missing death by inches on a routine basis.'

'You ever wonder what makes us keep coming back?'

'I think you've spent too much time doing nothing, my friend. All this introspection isn't healthy.'

Stroud pulled himself up into a sitting position. His leg ached, his head ached, he felt simultaneously nauseous and famished, but there was something about this moment – why, he had no idea – that made him want to get an answer from Raphael.

'Just tell me what you think, Vincent,' he said. 'You must have thought about it. I mean, the sacrifices we have to make. Relationships, family, security, stability, all that shit . . .'

Raphael leaned forward. 'That's the point right there, Stroud.'

'What?'

'Most of it is shit.' He smiled again, that knowing expression, forever implying that he was aware of something arcane that afforded him a unique perspective. 'I mean, if your family are anything like mine, you can do without them, right? And security? Doing what? Working in some mind-numbing job, never earning enough and never being given a chance to earn more.' He laughed. 'Banality and conformity are the suburbs of hell, my friend. I have seen my father work all his life, and what does he have to show for it? The high point of his week is cleaning the fucking car and going for the newspapers on a

Sunday morning. I mean, it's fucking awful to see what happens to people when they buy into that reality.'

'You're an anarchist,' Stroud said. 'Fuck the system and all that.'

'I'm not anything. I'm just me. I do what I do the best I can, and if other people don't understand it, so what?'

'What did you want to do when you were a kid?'

'To never grow up.'

Raphael reached for the bottle of ouzo and refilled both their cups.

'Here's to being someone that no one else understands for the rest of our very short lives.'

20

Stroud had merely pushed food around his plate, eaten next to nothing. Nina watched him, her expression unchanging. He was unreadable at times, other times an open book.

'So?' she finally prompted.

'I want to get into that flat.'

'You what?'

Stroud leaned forward and lowered his voice. 'I need to get into that flat. I want to see what's in there. I want to find out if this Hendrik Dekker is actually Raphael, and if he's not, then I need to find out why that name was on a picture of Raphael in Istanbul.'

'Can we at least go to Hilversum and check out the other Hendrik Dekker first, for Christ's sake?'

Stroud shook his head. 'No.'

'Why the hell not?'

'Because.'

Nina frowned. 'Because? That's all you're going to say? *Because*? Because of what?'

'Gut feeling. Intuition. Something about this smells very bad indeed. Dekker's name on Raphael's picture, and we wind up here, ten miles from the headquarters of Dutch intelligence.'

'I live less than ten miles from MI6, Stroud.'

Stroud looked at her intently. It was an unnerving feeling, as if he could see the thoughts she wasn't sharing.

'I do not expect you to come with me,' he said calmly.

'I have no intention of coming with you.'

He smiled.

'What?' she asked.

'Nothing.'

'Why are you smiling?'

'Because you're probably a whole lot brighter than me, and I don't believe for a second that you suspect nothing. I think you're as caught up in this as I am. You believe that Raphael is still alive, don't you?'

Nina didn't reply. She looked away. At last she nodded. 'Yes, I do.'

Stroud leaned forward. 'Why? Why do you think he's still alive?'

'Because I believe he was too smart, too experienced, to get caught out like that. I don't think he'd have got into that Land Rover, or he'd have seen it coming and got out of it fast.'

'Did you see the official report? The one from the Jordanian authorities?'

'No, I didn't.'

'It said there were no identifiable remains. Actually, it said there were no remains at all, nothing they could examine or use to verify identity. Teeth don't burn until you're way past a thousand degrees centigrade. An explosion like that, a hand grenade, cans of petrol... that's hot, for sure, but not hot enough to leave nothing.'

'Hang on a minute, you're supposed to be the sceptic here. You're the one who's been banging on about how he can't possibly be alive.'

'Reconciling yourself to something for six years, accepting it, convincing yourself that the official report is factual...' Stroud shook his head. 'I *am* uncertain. I really am. But this thing keeps nagging at me, this thing he said to me a couple of times, once when I was laid up with a bullet wound that had gone septic, another time in Vietnam.'

'What did he say?'

'The skin of the beast is not the beast.'

Nina frowned. 'What the hell does that mean?'

'As it sounds. The outward appearance of something is just its outward appearance.'

Stroud paused, closed his eyes for a moment.

'I can see his face. He looked at me so intensely. He said that the only way to make it out was to become someone else. And then he said that thing again. The skin of the beast is not the beast.'

'You think he really could have faked his own death? That this Hendrik Dekker is Dutch intelligence and he's somehow connected to Raphael, or maybe could even *be* Raphael?'

'I don't know. I guess if I had to bet on someone doing that and getting away with it, my money would be on Raphael. I just have to go on gut instinct, and there's something about this guy who works at Wassenaar that won't let me go.'

'Haig told me to keep an eye on you.'

'I know he did.'

'I guess I can't do that from outside in the street, can I?'

'I guess not.'

'Jesus Christ, Stroud, I'm beginning to think you guys have a death wish. But that's not my main worry. My main worry is that it's contagious.'

21

At the end of the street, a gang of lads were drinking cans of beer and laughing. Their noise was appreciated, attracting attention away from Stroud and Nina as they crossed behind the block of flats and headed along a dark alleyway that ran between the rear of the building and the neighbouring gardens.

'This is mad,' Nina told him. 'How do you even know which flat it is?'

'Flat three, remember? Third floor.'

'And what if he's there?'

'Well, the lights will be on and we'll see some movement or hear some noise, won't we? And the Timmerman guy said he'd only seen Dekker five times in the last year.'

'What if tonight is number six?'

Stroud stopped in his tracks and turned around. 'If it bothers you that much, then let me go alone.'

'I'm just scared, that's all. This kind of thing freaks me out.'

'I haven't exactly made a habit of it. I just want to get in there, take a look around, see if there's anything that connects this guy with Raphael.'

'Okay,' Nina replied, nervous agitation evident in her tone. 'All right. Let's go then. Let's just get it done.'

There was an external wrought-iron stairway and fire escape that ran right to the top of the building. There were lights in the lower two floors, but the upper two were in darkness. Within arm's length of the third-floor walkway was a small window, sizeable enough for Nina to get through, and this was the proposition that Stroud put to her.

'What if you can't get it open?' she asked.

'Then you won't have to climb through it, will you?'

'Oh for Christ's sake, Stroud. What the hell are we getting into?'

'I can't answer that until I know, and right now I only know as much as you.'

'There's no other way in?'

'Not that I can see, no.'

Nina stepped back into the shadow of the fence and watched as Stroud went up the stairway on the balls of his feet. He reached the third floor, and for what seemed like an age he inspected the window, his fingers beneath the frame, tapping the glass, peering over the edge to determine what kind of catch secured it from within.

Once down again he said, 'It should be easy enough. I just need something thin and strong, maybe four, five inches long.'

Nina went through her bag and passed him a nail file.

'That should do it,' he said. 'Stay here. I'll be as quiet as I can, but keep watch. If someone walks down the alleyway, cough and walk away. Stay out of sight until they've gone and then come back.'

Nina stepped back into the shadows as Stroud headed for the fire escape again.

Back at the window, he paused for a moment. He was scared. Not of being caught, but of what he might find out. Something or nothing, both were equally unsavoury outcomes. He was now beyond asking himself what he was doing. The nerves and self-doubt were a thing of the past; this was as real as anything he had ever experienced. He had not exaggerated when he'd said that a lie as significant and profound as this raised doubts in all other areas. If what he knew of Raphael wasn't true, then what other illusions and falsehoods were part of his life?

He was about to cross the line. Breaking and entering was serious in any language, in any country, and yet he knew that the choice that presented itself was actually no choice at all. There were some questions that required a definitive negative or positive. No half-measures.

He stepped towards the window and got to work. It didn't take as long as he'd imagined. He was able to work the nail file through the gap and ease the catch upwards. He felt it give, and then the window was open. He looked down. Nina was looking right back up at him. He waved his hand, and she started up the fire escape.

Pulling herself through the window, Nina tore a four- or five-inch rip in the thigh of her jeans. As the weight of her upper body complied with gravity, she found herself falling awkwardly over a bathroom sink and down to the floor. She landed heavily, painfully, and before she even inspected it she knew she'd done something bad to her left wrist.

To Stroud, it seemed like an eternity before he heard the latch on the inside of the fire door snap back. He stepped into the darkness, pulled the door to behind him, and as his eyes grew accustomed to the light, he could see that Nina was in some considerable discomfort.

'You okay?'

'I think I've broken my fucking wrist.'

'Seriously?'

'No, Stroud, it's a joke. I'm just saying that because I think it's funny.'

'Sorry.'

'I'm going to need a doctor. Can we do whatever we need to do and get the fuck out of here?'

Stroud reached through and pulled the light cord. Nina's

complexion was off-white and varnished with sweat. She looked as if she was ready to throw up.

'Let me see,' he said.

Gingerly she held out her arm. With great care, Stroud turned back the cuff of her coat. Her wrist was already swollen and discoloured, and though there was no sign of a protruding fracture or surface wound, it didn't mean it wasn't broken.

'Okay,' he said. He went through to the kitchen and grabbed a tea towel from a rail beside the sink. He soaked it under the tap, wrung most of the water out and then wrapped it as tightly as Nina could bear around her wrist.

'Do you know what you're doing?' she asked.

'Right now, or generally?'

She managed a weak smile.

'Sit on the toilet or the edge of the bath,' he said. 'Stay there. I'll be as quick as I can.'

He turned off the bathroom light and went back to the kitchen. Unadorned walls, plates, cups, saucers, cutlery all in its rightful place, the stove top clean, the sink dry. In the fridge, there was nothing that could spoil – no milk, no dairy products, no eggs, no meat. What he did find was jars and bottles, many of them unopened.

In the living room there were a couple of copies of *National Geographic*, one dated June of the previous year, one from November of the year before. The dust on the shelves and the top of the television was uniform and undisturbed.

Again the walls were unadorned – no family photos, no paintings – and there were no vases, no ornaments of any description on the sideboard or the small table by the window. There was an ashtray with some spent cigarette ends in it, but these were hard and dry. If someone lived here, they had not been home for some considerable time. That was the crux of it – it didn't feel like a home at all. It had the impersonal nature of a hotel room.

The bedroom was similar in all respects – clean bedding, a smooth pillow, a laundry basket with no laundry. The clothes in the wardrobe were few, and even as Stroud went through the pockets of the three or four pairs of trousers and the two jackets that hung there, he knew he would find nothing. His certainty of this was undone as his hand brushed along the lower hem of the last jacket. There was something there, no doubt about it. He took the jacket out and once again ran his hand along the fabric. Something unyielding and small. A coin, perhaps? He felt again. It was no coin. He believed it was a key. He laid the garment on the bed and went back to the kitchen for a knife. He checked on Nina on the way back to the bedroom. She asked him if he'd found anything.

'Not sure,' he said. 'You okay?'

'As can be. Really hurts, mind.'

'Be back as fast as I can.'

In the bedroom, he laid out the jacket. He hesitated, looking down at the stitching that secured the lining to the fabric. There was something about this that felt wrong. Not the fact that he was in someone else's flat, that he had gone through their possessions and clothes, that he was just about to unpick the lining of a jacket and find out what was inside; rather, the emptiness of the place, the fact that to all intents and purposes it was not a real home, set off alarm bells. *Safe house* was the phrase that came to mind. Somewhere to run to, somewhere to hide. Somewhere, perhaps, to change identity.

The stitching came away easily. He'd been right. It was a key – small, silver, unfamiliar in design – and it had been stitched to the fabric itself. This, as he had at first suspected, was not something that had fallen through a hole in a pocket and got lost. It had been secreted here intentionally. He cut it free. It sat there in the palm of his hand. He had no way to sew it back into the lining. He had no idea what it opened. He asked himself if he wanted to know, and the answer came back without hesitation: he *needed* to know.

He hung the jacket in the wardrobe. He went back to the bathroom.

'Anything?'

Stroud shook his head. 'No,' he replied.

He didn't know why instinct told him to lie. He would tell her later, when she was out of pain and they were away from this place. By that time it would be too late to undo his actions.

'Let's go,' he said. 'We need to get you to a hospital.'

22

The prognosis was not something they wanted to hear.

Nina sat on a gurney in a curtained booth. She looked pale and tired. Her left wrist was now twice its regular girth, and her fingers were pale. She had asked Stroud to stay. Dr Visser – young, confident, very direct – quickly established his medical authority.

'Miss Benson, you have to listen to me and understand what I am saying. This is not a sprain, nor is it a dislocation. You have broken your wrist. Snapped it. It needs to be properly cared for. The ramifications are serious if you do not do as I advise.' He turned to Stroud. 'You understand me?'

Stroud nodded.

'You need to have your arm splinted until the swelling goes down. That may take three or four days. Then we have to set it and put a cast on it. The swelling may reduce again, in which case you will need a second cast. I advise you to go back to London and get your treatment there. I will splint it now, but I want you to be very careful. You have to take this matter seriously. You need to rest. You need to keep your arm above the level of your heart. You cannot just behave like there is nothing wrong.'

Nina looked at Stroud. Both frustration and defeat were evident in her expression.

'So?' she asked.

'So I think you should do what he says.'

'And you?'

'We'll talk about that later.'

Nina looked back at Dr Visser. 'How long to heal? I mean, how long do I need to wear a cast for?'

'I understand what you are asking, Miss Benson, but a cast does not mean you can ignore the broken bone. Even with a cast, you need to take care. You cannot put undue stress on it. Broken bones, if they are not correctly treated and fully healed, can cause all manner of later complications.'

'I think what he's saying is that you can't come out to play any more, Nina.'

'I get that, Stroud.' She looked at Visser. 'Fuck,' she said.

Visser smiled. 'I appreciate your Anglo-Saxon directness. I understand your frustrations, but these are the facts. Do as I advise, all will be well. Do not do this, and you may have irreparable damage and permanent deformity.'

An hour and a half later, Stroud walked Nina out of the hospital and down the street. They took a room at the first hotel they found. It was close to eleven p.m. They were tired, ready to drop, but also hungry and thirsty.

Room service was slow, but the food and drinks were welcome.

After she'd eaten enough, Nina lay on the bed, three or four pillows behind her, and smoked and drank until it looked like she was fighting to keep her eyes open.

'I'll help you get undressed,' Stroud said.

She didn't quibble. She let Stroud remove her jeans, her blouse, the T-shirt underneath. He rolled her sideways while she held her arm up, and then managed to get her beneath the covers. One pillow beneath her head, another two to support her arm, and she was as comfortable as she could get.

'I can sleep on the sofa,' Stroud said.

'Stroud, just sleep in the bed. It's fine. Just don't roll over on me, okay?'

He stripped down to his underwear and climbed in beside her. He switched out the lamp and the room fell into darkness. A faint glow from the street lights outside the window gave form and distinction to the furniture after a little while, and when Stroud looked to his left, he could see Nina's profile, her dark hair splayed across the pillow, the shape of her splinted arm.

'This is not good,' she said. 'I don't want to go back to London.'

'You don't have a choice, Nina. You have to do what the doctor said.'

'You're going to stay behind, aren't you?'

'Yes. For a little while. I have to know if this Dekker is Raphael.'

'And if he is? And he works for the Dutch security services? What will you do then?'

Stroud didn't respond for a while. He heard Nina's breathing slow down and become deeper.

'I don't know,' he said. 'I really don't know.'

'Don't know,' she murmured.

'No.'

'Don't know what, Stroud?'

'Go to sleep, Nina. We'll talk about it in the morning.'

Despite his deep sense of fatigue, Stroud didn't sleep well.

Nina was restless, understandably, and that also served to keep him tense and unsettled. When dawn came, he stirred, sat up, felt the ache across his shoulders and neck. He slid out from beneath the covers as quietly as he could and went into the bathroom. While the water ran into the tub, he smoked a cigarette.

Nina was awake.

'Can you help me up?' she asked.

He did so, putting her blouse around her shoulders and supporting her as she made her unsteady way to the bathroom.

'I feel bloody awful,' she said. 'I shouldn't have had anything to drink. Not good with the painkillers.'

Stroud left her to use the toilet, and put the rest of his clothes on. In truth, he wanted to go back to London. He wanted clean laundry, a shave, a good meal and a few pints in a familiar pub, but there was reason enough to stay behind. He had broken into someone's flat, rifled through their belongings, cut a key from the lining of their jacket and stolen it. Now he needed to find out what it opened.

Nina appeared. He helped her get dressed. Once downstairs, they ate breakfast – a roll, some cheese, a cup of coffee – and then Stroud had the receptionist call a taxi for the airport.

'What do you want me to say to Marcus?'

'Just tell him that I have a couple of other things to check out. I don't intend on staying here any longer than I absolutely have to.'

The flight left a little after ten. Stroud waited until Nina was through the gate and out along the glass walkway. He waved. She smiled back weakly. She looked exhausted, but Stroud knew that her frustration would be of far greater significance. He left the lounge. He didn't look back. Before he reached the exit, he was already missing her.

23

Three key cutters told him that the key he had taken from Dekker's flat could be for any number of locks. A security deposit box, a personal safe, a filing cabinet, even a shop display cabinet. Stroud kept walking, kept asking. In the sixth shop he found someone who seemed to possess a far wider knowledge and far greater certainty.

The man was at first suspicious. 'So, how do you have a key and you don't know what it's for?'

'I'm going through my cousin's personal possessions for his wife. He died a month ago. He lived here in Amsterdam. She asked me to help her sort things out.'

'Of course, yes. I'm sorry to hear that.' He paused. 'The manufacturer's name is there. There is a five-digit product code as well.' He indicated a word along the upper side of the blade. *SCHILDSICHERHEIT*. 'Shield Security. It is a German firm. Any reason your cousin would have a mailbox or a security locker in Germany?'

Stroud shook his head. 'Not that I can think of, no.'

'Let's hope that whatever you find is not an unpleasant surprise for his widow, eh?'

Stroud returned to the hotel. In the room, he dialled for information, spelled the name of the key company. A few moments later he was calling a number in Oberhausen, Germany.

The receptionist who took the call didn't speak English with sufficient fluency to understand what it was that he was asking. She told him to wait while she checked if someone else was available to deal with his request.

'Yes, how can we help you?' a man asked.

'Oh, hello. I'm calling to make an enquiry about a key.'

'Yes. Keys. We make keys. Keys and locks and all related items. What is it that you need?'

'I have a key. It belonged to my cousin. He died recently. His wife asked me to help settle his affairs, and we found this key from your company. I wondered if it was possible for you to tell me what it's for if I give you the product code.'

'Yes, of course. What is the code, please?'

'FT one-one-seven.'

'The FT is Flughafen Tegel. This is for a security locker at Tegel Airport in Berlin.'

'A security locker?'

'Yes, sir, a security locker. For the use of passengers who reserve their luggage while they wait or have dinner. They are for storing personal possessions. You understand?'

'Yes, yes, of course. A security locker.'

'Good. Is there anything else?'

'No, that's all. You've been very helpful.'

'You are very welcome, sir.'

The line went dead.

Tegel Airport. Berlin. Hendrik Dekker – whose name appeared beneath a photograph of Vincent Raphael, said photograph in a dossier held by Turkish intelligence – had the key to security locker number 117 sewn into the lining of his jacket. Notwithstanding the fact that this could be entirely the wrong Dekker, Stroud was not surprised at the revelation. It seemed in keeping with the way everything else had unfolded thus far.

He picked up the phone again and dialled London.

Haig was out of the office. No one seemed to know where he was or when he would return. Stroud left a message with his secretary, Carole.

'Tell him that I called. Nina's on the way home. I have to check a few other things out but I shouldn't be much longer.'

'Very good, Mr Stroud.'

'Oh, and Carole?'

'Yes?'

'Tell him that the Doubting Thomas is weakening in his certainty.'

'The Doubting Thomas...'

'Just tell him. He'll understand.'

Stroud took a taxi back to the airport. Flight restrictions limited the number of airlines from which he could choose. Only those companies headquartered in the USA, France or the United Kingdom could fly through the Allied air corridor into West Berlin. The first out was with Dan-Air. He wouldn't get into Tegel until eleven, but better that than another Amsterdam hotel room. He had no idea how many lockers would be there, nor the level of security around them. Any suspicious activity would result in unwanted attention from airport security, perhaps the police, and then what? An arrest for breaking and entering and theft. The one saving grace in this ridiculous escapade was that he was not flying into the East.

He sat in the bar at Schiphol and drank three beers without even thinking about it. It was a bad habit, but knowing that didn't stop him. He should have stopped drinking and smoking a good while back. He was thirty-seven, but his last medical had revealed the blood pressure of a man a good fifteen or twenty years older.

'Bad diet, no exercise, alcohol and cigarettes, yes?' the doctor had asked.

'Sounds about right.'

'What are you going to do about it?'

'Eat better, take some exercise, stop drinking and smoking.'

The doctor smiled knowingly. 'And I am growing wings and will shortly fly unaided to the moon.'

'You don't believe me?'

'No, Mr Stroud, I don't believe you. You should cut back on all the bad, improve the good. You can do it in increments. I am not suggesting ascetic seclusion and self-flagellation, just an awareness of how a small change can make a big difference.'

The small changes had continued for a week or so, and then Stroud was back to his old habits. Granted, a lack of money had tempered his consumption, certainly of the hard stuff, but now he was on Haig's tab and could run riot. Considering what he was doing and the potential consequences should he screw it up, it was not a safe course of action. If he wasn't acting straight, he at least needed to think straight while he did it.

Notwithstanding the seriousness of the situation he had created for himself, he refused to waver in his intent to see it through. Whether that was driven by a real need to know the truth or merely stubborn bloody-mindedness, he didn't know. More importantly, he didn't care. He refused to be drawn into the temptation to analyse what he was doing, and now that he didn't have Nina to consider, he could make his own decisions and just follow them. He liked her, no doubt about it, trusted her too, but he was used to working alone. That was how it had always been. Yes, he'd had companions – Raphael, Haig, others too – but they were all independently minded and often had not taken the same road, followed the same potential lead or photo opportunity. Nina had been sent by Haig to keep an eye on him, and though he had roped her into participating in what was perhaps the most ill-advised venture of his life, still the fact remained that seeing her onto a plane and back to London meant that the risk of being caught was halved. Two people attracted twice as much attention as one.

Boarding was announced. It was a short flight. Stroud impressed himself with his refusal of a further drink on the plane.

24

Despite the late hour, the Tegel terminal building was still busy.

Once Stroud was through customs and passport control, he had no difficulty finding the bank of security lockers. There were thirty-six in all, racked four high, nine across. Number 117 was on the second-highest tier, the sixth along to the right.

He could feel the key in his pocket. The emotion he experienced was one of both anticipation and trepidation. Thankfully, a heavy frosted-glass partition separated the lockers from the main concourse. He would be little more than a blurred silhouette behind it. Regardless, a sense of unease slowly built, and by the time he stood there, the locker right in front of him, he could feel his own heartbeat. At first he was certain that his unease was caused by nothing more than concern for what he might find within, but then it became something else. What if the locker was being watched? What if someone had anticipated his finding the key, and it had been put there for no other reason than to bring him here? Such a possibility seemed ludicrous, but then there was a sound behind him. Footsteps approaching.

He turned, perhaps too quickly. A man passed him, smiled nonchalantly, went to his own locker and opened it.

Stroud did his best to observe him without making it too obvious.

The man glanced left towards him. Had he sensed that Stroud was hesitant, waiting for him to leave?

Stroud was making it worse, fuelling his own anxiety. He focused, took a deep breath, waited for the man to retrieve his belongings from the locker and move away. The man didn't look back, and Stroud was grateful for this. Nevertheless, he wondered whether the lack of attention had been intentional. Had the man gone to report a suspicious individual in the security locker area?

He tried to ignore the premonition of panic. He held the key in his hand. This was it. This was now the point of no return. If he didn't open the locker, he could never be connected to the break-in at Dekker's flat, but he would leave a question unresolved that would haunt him forever. He had to open it. He had to know.

He reached up. The key slid into the lock. He glanced over his shoulder. Silhouettes passed back and forth on the other side of the frosted glass. He turned the key. It started to move, and then it stopped dead. Stroud's heart stopped with it.

He withdrew the key, inserted it once again, turned it. Just as before, it travelled a few millimetres and then stopped. He turned it back the other way. Nothing. The key didn't open 117. He had assumed that the number on the key related to the number of the locker. He now appreciated the utter stupidity of such an assumption. It was a security locker. Who in their right mind would manufacture a key and put the locker number on it?

But it had to be these lockers, surely? It had to be Tegel. The key would open one of the other thirty-five lockers, save the one he'd already seen someone open. That had to be it. It just had to be.

He stepped back for a moment. He asked himself if there was any other way to do this than trying each one in turn.

Even as he was considering how best to approach the problem, a woman appeared to his right. With her was a small boy. She smiled, made her way towards the lockers, searching through her handbag as she did so.

The boy just stared at Stroud. Stroud smiled at the boy.

The woman found the key she was looking for, opened her locker and from it took an attaché case and a small travel bag.

Leaving the key in the lock, she started back towards the main concourse.

Stroud had not moved.

And then the woman stopped. She glanced back at Stroud. She frowned and said, '*Sie brauchen Hilfe?*'

Stroud shook his head. 'It's okay.'

'You are English?'

'Yes, English.'

'You need some help? You are having difficulty with the locker?'

'No, it's okay. I'm okay. Thank you.'

The woman hesitated.

Stroud smiled. He looked down at the boy.

It could not have been more than three or four seconds, but it felt endless.

Eventually she nodded, smiled back, and then, holding both bags in her left hand, she took hold of the boy's hand with her right and walked away. The boy continued to stare at Stroud.

Stroud breathed deeply. He didn't move for a good ten seconds. He expected someone to appear, to question what he was doing. He was either going to do this or he wasn't. There was no middle ground.

Beginning nearest him, he started with the uppermost locker and worked down to the lowest. Then to the next column. He couldn't rush it for fear of failing to ensure the key was fully home in the lock, thus missing the correct one. He went quickly but conscientiously, ever attentive to someone else appearing from either side of the bank of lockers. The silhouettes kept on moving. Nevertheless, he anticipated an interruption, a sudden word, another passenger taking the initiative and alerting an official.

Panic rose in his chest. It was becoming acute. The very real fear of being caught, what he would say, how he could ever explain himself. It undermined any element of certainty he might have had about what he was doing.

His hands had started to sweat, so much so that his fingers slid as he tried to put the key in yet another lock. He had reached the fifth or sixth column, and was already wondering if he had missed the right one. He looked back along the bank of lockers. Should he go back and start again? Should he try the last few once more? He was about to give up, to walk away and rethink this whole situation, when he glanced to his right and saw what he had most feared. The dark uniform and cap, the gun at his belt, his head cocked to one side as he patiently watched Stroud trying a key in one locker after another.

'*Brauchen Sie Hilfe?*'

Stroud's heart was in his mouth. He glanced away, looked back at the policeman, and then put the key in his pocket. His heart doubled up in pace, and a sense of real terror invaded the base of his stomach.

The policeman started towards him. There was nowhere for Stroud to go. He smiled as best he could despite the paralysing tension of the situation.

'*Was tun Sie hier?*' the policeman asked.

Stroud shrugged, didn't understand what he was being asked.

'American?'

He shook his head. 'English.'

'What are you doing here?'

Stroud tried to laugh. 'I have completely forgotten the number of my locker. I know, it's really stupid, but I cannot for the life of me remember it.'

The policeman didn't seem to relax at all, nor did the suspicious expression leave his face.

'Passport, please,' he said.

'Passport?'

'Yes, sir. Your passport.'

Stroud took it from his jacket pocket and handed it over. First rule: never give up your passport. Here he had no choice.

'You flew from where today?'

'Amsterdam. Schiphol.'

'Where is your ticket?'

Stroud produced it.

'This flight arrived less than an hour ago. You pay for a locker, leave your luggage, and have already forgotten the number?'

'Well, no, it's not that simple. I am collecting something for someone.'

'Who?'

'A friend.'

'And where is your friend?'

'In London. He's sick. He asked me to collect his suitcase.'

'Show me the key.'

Stroud was helpless. He couldn't refuse. There was no way out of this but to bluff it, and yet he had the inescapable feeling that this was not going to work.

He held up the key.

'You say that your friend's suitcase is in one of these lockers?'

'Yes, that's right.'

'But you said it was your key and you had forgotten the number.'

'I did, yes.'

'You didn't pay for this locker, correct?'

'No, I didn't.'

'And your friend in London does not know the number?'

'Yes, he does, and he told me, but I have forgotten it.'

'You cannot telephone him and ask him?'

'I could, but I thought it would be quicker to just try the key. There are not very many lockers.'

'So why are you flying from Amsterdam and not from London to do this?'

'I was already in Amsterdam. My friend called me and asked me to collect this for him on the way back to London.'

'You are a good friend?'

Stroud relaxed a little. 'Yes, I try to be.'

'But not such a good liar, Herr Stroud.'

'Liar?' Stroud did his best to look surprised, even offended.

'Yes, Herr Stroud. You are not a good liar.'

'What do you mean?'

'I mean that I do not believe what you are saying. I believe that you found this key somewhere and you are hoping there is something valuable inside the locker.'

Stroud frowned, stepped back. 'Why would you accuse me of such a thing? This is completely unacceptable—'

'You can explain it to airport security. We can contact your friend in London. If what you are saying is true, then it will be sorted out in a very short time and you will be free to leave.'

Stroud reached for his passport, but the policeman pulled it back.

'You stay here,' he said. 'You do not move.'

Stroud retreated one step, his back against the lockers. He was finished. He knew it heart and soul. There was no way out of this.

'*Flughafensicherheitsbüro*,' the policeman said into his radio. '*Terminal Eins. Unterstützung erfordelich.*'

Two of them came. They were not in uniform. For some reason that seemed all the more ominous. The policeman explained the situation. The older of the two security officers

139

took Stroud's passport and asked for the key. Stroud handed it over.

'Follow me, sir,' he said. 'I am sure it will not take long to resolve this matter.'

Stroud followed them without saying a word.

25

After searching Stroud, then going through the contents of his bag, Lange, the older of the two officers, stayed with him while the younger, Hahn, was sent to make a telephone call.

Stroud was sequestered in a small plain office. The sole entry and exit was through a heavy door, within which was a pane of toughened glass. The table at which he sat was bolted to the floor, as was the chair. This was an interrogation room, no question about it.

'On what basis are you detaining me?' he asked Lange.

'I am not authorised to answer any questions.'

'What do you mean, you are not authorised. Who are you?'

'The proper authorities have been informed and they will send some people to talk with you.'

'What authorities? Which people?' Stroud could hear the fear in his own voice. This was no game.

'The proper authorities, Herr Stroud. They will tell you who they are and they will ask you questions.'

'What right do you have to keep me here?'

Lange smiled patiently. This was what he did. This was his territory. He was in the business of arresting and questioning suspicious characters. Tegel was an international airport, and thus he was no stranger to such things. Stroud appreciated that he must have heard every protestation and denial in the book.

Lange opened a drawer on his side of the table and produced a flimsy aluminium ashtray.

As he set it down, he looked at Stroud. His face was implacable, emotionless, utterly matter-of-fact.

'You are permitted to smoke, Herr Stroud.'

With that, he rose and walked to the door. He opened it, and then paused. He turned and looked back at Stroud. Stroud expected him to say something, but Lange just looked at him again. Finally he went out through the door and locked it behind him. His footsteps grew ever quieter as he made his way back down the corridor.

Stroud lit a cigarette. His hands were shaking. He got up and started pacing. He walked to the door, tried the handle, even though he knew it was futile, and then attempted to see sideways along the corridor. He felt sick to his stomach, angry with himself, upset that he had been so ill prepared for such a scenario. He could have pre-empted all of this by appreciating that no security firm would put the damned locker number on a key. He could have taken a room somewhere, returned in the morning. There was a café within line-of-sight of the lockers. He could have sat there inconspicuously, watching as people accessed the lockers, eliminating them one by one and thus significantly reducing the number he would have to try. But no, he'd had to do it now. Always now. Impatient, headstrong, impulsive. That was what had prompted the theft of the key in the first place, and now here he was, in a holding cell in a German airport, awaiting 'the proper authorities'. The embassy would be involved; they would call Haig at *The Times*. If Dekker really was Dutch intelligence, it could turn into a full-blown diplomatic incident.

The footsteps came back down the hall. Stroud sat down again, stubbed out his half-smoked cigarette in the ashtray, then lit another without thinking.

The door was unlocked. Stroud looked up. Instead of Lange, he saw a dark-haired woman, perhaps early thirties, behind her a man carrying three cups on a small plastic tray.

The man stepped past her and set down the tray. Neither of them spoke. The man then left again, returning a moment later with a third chair. He set it against the wall to Stroud's right. The woman sat across from Stroud and – still without a word – passed him a cup of coffee.

'Thank you,' he said.

She gave him a brief smile.

The man sat down.

'If you don't mind, I would like to look in your bag,' the woman said.

'Someone already searched it.'

'Please, Herr Stroud.'

Stroud took his canvas holdall from the floor and put it on the table.

The woman took out his camera, a couple of lenses, a notebook, pens, his wallet, a change of underwear and a comb.

She picked up the camera, looked over it, and then opened the back.

'Hey!' Stroud said. 'Those are my pictures.'

She didn't even glance up. She popped out the film canister, then pulled the celluloid out of it until the entire roll was exposed.

'You can't do that!' Stroud exclaimed. Again, there wasn't the slightest sign of recognition from the woman.

She proceeded to go through Stroud's wallet, and then flipped through his notebooks, pausing every once in a while to scan a page or two. Once she was done, she put everything back in the bag and handed it to her colleague. He placed it on the ground between his feet, and then kicked it back under his chair.

The woman took Stroud's passport from her jacket pocket and placed it on the table. Then she looked up, again that brief smile, and said, 'My name is Christa Maier, and this is my colleague, Dieter Lehmann. We are here to ask you some questions, Herr Stroud, but before we do, we want you to understand that you are not obliged to answer them. If you wish, you can ask for a lawyer or a representative of your embassy to be present.'

'Why would I need a lawyer?' Stroud asked. 'I haven't done anything wrong. And who the hell are you people anyway?' His tone was defensive, overly so, and he knew he sounded both weak and guilty. For the first time since this whole thing had begun, he was genuinely afraid.

'We are BND,' Maier said. 'Do you know what that is, Herr Stroud?'

Stroud shook his head.

Maier smiled as if humouring a small child. 'No, of course you don't. We are from the Federal Intelligence Service.'

He felt the colour draining from his face.

'We work with the intelligence communities of other countries,' Maier explained. 'We investigate money laundering, extortion, arms and weapon trafficking, organised crime, such matters as these. However, our primary focus for the last few years has concerned acts of terrorism.'

Stroud glanced at Lehmann. The man was implacable, his face like stone. He felt his insides twist and weaken.

'So ... so why am I here? What the hell have I got to do with terrorism?'

Maier leaned back in her chair. She looked at him for a good ten seconds before she spoke.

'That, Herr Stroud, is precisely what we are here to find out.'

She paused, and then said, 'You are English, Herr Stroud.'

'I am, yes.'

'From London.'

'Amongst other places.'

'You are here to collect something for your friend.'

'Yes.'

'And the name of your friend?'

'I am not sure I have to tell you that.'

Maier nodded slowly. She didn't smile. 'Your friend, I understand, is ill, and therefore he couldn't come himself.'

'That is correct.'

'When did he leave his possessions in the security locker?'

'He didn't tell me.'

'And you do not remember the number of the locker.'

'No,' Stroud replied. Maier was simply stating what he had
already said. To Stroud, it felt like she was confirming the lies
he'd told.

'How well do you know your friend, Herr Stroud?'

'Well enough.'

'Do you trust him?'

Stroud smiled nervously. He didn't like the direction this was
taking. 'Trust? That's a difficult thing to measure.'

'You believe there are degrees of trust?'

'A friend helps you move house. A real friend helps you move
a body.'

'Funny,' Lehmann said, but his features displayed no amusement.

Stroud looked at the man. 'What do you want from me?'

Lehmann held his gaze for a few seconds, and then said, 'The
truth, Herr Stroud. Just the truth.'

'I have told you the truth.'

'We don't believe you,' Maier said.

'I don't care if you believe me or not,' Stroud replied, knowing
that the reality was quite the opposite. 'Unless you have some

specific reason for detaining me and confiscating my passport, you are legally required to let me go.'

'We have a very specific reason,' Lehmann said.

'Which is?'

'We'll get to that, Herr Stroud,' Maier said. 'However, it is a little unfair, no? You ask questions and expect answers, and yet you continue to lie to us.'

Stroud felt a wave of fear course through him. He was angry, sure, but so very much more afraid of what he had created for himself. The repercussions were potentially dire.

Maier reached into her pocket and produced the locker key. She placed it on the table. Stroud's instinctive thought was to snatch it and swallow it. Then he considered the overnight detention, the medical administration of laxatives, the humiliating consequences.

'Where did you get this, Herr Stroud?'

'From my friend in London.'

'Where did you get this, Herr Stroud?'

'I just told you.'

Maier smiled. 'Where did you get the key from?'

Lehmann leaned in. 'Tell us where you got the key from. Did you find it? Did you steal it?'

'Tell us the truth now, Herr Stroud,' Maier insisted. 'If you do, things will be a great deal easier for you.'

'I want a lawyer,' Stroud said. 'I want someone from the British embassy here.'

'It is too late for a lawyer now,' Lehmann said. 'You should have asked for this at the beginning. And no one is coming from the embassy.' His tone was strangely sympathetic, like an adult delivering bad news to a child.

'But I have every right—'

'It is really very simple, Herr Stroud,' Maier interjected. 'You tell us where you got the key, what you are doing here in Berlin, why you wanted access to this locker, and then we will tell you what is going to happen.'

'What's going to happen? You're going to return my passport, give me back my friend's key and let me return to London. That's what's going to happen.'

Lehmann leaned back in his chair. He breathed audibly and seemed to relax. Then he drank the last of his coffee and put the cup down on the floor beside his chair.

'Herr Stroud,' he said. Not only was his voice calm and unhurried, he also appeared to show not the slightest sign of vexation or impatience. 'We are from the Federal Intelligence Service. We are not the police, we are not airport security, we are not representatives of the West German diplomatic corps. This is not a game. You are suspected of involvement in matters that are very serious indeed, and nothing will change for the better until you start cooperating with us. Tell us where you got the key to this locker.' He reached out and closed his hand over Stroud's forearm. 'The truth, Herr Stroud. Where did the key come from? Tell us how it came into your possession.'

Stroud felt a surge of resistance. He resented their smug self-assurance, their arrogance. However, he knew that defiance and protest would only make things worse. They had his passport, they had him detained. He was going nowhere until he co-operated.

'I will tell you,' he said, 'but first I want my passport back. I want a return flight to London. And I want an official apology from the West German consulate or whoever the hell is responsible for official apologies.'

Neither Lehmann nor Maier responded, both of them wearing that same cold, businesslike expression.

'I found the key, okay? I found the key in my friend's flat.'

'And the name of your friend?' Maier asked.

'Dekker,' Stroud said. 'Hendrik Dekker. But that might not be his real name.'

Lehmann frowned. 'I don't understand. You say that someone is your friend, but you do not know his real name?'

'It's complicated, okay?'

'Then explain,' Maier said. 'We have time.'

'I have a friend,' Stroud said. 'He is dead. At least I thought he was dead. I am looking for him.'

Maier leaned back in her chair and crossed her arms. 'You are saying that your friend may or may not be dead. You are not sure of this friend's name. You take a key from his home and you come here from Amsterdam to open a security locker, but you do not know the number of this locker.'

'I know how it sounds, okay? I know it seems crazy, but it's true. There's more to it. A lot more, believe me.'

'And this is the problem, Herr Stroud,' Maier said.

'What?'

'I do *not* believe you. You lied, lied again, and now you are creating some ... some fantasy about dead friends with unknown names.'

'It's true. I swear what I am telling you is absolutely true.'

Maier looked at Lehmann. Lehmann sighed disappointedly and shook his head. Maier got to her feet. Lehmann followed suit, picking up Stroud's bag as he did so.

'I am sorry for your trouble, Herr Stroud,' Maier said.

'Trouble? What trouble? I'm telling you the truth. Just let me explain. Let me tell you the whole story, and then you'll know that I'm telling the truth.'

Maier smiled, something almost apologetic in her previously disdainful expression.

'I am sorry, Herr Stroud, but this matter is now out of our hands.'

Without a further word, she once again pocketed Stroud's passport and the key.

The sound of the door being locked was like a gunshot in the narrow confines of the room.

26

Of all the journalists killed in action, photographers had the highest fatality rate. In the trade they were known as bullet bait. The military referred to them as clay pigeons. Robert Capa, Larry Burrows, Dickey Chapelle, Charlie Eggleston. Even Sean Flynn, son of Errol, who had just vanished on Highway 1 in Cambodia in April of 1970, apparently seized by guerrillas. He had not been seen or heard of since; few doubted that he was still alive.

The list went on.

A camera implied distance when there was none. It was a shield that offered protection from nothing. The lens seemed to act as a magnet for snipers. So often, combatants were engaged in abuses of human rights and violations of wartime conventions. The last thing in the world they wanted was someone recording it. And yet to snatch that rare shot, to capture an image that would convey the essence of conflict for all the world to witness, required that the photographer get closer to the action than anyone else. Right in the very heart of it was where striking images were found, but there was also found the greatest risk.

It was October of 1973. As Watergate spiralled out of control and Nixon approached the end of his presidential career, Stroud and Raphael were in Israel. On Yom Kippur, the holiest day of the Jewish calendar, Egyptian forces launched a massive shock attack across the Suez Canal. While the Israelis prayed in their bunkers, their enemies built pontoon bridges across the waterway and stormed the seemingly impregnable Bar Lev Line. Simultaneously, the Syrians invaded the Golan Heights, captured Mount Hermon and advanced more than fifteen miles. Israeli radio broke the traditional silence to broadcast instructions. Troops were rushed to the northern front; the air force bombed Damascus.

In the midst of this madness – together, yet working for separate agencies – Stroud and Raphael were seized by Syrian troops. Westerners were assumed to be pro-Israeli. The English were no different from the Americans in that regard. They were told that they were going to be held indefinitely, perhaps traded for Syrian POWs, perhaps killed as an example to the other Westerners who supported Israel with arms and training and intelligence.

The men who had captured them looked broken and desperate, and yet Raphael seemed almost unperturbed by the situation.

'Don't antagonise them,' he said. 'Worst thing you can do is give them cause for alarm. They're all trigger-happy, exhausted, probably starving hungry. If they bait you, don't rise to it.'

They were blindfolded, their cameras taken, their boots too, then locked in the back of an armoured vehicle. The heat was unbearable, claustrophobic.

'Do you ever think about dying?' Stroud asked Raphael.

'No.'

'I do … especially right now.'

'Does it help?'

Stroud tried to smile. Resilience under pressure.

'Don't think about it,' Raphael said. 'I mean it. It serves no purpose. You can smell fear on a human being. Hunter-and-prey stuff, you know? Primal instincts and all that. No one respects a coward.'

'You think they're going to kill us?'

'I think it's fifty-fifty, Stroud.'

'This is not the way I planned for it to go.'

'Then what the hell are you doing here? Jesus, Stroud, isn't it a little late to be questioning your career path?'

'Does anything bother you, Raphael?'

'Sure. Lots of things.'

'Such as?'

'Cold horizontal rain. You know how it gets sometimes. The wind blows sideways, takes the rain with it, and not only is it freezing fucking cold, there's no escape. Umbrella is about as much use as a wooden frying pan.'

'We're blindfolded and bootless in the back of an armoured car, probably about to die, and you're thinking about rain.'

'Okay, so my turn for a question. You run around the place like a lunatic with a camera. You chase wars, you take pictures of things that would seriously disturb the vast majority of the population, and yet you never expected to find yourself in a situation like this?'

'No, I didn't,' Stroud replied. 'This kind of thing always happens to the other guy.'

Raphael was quiet for a moment. 'Good point,' he said. 'I suppose if we thought there was a real chance of it happening to us, then we wouldn't do it.' He checked himself and added, 'Having said that, I'm not so sure.'

'I don't think it'd make any difference. I think we'd still do it. I think that even if we knew the odds were stacked against us, we'd still get on the plane.'

'I think you're right.'

'You know anyone who was taken hostage?' Stroud asked.

'Sure. Three or four of them.'

'What happened?'

'They're all dead.'

Stroud couldn't see Raphael's face, but he could hear the smile in his voice.

'The worst that happens is you die ... or maybe they cut your hands off or something. You've got to have a bit more of a philosophical viewpoint about this kind of thing.'

'Philosophical. You're telling me to be philosophical about the fact that I've been captured by Syrians and might be dead before the day is out?'

'What else are you going to be? You could cry and beg and see if it makes any difference. You just have to do whatever you think is going to help, and if it's not going to help then don't do it. Worrying about what might or might not happen doesn't change the outcome.'

'True, but it's hard not to worry when you have visions of your dismembered body being paraded around before the world's news cameras as an example to other infidel Westerners.'

'Mordaunt, my friend. Thomas Mordaunt.'

'What?'

'One crowded hour of glorious life is worth an age without a name.'

Stroud was silent for a little while, contemplating how he had managed to cram so much into less than a quarter of a century. He'd been married, divorced, fathered a daughter; he'd seen conflict in a dozen or more countries; he'd seen JFK in Berlin, the Paris riots, the aftermath of the Munich Olympics massacre. He was in Cuba hours after the Bay of Pigs fiasco, and amidst all of that he'd seen the Vietnam War up close and personal on nine different occasions. He'd missed death by inches more times than he could recall, and there was every possibility that he might just miss it again.

'Reconcile myself to fate. That's what you're saying.'

'Reconcile yourself to the fate you can't change. Sounds the same, but it's not.'

They had been released after three days. Their boots were returned, but not their cameras. More than likely they were sold on for next to nothing. The two of them were picked up by a Canadian news team on a long stretch of road thirty or forty miles east of Damascus. They were dehydrated, famished and filthy.

'One day you'll look back on this as a character-building experience,' Raphael said.

'I doubt it.'

'Trust me, you will. One day you're going to need to hold your nerve, and you'll remember being blindfolded in the back of an armoured car wondering if you were going to get a bullet through your face.'

Stroud didn't reply. He never wanted to feel that way again. He said so.

'But at least you know you're alive,' Raphael replied. 'Proof of life. If nothing else, it's proof of life.'

27

It was an hour before Stroud heard footsteps again.

He expected Maier and Lehmann to return, but it was someone else – a new cast member in this disturbing theatre of events.

The man – early forties, blond hair, spectacles, similarly dispassionate and businesslike – said, 'Herr Stroud, you are to come with me.'

'Where?'

'Please, Herr Stroud, come with me.'

'Where am I going? I want my passport back. And I want to use the bathroom, for Christ's sake. Tell me what the hell is going on.'

The man stood there in silence. His patient expression merely served to wordlessly repeat the question. There would be no negotiation here.

Stroud got up. He put on his jacket. He followed the man out of the room. They turned left and headed down the corridor.

'What is your name? Who do you work for?' Stroud asked.

'My name is Kessel,' came the reply. 'I work for the airport.'

Stroud knew instinctively that the latter was not true. He doubted the man's name was even Kessel.

'So are you going to tell me where we're going, Herr Kessel?'

'We are going to take a car ride,' Kessel replied.

'And where are we going in this car?'

'You will see when we arrive.'

'And where is my bag? The other man, Lehmann, he took my bag. Where is he?'

Kessel did not respond.

Stroud understood the futility of protesting further. He couldn't change what was happening. Perhaps they would hold him on remand and have him make a court appearance. He didn't know. It didn't elude him that had this happened in the eastern sector, he would be in the hands of the Stasi. Chances were he'd never have been heard of again.

As he walked behind Kessel, every once in a while glancing back down the interminable corridor, he tried to feign some degree of composure. In truth, he was panic-stricken. His heart raced; his whole body was varnished with a film of cold sweat. He had been given nothing by Maier or Lehmann, and that had merely served to ramp up his paranoia to an acute degree. He remembered a half-dozen or more incidents where his life had been endangered. He had survived each and every one. The thought that struck him was that perhaps he'd used up all his lives. Was there any chance at all that he would learn the truth, that he would actually get to the bottom of this mystery? This was now so very much more than a delay or a diversion. It was a real and tangible threat to his personal survival.

His fragile composure took a further blow as he was ushered through the door at the end of the corridor and into an underground car park.

There was something deeply menacing about the long black Mercedes that waited for him. He could see the driver, as well as a second man on the other side of the vehicle, both of them stern and uncommunicative.

Kessel indicated that Stroud should sit in the rear of the car. He complied, his heart now hammering, his pulse racing. Kessel closed the door, then walked around and got in beside him. All four doors were locked. The sound possessed an ominous finality.

'Can you tell me where we're going?' Stroud asked again, knowing that the answer he'd get would be no answer at all.

'It is not a long journey, Herr Stroud. Please make yourself comfortable.'

It was dark. Street lights showed him a little of the outskirts of Berlin as they drove away from the airport. Tegel was north-west of the city, perhaps five miles or so, but Stroud had no bearings and couldn't determine in which direction they were travelling.

Kessel had been true to his word. No more than fifteen minutes into the drive, they turned left along a narrow street, and then left again into another underground car park. The Mercedes came to a halt alongside some lift doors. Kessel got out, accompanied by the man in the passenger seat, and called the lift. Stroud was asked to follow them. The fact that Maier, Lehmann and now Kessel had all been so polite made him feel like a man enjoying the courtesy of executioners.

Kessel entered the lift with Stroud. He pressed the button for the sixth floor. The doors closed and they went swiftly upwards.

The lift opened onto a corridor that could have been any hotel in any country. The floor was carpeted, the walls split-coloured, a dado rail separating cream and pale blue. They walked past numbered rooms; odds on the left, evens on the right. They stopped at 614. Kessel produced a key, opened the door and indicated that Stroud should enter. He himself followed and put on the lights, and much to his relief, Stroud found himself in a comfortable, spacious hotel room. To the right a bathroom, to the left a bedroom, and on a low table near the window a tray with a lidded plate, a bottle of beer, cutlery and condiments.

'Tonight you will stay here,' Kessel said. 'There is a meal.

There are fresh clothes in the bedroom. If you require anything else, please press this button near the door and someone will attend to you.'

'Can I just ask—'

'Goodnight, Herr Stroud,' Kessel said, and left the room.

As Kessel's footsteps faded into silence, Stroud tried the door handle. The room was locked from the outside.

He checked the room. Everything had been provided – clean slacks and a shirt, underwear, towels, soap, shampoo, even razors, toothbrush, toothpaste and dental floss. Back in the sitting room, he removed the cloche from the plate; beneath was a schnitzel and potato salad. He opened the beer, took a drink, and sat down to eat.

Once he was finished, he looked around the room again. There was nothing unusual about it at all, save the absence of a radio or television set. The windows looked out onto a brightly lit stone courtyard. They had no latches, nor any other visible means of opening, and there was a dense, heavy-duty mesh on the outside.

He checked the bedroom and bathroom. The windows were exactly the same, and from each of them he merely saw a different angle of the courtyard below. The realisation dawned on him. He was in a prison cell. More comfortable than most, but a prison cell all the same. He drew the curtains and returned to the central room.

He was somewhere outside of Berlin, locked in a room on the sixth floor of an unknown building. He had no means of exit, no passport, and even if he'd been able to leave, no money for a taxi to the airport. He had no idea who had delivered him here, nor what they were going to do with him. Kessel could be Federal Intelligence. He had no way of knowing. Maier had mentioned terrorism. Did they really consider him a terrorist? If so, he was in a far graver situation than he'd previously considered.

Stroud paced. He tried to think of anything he could have missed, anything he might have overlooked that could indicate what he'd got himself into, and, more importantly, what the outcome might be.

He could identify nothing that stood out. Of course, that didn't mean a great deal. He didn't know what he was looking for. Had he even thought of something, it might not have possessed any greater significance than anything else. He was adrift, his only option to wait until the next piece of the puzzle was presented.

Almost in echo of his thoughts, he heard something outside. He stepped to the door, pressed his ear against it, and caught the sound of footsteps as they reached his room.

The handle turned and he stepped back quickly, almost losing his balance.

He was near the low table when the door opened and a man entered the room.

He looked at Stroud and smiled. In one hand he held a bottle of brandy, in the other a couple of glasses.

'Herr Stroud,' he said. 'I am sorry for the late hour. I understand you must be very tired, but—'

'Who are you?'

'My name is Ernst Lügner, and I have come to have a chat with you.' He held up the bottle. 'I have some brandy. I thought it would make things a little more civilised.'

'Things? What things?'

'All in good time, Herr Stroud, all in good time.'

Lügner closed the door behind him and put the bottle and the glasses on the table. He indicated the sofa to the right.

'Please, sit,' he said.

Stroud did as he was asked.

Lügner fetched a chair from the bedroom and set it down near the sofa. He then opened the bottle and poured a generous measure of brandy for each of them. Stroud took the proffered drink.

Lügner raised his own glass and smiled. '*Zum Wohl.*'

Stroud frowned.

'To your health, Herr Stroud. To your very good health.'

28

'The simple truth, Herr Stroud, is that no one knows where you are.'

Stroud smiled reflexively. 'Of course they do.' He tried to recall if he'd told Haig's secretary, Carole, that he was going to Germany. He didn't think so. He'd just told her that Nina was on the way home and that he himself wouldn't be much longer.

Lügner shook his head. 'You came in from Amsterdam on a one-way ticket. You sent your friend home to London with a broken wrist. She has arrived, of course, and I do not think you told her about the key. Until you knew what it was for, there was no way to know what your destination would be. This is correct, no?'

Stroud looked at him. He knew the colour had drained from his face.

'Don't act so surprised,' Lügner said, and laughed. 'You think we don't know who you are?'

'I am a journalist. A photographer.'

'And who do you work for?'

'*The Times.*'

'You say this, and yet you have no valid press credentials. Whatever official status you may once have had has expired. You are acting alone. At least that seems to be the case. However, I do not believe it for one moment.'

'What do you mean?'

'Who are you looking for, Herr Stroud? What mission is this you have undertaken? Why were you in Istanbul, Amsterdam, now Berlin? Why did you come here with a key to an airport security locker that is not registered in your name?'

'I assure you—'

'I don't think you can assure me of anything, Herr Stroud.'

Lügner leaned back in the chair. He raised his glass and sipped. 'Drink, Herr Stroud. It is good brandy, and it will calm your nerves.'

Stroud, unthinking, downed the contents of his own glass in one go. The brandy was strong; it burned in his throat and chest.

Lügner leaned forward. He placed his glass on the table. He rested his elbows on his knees and steepled his fingers together.

'In the realm I inhabit, there are no degrees of truth,' he said. 'Mine is a black-and-white world. You would think that this makes things very simple, but it does not. You see, Herr Stroud, I find myself in the company of individuals who believe that truth is a commodity that can be diluted and divided and shared out in small pieces. Of course, I do not expect you to understand what I am saying because I cannot give you any context—'

'Who are you?' Stroud asked. 'And where am I, for Christ's sake?'

'I am Ernst Lügner, and you are here as a guest of my country.'

'I know your name, but what do you do? Who do you represent? On what grounds am I being held here?'

'You know precisely why you are being held here. You know precisely the answer to the questions I have asked you, and yet you continue to play this little game of half-truths and subterfuges.'

'I am sorry, Herr Lügner—'

'I do not want an apology. I want the truth. You must understand that no one will come from the British embassy, and no one from the London *Times* will make enquiries about you because they do not know where you are. Even if you managed to escape from this facility, it would serve no purpose, for you have no passport.'

'I have certain rights—'

'Which you relinquished when you crossed the border into my country with stolen property in an effort to gain access to a security locker that does not belong to you.'

'My friend—'

'There is no friend, Herr Stroud. We both know that whatever name you give me for the registered holder of this locker will not be correct.'

'I demand that my human rights be respected. You can't lawfully hold me here. You can't just lock me up and tell no one that I'm here.'

'And yet we have.'

Lügner leaned forward and refilled Stroud's glass.

Stroud knew he was running out of corners in which to hide.

'Please understand what I am saying. You simply need to tell me the truth, and the consequences and repercussions will be minimal. The longer you play this ridiculous game, the less patience I will show.'

'What the hell is that supposed to mean?'

'You know what it means, Herr Stroud. You are not naïve, nor are you unfamiliar with the game of war.'

'War?'

'Yes, Herr Stroud. War.'

'I don't understand. How does this have anything to do with war?'

'The world is at war. The world has been at war for centuries. This is what we humans do. We fight. We kill. We find new ways to fight and kill. This seems to be our nature, and no civilising power has ever managed to quell or subdue this instinctive impulse. We are small-minded, territorial creatures and we never seem to grow tired of this relentless battle.' Lügner smiled. 'But why am I telling you this? You, of all people, know exactly what I am talking about.'

'Me?'

'Yes, Herr Stroud.'

'Why would I know about this?'

Lügner laughed. 'Come now. Vietnam, South Africa, Cyprus, Palestine, Bangladesh—'

'Okay, so you know where I've worked. Finding that out would not be so difficult. It also tells you that I am a bona fide photojournalist.'

'A man can be many things.'

'Meaning?'

Lügner didn't reply. He merely sat there and looked at Stroud. It was an old trick, but it worked.

'Who do you think I am? You think I'm working for someone?'

'That is one thing I do not know, Herr Stroud. I have no idea who you work for.'

'I work for myself.'

'You said you worked for *The Times* newspaper.'

'I am freelance. I work for myself, and I am also under contract to many newspapers.'

'Then why do you not have a valid press pass?'

'It expired. I stopped working for a while and it expired.'

'And what were you doing when you were not working for newspapers?'

'That's none of your goddamned business!'

'Everything that happens in this room is my business. Every answer you give me is my business. Same with the answers you do not give me, and those are the answers I am interested in. I am not the one who has broken the law, Herr Stroud. You are. I didn't enter West Germany with the intent to commit a crime.

You did. This is a simple matter, and it can be resolved very quickly. Tell me the truth and we will talk about your passport, how long you will remain here, whether there is anything else we wish to know. Continue this charade and things will very quickly become a great deal more complicated.'

'I told Maier and Lehmann. The key came from the flat of someone I know, a man called Dekker.'

'You gave this name before.'

'I did, yes.'

'And this man is a friend of yours? This Dekker?'

'I don't know. I'm not sure. I am actually trying to find someone else.'

'Someone else?'

'I was going to explain it to the other two at the airport, but they didn't give me a chance. I had a friend. We worked together for many years. I thought he was dead, but I was shown a photograph and was told that it was him.'

'He came back from the dead, this man?'

'That's what I don't know.'

'Go on, Herr Stroud.'

'I went to Istanbul, which is where this photograph was taken. I was in the French embassy, and I saw a picture of my friend, and it had this name, Hendrik Dekker, underneath.'

'And so you went to the Netherlands to find this Dekker to see if it was really your friend.'

'Yes. Yes, exactly. I went to the Netherlands to see if Dekker existed. To see if it was my friend with a new name.'

'The friend who returned from the dead.'

Stroud hesitated. He knew then – in that moment – that he should give up Raphael. He had no idea if this was who they were after, but it was the very last piece of the truth he possessed. He asked himself what would be gained by holding onto it, whether telling Lügner everything he knew – right from the very first meeting with Haig – would change what was going to happen.

'And the name of your friend, Herr Stroud?'

'His name?' Stroud said.

'Yes, Herr Stroud. What is the name of this man who has perhaps risen from the dead?'

'Raphael,' he said. 'His name was Vincent Raphael.'

Lügner didn't respond. He sat silently, as if he was processing the information that Stroud had given him, evaluating its credibility, determining for himself whether he believed what he was being told.

'Very good,' he said eventually. 'We are finished with our conversation, Herr Stroud. I believed you were a reasonable man, and I have tried my best to reason with you. But now my hands are tied. Let me just say that what happens next is exactly what I was trying to avoid.'

'But I've told you—'

'Enough now, Herr Stroud.'

Lügner indicated the glass of brandy in front of Stroud.

'I cannot leave the glass here.'

Stroud handed it to him.

'I trust you will come to your senses before this situation becomes even more troublesome and distressing for you.'

'I have told you everything. I have told you about Dekker, about Raphael. I don't know what else you think I know,' Stroud said.

'You will have some time to consider that.'

'So what happens now?' Stroud asked, trying his best to mask the fear that was so obvious in his voice.

'What happens now is that I wish you farewell, Herr Stroud.'

Lügner retrieved his own glass and the bottle of brandy. He walked to the door and knocked on it once. It opened immediately. In the moment before he stepped out into the corridor, he turned and smiled at Stroud.

'Goodnight, Herr Stroud. And pleasant dreams.'

Perhaps it was the brandy, perhaps the sheer stress of the situation, but within minutes of Lügner's departure, Stroud was overcome with the most profound exhaustion.

Barely able to keep his eyes open, he stumbled through to the bedroom and fell face-down on the mattress.

Pleasant dreams, Lügner had said.

It was only as he passed out that Stroud realised he'd been drugged.

29

Her skin was pale and unblemished. In her eyes you could still see the child she had once been. Even though there was only a few years between them, they were worlds apart. He had seen war, so very much of it, and had somehow become inured to its brutality. She had seen nothing of any life but the one into which she'd been born – simple, uncomplicated.

Stroud watched her as she slept, her eyelids flickering in response to whatever images had been burned into her mind. Or perhaps not. Perhaps she dreamed of something far distant from the nightmare she'd survived.

They had not known peace for decades here. Before the Americans, the French were here, treating the Vietnamese as if they were tenants in their own land. And now the communists wanted their home back, and out of some misguided sense of protectionism, the almighty, God-fearing, freedom-loving United States of America had deemed it necessary to intervene.

Their ethos was simple: if you drop enough bombs, you can bring a nation to its knees without ever looking into the eyes of a single casualty. There is no guilt. In perfect step with military advances, conscience can be erased by degrees. To Stroud, war seemed to be a commercial enterprise. Perhaps it always had been, time and technology merely having served to improve efficiency.

In that moment, he believed that the sleeping Vietnamese girl signified all that was wrong with this hopeless conflict.

Her right arm was missing from just beneath the shoulder, the left side of her face was bandaged, and beneath the dressing were burns of such severity that she would never again see through that eye, nor hear through that ear, nor ever walk a street without attracting expressions of horror and abject disbelief.

Stroud never learned her name. He knew nothing about her, save that she had been raped a dozen times and left for dead. Raped by Americans. Young Americans. Americans who had been trained to destroy anything that wasn't 'us'. It was easy to forget a person's human rights when you didn't consider them human.

Stroud was there taking pictures for *Life*. His press credentials would take him anywhere he wanted to go. He could command use of a helicopter, a jeep, a military escort, whatever he believed would assist him in documenting the fine, upstanding, gung-ho endeavours of the United States Army as they brought democracy and peace to the people of Vietnam.

He was here to show how grateful the South Vietnamese were for the tremendous effort that was being made to defend and protect them from the tyranny of the North. He was here to deliver pictures that would exemplify the heroic actions of ordinary American infantrymen as they pushed back the enemy and restored order from chaos.

He was not here to show the other side of the story. He was not to photograph the murders and interrogations, the wholesale slaughter of entire villages by helicopter gunships. He was not here to display the true horror of napalm as it ripped through vegetation and undergrowth, as it adhered to skin and burned white. People eating wholesome breakfasts in clean kitchens didn't want to see phosphorus wounds, decapitated teenagers or women holding dead babies. It was a war of propaganda and falsehoods; a war where the busiest of all were those telling the lies.

Afterwards, Stroud knew he would no longer be surprised by any human or inhuman act.

That night, he stayed awake. He watched and waited while the girl slept, and as the sun broke the horizon and bathed the tent in a thin, ethereal light, she murmured names and disconnected phrases and then she died. In death, there was no calm respite in her expression. She died alone and in pain, her lips stretched back in one final, stricken grimace. It was a terrible end to a too-brief life, and Stroud shed tears for her – this young, beautiful, broken stranger – and lost yet another facet of his own frail humanity.

'You cannot identify,' Raphael told him later. 'The camera is another eye, an eye through which you see a world that isn't yours. Your world is elsewhere, hundreds, thousands of miles away. Your world is the one you leave, the one you look forward to returning to, while all of this ...' He held out his arms, and within their span he encompassed the smoke-filled sky, the smell of blood and cordite and sulphur and death, the fear, the panic, the loss, the rage, the futility of it all. '... this is someone else's world, and you are just a tourist.'

'A tourist in hell,' Stroud said.

Raphael smiled. 'Everyone has their own version of hell. Ours is banality and conformity, complacency, being blinded by false values and hypocrisy. Our hell is forever wanting to be something that we're not, and never being satisfied.'

'I think this is worse.'

'Do you?' Raphael said. 'This is simple. Do I have enough to eat? Can I feed my children? Do I have somewhere for us to sleep? Can we make it through another drought, another famine, another monsoon, another war? This is survival, Stroud. Real survival. We are shallow, ignorant Westerners, concerning ourselves with our reputation, with others' feelings, with whether or not people will like us or remember us or get the wrong impression about something we say. It's pathetic, Stroud. That's what it is. Pathetic. I've been escaping from that shit ever since I was able to think an independent thought. I am still escaping from it. Maybe that's why I'm here. Maybe that's why I get on planes and fly into this madness. At least here the people are real. As real as the bullets and bombs, as real as the dead and the dying. And I'm not talking about the fucking Americans. They're just tourists too. This war will end and they'll all go home, and these people will go back to whatever it was they were doing before we got here. They'll go back to doing what they've been doing for hundreds of years. Nothing changes, man. Nothing ever changes. The idea that we're going to make a difference is nothing more than a fucking delusion.'

'So why do we bother?' Stroud asked. 'Why do you bother? You take pictures, you send them home, you get paid for them. Why go on doing that if none of it makes any difference?'

Raphael laughed. 'Because I was like you when I started. All fired up and motivated, ready to see the truth and pass it on and make the world understand what was happening. It took me a long time to understand that it's all fucking pointless, and now I am too stubborn and too stupid to do anything else. This is the life I created, and I have no choice but to live it.'

'Is anything good going to come from what we're doing?'

'Oh, I very much doubt it,' Raphael replied, 'but then again, you never know.'

Stroud thought of the dead Vietnamese girl, her body lying out behind the medical tent.

'Don't look so down,' Raphael said. 'Get some sleep, find some breakfast, load up your camera. Tomorrow's another day. Tomorrow you could get the picture of the decade and have wannabe combat snappers buying you drinks for the next five years.'

Stroud laughed.

'That's good. Laugh it off. Get serious and you are truly, truly fucked.'

30

When Stroud opened his eyes, he knew that everything had changed.

This was no longer a matter of extricating himself from an awkward situation with the possibility of deportation. This was now a potentially disastrous reality.

He was seated on a plain wooden chair. His feet were bare, his ankles tied to the legs of the chair. His hands were down by his sides, his wrists secured to the crossbeam beneath the seat.

The room – perhaps twelve feet by fifteen – was without adornment. No window, a door – in which there was no visible lock nor handle – directly ahead. Above him was a bare light bulb, the glare unrelenting.

His heart started beating more rapidly. He wrenched both wrists and ankles against the ties, but they were immovable. He was aware of an emptiness in the middle of his body. He didn't know how long he'd been out, but he was famished. His thirst was comparable, the inside of his mouth and throat parched, his tongue rough and swollen.

He tried to shift the chair, but quickly realised it was bolted to the floor. Panic rose in his chest and he fought to maintain his bearings. The worst thing he could do was succumb to it. This was no random opportunistic seizure of a Western journalist in a war zone in the hope that he might be of use; this was a calculated drugging, incarceration and … and what? Torture? Deprivation? Beating?

'Hey!'

The sound of his own voice ricocheted back at him from the walls of the room.

'Hey! Let me the fuck out of here!'

He checked himself. Sounding terrified and desperate – even if he felt that way – would not help his cause. He had to maintain the story he'd told. He could not allow himself to be bullied and intimidated into some other explanation that would complicate things even further.

He forced himself to breathe more slowly, to get his emotions under control. He needed to think, to figure out precisely what he was going to say.

Above him the light went out. The room was plunged into complete darkness.

The effect was dramatic. Even though he knew what was around him – the handle-less door, the four walls, the ceiling with its bare light bulb – it was as if he had been thrown into some limbo where anything or anyone could be mere inches from his face.

After a minute, perhaps two, the light came back on. The door, the walls, the floor beneath him. Relief flooded through him. He breathed deeply. He willed his pulse to slow down.

The light was extinguished once again.

Instinct drove him to call out, to react, but he held his nerve.

Beneath the panic, he understood that the fear of detainment would soon become a fear of darkness. Despite him knowing that this was nothing more than the most basic denial psychology, it was working. Understanding it didn't make it any less intimidating.

The light came on. Was it brighter? It was. It was definitely brighter.

Stroud glanced up. He could barely look at the bulb directly. Then the light started to dim. Or was it his imagination? No, he was sure it was getting less intense. He could now look at it without it hurting his eyes. It became less and less bright, and then he could barely make out the door ahead of him.

'Enough!' he shouted, almost without thinking. It was an instinctive response. He started to cough. The dryness of his throat made it difficult to speak clearly. The coughing attack subsided. He tried to swallow, but there was nothing to swallow. His tongue was sticking to the roof of his mouth.

He heard something. Did he hear something?

Was someone coming?

There was a sound outside the door. He was as sure of it as he could be. Was that a bolt being drawn?

The light went out completely.

Then he heard the door open. He was sure of it. The door had opened.

He sensed someone entering the room. He heard the sound of rubber-soled shoes on the floor. He could smell them. The faintest hint of cigarette smoke.

Suddenly a vice-like grip held the back of his neck.

He was too shocked and disorientated to speak. The hand tightened, and his head was held steady.

Something against his lips. The rim of a cup. Liquid against his lips now. Instinctively he resisted, but then he realised it was merely water. He drank greedily, felt it quench his tongue, his mouth, his throat, easing the tightness in his chest. He wanted more, needed more, but the cup was gone.

He didn't hear the sound of the shoes receding, but then the door was again opened and closed.

The darkness remained for just a moment, then the light came on again – bright, brilliant, piercing. He closed his eyes and lowered his head, but somehow the light found him. He could feel it penetrating his eyelids, to the point of causing pain.

And then it dimmed once more.

Stroud opened his eyes and looked around. The door, the walls, the ceiling with its single bare bulb above him. His hands and ankles tied, the chair bolted to the floor. Everything was the same. Nothing had changed. His heart was thudding in his chest. He felt frightened, overwhelmed and sick. That was how they wanted him to feel. He resisted. He forced himself to focus on something else. Eva. He thought of Eva. He pictured her face. His heart slowed down. He felt calmer. He had been in worse situations and survived. He would get out of this. He knew he would get out of this.

He didn't know how long he'd sat there. His watch – not that he would have been able to see it – had been taken along with his shoes and socks. Before that, at the airport, they had taken his bag. His passport, his camera, his notebooks – everything was gone.

A deep fatigue began to cloud his concentration. He tried to formulate clear thoughts, but he couldn't. He focused his mind on retracing the sequence of events that had brought him here – all the way from that first flight from Amsterdam to London, the meeting with Haig, the trip to Turkey, to the Netherlands, and then to Tegel. It was like trying to recall the tangled threads of a confused dream. He could see himself in the restaurant in Istanbul, the way Orhan Yilmaz had spoken to him; then he was with Nina as they searched through endless newspaper archives. The next image was of Haig saying something, followed swiftly by his last memory of Raphael, and then he was back in the room at the airport with Christa Maier as she spooled the film out of his camera and exposed it.

How the hell had he managed to get himself here – tied to

a chair in some unknown location in Germany, not one person aware of where he actually was?

He felt an inadvertent tension in his lips. It was mania, nothing else. It was born out of an instinctive fear for his own well-being. It was inevitable and unavoidable. He was going to be tortured. It was going to be worse than anything he had ever experienced, perhaps far worse than anything he could imagine. They believed him to be somebody other than who he was. They suspected him of some complicity in terrorist activities, and here in Germany of all places, with recent memories of the Munich Olympics massacre, of Baader–Meinhof and Black September and Christ only knew what else. The tension built, and then he started to shake. He couldn't control it. Like an electrical charge running through his entire body, it caused muscular spasms, a sudden rush of nausea. He was going to be sick. He knew it. He felt the reflux of water in his throat, and he started to cough and gag.

And then it stopped as rapidly and unexpectedly as it had started. A second rush of nausea invaded his body and he retched drily.

He forced himself to focus on being alive, the idea of tomorrow, the day after. Think about getting back to London, about seeing Haig, Nina, telling them what had happened. He wanted so badly to see Eva. He *had* to see his daughter again.

It became difficult to maintain a single thought. His mind wandered. At one point he felt as if he was suffocating. He started to breathe deeply again – inhale, exhale, inhale, exhale. He felt light-headed, but he kept on going. Soon a degree of real mental clarity returned, and he started to seriously consider what he was going to tell them.

There were sounds outside the door.

He waited. He realised that he was holding his breath, and exhaled once more.

The door opened. It was dark in whatever corridor or hallway lay beyond.

A woman wearing a white lab coat entered. She was carrying a box.

'Hey!' Stroud said. 'Where am I? What's going on here?'

The woman didn't look at him. She acted as if she was the only person in the room. She stepped to the right and set the box down. She removed several items and laid them on the floor.

Almost immediately, a second woman entered the room carrying an identical box.

As the first one stood up and left, the second one replicated her actions and started setting things down on the floor. The woman blocked Stroud's view; it was not until she stood up and walked away that he could see what was there.

Batteries, coils of wire, brown-paper-wrapped blocks with serial numbers printed on them. There were three handguns, a box of small glass cylinders, an alarm clock, a plastic tub filled with bullets, a canvas holdall much the same as his own, a number of passports, a thick wad of banknotes secured with a rubber band. Aside from this, there were assorted documents, notebooks, a newspaper, a sheathed combat knife, a pair of heavy-soled boots and three black balaclavas.

It was with a heavy sense of dread that Stroud realised that these things were more than likely the contents of the Tegel security locker.

All of a sudden, Christa Maier's reference to terrorism made sense.

Stroud had walked into a nightmare.

The bare walls of the room closed in around him, and for the first time in a decade or more, he genuinely feared for his life.

31

Time passed. Ten minutes, an hour, half a day. Stroud had no way of knowing.

His stomach growled. His head ached. His ankles and wrists felt twisted and bruised.

He was cold, then hot. The light stayed constant, or so it seemed, but it became ever more aggravating. At last it seemed so intense that he was sure it was burning right through the top of his skull.

He wanted to be sick, but there was nothing inside him to give up. He needed water, he needed to eat. He needed to sleep, but doubted that he would have slept even if given a bed. A tangible feeling of panic coursed through him, and he resisted it fiercely. It was both exhausting and electrifying, a profound nervous hysteria that felt more physical than psychological. He knew he was weakening. He knew that at some point he would give answers to anything they asked. Even if he didn't know the answer, he would say whatever he imagined they wanted to hear in the hope that it might end this intimidation. Everyone had a tipping point. It was then that self-preservation became so much more important than loyalty.

But what was he really afraid of? What was he hiding? Nothing of any real significance. In truth, it was not the consequences of telling the truth that frightened him. What frightened him was that he was being treated as a terrorist. Now, more than anything else, it was who they thought he was that mattered.

And then something changed again. He seemed to push through some barrier of internal doubt and mental anguish. He focused on the feeling, and for some considerable time he couldn't identify what it was. At first he thought it was nothing more than stubbornness. But that was not it. It was determination. But not for himself. Not just for himself.

And then he thought of Eva again, and the sense of absence and longing that the thought precipitated was unlike anything he'd experienced before. It was as if a hollowness had always been there but he'd never confronted it. He'd been aware of it, yes, but had never really understood or appreciated its significance.

His child. His daughter. Someone out there who was an extension, a reflection, a facet of himself.

He pictured her face. He recalled the very first moment he'd held her in the hospital, the profound joy he'd felt. He remembered birthday parties, her first Christmas, the way he and Julia would look at one another as if to question whether they'd really brought this human being into the world. It was Eva that Stroud held onto. That idea – that he might never see her again – gave him reason and motivation amidst the whirlwind of tormented fears and anxieties he was experiencing.

And then Raphael's words came back to him: *Reconcile yourself to the fate you can't change.*

His life rolled out in playback. People he'd known, events he'd witnessed and documented, moments of history never to be repeated that he'd captured for eternity. It had been a life, no doubt about it, and not a wasted one. It had been a life of unpredictability, challenge, nothing superficial, nothing banal. Perhaps he had been depressed, even pessimistic, but he had never felt sorry for himself nor had he been defeated.

He knew he would see Eva again. This time he would say the things he wanted to say, tell her the truth of what had happened, and if Julia or her father – or anyone else, for that matter – got in the way, he would smash right through them and to hell with the consequences.

Stroud looked up.

As if on cue, the door opened and Lügner appeared.

He closed the door behind him and stood looking at Stroud.

He had on a white shirt, sleeves rolled to the elbows. He had removed his tie, but left the buttons fastened up to his neck. He had no belt, and on his feet he wore black flat-soled plimsolls.

'Herr Stroud,' he said. 'As you can see, we have emptied your friend's locker.'

Stroud didn't reply.

'You do not deny that the locker belongs to your friend.'

Stroud remained silent.

Lügner sighed and shook his head. A disappointed school-teacher. Stroud had failed to achieve the expected results.

He backed up and tapped the door. It opened. From outside, a low wooden stool was passed through. Lügner took, set it down in front of Stroud, and then walked around the room and surveyed the objects on the floor.

'Timers, batteries, explosives, guns, bullets, money, counterfeit passports,' he said. 'Bomb maker. Terrorist. Kidnapper. Killer. You keep interesting company, Herr Stroud.'

Stroud didn't look at Lügner, nor at the objects on the floor. He looked directly ahead. He focused his attention on a precise point on the wall. He used it as an anchor for his attention, a lifeline to something real and solid and unchanging. He didn't think about the implications of what was being said, nor about the hunger that gnawed in the base of his gut, nor the parched desert that was his mouth and throat. He thought about the point on the wall, nothing but that, and he pictured Eva's face

– Eva smiling, Eva laughing, Eva when she called him *Dadda*, Eva when she told him she loved him.

Lügner stepped around him and sat down.

'Where is Dekker, Herr Stroud?'

Stroud flinched at the name.

Lügner smiled.

'Where is Dekker, Herr Stroud?'

Stroud looked right through Lügner's face to the point on the wall.

The pain that lanced through the side of his face as Lügner struck him was indescribable. At first it was the shock. Then came a burning jolt down the entire left-hand side of his body. That was followed by whiplash generated by the sudden motion of his head to the right.

Stroud closed his eyes; he took a deep breath and held it.

Lügner struck him again.

'Where is Dekker? Tell me about Dekker. When did you see Dekker? When was the last time you saw Dekker? Where is Dekker? Dekker, Herr Stroud. Where is Hendrik Dekker?'

Lügner struck him yet again. The impact was audible – like a gunshot that reverberated and ricocheted inside his skull.

Stroud gasped. 'I have told you everything I know!'

Lügner raised his hand.

'Fuck you!' Stroud screamed. It was instinctive, almost primal.

Lügner hit him again.

The pain in Stroud's neck was indescribable. His left side was pulsing, his body kicking back against the agony with everything it possessed.

Lügner struck him yet again.

'Dekker!' he shouted. 'Where is Dekker? Tell me where Dekker is! Tell me now!'

Again a thundering collision – the flat of Lügner's hand across the side of his head.

'I don't know Dekker!' Stroud screamed. 'I don't know anyone called Dekker! I have told you everything. Everything!'

'Tell me about the others,' Lügner said. 'Hausner. Krabbe. Rössner. Wessel. Taufer. Tell me about Stockholm. Tell me about Günter von Drenkmann. Tell me about Peter Lorenz.'

Stroud knew that name. Lorenz. Peter Lorenz. Last year, something had happened. Something important. Lorenz.

And then it came to him. Peter Lorenz. Christian Democratic politician. The 2 June Movement kidnapping.

As realisation dawned, his expression changed. Lügner recognised the momentary shift in his focus.

'Peter Lorenz,' he said quietly, and leaned forward. 'Tell me about Peter Lorenz. Was Dekker involved in the kidnapping of Peter Lorenz?'

Stroud glanced away to the right.

Lügner slapped him again. Now the pain was like fire unleashed inside his head. He screamed unintelligibly at Lügner, screamed right into the man's face. 'Fuck you! Fuck you! Fuck you!'

Lügner didn't blink. He didn't flinch. He struck Stroud again.

'Tell me about your friend Dekker,' he said. 'Is he in London? Did he give you the key in London? Did he give you the key in Amsterdam? Did you steal it from him? Did you and Dekker have a disagreement? Tell me where he is now, Herr Stroud. Tell me exactly where I will find Hendrik Dekker.'

'I don't know anyone called Dekker,' Stroud said. The words came out with difficulty. He had reached a point where he knew he had to say something else, if only to stop the beating. It took everything he possessed to control his rage, his fear, his sense of utter despair. His head felt as if a bomb had been detonated inside it.

They – whoever *they* were – thought he knew this Hendrik

Dekker. They thought he was involved in some terrorist activity that Dekker was engaged in. For whatever good it now did him, that had confirmed for Stroud that Dekker and Raphael could never be one and the same person. He had stolen the security locker key from the flat of a known and wanted terrorist, and he had only himself to blame for the consequences. He should have done what Nina suggested and tracked the third Dekker down in Hilversum.

And then he remembered what the guy in Dekker's apartment building had said. Dekker worked in Wassenaar. Wassenaar was where the Dutch Foreign Intelligence Service was head-quartered. Did the Dutch have an insider working in Germany, someone who had infiltrated a terrorist cell that was connected to the 2 June Movement, to Baader–Meinhof perhaps?

Stroud's mind, already stretched in every imaginable way with disconnected threads and unanswered questions, was disorient-ated even further by this possibility. He was in Germany, being interrogated about someone he didn't know, someone who was being sought by German intelligence as a terrorist with inter-national links and responsible for the kidnapping of a mayoral candidate.

He had engineered himself – with impatience, lack of fore-sight, sheer stupidity – into a situation that went far beyond the mystery of Vincent Raphael's death. He was being tortured for something he couldn't tell them, and all for the sake of two thousand pounds that he would never see.

He closed his eyes and lowered his head. He longed for silence, for water, for a bed, for anything but this.

'Herr Stroud.'

Stroud didn't raise his head or respond.

'Look at me, Herr Stroud.'

He stayed right where he was.

'I have something you may want to see.'

More from reflex than anything else, he opened his eyes. He raised his head a fraction and saw a dark blue shape in Lügner's hand.

'I have your passport, Herr Stroud. This is your ticket out of this place. This is what you need. Without it, you will be trapped here indefinitely.'

Stroud focused. It was his passport, no doubt about it. What a way to taunt him. To have his passport right there in the room, his hands and ankles tied to a chair, a door without a handle, and no clue as to his whereabouts.

Lügner produced something else from his other pocket.

The snap, click and sudden burst of yellow made it very clear what would happen next.

As he held the lighter ever closer to the corner of Stroud's passport, the cruel smile on Lügner's face became more pronounced.

'No!' Stroud said. 'For Christ's sake, I don't know what you want. I don't know Dekker. I told you already. I am looking for my friend. That's all I'm doing here. For Christ's sake, don't burn it!'

'I don't believe you, Herr Stroud.'

'It's true! It's absolutely true, I tell you! I saw a picture of my friend in Istanbul. It had the name Dekker on it. I came here looking for Dekker because I thought he might be Raphael. That's all I know. I don't know anything about Peter Lorenz or kidnappings or anything else—'

The flame caught, the passport started to burn, and suddenly Stroud's eyes were watering with the smoke. He felt it in his mouth, his throat, his lungs.

'No!' he shouted. 'No! Don't burn it! Put it out! Put it out!'

Lügner rose from where he was seated and walked towards the door. He set the passport down and watched the flame take hold.

'No one ever gets out of here unless I say so,' he said.

He tapped the door, and it opened.

'Once again I advise you to consider your options, Herr Stroud. They may be limited, but I believe they are very clear.'

32

Stroud watched his passport burn down to nothing but a few remnants of paper and card. The smoke – at first acrid – dispersed quickly, and at last there was nothing left but the upper charred corner and the spine of the document.

It was as conclusive and final an act as he had ever witnessed – more severe and constraining than any locked room or barred cell. He didn't even know where he was, and he had no idea for whom Lügner worked. He assumed the Federal Intelligence Service, but Stroud was not naïve. The known government agencies were the front. Behind them were vast mazes of further intelligence units, special ops divisions, controllers, operators, and a host of unnamed departments whose personnel were known only to those individuals within the political inner sanctum. Just as the NSA dwarfed the CIA and yet remained almost anonymous and unidentifiable, so there would be a layer of security and espionage behind Federal Intelligence, and yet again behind that.

He had told them about Raphael. He had told them why he was looking for Dekker. That had not worked. They wanted something else, and he had nothing else to give them.

No one knew where he was. Even if he was tracked through the airline's records to Tegel, there was nothing to prove that he hadn't just walked out of the airport of his own volition and disappeared.

Stroud was a ghost. That was the fact of the matter. From the moment he'd been stopped while trying to find the security locker, he had ceased to exist in the same matrix or framework as anyone who knew him.

He drifted back and forth between a strange, almost delusory awareness and waves of semi-consciousness. The images in his mind were fractured and distorted, relating in no way to where he was or what had happened, but somehow possessing the same sense of intimidation. He would start awake suddenly and find that he had been kicking his feet away from the legs of the chair. His ankles were swollen and bruised, he was thirsty and starving. His body was overwhelmed with pain and stress.

Finally, there were sounds. Were they real, or was this some other hallucination? Were his frayed nerves and senses now deceiving him too?

The answer came as the door opened.

Lügner stood there. He wore the same clothes, but in his left hand he held a small bottle. The liquid within was pale yellow in colour.

He stepped across the threshold and closed the door behind him.

From his right pocket he took a handkerchief. He unscrewed the lid of the bottle and placed the handkerchief over the open end. He tipped it up, held it for a few seconds, and then replaced the lid. With two rapid steps he was in front of Stroud. Before Stroud had a chance to react or resist, Lügner had gripped the back of his neck.

Stroud pulled back instinctively, but the more he pulled, the tighter the grip became. He felt the pressure of the handkerchief over the lower half of his face. His nostrils were filled with the stench of some potent and invasive chemical. He could taste it in his mouth, feel it filling his lungs, and even as his muscles relaxed and weakened, he perceived a sense of clarity.

He looked at Lügner. The man's eyes were bright and intense. He could see the pores of his skin, every detail of the man's features as if through a magnifying glass. Colours changed, became monochromatic. Perspective and angles shifted. The pain in Stroud's body eased. He experienced intermittent waves of calmness. What had Lügner done to him? What the hell was in that bottle?

'You have a daughter, Mr Stroud. What's her name?'

'Eva. Her name is Eva.'

The word left his lips without any thought or consideration behind them. Lügner asked the question, Stroud gave the answer, and there was no other choice.

'How old is she?'

'F-fourteen.'

'What is her date of birth?'

'May ... it's in May ... the eleventh of May.'

'What is the name of her mother?'

'Julia.'

'What is *her* date of birth?'

'The fourth ... the fourth of January.'

'What is the name of the girl who accompanied you to Amsterdam?'

'Nina. Her name is Nina Benson.'

'Who sent you here?'

'Marcus sent me. Marcus Haig.'

'What did he tell you?'

'He told me to find Raphael. He told me to find out if he was alive.'

'Vincent Raphael?'

'Yes, Vincent Raphael.'

'Is Raphael alive?'

'I don't know.'

'Are Raphael and Hendrik Dekker the same person?'

'I don't know.'

'Are Raphael and Dekker the same person?'

'I don't know! I don't know!'

'Is Raphael alive?'

'I don't know. I don't know anything about Raphael.'

'Is he dead?'

'I don't know.'

Lügner's hand came out of nowhere. Stroud felt the impact of it against the side of his face. The pain was extraordinary, and yet he couldn't scream.

'Is Raphael alive?'

'I don't know! I don't fucking know!'

'Who is Dekker?'

'I don't know who Dekker is.'

'Do you know Karl-Heinz Dellwo?'

'No.'

'Have you ever met him?'

'No.'

'Have you ever spoken to him?'

'No.'

'Do you know Bernhard Rössner?'

'No.'

Lügner struck Stroud again. Stroud felt the bones crack in his neck.

'Do you know Bernhard Rössner?'

'No!'

'Have you ever met Bernhard Rössner?'

Again a lance of excruciating pain across Stroud's face that reverberated right through his skull.

'Have you ever met Bernhard Rössner?'

'No, I have never met Bernhard fucking Rössner!'

'Have you ever spoken to Bernhard Rössner?'

'No. I don't know who he is. I don't know who this person is!'

The handkerchief was clamped over Stroud's face once again. He tried to resist, but it was futile. The chemicals filled his chest. He coughed, he retched, but he possessed insufficient strength to fight what was happening. The room folded at the corners. He looked at Lügner as if through a funhouse mirror.

'Who do you work for?'

'I don't work for anyone!'

'Who sent you here?'

'No one sent me here. I am looking for Raphael. I am looking for Vincent Raphael. I am trying to find out if he really is dead.'

Lügner stepped back. He let fly with a kick to Stroud's right shin. A fierce and indescribable wave of excruciating agony ripped right through him. He opened his mouth to scream. His head back, his eyes clamped shut, his lips bared, that scream seemed to come from some primal place within him, and yet there was not a sound.

'Who do you work for?'

'I don't fucking work for anyone! I don't work for anyone!'

'Why did you come here?'

'I was trying to find out who Dekker was.'

'Where did you get the key?'

'From Dekker's flat. It was in a jacket. In the lining of a jacket.'

'How did you find out it was for a security locker?'

'I found out from the number on the key.'

Lügner took two steps back, and then kicked the other shin.

An anguished roar erupted from the very base of Stroud's lungs. He started to sob, to gasp for air. He felt sick with the pain. His legs felt as if they had been broken in numerous places. He was utterly terrified. He knew he would never walk again.

'Where is Vincent Raphael?'

'I don't know! I don't know where Vincent fucking Raphael is!'

Lügner stepped back again. Stroud braced himself for another kick, but it never came.

Lügner's voice was softer, less aggressive. 'If you tell me the truth, the pain will stop, Herr Stroud. I can stay here forever. I can bring you such pain that you will plead with me to kill you. You will cry and beg me to stop the pain.'

Stroud looked up at Lügner. He could see him through a haze of tears. He knew that he couldn't tell them anything else. He didn't know what they wanted. This was where it would end. After all the war zones and conflicts, after the horror he had seen, this was where he would finally meet the end of his life – in a featureless room somewhere outside Berlin, his heart giving out as he was tortured for information he didn't possess. And then his body would be burned or buried and no one would be any the wiser. Would anyone come looking? Would anyone persevere in finding the truth of what had really happened? Would Eva ever know that she was his very last thought as the lights went out?

The irony struck him with the same force as another blow from Lügner. He really had followed in Raphael's footsteps. He'd stood so close to the edge of the abyss that he'd tumbled in headlong.

'I don't know what you want,' he said. His voice was broken and exhausted. 'I can't tell you what I don't know. I came looking for Raphael. I thought he was dead. I still believe he is dead. I thought he and Dekker were the same person. I don't know why. I don't understand how any of this fits together. Nothing makes sense. I just wanted to find out if my friend was really dead or not.'

'What happened to him, Herr Stroud?'

'He died in Jordan, in a Land Rover. Someone threw a grenade into the Land Rover and he was killed in the explosion.'

'When was this?'

'Six years ago. September of 1970.'

'Have you seen Raphael since that day?'

'No. I haven't seen him. Of course I haven't fucking seen him! He's dead!'

'Is he alive, Herr Stroud? Is Vincent Raphael alive?'

'No, he's dead.'

'Do you believe that he is dead?'

'Yes, I believe that he is dead.'

Lügner paused. He smiled reassuringly, then took a step back. Stroud knew he was going to kick him again. He didn't think he could bear more pain like that.

'Stop!' he screamed. 'For Christ's sake, stop! I have told you everything I know! I don't know anything else! I can't tell you what I don't fucking know!'

Lügner didn't move. Again he smiled. He looked down at the floor, and then he put his hands in his pockets and sighed.

After a moment, he backed up and knocked on the door. The door opened. He said a few words in German, and then a woman came into the room. In her hand she had a hypodermic needle.

'What? What are you doing?' Stroud pleaded. 'What are you doing to me?'

Before he could even turn his head, the woman was behind him. He felt the sting of the needle in the side of his neck.

Blackness rushed down on him like a waterfall.

33

Stroud surfaced like a man believing he'd already drowned. The lights above him Catherine-wheeled in myriad colours. He twisted sideways and retched. Pain shot through his lower legs and he cried out. Then he retched again. Still leaning sideways, he tried to open his eyes just a little. He could see white, nothing more. His head pounded. His right hand instinctively gripped the edge of something. It was soft, yielding, and he ran his hand along it to determine what it was. Something covered his body, too. It was smooth and cool. He could smell something antiseptic. He lay still for a moment. Lügner. He remembered Lügner. He remembered the cloth over his face and not being able to do anything but answer the man's interminable questions. And then the needle. What had they injected him with? What the hell had they done to him?

He tried to right himself, fighting against the urge to just lie still and take whatever punishment they had concocted for him. The pain in his legs was fierce, but he somehow managed to roll onto his back, his eyes still shut tight, resisting the urge to retch again.

'Herr Stroud?'

Was he imagining this? Was someone saying his name? Whose voice was he was hearing? Was this some new horror of a human being come to torture him?

'Herr Stroud?'

Stroud opened his mouth to speak, but nothing happened. His lips were dry, his tongue swollen, his throat torn and cracked from screaming.

'*Wasser*,' the voice said.

There was movement, a sound, and then the feeling of a hand behind his head. He shut his mouth, his teeth grinding against each other, determined not to let them make him drink whatever poison they were planning to administer.

'It is just water, Herr Stroud. Just water. You are very dehydrated. Please drink a little.'

Stroud opened one eye just a fraction. The bright light, a white shape that came more and more into focus as he concentrated.

A young man. White lab coat. Smiling.

'There you are,' the man said. 'It is okay, Herr Stroud. You are okay now. My name is Dr Möller. I am here to look after you. Please drink a little water. You will feel better.'

Stroud turned his head. He could see a young woman, a nurse. She was right there next to him, and it was she who held the back of his head, trying to incline him so he could drink a little.

He did so. The water was cool, and it eased the dryness in his mouth and throat.

He tried to move. He winced as pain once again shot through his lower legs.

'Your shins are very badly bruised. Not broken, however. Very swollen, some deep lacerations, but they will heal.' Möller smiled knowingly. 'I think it must have been a very wild party, Herr Stroud.'

'Party?' His voice was hoarse, little more than a whisper.

'You were in a very bad state. You were outside on the road. I think you knew enough to get yourself here, but you were very sick and you were already unconscious when we found you.'

'What party?'

'Your blood alcohol level was exceptionally high. Your clothes were dirty, your trousers bloody from the wounds on your legs. You were covered in alcohol and vomit, Herr Stroud. You were in a very poor condition altogether.'

'There was no party.'

'No party?'

'Where am I?'

'You are at the Berlin Gesundheitszentrum.'

'Is this a hospital?'

'A medical centre, yes. We are a medical centre, not a hospital. We do not undertake the surgeries here, but we can treat injuries.'

'What day is it?'

'It is Saturday, Herr Stroud. July the twenty-fourth.'

Stroud looked at Möller closely. He squinted until the man was clearly in focus. 'How do you know my name?'

'You had a bag with you. There was a camera, some notebooks. Your passport was there. We know your name from your passport.'

'My passport?'

'Yes, Herr Stroud, your passport.'

'But it was burned.'

Möller frowned. 'Burned? You thought you had burned it?'

'No, I didn't burn it. Someone else burned it.'

'Who, Herr Stroud? Who would burn your passport?'

'Lügner. A man called Lügner. I saw him burn my passport.'

'Well, we have your bag here, Herr Stroud, and we have your passport. You are English, no?'

'Yes, I am English.'

'Do you remember how you injured your legs?'

'Lügner did it. He kicked me. Lügner kicked me. He put something over my face, and then someone injected me with something and I was unconscious.'

'And it was this same person that burned your passport?'

'Yes. That's what I thought. I saw him burn it.'

'Indeed,' Möller said. 'But now your passport is here.'

Stroud didn't reply.

'I think you have experienced some trauma, Herr Stroud. I am not saying that you have imagined this, but I am wondering if there was such a person as this Herr Lügner.'

'What? Of course there was! You don't think I made it up, do you? You don't think I burned my own passport, surely?'

'No one has burned your passport, Herr Stroud.'

'Yes, I understand that now, but that's not what I believed was happening. And what about my legs? You saw that they're cut and bruised. Someone did that.'

'I have seen such injuries from someone falling over a low wall. Perhaps running into a barrier of some sort. People drink too much sometimes, Herr Stroud, and they don't always clearly remember what it was that happened.'

'I am not making this up, for Christ's sake. I was at Tegel. I was taken somewhere. I was asked questions. I was tortured.'

'Tortured?'

'Yes, I was tortured. I was interrogated and tortured.'

'Why, Herr Stroud? Why would someone want to interrogate and torture you?'

'I don't know, okay?'

'And who did this to you? This man Lügner?'

'Yes. Lügner. He questioned me and he hit me. He kicked my legs. He hurt me. He kept asking me questions about things I don't know anything about.'

'And you don't know who he was?'

'No. I don't know anything. I have no idea what's happening.'

'And you are absolutely sure this man's name was Lügner?'

'Yes! Yes, it was Lügner. That's what he said.'

'You speak no German, Herr Stroud?'

'No. No, I don't speak any German.'

'I think perhaps that this man didn't give you his real name.'

'I would have thought that was pretty bloody obvious, wouldn't you?'

'Perhaps, yes. But Lügner is actually a German word, Herr Stroud. It means liar.'

They kept him overnight. Stroud slept fitfully for three or four hours, his mind still troubled with images of walls closing in on him, of questions being screamed relentlessly, of people with needles. He woke sweating and afraid. He lay awake until dawn broke, just grateful to be alive.

Möller returned to see him. He recommended that Stroud see a resident psychiatrist, but Stroud refused. He was not deluded. He knew what had happened. It was of no concern to him whether anyone else believed him. Finally Möller accepted that there was no actual reason to detain him, and his discharge papers were signed. His bag, his camera, his notebooks and passport were returned. His clothes were a mess, but they would suffice until he got back to England.

He called Nina from the airport, gave her a very brief and cursory excuse for his absence and lack of contact. He was on the way back, and that was all that mattered. He was taking the first available flight out of Tegel.

She asked him for his time of arrival at Gatwick, said she'd be there to meet him off the plane. He said it wasn't necessary, but she insisted.

'Enough, Stroud. I'm coming to get you.'

Something in her tone conveyed the definite impression that she actually gave a damn. It felt personal, and he appreciated it. It seemed like an eternity since someone had wanted to do something for him without expecting something more in return.

'I was really worried about you. Five days, Stroud. Five days without a single word from you.'

'Nina, I'm sorry. I will explain everything when I see you.'

Stroud sat near the window on the plane. He nursed a double Scotch, and in his pocket were another two small airline bottles. His head ached. His whole body ached. His legs were killing him. He could feel how swollen and tender they were even beneath the substantial bandaging. Möller had given him some painkillers, had made him promise to take no more than two every three or four hours. He'd also admonished him against taking them with alcohol. Stroud had blatantly ignored the instruction, had taken six with plenty of alcohol, but they nevertheless seemed to be doing nothing to ease the pain.

Nina was as good as her word, standing right there – her arm in a sling – as he came out of arrivals and started toward the concourse.

'Jesus Christ, Stroud, what the hell happened?' The shock was evident in her expression. He was limping painfully, everything blunted by painkillers and Scotch. It wasn't until the taxi pulled out of the airport car park that he started to talk.

He told her everything, keeping his voice low, conscious that the cab driver would perhaps overhear. He started with how he'd found the key in Dekker's flat, his trip to Berlin, his arrest, his detainment by Maier and Lehmann. And then came Lügner, the room in which he'd been held, the beating, the injuries to his legs, the injection they finally administered and how he had woken in a medical facility.

Nina listened and didn't interrupt. Stroud could feel her shock and disbelief. The atmosphere within the confines of the taxi was tense and uncomfortable. As he came to the end of his monologue, he wondered if she would respond in the same way as Möller – a sense of incredulity closely followed by immediate suspicion regarding what drugs he might have taken.

But there was nothing like that. She was quiet, absorbing everything he'd said, and then she leaned her head back and closed her eyes. She sighed deeply, then moved to better see him, all the while holding her arm away from her body so as not to aggravate her own injury.

'What have we got ourselves into?' she asked.

Stroud shook his head. He looked out of the window. The sky once again was that same flat gunmetal grey, but the heat had not abated. Any promise of rain was a cruel deception.

'Do you think this Lügner was German intelligence?'

'I don't know, Nina. I don't know who he was or what they thought I knew. I told them everything I could. There was no way not to.'

She reached out and took his hand, squeezing it reassuringly. 'I understand,' she said. 'I understand completely. I can't even begin to imagine what you must have gone through.'

'He kept asking me if Raphael and Dekker were the same person. He asked me about people who were part of Baader–Meinhof, and the things they brought from the security locker—'

'The things they *said* were from the security locker.'

Stroud nodded. 'Sure. Yes. The things they said were in that locker. I had the key, for Christ's sake. I had to tell them where I'd taken it from.'

'I know, I know. I know you had to tell them.'

'It's easy to think you wouldn't say anything, but the fear, the pain...'

'It's okay,' Nina said. 'You're here now. You're out of it. Let's get you back home for some rest. We can get a doctor to see you, and then we can talk about it, okay? We can talk about all of it and figure out what we're going to do now.'

Stroud turned and looked at her. Never had he been so relieved to see someone, to be able to tell her what had happened without having his sanity called into question. In that moment he believed that she and Haig were the only real friends he possessed in the world.

'Thank you,' he said.

'For what?'

'For not telling me that I'm mad.'

'I believe you, Stroud. There's no reason for you to make up something like this, and I sure as hell don't think you imagined it. We're going to figure it out, okay? Somehow we're going to try and make sense of all of this and ...' She paused, looked away.

'And what?' Stroud prompted.

'I need you to tell me what's happening, okay? The key. You took that key and you didn't tell me.'

'I know. I'm sorry.'

'You have to trust someone, Stroud, and if you don't feel you can trust me ...'

'I can,' Stroud replied. 'I can and I do.'

She nodded, squeezed his hand again.

After a while, she looked at him and said, 'Are you scared?'

'Yes,' he said without hesitation.

'Good,' she replied. 'Then I'm not alone.'

34

'Jesus Christ almighty,' Haig said. 'I am at a loss for words. I mean, look at you. Nina comes back with a broken wrist, we don't hear a word from you for the best part of a week, and then you drag yourself into the building like the walking wounded with this story about being kidnapped and interrogated by some German—'

'It's not a story, Marcus. It actually happened, okay?'

'And this... what was his name?'

'Lügner,' Stroud said. 'It's German for liar.'

'Right, yes. I get the irony.' Haig shook his head. He stood up, sat down again, looked at Stroud, at Nina, back at Stroud.

'He didn't say he was German intelligence.'

'He didn't say anything, Marcus. He just kept beating me and asking me questions, and then he beat me some more. Then he put some chemical on a cloth and put it over my face, and I didn't know what the hell was happening but I had to tell him everything I knew. I told him about you and looking for Raphael. I told him where I got the key, about Dekker. He kept asking if Dekker and Raphael were the same person. He asked me if I knew a whole bunch of different people. The people who kidnapped Peter Lorenz. The people who took over the embassy in Stockholm. All those connected with Baader–Meinhof, the Red Army Faction, Black September.'

'They thought you were a terrorist.'

'They thought I was something other than a journalist, that's for sure. Lügner also made me believe that he'd burned my passport. This wasn't some amateur operation, Marcus. They knew about Julia, about Eva.'

'What?'

'The questions he asked me after he put that stuff over my face. They were like test questions, asking me things that I would know, provable facts ... I guess to determine whether or not whatever it was they gave me was working.'

'A truth drug?'

'I don't bloody well know, do I? It was some sort of chemical. It was like ... Christ, I don't even know what it was like. He just put that thing over my face, and everything started moving in different directions and I felt utterly compelled to answer whatever he asked me whether I wanted to or not.'

Haig got up and walked to the window. He stood in silence for some time, immobile, his thoughts almost audible in the silence of the room.

Eventually he turned. 'Well, I don't think either of you is going anywhere very far in the state you're in. I don't even know what to think about this. I feel like I've walked you into some kind of ... what? What the hell have we stirred up here? We were looking for Raphael, and that was all. Based on what? An uncertain and unsubstantiated photograph that was apparently taken by MI6.'

'And the rumour that both Mossad and the French Ministry of Defence were looking for him,' Stroud added.

Haig waved aside the comment as if it was irrelevant. It was not. He was simply distracted and paying attention to little but his own thoughts.

'What now?' Nina asked. 'Do we carry on?'

Haig returned to his desk and sat down. He looked harried. 'I don't know,' he said. 'I need time to think. I want to make some enquiries. I want all the names of these people, these German people. I want to find out if there is anyone called Lügner. I am pretty much certain there isn't, but I want to check anyway.' He looked toward some indistinct point in the middle of the room. 'Bloody hell,' he said, his voice almost a whisper. 'I don't even know *how* to think about this, let alone what to do next.'

'Marcus, if you're worried about the money, it stopped being about that almost right away,' Stroud said. 'As soon as I saw that picture of Raphael in the embassy in Istanbul, it became something else entirely.'

'That is the very last thing on my mind. As far as I'm concerned, you've earned the money twice over. If I'd thought for a moment that this . . .' He waved at Stroud and Nina, indicating their injuries. 'If I'd believed for a moment that you'd wind up in this kind of trouble, I wouldn't have asked you to go out there.'

'It's not your fault, Marcus,' Nina said. 'No one could have known what we were getting into.'

'Nevertheless, I can't help but feel responsible for what's happened.'

'There is one thing we could check out,' Nina said.

Both Haig and Stroud turned and looked at her.

'The other Dekker, the one in Hilversum. If the one in Leiden wasn't Raphael, then there's always the possibility—'

'Right now I don't want to know,' Haig said. 'And I don't want either of you to do anything. Just take a day or two. Stay out of it and let me think this over. I'll find out what I can, and we'll have another conversation about this, okay? Nina, take a couple of days' leave. Give me a call on Wednesday morning. We'll meet up again, talk about it some more, see if I've been able to find out anything useful.'

'If that's what you want, Marcus,' Nina said.

'Yes,' he replied. 'Yes, I think that would be for the best right now.'

Both Stroud and Nina got up. They left the room without another word.

Stroud glanced back as he closed the door behind him. Haig was just sitting there, his expression vacant, as if everything he knew to be certain had just been disproved.

35

'I was the world champion at making promises,' Stroud said. 'Current title holder for breaking them too.'

Nina smiled as if she knew precisely what he meant.

'I guess I just tried to be normal in every way possible, but none of it stuck, you know? Regular job, settling down, being a parent, all that stuff. I gave it a good try, but this other life just kept pulling at me. I had to keep moving, keep throwing myself into the most dangerous situations I could find. And that, just so you know, is not the best way to keep a marriage together.'

Stroud moved his legs. They ached relentlessly. He leaned back on Nina's couch and looked over at her. She'd tied her hair back, had her knees tucked up under her on the armchair. She looked less worn out, and very beautiful in that moment. Was it true that the more you got to know someone, the more you saw who they really were, and thus your perception of them changed? He remembered an Italian journalist in Cyprus. She was there with some TV station. She got drunk with him and Raphael the night before she left.

'Men,' she told him, 'fall in love with bodies. Woman, however, fall in love with minds.'

He knew there was nothing between himself and Nina, but he had surprised himself with the change in his feelings towards her. She was no longer a colleague. Shared experience aside, he now considered her a friend, someone he could confide in, someone he could trust.

'What's she like? Your ex-wife.'

'Well, if she's the same as the woman I lived with, she's smart, funny, good-looking, but she's tied to her family, her father especially, in a way that prevents her from ever really being completely herself. Of course, I have only understood this in hindsight. The basic problem is that she's never had to work, and I think that's very destructive for a person. They get into a thing where everything comes too easy, no challenges, and then when things don't go the way they want and money can't fix it, they're buggered.'

'Rich family?'

'Self-made father. Knows what he knows and nothing else. Has an opinion about everything, and it's a problem if you don't see things his way.'

'And you never got the papal blessing.'

Stroud smiled. It was a good way of putting it. 'I was about as far from the plan as you could get. I don't know what he wanted for her. A banker, maybe. Suits, ties, hand-made shirts. Cambridge rowing blue, drives an Aston Martin. Christ knows, Nina. Someone who could elevate the family without diminishing his status. That game is all about how things appear, not how they are.'

'Tell me about your daughter.'

Stroud looked down at his reflection in the glass of wine in his hand. 'Eva,' he said. 'She turned fourteen in May.'

'Did you see her for her birthday?'

'No, I didn't.'

'Did you send her a gift?'

'I sent money in her birthday card.'

'How much?'

'Enough that she would know I cared.'

Nina looked at him. Stroud looked back at her. Neither of them spoke nor changed expression for a good ten seconds.

'I'm damaged goods too, you know,' she finally said.

'How so?'

'I'm twenty-nine, single, longest relationship has been less than a year, and I haven't had one of any kind for close on two. I don't speak to my parents, have no interest in being a mother, haven't had any contact with my brother since we were teenagers, and I'm only doing the job at *The Times* because there really wasn't anything else I could find. I don't think about tomorrow. I think about today. This thing, whatever this is, is the most excitement I've had in years.'

'Excitement?' Stroud said. 'I wouldn't call breaking your wrist or getting the shit kicked out of you by some German lunatic excitement.'

'You know what I mean, Stroud. I *know* you know what I mean. Same reason you go running towards things that everyone else is running away from. In truth, I think the answer's pretty simple.'

'You do?'

'To feel alive. To feel that what you're doing matters. To feel like you make a difference, or *could* make a difference. Like Thoreau, right? To reach death only to discover that you had never lived.'

Stroud laughed. 'And now you remind me of Raphael. He used to quote Mordaunt at me. One crowded hour of glorious life—'

'Is worth an age without a name.'

'Exactly.'

'Do you believe that he's still alive?'

'Yes,' Stroud replied. 'Now I do.'

'Why?' Nina asked. 'What changed your mind?'

'In Berlin with Lügner, or whatever the hell his name was, the thing he kept asking me was whether Raphael was still alive and whether Dekker and Raphael were the same person. Over and over like a broken record. He wanted to know if Dekker was involved in the kidnapping of Peter Lorenz. You remember that, right?'

Nina nodded.

'And then he started rattling off names of people who are probably Baader–Meinhof, Red Army Faction, all that German terrorist movement stuff. Not only does he think Dekker's involved with terrorist cells, I also think he believes that Dekker and Raphael are the same person. And that doesn't take into consideration that the Hendrik Dekker in Leiden worked in Wassenaar, and that may very well mean that he is Dutch Intelligence Service.'

'There's the third Dekker, the one in Hilversum. We need to rule him out.'

'I have no intention of going back to the Netherlands,' Stroud said.

'Nor do I. There must be some other way to find out.'

'So say we do that. Say we determine that the Dekker in Hilversum is not Raphael, we still have no idea what the Dekker in Leiden even looks like. We are actually no further forward on that.'

Stroud inhaled deeply, exhaled again. 'Right now I have no intention of doing anything but sitting here, drinking the rest of this wine, finding out what else you've got in the house that I can drink and drinking that too. Oh, and a good deal of feeling sorry for myself.'

'Are those painkillers helping at all?'

'Not that I'm aware of, but then I have no idea how I'd feel if I wasn't taking them.'

'Would you like something stronger?'

'God, no. I'm just going to sit here and suffer. It makes me feel noble, like a martyr to the cause.'

'Now I can appreciate how being married to you would be a thoroughly miserable business.'

Stroud nearly choked with laughing. 'Oh, you have no idea,' he said. 'You've seen me at nothing but my best.'

Nina was quiet for a little while, just looking at him with an implacable expression.

'What?' he asked.

'What was it like?'

'What was what like?'

'In Germany. Lügner. Being locked in that place. What he did to you.'

'It was terrifying. That's what it was like. I thought they were going to kill me.'

'You seem to be dealing with it, at least a hell of a lot better than I could deal with it. I think I'd have had a nervous breakdown.'

'Maybe I did, and I haven't realised it. Or the nervous breakdown is yet to come. I still have moments when I think I'm dreaming this and I'm going to wake up back in that room. To be honest, anything I've experienced like that has been in times of war. I don't really have any frame of reference. There's no box with a label that I can put it in so it makes any kind of sense.'

'And now? How do you feel about what happened right now?'

He smiled, shook his head. 'What, all of a sudden you're my counsellor?'

'I'm interested. I want to know what went through your mind.'

'Did my whole life play out before me like a film, you mean? Did I think about all the things I've done that I regret? All the things I should've done and never did? That kind of thing?'

'You're making fun of me.'

Stroud set his glass on the coffee table and leaned forward. 'I'll tell you what went through my mind, Nina. You think about how the fuck you're going to get through it. You think about every possible angle that might give you some more information, an advantage, a degree of leverage. You try to think of anything that will make you feel less like your fate is completely out of your control. You think about how you're going to survive. That's what you think about.'

'If you'd known that something like that would happen, would you still have gone to Germany with that key?'

It wasn't long before Stroud answered, but he did consider it, even if only for a handful of seconds. 'Yes,' he said. 'I would still have gone.'

'Why? Why put yourself through something like that?'

'Christ, Nina, I don't know. Because we instinctively err on the side of believing in our own invincibility, I guess. Because we think that we'll live forever, that we're indestructible, that we're bulletproof.'

'Only that?'

'And the truth. Something like this happens, you want to know the truth. It's got me completely. Right now the truth about Raphael, whether he's still alive and why he's covered his tracks so thoroughly, it's more addictive than...' He shook his head. 'More addictive than what? I don't know. Heroin? I've never done it, so I couldn't tell you. I just know that I have to find out. It's become a crusade. If he did fake his own death, if he has been off the grid for all these years, then he's a great deal smarter than I ever gave him credit for. And if he's that smart, he knows that we're looking for him, and yet he still chooses to be invisible. That makes it personal, I guess.'

Stroud looked up. His expression was intense.

'That means he's hiding from me,' he said. 'And I want to know why.'

36

Nina made up a bed for Stroud in the box room. A heap of blankets on the floor, a sheet over him, and by the time he lay down he was so drunk he wouldn't have noticed if she'd left him out on the pavement for the night. The heat was still unbearable and gave no indication of abating. The summer was already reported to be the hottest on record, and the temperatures seemed set to rise even further.

Had she not frantically woken him a little after noon on Tuesday, he perhaps would have slept through the day.

'Stroud! Stroud! Wake the fuck up, for Christ's sake!'

Her voice was urgent, panicked, and he slurred into consciousness, imagining himself dreaming, that he had never left Berlin, that he was still trapped in that room with Lügner and his relentless, unanswerable questions.

'Stroud! Get up! The news! Come and see the news!'

Enormously relieved to have his nightmare interrupted, and ignoring the pain in his legs, he made it through to the living room.

'...at this time unable to verify that the body was that of suspected terrorist Hendrik Dekker. The apartment was rented in the name of Dekker, reputedly connected to Baader–Meinhof and other West German terrorist factions.'

An indistinct image appeared – a man in his late thirties or early forties, a three-quarter view, glasses, unkempt dark hair, the photograph of such poor quality that it really could have been anyone of similar age and complexion.

The image disappeared.

'The explosion ripped through two floors of the building, killing both the occupant and several other tenants.'

On the screen, Stroud could see a pall of black smoke rising from the shell of a burned-out building, the very same building he and Nina had broken into just eight days earlier.

'Dutch police and anti-terrorist agencies have declined to make any further comment, stating that they have initiated a collaboration with West German authorities to thoroughly investigate any links between this incident and active terrorist cells in both the Netherlands and Germany.'

Nina stepped forward and switched off the television set.

She turned to face Stroud. He looked like he'd been slapped, and hard.

'They killed Dekker?' he asked.

'Or they made it appear that way,' Nina replied. 'According to the report, there was very little left to identify. They say he was building some sort of explosive device and it went off.'

'Christ almighty.' Stroud backed up and sat down on the sofa. He stared at the TV screen, looked up at Nina, then back to the TV screen as if he expected it to come to life of its own accord and give him further information.

'The photo—' she started.

'Could've been me, could've been Haig, could've been pretty much anyone.'

'Could have been Raphael,' she added. 'Maybe they found him, and have now made sure you can't.'

'And who would *they* be in this context, Nina? The Turks, Mossad, the French, the Dutch, the Germans, MI6?' He shook his head. 'The further this goes, the more unbelievable it becomes, the less I want to do with it and the more I have to find out.'

'We have to know about the third Dekker,' Nina said. She sat down facing him. 'We need to rule him out as a possibility. We have to make sure that—'

'I know, I know,' Stroud interjected. 'Let me think for a minute.' He reached for his cigarettes and lit one. 'Any chance of some coffee?'

'Sure.' She got up.

'Throw a shot of something in it, would you?'

Nina looked at him, her eyebrows raised.

'What?' he said.

'You really think that's a good idea?'

'I think I am way past the point of knowing what is and isn't a good idea.'

'I'll get you some coffee. Black, strong, no sugar.'

She left the room. Stroud got up and followed her. He sat at the kitchen table and watched her go through the motions of making coffee, but his mind was elsewhere.

Had Dekker really been killed, and was Dekker really Raphael? Had he just inadvertently colluded in the greatest irony of all? Had he been instrumental in killing his oldest friend, his mentor, and a man who had already been dead for six years?

Nina put the coffee in front of him and sat down.

They looked at one another for a few moments, and then Stroud leaned his head back, closed his eyes and took a deep breath.

'If Dekker was Raphael—' Nina said.

'Then taking that key and trying to find that security locker at Tegel means that I killed him.'

'You didn't kill him, Stroud. You can't let yourself think like that.'

215

'Then how the hell am I supposed to think?'

'We don't know if Dekker is even dead. That photograph could've been anyone, just as you said. This whole thing could be another disappearing act, just like in Jordan.'

'If he did it once, there's nothing to say he couldn't do it again, right?'

'I think we have to stop being naïve,' Nina said. 'I think that if Dekker and Raphael are the same person, whoever he works for, we're dealing with organisations that are more than capable of changing names, faces, identities and Christ only knows what else. Making people disappear, killing them, bringing them back to life...'

'You're going all conspiracy theory on me.'

'I'm not going anything, Stroud. Look at what's happened. Just look at it for a minute without any opinions or bias or pre-conceptions. You think whoever is doing this doesn't know about you? About me? Seems that everywhere we've gone, someone's been waiting for us. Every step we've taken has been pre-empted by someone else. Every time we think we're a little bit closer to finding out what the hell happened six years ago, we're faced with something else that makes it even more confusing and surreal. And now this. You take something out of this flat in Holland, you wind up getting the shit kicked out of you by a German who calls himself Liar, and then the flat is blown up with the guy we're looking for inside.' She paused. 'Supposedly.'

'I know all this—'

'You were the one who was most adamant that Raphael was dead, and now you think he's not. Let's go to the paper. Let's see if we can actually get some real information about what the hell happened in Leiden.'

'Okay, okay,' Stroud said.

'So what are we waiting for?'

'Can I take a shower first? And I need some clothes. I really need some different clothes, Nina. I look like I slept in a fucking dustbin lorry.'

'Okay. Shower, clothes, and then we go to *The Times*. We get Haig onto this and see if we can't find some actual truth here.'

37

The *Times* foreign desk seemed far more interested in Soviet chess grand master Viktor Korchnoi asking for political asylum in Amsterdam than a clumsy terrorist in Leiden. There was little more to be gleaned from the wires that had come in.

An explosion, believed to have been caused as Hendrik Dekker constructed an incendiary device, had torn through the upper two floors of the apartment building. Again, it seemed the only photograph of Dekker was a grainy, indistinct image.

'Looking at that,' Nina said, 'do you think there's any way it could be Raphael?'

Stroud shook his head. 'Same as the picture Marcus showed me right at the start of this thing. That could be pretty much anyone.'

Nina called up to Haig's office and spoke to Carole. Haig was out, wouldn't be back for an hour or more.

'I think we have to make a decision on this,' Stroud said. 'First thing is to find out about this other Dekker in Hilversum.'

'You still have the address?'

'Somewhere, yes.' He fetched a notebook out of his bag, leafed through it. 'Here we are.' He handed it to Nina.

Nina called international directory enquiries, gave the name and address, waited for the number.

She wrote it beside Dekker's name, handed it to Stroud.

'You call him,' Stroud said.

'And say what?'

'I don't bloody well know. Tell him you're doing a national survey. Tell him you're from the Netherlands Office of Statistics or something. Just make up any old crap and ask him his age and marital status and whatever.'

'We need someone who speaks Dutch,' she said.

'Fuck it, give me the phone. I'll call him.'

Stroud dialled the number. It rang. He could feel the tension rising in his chest, his increased heart rate. What if he heard Raphael's voice? What if Vincent Raphael himself answered the phone?

'*Hallo?*'

It was a woman's voice, elderly.

'Er ... yes ... hello. I'm looking for Mr Dekker.'

'*Wie is dit? Wat wil je?*'

'Mr Dekker. Hendrik Dekker. Is he there, please?'

'*Ik begrijp niet wat u zegt. Wacht hier.*'

The sound of the receiver being set down.

Stroud frowned.

'What happened?' Nina asked.

'A woman. She doesn't speak English. I think she's gone to get someone.'

'Hello, who is this?' a voice said. Younger, a man.

'Hello there. I was looking for Mr Hendrik Dekker.'

'And who are you?'

'I'm calling from the Office of National Statistics, and we're conducting a survey of—'

'Mr Dekker is dead.'

'I am sorry.'

'This is his son. My father is dead. He died six days ago. I am here making funeral arrangements with my mother.'

'I am really very sorry. I had no idea. I hope you will accept my apology for disturbing you at this time.'

'Please do not call again,' the man said. The line went dead.

Nina looked expectant.

Stroud put the phone down. 'Our Hilversum Dekker is dead. Six days ago. The guy on the phone said he was Dekker's son, that he was arranging the funeral. If that's true, then it makes things a great deal easier. At least we don't have to go back to Holland.'

'So all we actually have is an unknown German agent who thinks that Dekker and Raphael might be the same person.'

Stroud didn't speak for a while. Then he leaned forward and took his notebook from the desk. 'This started with a picture, supposedly taken in Istanbul by the French. That picture was no clearer than the one they're showing on TV, but there was a photo of Raphael in that file in Istanbul with Dekker's name on it. That is the one thing I can't explain. Haig said there was a rumour that Mossad were interested in him as well. There's the possibility that he was also inside Dutch intelligence, unless working in Wassenaar was simply a coincidence.'

'So both French intelligence and the Dutch are using pictures that are so vague that identity can't be determined.'

'Right.'

'Are you wondering whether that is on purpose?' Nina asked.

'I'm sure it's on purpose. If our Hendrik Dekker in Leiden was an insider and the Dutch found out, they'd want him gone.'

'Yes, of course, but I'm also thinking about the photo in Istanbul.'

'What? That someone wanted me to think that Raphael and Dekker were the same person?'

'Hey, you agreed with me when I said that every step we've taken seems to have been pre-empted by someone else.'

'Well that's another angle,' Stroud said. 'Someone wants us to think that Dekker is Raphael, and then Dekker is reported dead.'

'Without us ever being able to identify one or the other.'

'And this doesn't even take into consideration the first discovery we made.'

'The first discovery?' Nina asked.

'That the real Vincent Raphael died when he was four days old.'

'The whole thing is smoke and mirrors. I feel like a chess piece in someone else's game.'

'Haig needs to give us something else,' Stroud said. 'And if he hasn't got anything else, then he needs to find it. He's got contacts. I'm sure he could find out something that would move this thing in one direction or another.'

'And if he doesn't, or can't?'

Stroud shook his head. 'I am not even going to consider that right now. I just want to talk to Haig.'

38

'Like who, Stroud?'

'I don't bloody well know, Marcus. Editors, chief editors, newspaper publishers. Call someone in Holland and ask a favour. There must be some kind of network of newspaper people all over Europe. I have no doubt that someone somewhere has a real honest-to-God photograph of the man who was supposedly killed in that flat in Leiden.'

Haig looked at Nina. 'Has he been drinking?'

'I agree with him, Marcus. We need something else. We've chased this thing as far as we can and we need some other lead or clue or something. We need your help.'

'Do you have any idea what you two look like?' Marcus said. 'You look like you've gone ten rounds with Ali. Looks like he used one of you to beat the crap out of the other.'

'You asked me to do this,' Stroud said.

'I know I did, and the more I think about it, the more insane it seems.'

'Hell, this is what we do, for Christ's sake. Where the fuck is the lunatic Marcus Haig that used to run through gunfire with a fucking Leica, eh? What the hell happened to him?'

'He got shot at too many times. That's what happened to him.'

'You're not dead, are you? That's the only time you know you've been shot at too many times.'

Marcus laughed, but there was no humour in it. 'Look, Stroud, we're not all the same as you and Vincent. It seemed like a good idea, okay? There was a rumour. There was this little unsubstantiated rumour that Vincent might still be alive and I got interested. That was all, and it was from a purely professional point of view. As far as I was concerned, the man was dead, had been for six years. How many times did I think about him? Maybe ten or twenty times in all those years, and only when something prompted me to. People change. They get older, they grow up, their priorities alter. You know, if there was someone who could actually calm you down, then you might actually discover that having some degree of predictability and stability in your life isn't anywhere near as bad as you think. And as far as kids are concerned, I only have to mention Eva and you look like your heart has been dragged out of your chest and kicked around a football pitch.'

'Oh, fuck off—'

'No, Stroud, you fuck off. I didn't make any lifelong deal with you or Raphael. I was on a mission, certainly, but my thoughts were directed a little further forward than whether or not I would survive the next gunfight or the next hair-raising fucking helicopter ride out of some godforsaken shithole on the other side of the world.'

Stroud didn't speak. He had no leverage. Haig was right. He'd also floored him with the comment about Eva.

'I don't want to quit,' Nina said. 'Marcus, I really don't want to quit. Too much has happened.'

'Nina, look—'

'No, Marcus, don't *Nina, look* me. We need your help. We need something else to work with. Call some people, use whatever influence you've got and get us a picture of the man who died in the flat. Or something else. I don't care. We're stalled

223

right now, and we need to change something before we break down completely.'

Marcus frowned, half smiled. 'Why is this so important to you all of a sudden? You're not getting a hefty pay-off like Stroud. Are you just so mind-numbingly bored down in copy-editing that you'll risk getting killed for the sake of a little excitement, or what?'

'Let's just say that,' Nina replied. 'Let's just say I'm stubborn or obsessed or whatever you want. It doesn't matter why I'm so determined. I don't even know why myself. Seems to me that both of you, Raphael as well, seem to have spent most of your lives addicted to finding the truth. Maybe that addiction is contagious. I just know that I don't want to let this go. I can't let it go, Marcus, but right now I don't know where else to look.'

'I really have created a Frankenstein's monster here, haven't I?'

The question was rhetorical. Neither Stroud nor Nina responded.

'And if I paid you to drop it?' Haig asked.

'Why would you do that?'

'To stop you getting into any more trouble.'

'I think we're way beyond that, Marcus,' Stroud said. 'We're already up close and personal with the Turks, the Dutch and the Germans, and if the French Ministry of Defence and Mossad have their wits about them, which I don't doubt for a second, then we're on their watch list too, for sure.'

Haig sighed deeply. 'Okay, okay. Leave it with me. Let me see what I can do.'

'Thank you.'

'You know, I regret ever having—'

'Regret is pointless, Marcus. Didn't Raphael teach you anything?'

39

Haig didn't call until the following afternoon. It was a little before two o'clock, and both Nina and Stroud had spent much of the intervening hours doing nothing but eating, sleeping, drinking and watching TV.

Breakfast was actually lunch, and that was when the call came through. Haig told them to get over to *The Times* as fast as they could. They took a taxi and went up to his office.

'I have someone who will talk to you,' he said. 'Someone in the Netherlands.'

'Who?' Stroud asked.

'He doesn't want me to give you his name.'

'Because...?'

'Because he doesn't want you to know who he is, that's why. I don't think it's complicated, Stroud. For Christ's sake, the guy won't even talk to me. Said he won't deal with the press officially, but he will speak to someone who's not with the paper.'

'And you really have no idea who this person is?'

'I spoke to someone I know at *De Telegraaf*. He said he could maybe help. He called me back and said he had a contact who worked near where this Hendrik Dekker's flat was.'

'Wassenaar,' Stroud said.

'What?'

'There's a place called Wassenaar. It's not far from Leiden. It's where the headquarters of the Dutch Intelligence Service is.'

'I haven't a clue, Stroud. What I've told you is all I've got.'

'And I'm to phone him, or what?'

Haig leaned forward and handed Stroud a slip of paper, on which was written an overseas number.

'I appreciate this, Marcus.'

'Best I could do. Whether anything comes of it … well, you're going to find out, right?'

'Right.'

'And don't phone from my office, okay? Use one of the public phones in the lobby downstairs.'

Stroud went down with Nina. They gathered up all the coins they had between them and placed the call through the international operator.

For what seemed like an interminable time the phone rang at the other end. The operator cut in and asked Stroud if he wanted to stay on the line.

'Please, yes,' he said.

No more than a handful of seconds later, the line connected.

'Yes?'

'Yes. Hello. I'm calling from London—'

'Yes.'

'I am—'

'I know who you are. I don't need your name.'

Stroud hesitated. The accent was almost certainly Dutch.

'Okay. No, of course. So as you know, I am trying to get some information about what happened in—'

'No names. No places.'

'Some information about what happened. I was told you might be able to help me.'

There was a long pause, and then Stroud could hear a smile in the voice at the other end. 'I am your Deep Throat, no?'

Another pause. Stroud wondered for a moment if they had been disconnected.

The line went dead.

Stroud stood right where he was with the receiver in his hand, the expression on his face one of utter disbelief.

'What?' Nina asked. 'What did he say?'

'He told me that this had nothing to do with the French, and that there was nothing of interest in Paris.'

'Huh? What the hell use is that?'

Stroud smiled, but he was still looking inward. 'I never asked him about the French. I never brought it up.'

He hung up the receiver. 'I think I just got confirmation that Raphael and Dekker are the same person.'

'And he's dead?'

Stroud slowly shook his head, as if he was trying to both absorb the information he had and relay it at the same time.

'No,' he said. 'No, he's not.' He looked at Nina. 'Raphael is no more dead than me.'

40

'So you think this person on the phone was Dutch intelligence?' Haig asked.

'Yes, I do. Your contact told you that this guy worked near Leiden, right?'

'That's what he said.'

'Leiden is about six miles from Wassenaar, and Wassenaar, like I said, is home to Dutch foreign intelligence.'

'That's your assumption,' Haig said. 'Dekker could've worked in a sodding newsagent for all we know.'

'True, but I don't believe in coincidences.'

Haig laughed. 'People believe in coincidences when it suits them, Stroud. Don't go down the route of having a theory and crowbarring everything to fit it.'

'So what do *you* think, Marcus?'

'I have no bloody idea.'

'Well I have no clue what his real name is, but he took the identity of a baby who died aged four days. For some reason he had to vanish. So he did, vaporised in a fireball in Jordan. He came back from the dead as Hendrik Dekker, or maybe there was another name in between and Dekker is a more recent addition to the roll call. I'm in the process of verifying that Dekker is actually Raphael, but – oh my fucking God! – he just happens to be a spectacularly clumsy terrorist who blows himself to kingdom come with some home-made incendiary device.'

Haig closed his eyes and leaned back in the chair, his fingers against his lips, his thumbs beneath his chin. He looked like he was praying for forgiveness. After a while, he looked up. 'You want to go to Paris, don't you?'

'Yes, Marcus, I want to go to Paris.'

'And what makes you think that your reception there will be any less hostile than the one you got in Istanbul and Berlin?'

'Because I am going to go under a pseudonym.'

'You what?'

'A fake passport, Marcus, and I'm going to get into France without everyone knowing it before I even arrive.'

'Seriously? And if you get caught?'

'Then I get caught. I'll be arrested and charged and probably do a year in prison. Fuck it, it's three hots and a cot, as our American cousins say. I might even manage to get a few good nights' sleep while I'm inside.'

'You're mad. You're absolutely bloody mad. You do realise that, don't you?'

'I am, always have been, and so were you once upon a time.'

'This is not spirit of adventure, Stroud, this is straightforward certifiable lunacy.'

'Hasn't this thing got right inside you, Marcus? I mean, for Christ's sake, the man we lived and worked with for all those years isn't even Raphael. Don't you want to know? Aren't you just dying to know the truth?'

'I was, right up until Nina came back from Amsterdam with a broken wrist and you showed up looking like you'd been run over by a train. Did what happened in Berlin not dissuade you at all? They could have killed you and buried you in the fucking woods and none of us would have been any the wiser. We tried to find you, you know? We got as far as Tegel. We finally got someone in the airport to confirm that you did come in on a flight from Schiphol. That was it. The trail went cold. We called hospitals, police stations, whoever we could think of, but there was nothing. Finally we accepted that you were going to do what you wanted to do, and the more attention we attracted the less helpful it might be.'

'Well, maybe the attention that you did attract was one of the reasons they let me go.'

'Maybe. Maybe not. It could have been that they simply realised you knew nothing.'

'That's the conclusion I came to as well.'

'And now you want to go to Paris with a false identity.'

'Yes.'

'And when you get there?'

'I don't know yet.'

Haig looked at him. He raised his eyebrows, as if waiting for the punchline. It never came.

'You don't know yet? Seriously? And you expect me to support this venture of yours?'

'I don't expect anything. You said you'd give me two grand to prove one way or the other whether Vincent Raphael was dead. Well, the original Raphael was dead at just four days old. I've proven that, so I guess we're done.'

'You know what I mean.'

'Yes, Marcus, I know what you mean. You asked me for something. I didn't want to do it. The two grand convinced me. Now it's something else, and if I wind up spending that money satisfying my own curiosity, then I am quite prepared to do it.'

'But is it worth your life?'

'You want me to throw in the towel, call it quits? Is that it?'

Haig didn't reply.

'Honest answer, Marcus. No bullshit. Don't say what you think I want to hear. Do you actually want me to stop looking for Raphael?'

Haig sighed. 'Honestly? I think you know the answer to that question.'

'So this is just some concern you're feeling for my personal well-being?'

'We're friends, Stroud. For Christ's sake, I'm the one who got you back from Amsterdam and into this mess in the first place.'

'I think you bringing me back from Amsterdam saved my life.'

'Really? It was that bad?'

'I was on a bender. Big self-destruct bender. No other way to look at it. Another six months, a year at best, and I think I would have drunk myself in front of a tram or into a canal. I've got a reason now, Marcus. It may not be much of a reason, but at least I've got something to do every day, and it's better than simply finding my way to the next bar.'

Marcus was silent for a moment. 'I hadn't realised. What do you need from me?'

'I need you to make Nina stay here. Aside from the broken wrist, I really don't think she should come.'

'I think Nina Benson is a good deal tougher than you give her credit for.'

'I know she's tough. That's not the point. I'm just not going to have someone assume that she and I are so close that hurting her would be a good way to get to me or back me off.'

'Understood. What else?'

'I need someone who can make me up a passport in a hurry.'

'Christ almighty, Stroud, who the hell do you think I am?'

Stroud smiled. 'Marcus Haig, that's who. One-time lunatic and war junkie, a man who speaks to more people in a week than I do in a year. If you don't know someone who can do this, then you know someone who knows someone.'

'You're bloody well paying for it, then. It comes out of the two grand, okay?'

Stroud grinned. 'And there he is, ladies and gentlemen, the Marcus Haig we all know and love.'

41

Standing in the queue on Saturday morning to board the Paris flight, Stroud looked at his own face in the passport, beneath it the name *Robert Mason*. He wondered about this person – who he was, how old he was when he died, who he would have become had he lived. Stillborn, a cot death, a childhood accident, or had his life been snatched away as a result of a far more violent and sinister occurrence?

'Sir?'

He looked up. The gate clerk held out her hand for his ticket and passport.

She looked at the passport. Did she frown?

Stroud's stomach tightened. Anxious then, realising that he hadn't actually considered what would happen if he was caught.

'Thank you, Mr Mason. Enjoy your flight,' the clerk said. She smiled as if there was nothing untoward at all. Stroud thanked her, retrieved his documents and walked on towards the stairwell. He felt his heart slow down. He relaxed.

As he took his seat and put his passport away, he realised that he was becoming ever more like Raphael. He was living the same lie that Raphael had lived for as many years as he'd been alive. It was an unsettling thought, but there was something about it that gave him a strange sense of comfort, as if this simple act of deceit and subterfuge had brought them closer than they'd ever been.

The flight was short, barely long enough for him to really gather his thoughts. He'd exchanged some of his cash at the airport. He had two hundred in sterling, and two thousand francs. He'd tried to keep track of what he'd spent, but there were gaps. Once this was concluded – *if* it concluded – he'd have that conversation with Marcus. He had no doubt Marcus would keep his word. Expenses would be covered.

The previous evening, having done his best to circumvent the details of what he was doing, he had finally told Nina he was going to France without her.

Her expression said everything. She was frustrated. She felt redundant. Carole had told her she was on sick leave until she could use a typewriter again. Both Nina and Stroud figured that Haig actually wanted her out of the building until there was some conclusion to this thing. What she did from home would give him a thin hope of deniability.

Stroud had looked at her, was ready to tell her about the passport, but checked himself. It was for her own safety. She couldn't be held accountable for what she didn't know. Later, though, as he thought about it, he realised there was another factor in play. He didn't want her to know, not to protect her, but to protect himself. It was the same motivation that told him not to give Haig the name in the passport. Only he and the forger would know that he was entering France as Robert Mason.

'So go,' she'd said. She pouted like a spoiled child.

Stroud laughed. 'You know, I think we should have started a relationship. This kind of thing would have been so much more melodramatic and personal. You could have really held it against me.'

'Sometimes you are such a wanker, Stroud.'

'So do you want to go out to dinner, or what?'

'Yes,' she said. 'Somewhere really expensive. And just so

you know, I intend to drink a lot. I plan to get very drunk and embarrass myself and you in the process.'

'Whatever floats your boat,' Stroud said.

They had not drunk a great deal. They had kept it together and talked. Nina was hard work; she gave away little, and all of it in fragments. Stroud was left with the impression that somewhere along the line she'd been hurt – perhaps badly – and now considered that her best form of defence was anonymity. He didn't pry. What had happened in her personal life was really none of his business.

Looking now from the window of the plane as he crossed the Channel, something that she'd said came back to him. At the time he hadn't given it a great deal of attention, but it had stayed with him.

'I have come to the conclusion that it is actually possible for someone to just disappear. However, I also believe that no matter what steps you take to hide, you can always be found.'

Did he believe that too? Did he really think that if he just kept at it, then the life and death of Vincent Raphael would be fully revealed? For Raphael was dead, for the first time at just four days old, and then again in Jordan, subsequently rising from the ashes as Hendrik Dekker. After the Netherlands phone call, he could no longer doubt that Raphael and Dekker were one and the same person. He had to have an anchor, a truth – whether substantiated or not – upon which he could rely. In the absence of a provable truth, he had to decide what to believe. He had decided to believe that Raphael had become Dekker.

It was Dekker who had been photographed by the French in Istanbul, and that was why the name appeared on Raphael's picture. Who he really was, who he actually worked for, what purpose he served, whether he was in hiding for fear of his own life or on the run as a committed terrorist was yet to be determined. Stroud had to keep going. He didn't consider there was any other option. He *had* to find out, no matter how long it took. That same bull-headed, stubborn, ignorant, self-serving compulsion that had taken him away from Julia and Eva so many times was now driving him to keep on looking until the truth came to light.

And if he went too far? If he upset too many people and something far worse than Tegel happened to him, what then?

Well, then he would be dead, and the dead had no regrets.

42

Stroud had not been in Paris since the riots of '68. Back then – not yet thirty years of age – the events of those weeks had been of immense significance to him. In a strange way, it was a baptism of fire, and so very different from the war zones he'd experienced. Paris was a modern, Western city. It was a city of art, of culture, of sophistication and style, and yet almost overnight it had become a battleground. Following support for the initial demonstrations at the university in Nanterre, more than twenty per cent of the population had gone on strike. Factories and universities were occupied by *soixante-huitards*, street battles ensued, and the response from the police – apparently incited and encouraged by the state's own agents provocateurs – grew ever more violent and heavy-handed. Finally de Gaulle fled to a French military base in Germany. The National Assembly was dissolved and new elections were held.

Despite the black humour of the chants – 'I'm a Marxist, of the Groucho tendency!' and 'I love you! Say it with paving stones!' – there was a real fear that the ruling class would collapse and anarchy would reign. It had happened before, and a lot of heads had been lost.

Raphael and Stroud were side by side during those fraught and desperate weeks, one day amidst the crowds gathered on the Rive Gauche, the next hurtling down narrow streets in the Latin Quarter, clutching their cameras, knowing all too well that if they were cornered by the police, they would lose not only their pictures, but also their freedom. Whatever was going on, the government didn't want it publicised to the world.

Ironically, when the fury had somehow burned itself out, the Gaullists emerged stronger than ever. The protests and demonstrations evaporated as rapidly as they'd started, and order – at least superficially – was restored.

Of course, such a tidal wave of political upheaval had sent shockwaves through French political society, and many societies beyond. If this could happen in Paris, then perhaps it would also be seen in London, in Rome, in Berlin. Effects would be felt for years, even decades. All the same, it taught Stroud a lesson that he was to see time and again in so many places around the world. Human beings, no matter what they said and did, ultimately erred in the direction of order. The wars, the civil conflicts, the riots and protests always ended, and in their place – alongside a huge sense of relief for the vast majority of ordinary people – came a renewed effort to establish a stable society. That it became unstable again was evidence of man's ultimate dissatisfaction with inequality, injustice and the gulf between the haves and the have-nots. It was a scenario that had played itself out generation after generation, irrespective of the culture, irrespective of the country.

Nevertheless, the Paris in which he arrived – with a different name and a different purpose – was still Paris. It was a city like no other, a city that was so very easy to love.

Stroud took a taxi into the 5th arrondissement. He had no plan, no predetermined strategy, and once he'd found a hotel and taken a room, he stood at the window and took stock of what he'd done.

Once more, driven by an innate compulsion to do everything at once, he had taken steps without considering the precise destination. He couldn't look for Vincent Raphael. He couldn't look for Hendrik Dekker. They were dead. What name was now being used – if the man behind those names was even alive – he didn't know, and there was no way to find out. Based on nothing more than the indefinite words of an anonymous source, he had crossed the Channel under an assumed name and was now adrift. All he had was Jean-Michel Fournier and some connection to the French security services. That was where this thing had started, and it had now come full circle.

Whether or not Fournier was back in France would only be known if Stroud went looking for him, and that – as far as he could see – was his sole course of action. Merely asking after the man seemed clumsy and ill-advised, but what other option did he have? Fournier might very well be nothing more nor less than who he professed to be – a member of the French embassy staff – but Stroud doubted that. He understood the dynamics of an embassy too well. Diplomatic immunity and privilege were a green light to many undercover operations. Individuals could be spirited in and out of cities under the aegis of ambassadorial protection. Coups had been organised, assassinations planned, military strategies devised and implemented by men whose business cards merely said *Political Adviser* or *Assistant Administrator*.

From what Stroud remembered, Fournier had very pointedly denied any knowledge of Raphael, and then the following morning, Stroud had learned with one phone call that there was no such office as assistant to the deputy ambassador. As far as he was concerned, Fournier was the agent of an interested concern, presenting himself as embassy staff, in reality an operative for Direction Générale de la Sécurité Extérieure. It was a long shot, but it was the only shot he could think of. If the DGSE – as Haig had said – was now under the Ministry of Defence, then the Ministry of Defence was where he had to go.

Stroud had arrived early on a Saturday afternoon. He had to

assume that the wheels of government, especially within those offices and departments in which he was most interested, didn't grind to a halt for the weekend. Spooks were not the kind of people to maintain sociable hours. However, waltzing into the Hôtel de Brienne – the headquarters of the French Ministry of Defence in the 14th – and loudly announcing his wish to have an audience with Jean-Michael Fournier was perhaps not the wisest course of action. He needed Fournier unguarded, a meeting on neutral ground, but making contact with the Ministry of Defence was going to be necessary to determine whether he was even in the country. If he had no success with that, he would have to go via the embassy. That, without doubt, would require that he prove his identity with his passport, something he very definitely wished to avoid.

He found the Hôtel de Brienne on a map. The 14th bordered the 5th. It would take no time at all to get there. And it was in that moment – as he realised the proximity of this building – that he also comprehended the foolishness of such an approach. If he needed Fournier alone, he needed to find out where Fournier was when he was alone. His home. The journey between where he lived and where he worked. The bar he frequented, the restaurant he preferred. This was where he needed to be looking. This was where he might catch the man off-guard, and thus find out why he had a picture of Raphael in his possession. And more importantly, why that picture had Dekker's name on it.

The telephone directory gave him three J.-M. Fourniers, only one of whom had an unlisted telephone number. The address was in the 7th, a stone's throw from the Eiffel Tower. Stroud doubted very much that Fournier garnered a salary sufficient for such an address. It made sense that it would come with the job, state-owned and state-funded.

He left his hotel and took the Métro. What little he knew of

French was sufficient to get the right station, the right ticket, the right direction. He looked at the people who alighted and departed at each station en route – young, old, elegant, awkward, each of them travelling from somewhere to somewhere else, their reasons and motivations known only to themselves. How many of them were actually who they were purporting to be? How many of them wore a face for the world that was not their own? How many of them were operating under an assumed name with fabricated identity papers? Perhaps very few, perhaps none at all, but Stroud's experiences thus far had contributed to another shift in viewpoint.

The times he had spent with Raphael had not been spent with Raphael at all. South Africa, the Congo, Berlin, Cuba, and finally the Allenby Bridge in Jordan, where a stray hand grenade had been thrown into Raphael's Land Rover and wiped him from the face of the earth. All of them were fabricated, both in reality and in his memory. If Raphael was not Raphael, then who was he? How much of what he had said was a reflection of himself, rather than a reflection of who he was pretending to be? And what had happened that had necessitated his disappearance? More than that, in fact – what had necessitated that his life, at least as Vincent Raphael, had to come to an abrupt and violent end?

It was interesting that those who knew him were not surprised by the nature of his death. Such an end could be the only fitting one for Raphael, they said. Stroud remembered his memorial service. He remembered the shock they'd all felt, and yet beneath it there had been a sense of karmic inevitability. This was Raphael. This was his life. This was his death. But it was all a lie. This was not Raphael, neither his life nor his death. It was theatre, an illusion, sleight of hand. Now you see me, now you don't. And even when you see me, the person you believe me to be is not who I am at all. Shame on you, suckers.

Stroud felt anger for the first time. He felt that deep wound of personal betrayal. He had been lied to, deceived, misled. More than his parents, more than any childhood friend, more so even than Donald Montgomery's influence over Julia, Raphael had been a constant certainty. For all his idiosyncrasies, his lunatic escapades and death-defying leaps into the unknown in search of the bigger headline and the better picture, he had been for-ever reliable. If nothing else, the one thing that could always have been said of Raphael was that what you saw was what you got. Except that it wasn't, and never had been.

Stroud got off at Bir-Hakeim and started walking. He found the correct street, and the apartment building within which J.-M. Fournier lived was right there on the corner. He was listed as one of the occupants on the external intercom, and Stroud thought to buzz it and see if there was an answer. The first thing he had to establish was whether this was the same man, and whether he was even in the city.

Standing there in the doorway, he caught sight of the concierge. He got her attention. She came out to him and he asked – as best he could in his pidgin French – whether Monsieur Fournier was home.

The woman smiled. 'It is okay,' she said. 'I can speak some English, yes?'

'So, Monsieur Fournier. He is at home?' Stroud asked.

'I do not know, monsieur. Perhaps here. Perhaps he is away for his work. You would like for me to call his apartment?'

'No, it's okay,' Stroud said. 'But he is back in France?'

'Oh yes. You are his friend?'

'No, we work together. I am also at the Ministry of Defence.'

The concierge frowned. 'You are English, no?'

'Yes,' Stroud replied. 'I work for the United Nations. I am a consultant. I have been at the Hôtel de Brienne for some weeks.'

'Ah, yes, I understand. Well, Monsieur Fournier is here and

there all the time. He is not home for a week, sometimes a day, then he is here again. It is this way with the government business.'

'Thank you,' Stroud said. 'You've been really helpful.'

'*De rien, monsieur!*' she replied, and closed the door.

Stroud headed back up the street and found a café with a clear view of the front of the apartment building.

He had succeeded in locating Fournier's place of residence. He had succeeded in confirming that this was the right Jean-Michel Fournier. He knew the man was no longer in Istanbul. Three out of three. Maybe his luck was turning. Maybe he was getting a little closer to finding out the truth of this thing, whatever this thing was.

He knew he would wait as long as it took. He could be accused of many things, but a lack of patience was not one of them. He had come this far. There was no turning back. Such a possibility didn't even enter his mind.

He took a window seat, ordered coffee, and sat with his cigarettes and his thoughts.

43

It was a Saturday. Somewhere outside Hereford, an old timber-raftered pub called the Dog & Duck was the rendezvous for a ragtag collection of the weary and the frayed.

Stroud was subdued, propping up the bar and on his third Guinness, keeping himself to himself.

'You know where he would be right now?'

He turned at the sound of a familiar voice. He hadn't seen him since Biafra in June of the previous year.

'Marcus. Jesus. Hello. How are you?'

'As good as can be expected, considering the circumstances.' He looked around at the collection of journalists and cameramen who had congregated for Raphael's memorial.

'So, where would he be?' Stroud asked.

'You heard what happened on the twelfth. The planes the Palestinians blew up in the desert?'

'Yes, I heard about it.'

'Hostages, eight of them British, hijacked planes, the Popular Front for the Liberation of Palestine. The only other thing you'd need to throw into the mix would be several bottles of something at forty per cent proof and a couple of air hostesses. That would be Raphael's idea of heaven.'

'I don't doubt a word of it,' Stroud said. His attention went to an outburst of laughter from a group of strangers at the other end of the bar.

'Who's that lot?' he asked Haig.

'A few from Reuters, AP, Magnum. The agencies, you know? But mostly SAS.'

'SAS?'

'Hereford is SAS country.'

'Yes, I know that,' Stroud said, 'but how come Raphael knew them?'

'Christ only knows. Another question we'll probably never find out the answer to.'

Stroud watched them for a few moments. They possessed the blunt-instrument look of seasoned military veterans. They were used to being thrown at something unforgiving with the expectation that it would be swiftly overcome. It took a very particular type of human being to live that life. Stroud had seen so many of them come and go. There were some who were too brutal for the army. Discharged, they would go into gun-for-hire mercenary work. The Dutch seemed to have a penchant for such a life. South Africans, too. And the British. Ex-paras, ex-commandos, ex-SAS. It didn't matter who you spoke to – Mossad, Sayeret Matkal, even SEALs – the SAS was still ranked as the most formidable special forces unit in the world. When such a man was taken out of that elite cadre, where everything done had been done with contemporaries ahead, behind and on each side, something came unhinged. A human being built by war could only survive in war, and he would go on surviving until war killed him.

Stroud didn't spend a great deal of time considering this until later, but then – alone, the memorial finished, the pub emptied out – he understood that there must have been so very much about Vincent Raphael that he didn't know.

Haig stayed behind with him. They talked, shared anecdotes, drank far too much to drive anywhere and ended up staying the night at a local B&B. In the morning, each of them staring helplessly at a full English, they agreed to stay in touch, to get together occasionally.

'I'm looking at staying here,' Haig had said. 'You know I got married?'

'Yes, I heard. I was away at the time.'

'Hell, Stroud, you're always away. You and Raphael were born from the same egg.'

Stroud frowned and shook his head. 'I'm not so sure about that.'

'What d'you mean? You were always together, weren't you?'

'On assignment, yes,' Stroud said, 'but not when I was back home. Julia didn't like him ...' He checked himself. 'Actually, that's not completely fair. She didn't know him enough to dislike him. He unsettled her.'

'Stroud, he unsettled everyone. I bet he even unsettled some of those SAS bruisers we saw last night.'

Stroud was quiet for a moment, looking away towards the window.

'What did you make of him?' he asked Haig.

'What do you mean?'

'Your honest opinion, Marcus. What did you really think of him?'

Haig was pensive for some time. He smiled, shook his head, looked down, looked away. Finally he turned to Stroud and said, 'You know, I don't really know.'

'What the hell is that supposed to mean?'

'What I say. I don't really know. I knew him for what? Ten years. I say *knew* him, but that's in the very loosest sense of the word. I mean, what can you actually say about Vincent Raphael? The Transvaal. Sharpeville, right? That was the first time all three of us were together, wasn't it?'

'The three of us, yes.'

'So when did you first meet him?'

'London, '59. I was delivering something to *The Times* and he sort of flew in and flew out. Indirectly, the fact that he happened to show up while I was there was how I ended up with a job. I took some of Raphael's pictures up to Barry Hunter—'

'Christ, yes. Barry bloody Hunter. I'd forgotten about him.'

'That was the first time I met him. The first time we worked together was when Khrushchev went to DC.'

'Right, right, of course.'

'So in truth, I really didn't know him any longer than you.'

'But you worked with him a great deal more. I did maybe five or six trips with the two of you. You must've done a countless number.'

'Sure, yes, but you know how it is. You're always moving, following units, getting stranded somewhere. The only time you ever really get a chance to talk is when you're in the airport waiting to come home. And by then you're too shell-shocked and worn out to say anything.'

Haig smiled as if it was a pleasant memory.

'So, back to my question,' Stroud said. 'What did you really think of him?'

'I thought he was a lunatic. Charming, hilariously funny, unpredictable when it came to the unimportant, utterly dependable when it mattered. He was the kind of guy we all wished we could be, but we just didn't have the balls.'

'He saved my life, you know. Twice.'

'Is that so?' Haig said. 'Must be strange knowing that you're alive because of someone who isn't.'

'Like anyone who's ever lost a parent.'

'I guess so. And what did *you* think of him?'

'I'm thinking that the more I find out about him, the more I realise I knew nothing at all,' Stroud said.

'I can understand that.'

'It's like trying to remember someone you met in a dream, you know? I don't know how else to describe it.'

44

The better part of two hours into his watch, Stroud was already asking himself if there was any other way he could have approached this. He could think of none. This was the realm of police, private investigators and bail bondsmen. Half of the work was waiting, the other half was finding out you were waiting in the wrong place. He really hoped it would not be futile.

He had nothing but his canvas holdall, his notebooks, camera, the francs he'd exchanged. If he did see Fournier and needed to follow him, he would need to make some slight effort to remain inconspicuous. He had observed agents of foreign governments and industrial corporations at work in numerous places around the world, but he knew very little of their tradecraft.

He left the café and made his way to a souvenir shop at the end of the adjacent block. He purchased a cheap pair of sunglasses and a baseball cap with the Eiffel Tower on it. He hurriedly returned to the same seat in the café window, having lost line-of-sight on Fournier's building for no more than three or four minutes. Had he left for the shop any later, his patience would have gone unrewarded. No sooner had he ordered another espresso and lit a cigarette than the man himself exited the building and turned left. Stroud left money on the counter and went after him, pulling the peak of the cap down as far as he could.

Fournier walked towards the Champ de Mars public garden. It was Saturday, the weather was good and the park was crowded with people enjoying the sunshine. Stroud stayed well back, ever watchful, never losing sight of his quarry, and when Fournier made a beeline for the Métro station, he hurried on so as not to lose him in the maze of tunnels beneath.

He had to buy a ticket without knowing where he was going. In the brief confusion of trying to explain that any ticket would do, he nearly lost sight of Fournier. As he shoved his way through the turnstile, he caught sight of him hurrying down the stairs toward the platforms. Stroud took an adjacent stairway and arrived on the platform through another archway. Fournier was looking down the track. Stroud stepped back. He possessed one advantage. Fournier didn't yet know he was being followed, nor could he possibly imagine that it would be Stroud who was following him. The human mind rationalised the unexpected within acceptable parameters. It was not realistic that Stroud – their last meeting having taken place in the French embassy in Istanbul – would now be in Paris, on the same street, even in the same Métro carriage and headed in the same direction. Regardless, Stroud took care to stay amongst the crowds on the platform. Fournier maintained his gaze in the direction from which the train would come, occasionally glancing at his watch and then back down the track.

The train arrived on schedule and Fournier boarded. Stroud hung back and then boarded the same carriage at the other end. He couldn't clearly see Fournier, but he could see the door through which he would exit.

He alighted at Musée d'Orsay. Stroud waited until the very last moment, then stepped onto the platform, the doors almost trapping his bag as he moved away. Fournier seemed to be in a hurry. He took the steps two at a time, turned right at the top and made his way towards the exit. Stroud went after him, and once through the gate and into the street he scanned left and right. Fournier was standing at the crossing. Stroud waited for just a moment, and when the lights changed and Fournier made his way to the other side of the road, Stroud did the same, all the while taking care to stay behind someone else.

He followed Fournier for the better part of half a mile. The man walked purposefully, slowed only at corners by traffic or a huddle of pedestrians blocking the pavement.

Finally, down a side street off Rue Saint-Dominique, he entered the canopied doorway of a restaurant called Lumière. Stroud paused on the other side of the junction and stepped into a newsagent. Never taking his eye from the restaurant doorway for more than a moment, he bought a packet of cigarettes and a book of matches. Once outside, he retraced his steps to the entrance of a private garage, from where he could watch the facade of Lumière without being seen. He put a telephoto on his Nikon and took three or four photos of the doorway. He set himself to waiting once more, conscious of his hunger, the fact that it was now approaching the end of the afternoon and he had eaten nothing since breakfast. Fournier had made his way here in a hurry. Of that Stroud was sure. He had acted as if he'd been summoned, or had finally secured a rendezvous for which he'd been waiting.

Stroud went through a half-dozen cigarettes. The air chilled as late afternoon became early evening. He considered the possibility that Fournier might have been aware of him, that he had led him to Lumière, and had then left the restaurant by a rear exit and vanished.

After two hours, he felt certain that this was the case. Fournier was not in Lumière. He was somewhere on the other side of Paris, laughing to himself about the stupidity and predictability of the ignorant Englishman.

Stroud gathered his nerve and walked back to a point where he could cross the street as inconspicuously as possible. He turned right, crossed again and made his way along the pavement from the other side of the restaurant. The entrance was now ahead of him, and he could see back across the junction to the parking garage. The windows of the restaurant were around the corner and would be on his right as he passed. He pushed his sunglasses up the bridge of his nose, pulled the peak of the cap down a little further, and set off.

It was a mere moment, a sideways glance, a split-second registration of Fournier's face right there at a table close to the window. He was not alone. Stroud only saw the back of the man facing him. Fournier never once looked away from his companion.

He kept going, cleared the far end of the block before turning around, and then headed back the way he'd come on the opposite side of the street.

He took up his place in the lee of the garage entrance. He had accomplished what he'd set out to do. Fournier was in there. Now he had to just wait it out and see where he went once he left.

He tried not to think. He tried not to consider the ramifications and repercussions of being discovered, identified, perhaps turned over to the police in possession of a false passport. He couldn't retrace his steps and choose a different course of action. He couldn't undo what had been done.

He asked himself what Raphael would have done had he been here. Would he have possessed the necessary tradecraft? Would he have already had an answer for all of this if the roles had been reversed?

254

Vincent Raphael – now twice dead – might well be the only person who understood enough of this to offer up an honest explanation.

45

'We are a breed apart, Stroud,' Raphael said. 'We are that rare human being that wishes to associate with all that is inhuman.'

'A wish implies that there's some degree of choice in the matter.'

Raphael smiled as if he knew something hidden to everyone else. It was a familiar expression, and yet sufficiently artless to suggest neither superiority nor amusement.

They were drunk, as was so very often the case. Seated in the shadows at the back of a makeshift unlicensed bar in the outskirts of Havana, the air thick with the smoke of Bolivars and Cohibas, they had manoeuvred their way through half a bottle of rum and seemed intent on finishing it. It had been a rough day. People had died, and a good number of them. Stroud had blood in the welts of his boots, and he could still smell cordite despite the pall of cigar smoke.

'You don't think it's a choice?' Raphael asked.

'I don't,' Stroud replied. 'I think anyone who does something off the grid, anything that isn't filing documents in an insurance office or hawking shoes in a department store, is pulled by something.'

'Pulled?'

'You know, impelled to do something. Athletes, painters, people who do ballet or whatever.'

'So how do you differentiate between these two types of people?'

Stroud thought for a moment. He was expressing opinions without really thinking, and it was taking a considerable effort to back them up with anything sensible. He knew better than to have conversations any deeper than a coat of paint when he was drunk.

'Maybe it's the difference between what we need and what we want,' he finally said.

'Explain.'

'Well, there are jobs that people do that provide us with what we need. Insurance, clean cars, food in the supermarket—'

'Brandy in smoky bars,' Raphael interjected, and raised his glass.

'Right. So there are people who do something because it pays the bills. And then there are the people whose life is their work. There isn't anything outside. Not really. There are people who give us what we have to have, and there are people who give us what we want. Entertainment, art, music, sport. Stuff like that.'

'So you think we do this because we can't help it?'

Stroud shrugged drunkenly and almost lost his balance. 'What're you asking me for? How the fuck would I know?'

Raphael started laughing. He emptied his glass, refilled it, refilled Stroud's, and they both raised them.

'To the bliss of ignorance and the unbridled happiness of fools,' he shouted.

Stroud brought his glass to his lips in the same moment that the door was ripped from its hinges and blown across the room. It felt as though the sound of the explosion came from inside his head and tore outwards. There was no other possible way to describe it. He tasted blood in his mouth, and the dust in his eyes almost blinded him. When he started breathing again, he was breathing smoke, the scorch of flame and the stench of burned flesh.

Raphael was over him, and it was only then that he realised he was on his back on the floor. He had instinctively put his arms up and over his face, but still the force of the blast was sufficient to find him. He coughed and retched. He tried to speak, to ask Raphael what had happened, but there were no words. His ears rang incessantly, the pitch and volume such that it physically hurt him.

Raphael was helping him up, his arms beneath his shoulders, dragging him to his unsteady feet and manhandling him towards the exit behind the bar.

Another explosion followed, just as loud, just as fierce, but without the obstacle of the heavy wooden door, the fire and smoke came roaring through like a freight train. A man – his hands clamped to his face, blood on his clothes, in his hair – staggered past them and just folded awkwardly to the ground.

Raphael kept pushing Stroud, forcing him over the bar and onto the floor. The sound of gunfire, automatic gunfire, and then the sense of moving once again. He used Stroud like a battering ram, shoving him forward with every ounce of strength he possessed, and the pair of them broke through the door and fell into the alleyway behind the building just as the sound of gunfire intensified within.

'Run! Run, for fuck's sake!' Raphael was screaming, and his voice, though he bellowed at the top of his lungs, came through the smoke and dust and Stroud's blood-clotted ears like a distant whisper. Stroud couldn't move. He was shocked, stunned and disbelieving. One moment he was drunk, laughing, bullshitting with Raphael, the next he was staggering blindly into an alleyway, disorientated, unable to think, to focus, to even comprehend what was happening.

Raphael dragged him. He knew that much afterwards.

Raphael, himself injured, bleeding, similarly deafened and stunned, dragged Stroud a good quarter of a mile through narrow streets and across a square that gave onto a courtyard beyond. Here the gunfire seemed distant, consigned to history or imagination, and they lay on the cold stones and tried their very best to determine if they were wounded, dying, perhaps already dead.

The third and final explosion sent a plume of bright light and smoke high into the air. It ripped a hole through the night, and the shroud of smoke it left behind seemed to hang there for hours. Stroud passed in and out of semi-consciousness. He was aware of being told to sit up, and then Raphael was helping him, bringing something to his lips from which he drank greedily. And then he was on his side again, the pain in his head and chest like nothing he'd ever experienced before. It was daylight before he understood that he was in fact alive, Raphael too, and that they had somehow managed to escape a rebel hideout by the very skin of their teeth.

Only later did they really comprehend the extent of reprisals carried out for the failed Bay of Pigs invasion. They didn't escape Cuba until the last week of April. They spent those days in hiding, hearing word of widespread rebel captures, the torture, imprisonment and execution of plantation and factory owners, businessmen, students and soldiers still loyal to Batista. On the nineteenth, just two days after the invasion, a trial was held in the Pinar del Río province. Seven Cubans and two CIA-hired American citizens were found guilty and executed. There were executions too at Fortaleza de la Cabaña and Morro Castle. By the time Stroud and Raphael were finally on British soil, the catastrophe had become world news. It was portrayed as a shameful exposé of the CIA's black-ops mandate, and Kennedy himself was considered directly accountable.

All that Stroud knew was that Raphael had saved his life.

Three and a half months later, he married Julia, perhaps more from need than want. She represented all he didn't have – stability, certainty, security, permanence. With that marriage, he promised both himself and his new wife that things would change, that life would be different, that the risks he took to get the bigger story or the better picture were risks no longer worth taking.

It was a promise that was quickly broken, for the impulse, the motivation, the force that drove him to seek ever more threatening realities didn't come from without, but from within. He had believed it would never be tamed. He had believed that it would always take precedence over love, honour, even his word. And he was right. It did always take precedence. What he'd said to Raphael was something he believed. There had been no choice. It was something he *had* to do.

Until Eva. Becoming a father was when it changed, and it changed forever.

He understood that if anyone had truly saved him, it was someone who didn't even know it. Perhaps one day he would have an opportunity to tell her. Perhaps one day she might even understand.

What was done could never be undone.

For that alone he would be eternally grateful.

46

By the time Fournier left the restaurant, it was close to seven. He didn't leave alone. Whoever had been sitting with him walked by his side. Stroud took one picture after another. He was unable to see either of their faces clearly, but if it later proved significant, he wanted a record of this meeting. He hoped that he would have an opportunity to get a clear shot of the pair, side by side, perhaps in conversation. Whether it would be of any relevance was something he would only know in hindsight.

The men walked at a leisurely pace. They talked, they smoked, they paused every once in a while as one seemed to emphasise a point in their conversation. The effect created was one of intensity, as if matters of importance were being discussed, though perhaps this was just Stroud's interpretation because he wanted it to be that way. Maybe Haig was right. People believed in coincidences when it suited them. They formulated opinions and then interpreted everything else to fit them.

Fournier and his companion didn't take the Métro. They passed one station, then another, and Stroud began to wonder if they were making their way to another rendezvous. They were not walking in the direction of the 7th, that was for sure. Back towards Eiffel would have been west, but the two men walked around the south-easterly corner of the Jardins des Tuileries and into the 2nd. So engrossed were they in their discussion that they never looked back. Stroud wondered whether he could cross the street and get ahead of them, somehow managing a shot from the other side of the road before the light failed completely.

As it transpired, he didn't need to go to any extra lengths. The men slowed as they approached the Métro station at Grands Boulevards. They had been walking for the better part of forty minutes, even though the distance couldn't have been more than a mile and a half. It was here that they stopped, right there on the pavement, and concluded their conversation. The light was dim, and Stroud was some distance away. Even with the telephoto he couldn't clearly see the face of Fournier's companion. He would have to get the pictures developed, push the film as much as he could in the darkroom, and underexpose the print. Maybe then the features would be discernible, and he would have someone else to attach to this cast of characters.

The men parted company, Fournier into the station, the second man on towards Rue Rougemont. Stroud let him go. Fournier did as Stroud expected: took a route back towards Champ de Mars with a change at Invalides. By the time he was through the lobby and heading for the stairs in his own building, Stroud was already walking back in the direction he'd come. He needed to find a place that could process film. Tomorrow was Sunday, and he couldn't wait until Monday to find out who it was Fournier had met, and with whom he had maintained such a lengthy and intense discussion.

If there was one thing that broke all language barriers, it was money. Not far from the corner of Avenue de la Bourdonnais and Rue Marinoni, Stroud found a photographic studio. The sign on the door read *CLOSED*, but there were lights still on in the back and up above. He knocked on the door, and kept on knocking until a woman appeared. She gesticulated at him, making it clear that they were done for the day. Stroud held up a film canister in one hand, and in the other a fifty-franc note. The woman came out of the shadows. She was in her late twenties or early thirties, her hair fashioned into an unkempt bob that was nevertheless elegant and sophisticated. She was beautiful in that no-nonsense French way, both alluring and slightly intimidating.

'*Qu'est ce que vous voulez? Nous sommes fermés.*'

'*Assistance, s'il vous plaît.*' Stroud help up the canister. '*J'ai un film. J'ai besoin de photos.*' He showed her the fifty-franc note. '*Argent, ici.*'

The woman opened the door but didn't slide off the security chain. '*Americain?*'

'*Anglais.*'

'Your French is pretty bad,' she said.

Stroud smiled and shook his head. 'Three years, one hour a week, and that was more than twenty years ago. I can remember something about the pen of my aunt being in the garden.'

'So what do you need?'

'I need to develop and print this film,' he said. 'Fifty francs.'

The woman shook her head. 'A hundred, and that's only if it's black and white. You will make me very late for a dinner with my friends. It is Saturday evening, Mister English.'

'It's mono, yes,' Stroud replied. A hundred francs was something like ten or eleven pounds. He was being fleeced within an inch of his life, but he couldn't afford to wait. The only thing that lessened the feeling of daylight robbery was that it was Haig's money he was spending.

'A hundred francs,' he said, 'and I'll get it done as fast as I can.'

'You want to do it yourself?'

'I would prefer to.'

'You can do it if you like. It will cost the same.'

The woman slid off the security chain and opened the door. Stroud stepped inside.

'My name is Stroud,' he said.

'And I am Daphne.' She held out her hand and they shook.

'This is your studio?'

'Yes.'

'What do you do? Portraits? Weddings?'

'Yes. Whatever you want. Cats, dogs, kids, anything. And you?'

'Death, mayhem, war, famine and natural disasters,' Stroud said, 'and that's just in my immediate family.'

Daphne laughed. 'Really? You take pictures of war?'

'I do, yes. Or rather, I did. I don't any more.'

'This way,' she said, and Stroud followed her behind the display panels and into a small kitchen area.

Outside, there was a covered yard, a toilet to the right, and to the left a door that said *CHAMBRE NOIRE*, beneath it, *ARRETEZ! Si le voyant rouge est allumé, n'entrez pas!*

'Here,' Daphne said, and opened up. The all-too-familiar aroma of developer and fixer cleared Stroud's nostrils like ammonia.

Inside, she latched the door and handed him a spool and developing canister, then switched out the light. With the dexterity of the seasoned pro, Stroud popped the film lid, threaded the celluloid into the spool, wound it through and dropped it into the black container. He secured the lid and said, 'Okay.'

Daphne flipped a switch, and they were bathed in the rich red light of the darkroom.

Stroud let Daphne take over. She knew what she was doing, which chemicals were in which bottles, and she went through the motions with the same degree of familiarity and expertise as he himself would have done.

'It's a one twenty-five ISO,' he said. 'Can you push it to eight hundred or thereabouts?'

'Of course.'

She glanced at the clock above the enlarger.

'So, war?' she asked. 'What war?'

'Oh, I'm not picky,' Stroud said.

She frowned. 'Picky?'

'Fussy. Choosy.'

She shook her head.

'I will go here, but not here. I will do this, but not this.'

She laughed. '*Difficile!*'

'Yes, difficult. I am not difficult.'

'This is the English sense of humour, yes? You will go to any war. It does not matter for you.'

'Right. South Africa, Cyprus, Cuba, Vietnam—'

'Vietnam?'

'Yes, I was in Vietnam.'

'For a long time?'

'I went many times. I don't remember exactly. Eight or nine, perhaps.'

'You know it was a French colony.'

'Yes, of course,' Stroud replied.

'We were there a long time before the Americans.'

'I met a lot of French over there. Some of the plantations were still owned and run by families that had been there for generations.'

'It was bad?'

'All war is bad, no matter the reason for it.'

Daphne was quiet for a while, rotating the film drum, ensuring the developer was evenly reaching the celluloid within.

'And why are you here with this urgency now?'

'I am looking for someone,' Stroud said. 'Looking for a friend.'

'And this friend is here in Paris?'

'I don't know. I don't know where he is.'

'It is a man?'

'Yes. Someone I've known for a long time. Someone who

went to war with me. I thought he'd died in the Middle East, but now I don't believe he did. I think he is still alive, and I am trying to find him.'

'Okay,' Daphne replied, almost as if she had heard enough of this saga and didn't wish to know any more.

'Your English is really good. Did you live there?'

'Canada,' she said. 'I studied and worked in Canada for three years.' She looked at the clock above the enlarger. 'We are done.'

She took the stopper from the top of the drum and emptied the developer into the sink. She used a stop-bath solution before the fixer, and together they waited the few minutes necessary for the chemical to do its job. The film came out of the spool and was cut into six sections. The last two were blank. Stroud had used only the first two thirds of the film. Daphne put the blanks in the bin and clipped the four six-negative strips to a string with clothes pegs.

Stroud looked at the last images taken. A reverse image of faces he had been unable to discern at such a distance and in low light.

'I can dry them more quickly with a hair dryer,' Daphne said, 'but sometimes it can melt the emulsion.'

'I can't risk that possibility,' Stroud said.

'So come to the dinner with me.'

'What?'

'Come to the dinner. It's just a few friends. French academics and artists, you know? People with too many opinions and too little money. We will eat cheese and drink cheap wine and smoke too many cigarettes, and maybe someone will have a Serge Gainsbourg LP.'

Stroud laughed. 'You're teasing me.'

'Just a few friends is true. They're nice people. You will like them. We just go for a couple of hours, then we come back and make your prints.'

'I don't want to put you to any more trouble, Daphne.'

She laughed and nudged his arm. 'Such an Englishman. You can buy the wine, okay?'

'You're sure your friends won't mind?'

'Don't be so *difficile*. Come on. We go.'

47

The apartment where Daphne was meeting her friends was close. They stopped en route for wine. Daphne recommended a Saint-Émilion, and Stroud bought two bottles.

There were six people already there – two girls and four men. Daphne introduced Stroud, and within minutes two more girls, Odile and Françoise, and a man called Sébastien arrived. Eleven people in all, and within the confines of the living room and kitchen it was difficult not to be involved in numerous simultaneous conversations.

It was only when they sat down to eat in the dining room – at a table that spanned the length of the room and could have seated another two or three – that Stroud seemed to become the focus of interest. Food had been served – a cassoulet – and he added his two bottles of wine to the half-dozen that were already opened.

It seemed that they all spoke English to some degree or other. One or two seemed to struggle and requested translations. Daphne sat beside Stroud and encouraged him to engage with everyone. It was so very European, far more relaxed and informal than any similar such circumstance in England. Stroud was reminded of the time he'd spent in Amsterdam before Haig called him back. Despite the fact that three and a half weeks had elapsed, it seemed like something from a different life altogether. He had become far closer to the person he'd once been – driven, even obsessive, impelled by some indistinct need to do something, to find something, to have a story worth telling. And yet at the same time, he had a different perception of the future. That it was out there, that he would be in it, that he didn't wish to be alone.

'So, you are English?' Jean-Luc asked.

'I am, yes.'

'And how do you know Daphne?'

Stroud smiled. 'I don't. I just met her this evening. I needed some film processed and she was willing to help me.'

'You are a photographer?' Elodie asked.

'Yes. For the newspaper, magazines, you know?'

'What kind of pictures do you take?' Gabriel asked.

'Well, in the past I have covered a lot of war, political uprisings, civil conflict. Things like that.'

Gabriel hesitated. Stroud's answer seemed to displease him. He didn't say anything directly, but his expression was one of disapproval.

'War?' Arnaud asked. 'What, like Vietnam or something?'

'Yes, I went to Vietnam several times.'

'When?'

'Oh, I don't know. It was a three-year period between 1965 and 1968.'

'You were in Vietnam for three years?' Clémence asked.

'No, I went home in between. I was out there maybe eight or nine times for several weeks each time.'

There was a brief and awkward silence.

Stroud glanced at Daphne. Her expression was odd, as if she was somehow enjoying the fact that she'd delivered a strange Englishman to dinner and he'd done something to upset the atmosphere.

'And what did you see?' Arnaud asked.

'See?' Stroud asked.

'Yes. In Vietnam. The things you saw must have been terrible, no?'

Stroud looked down at his food. He was famished. He'd already had two glasses of wine and he was aware of its effect on an empty stomach.

'Let him be,' Sébastien said. 'He is Daphne's guest. He does not want to speak of such things, I am sure.'

'It's fine,' Stroud said, conscious of the fact that he was indeed Daphne's guest, that his negatives were drying in her darkroom, and the last thing he wanted to do was upset anyone here. Perhaps it had been a mistake to come.

'So tell us,' Odile said. 'What things did you see in the war?'

'You mean what terrible things?' Stroud asked. 'Or what acts of bravery? What acts of humanity?'

'How can you use a word like humanity when you speak of war?' Gabriel said. An undertone of aggression was there in his voice, his mannerisms. 'Humanity is the first sacrifice of war, *non*?'

'Gabriel,' Daphne said. Just his name. Nothing else, but in those three syllables were layers of history. Perhaps he was known for his attitude, his willingness to challenge. Perhaps here was a man who made his presence felt by argument and conflict. If that was the case, Stroud really could have done without it.

'Let your English friend speak, Daphne,' Gabriel said. 'Let him justify his war.'

'They are not *my* wars, Gabriel.'

'No, of course not, but you rationalise them and you agree with them.'

'I don't agree with them,' Stroud said, doing his utmost to remain calm.

'You must agree with them, or you would not keep going back like ... like this ... what is this bird that eats the dead?'

'Vulture?' Jean-Luc said.

270

'Yes, this vulture. You keep going back to look at the dead bodies like a vulture. You take your pictures and you make your money, and then you go home.'

'Gabriel, this is Daphne's friend,' Sebastien said.

'They are not friends. He just met her this evening.'

'*Arrête d'être un connard,*' Arnaud snapped.

Stroud knew enough to understand that Arnaud had just told Gabriel to stop being an arsehole.

'Your conscience is the lamb you sacrifice to fame,' Gabriel said to Stroud, sneering condescendingly.

'I don't think fame has anything to do with it,' Stroud replied. 'I am anything but famous, and I don't think that was the reason for doing it.'

'For money then, eh? You did it just for the money.'

Stroud looked around the table. The expressions he saw ranged from sympathy to apology to bewilderment.

'I really didn't come here to argue with anyone,' he said. 'For fifteen years or more I've worked as a photographer and a journalist. I was here in Paris during the riots of '68. I have been to Vietnam, to Cuba, to South Africa, to Cyprus. I have been all over the world, and I have seen some truly terrible things. I have also seen some things that were uplifting and inspiring. But I can't agree with what you say, Gabriel. I certainly didn't do it for fame, and I didn't do it for money. I am neither famous nor rich. In fact, it's true to say that I own nothing but my cameras, my notebooks, the clothes I'm wearing.'

'Ignore Gabriel,' Elodie said. 'He is being a fucking child.'

Gabriel turned on her, but Jean-Luc spoke before he had a chance to say anything.

'We're having dinner, Gabriel. We are going to talk about other things. We are going to drink some wine and—'

'Do you feel guilty?' Gabriel asked Stroud. 'Do you feel guilty

271

for taking advantage of these people? Selling your pictures? Taking money for their misery, eh?'

Stroud closed his eyes and took a deep breath. He was tired. So fucking tired. He didn't need this. He didn't need to be challenged, or told what was wrong with his life, or shown how everything he had done had been worthless. He looked up.

Daphne put her hand on his arm. 'Don't,' she said. 'Pay him no attention.'

'What do you want from me, Gabriel? You want me to apologise for who I am? Okay, I'm sorry. I am so very fucking sorry for being a worthless piece of shit and offending your self-righteous fucking sensibilities. Tell me everything that's wrong, my friend. Tell me all the mistakes I've made. Let me beg you for fucking forgiveness. Is that what you want? Are you my judge and jury? Huh? Are you ready to give me my sentence? Tell me what I have to do to be worthy in your eyes.'

Gabriel said nothing. He continued to look at Stroud with a mean, supercilious expression.

'So if you're so damned perfect, what is it that *you* do? How are you so much better than me?'

'Gabriel is the son of a very wealthy man,' Françoise said. 'Gabriel has never done a day's work in his life, and he probably never will.'

'*Va te faire foutre, Françoise!*'

Françoise laughed. She looked at Stroud. 'He told me to go fuck myself.'

Stroud set down his knife and fork. He shifted his chair back. 'I am really sorry,' he said. 'I shouldn't have come. I didn't intend to upset your dinner—'

'Sit down,' Daphne said.

'Yeah, sit down, Englishman,' Arnaud said. 'Gabriel is leaving.' He turned and glowered. 'Aren't you, Gabriel?'

Gabriel looked awkward for a moment, and then he looked

very angry. He got up slowly, glancing around the table as he did so.

'*Vous pouvez tous aller vous faire foutre!*' he snapped, and knocked his glass over. It didn't break, but wine spilled out across the cotton cloth like blood.

He came around the table and made his way towards the door. As he passed Stroud, his elbow caught Stroud's shoulder with some force. There was no doubt that it had been intentional. Before Stroud could even evaluate what he was doing, he was up on his feet, had pushed Gabriel back against the wall and had him around the throat. He instinctively turned his body sideways and used it to force Gabriel back, all the while conscious of the other man's feet and knees. The muscle memory of things he'd been shown and taught on assignment, self-defence actions, things that would give him some slight chance or advantage against an assailant, came back to him. He was no fighter, but perhaps he could make-believe sufficiently well to back Gabriel off.

'I really think it might be a good idea if you left,' he said. 'I feel that would be the polite thing to do.'

Gabriel pushed back. Stroud didn't give.

'I am going!' Gabriel said. 'Get off me, you fucking asshole. I am going.'

Stroud took a step back. He eased up a little. Gabriel didn't kick or swing at him. He looked angry, but it was clear that he knew retaliation was not wise.

Stroud let him go.

Gabriel looked around the room one final time and then stormed out. The front door slammed as he left; he shouted once more from the bottom of the stairs, and then he was gone.

Stroud turned to face the people seated around the table.

'I can't tell you how sorry I am,' he said. 'I really don't know what I said or did to upset him.'

273

'Come and sit down,' Daphne said. 'He was being a child. He does this so much. Eat your dinner. Forget about him, okay?'

'Yes, come and sit,' Arnaud said. 'It is okay. Someone needed to tell him to shut up. I have wanted to kick him so many fucking times myself, but I never did.'

Clémence laughed. Odile too.

Stroud sat down. Sébastien refilled his glass, and then indicated Stroud's plate, his food barely touched.

'Eat, eat,' he said. 'We have a lot of wine to drink, and it is not good to drink so much without eating also.'

Stroud picked up his knife and fork. He looked around the table. They all seemed relieved. That was the way he read it.

He felt Daphne's thigh against his own, and then her hand on his leg.

She leaned close. 'I think perhaps you should stay at my place tonight,' she said. 'Just in case Gabriel has gone to fetch his big brother.'

Later, walking back, she told him to ignore what had happened.

'He and I have a history,' she said. 'Not the one you think. He has chased me for a long time, and I have refused him.'

'Jealous,' Stroud said. 'He thought I was your lover, perhaps.'

'It would not matter. That you came with me, that we were perhaps friends, would have been enough to make him crazy.'

She slid her arm through Stroud's as they walked, pulled him closer. He was a little drunk, as she was, but it didn't matter.

'Where are we going?' he asked, aware that they were retracing their steps.

'I live above the studio,' she said. 'It is small, but it makes life easy. And it is not expensive for me.'

He didn't say anything in response.

'You are okay?' she asked.

'I am okay.'

48

Perhaps there could be nothing so intimate and yet so impersonal as sex with a stranger.

So Stroud considered as Daphne took his hand and led him up the stairs behind the studio to her apartment.

Everything was new and unknown. There were expectations, but without the routines and certainties of a familiar lover. It was not making love, for there was no true love, except perhaps the love that one human being felt for another. If such an emotion could be verbalised, it would say, *We are all in this together. This world is strange and dark and often fearful, but it is the only world we have. We must make the best of it, even if only for this handful of moments.*

You didn't lie down with all the earlier times, the elsewhere thoughts, the everyday accumulation of faults and failings, the quiet disappointments and greater despairs.

You lay down with a stranger, relieved to possess no history at all, driven by lust, passion, impulse – whatever other self-serving reasons might be present. Perhaps it was little more than a primal urge to make yourself known, to prove the existence of self, to find some small degree of recognition. *Tell me that I matter. Tell me that I am needed.*

And yet for all the strangeness, there could be moments – fragile and fleeting – when you looked at this person and saw not who you imagined them to be, nor who you wanted them to be, nor indeed the face they themselves wore for the world, but who they truly were.

So it was with Daphne.

Stroud didn't know her last name, and she didn't know his first. Again, it didn't matter.

She pulled him close and kissed him. He tasted the raw funk of wine and cigarettes in her mouth. She seemed almost angry, tugging his jacket from his shoulders, tearing at his belt. And he, feeling things that he had not felt since those first few months with Julia, wanted more than anything in the world to escape from reality into this woman's unfamiliar embrace.

She led him down the hallway of her tiny apartment towards the bedroom. It was like a cell, but beautiful. Photographs lined the walls, framed, taped, stuck with pins, the plaster beneath several shades of burned orange, faded with time, the window curtained with a sweep of dark red velvet that ran to the floor. The only light came from the hallway. It was like stepping into a chamber of the heart.

They were both awkward and graceless, trying to find some way to express what needed to be expressed, and yet afraid to communicate the unwanted.

At one moment she started laughing, but it was something free and unfettered, and there was nothing judgemental or strange in the sound. She was laughing simply because – for however long – she had separated from the noise, the fury, the mundane, the banal, the senseless and suppressed. Here, now, in this moment, she was herself, and no one demanded that she be anything else.

What had happened with Elise in Montpellier had hurt Stroud. Perhaps more than he was willing to accept, his trust in himself to love, to be loved in return, had been bruised and battered. He didn't know what he was doing here, but it felt good and right and truthful. Perhaps he and Daphne were each as lost as one another, and just finding someone who understood that reality was enough.

Later, body filmed in sweat, smoking, naked, lying amongst a tangle of sheets, she turned and looked at Stroud. Her hair was in disarray, her lipstick gone, her mascara speckled across her cheeks, and Stroud couldn't remember ever seeing anyone quite so beautiful.

'What do you believe in?' she asked.

'What do you mean?'

'God, fate, destiny, luck, hell, nirvana. Anything.'

Stroud shifted slightly. He moved closer so as to feel the full length of her body against his own. He looked at the ceiling. He didn't know why – perhaps because he had known her for merely a few hours – but he wanted to talk.

'I'm frightened,' he said.

'Of what?'

'It's not a specific fear. It's just fear. That I have failed too many times, that I have fucked up too many things, that too many things are broken and can't be repaired.'

'Do you love someone?' she asked.

'Not in the way you're asking.' He looked at her intently. 'I was married. I had a wife. I have a daughter.'

'Where is she?'

'She is with her mother.'

'And you see her?'

Stroud closed his eyes. 'No,' he said. 'Rarely. Not enough. I'm scared that she thinks I abandoned her.'

'Did you?'

'No. No, I didn't abandon her, but I could have done more to ensure she didn't feel that way.'

'But everything in life is like this,' Daphne said. 'Everyone has things they would do differently.'

'I know, but you don't know about those. You only know about your own.'

'And what you were saying at dinner. About your work. The wars you have seen, the terrible things that people do.'

'Which they have been doing for thousands of years, and will continue to do long after I am gone.'

'Which makes you feel... how do you say that, when you have no purpose for being there?'

Stroud opened his eyes. 'Redundant. Impotent. Futile.'

'You feel like this about your work?'

'I feel like I wasn't doing it as work. Maybe I was doing it to escape, to hide, to fool myself into thinking that I had a real reason for being alive.'

'And you still feel this way?'

'Less,' Stroud said. 'I am looking for someone, and the more I look for him, the more I am finding out about myself.'

'So there is hope?'

'Maybe. Just a little.'

'I think you and I are the same. Different, but the same.'

'How so?'

'Noisy lives, surrounded by people, but still alone.'

'I sometimes wonder whether I keep everyone at a distance to save them from me.'

'Is that what you feel in this moment?' she asked.

'No,' Stroud said. 'In this moment I feel fortunate.'

She laughed gently.

'I don't know what to think, Daphne. I don't know what to say about who I am or how I have lived my life. I don't know what to say about the weight of memories I carry. Sometimes I struggle to remember much of anything at all, and then it all seems like it's happening right now and it's relentless and I'll never escape from it.'

'Do you believe there is a reason for us? A bigger reason. Something more than just eating and sleeping and breathing and fucking.'

'Yes.'

'I believe it, too. But I have no idea what it could be.'

'I have no idea either,' Stroud said.

'Do you want some wine?'

'Yes.'

Daphne slipped from beneath the sheet and walked to the door. She was nothing but a silhouette in the darkness, but Stroud couldn't take his eyes from her. She went down the hallway to the kitchen and returned moments later with two glasses and a bottle. It was half empty, the cork lodged in the neck.

She sat cross-legged on the bed, unashamedly naked, and with her teeth she prised the cork from the bottle and spat it across the room.

Stroud smiled. 'Like a pirate,' he said.

Daphne laughed, poured the wine, handed Stroud a glass.

'So, where do you go now?' she asked.

He shook his head. 'I have no idea. I am following a ghost.'

'A ghost?'

He told her then. All of it. Driven, perhaps, by nothing more than the need to hear it out loud. From Haig's first phone call to the moment he'd hammered on her studio door with a fifty-franc note and a roll of film in his hand. He showed her the marks on his shins, and he tried to explain how he'd believed that his life had come to an end in a featureless room in Berlin. He told her about Istanbul, about Jean-Michel Fournier. He told her everything, holding back nothing, and when he was finished she sat for some time and didn't say a word.

'That is why Raphael is a ghost,' Stroud said.

'He is alive.'

'Yes, I really believe he is.'

'And you are not the only person who is looking for him.'

'No.'

'This is like a spy novel,' Daphne said. She lay down on her side, leaning up on her elbow, her feet touching Stroud's.

'And now you are part of it,' he said.

'Do I appear in just one chapter?'

Stroud looked at her and smiled. 'I hope not,' he said. 'I really hope not.'

She reached out and placed the flat of her hand on his face. 'I have never seen a man so tired,' she said. 'I have never seen a man so haunted. I think when this is done you need to choose a different life.'

Stroud nodded. 'Yes,' he said. 'A different life. I think so.'

'But now we are here, and we can sleep and eat and breathe and fuck.'

'And drink wine,' Stroud said, and he pulled her close and kissed her.

49

Daphne turned from the stove with a coffee jug. She put it on the table and sat down.

She looked at Stroud without saying a word for a good ten seconds.

'What?' he asked.

'I meant what I said last night. That perhaps it is time for you to find a different life.'

'Maybe I will move to Paris and take pictures of cats and dogs with you.'

She smiled. 'Maybe you will.'

'Seems to me that life is a game of sacrifices,' Stroud said. 'Takes a long time to figure out which ones mean something and which ones don't. Maybe death is the last great sacrifice we make, hoping that we finally found out what the fuck all the heartbreak was for.'

'This is a very negative viewpoint.'

'I am a very negative person.'

'I don't believe that,' Daphne said.

'You don't know me.'

'So we have coffee and then we make your prints and then you disappear like your friend.' She looked at him, her expression unchanging.

'If he is still alive, there has to be a very good reason for what he did.'

'Maybe he was like you,' she said. 'Maybe he had enough of this life and wanted to change.'

'I don't think so.'

'Why not?'

'Because that would not have been like Raphael at all.'

'How do you know what he was like? You don't even know his real name. He lived a lie the whole time. You are like the wife who never doubts her husband, and then she learns that he has a mistress for ten years.'

Stroud didn't reply. Daphne was right. He saw Raphael as a stranger. Beyond even that, a liar, a fraud, an illusion.

'We should make your prints, no?'

Stroud nodded. 'I think I'm afraid to do it. What if I can't see who it is? What if it's no one, just a friend, someone unconnected to this?'

'What if it's Raphael?' Daphne asked.

Stroud felt his heart skip a beat. The thought unsettled him. Had the prospect of actually finding Raphael become even more challenging than proving he was dead? Which of these two outcomes did he want? Perhaps neither. Perhaps he wanted to turn back time and never return to London, never accept Marcus's offer; to remain with the certainty that what had been reported was the truth. Raphael was dead, and that was all there was to it.

'I don't know what to think about that,' he said.

'I think we should go and find out.'

Back in the darkroom, everything bathed in red light, Stroud watched as Daphne set up the enlarger, the trays of chemicals, as she first made contact prints and had him show her which ones he wanted enlarged.

'This section here... and here... and this one too,' he explained. 'See if you can bring up the shadow. I'm trying to get this man's face as clear as possible.'

She understood exactly what he needed. She just did what he asked of her, effortlessly professional in every aspect. Stroud felt something. Perhaps a great many things. It was as if he'd been given a brief reprieve from the strange madness of this pursuit. Some higher power had taken pity on him, granting him a few hours of peace with a beautiful, uncomplicated woman. He didn't know her surname, her age, anything of her history save the fact that she had spent three years in Canada. Perhaps she had wanted to share such things, but seeing that Stroud was burdened by so much, she'd chosen to withhold them.

A woman like this could save him, he thought, but would he kill her in the process?

Daphne took photographic paper from the envelope and laid it flat. She threaded the negative through the enlarger, flicked the switch and counted.

She handed the paper to Stroud and he slid it into the developing bath.

'Still too dark,' he said, pulling the paper from the bath even as the face began to emerge.

Daphne underexposed a little more, and again Stroud watched as the outline of the face appeared.

'This one isn't going to work,' he said. 'Try the next one.'

Daphne reset the enlarger, changed the negative, exposed the picture.

'Again, just a second or so less,' Stroud said as the print failed to give the detail he needed.

'Maybe we won't get it,' she said. 'Maybe it was just too dark.'

'Perhaps,' Stroud replied, 'but give it a go.'

She flicked the switch, counted off the seconds, handed the paper to Stroud. Into the bath it went, and slowly the outline emerged. The forehead, the brow, the eyes and then the lower half of the face appeared.

There was no word in Stroud's vocabulary to express what he

was feeling. Disbelief didn't even come close. Shock and dismay were in there somewhere, as was the stunned realisation that none of what had happened could be a coincidence. Fournier was connected, but how and in what way Stroud couldn't even begin to comprehend

All he knew – and whether it would do him any good or not, he would soon find out – was that Fournier had answers. Stroud needed to confront him with the evidence of his complicity. If that placed him in an even more dangerous situation, his life truly threatened, then so be it. It was now too contrived, too manipulated, too complex a puzzle for him to ever escape without understanding it. Collusions had been engineered, people had conspired one with another, and all in the direction of withholding the real truth of Vincent Raphael.

Stroud told Daphne that he needed to go, and go immediately.

'I don't even know you,' she said. 'But I do know that I want to see you again.'

Stroud took the Métro back to the 7th. He returned to Fournier's apartment building, spoke with the same concierge, acting as nonchalantly as he could as he explained that Fournier had called him over to go through paperwork.

'Always working,' she said. 'It is Sunday.'

'Like you,' Stroud said, smiling. 'Sometimes we have to, no?'

'I shall telephone him and say you are here?'

'No, it's fine. He's expecting me.' He started towards the stairs. Half a dozen steps up, he called out, 'The number?'

'Number seven, *monsieur*,' the concierge said, and went back to her dusting.

Stroud reached the second floor. He knew Fournier was in. Had he not been there, the concierge would have told him. His heart clamoured frantically in his chest. He didn't know what he was doing. Fournier could be armed, could be expecting him, could be anything. The man might have his family here, he and his wife and children all home for the weekend.

Stroud didn't care. Fournier had been in possession of Raphael's photo with Dekker's name, and now, with the rendez-vous at Lumière, his complicity in this... this what? Conspiracy, subterfuge? Stroud didn't even know what it was, but Fournier was right there in the middle, and he had to find out what he knew.

Standing on the fine, deep carpet on the landing, Fournier's apartment door no more than six feet from him, Stroud wondered once again if this was where he would find the truth about Raphael. It was certainly ill-advised, potentially very dangerous, but he couldn't stop himself.

He set down his bag, raised his hand and knocked on the door. He stepped back so as not to be seen through the spyhole.

He waited, his heart racing, his mind unravelling.

There was nothing. Not a sound from within.

He knocked again louder, more firmly, staying to the left of the door in case Fournier was on the other side trying to see who was interrupting his Sunday morning.

Suddenly, a voice from within. '*Oui?*'

Stroud did his best to mask his voice. '*Monsieur Fournier?*'

'*Oui, c'est moi.*'

'*Livraison, monsieur.*'

'*Livraison?*' Fournier said.

Stroud knocked again, hoping to create some sense of urgency. Perhaps Fournier's impatience or irritation might cause him to open the door, if only to see why someone would be making a delivery on a Sunday.

His judgement was right. The door was unlocked from within and the handle started to move. Stroud waited until it had made a complete turn, and then he lunged forward, shoulder first.

The sound of the door slamming back against the wall was like a gunshot. Fournier was thrown backwards to the hallway carpet. Stroud was younger, heavier-set, and surprise alone gave him the advantage. As Fournier tried to get up, Stroud moved behind him and got his arm around the man's neck. He pulled back until he was kneeling. Fournier gasped for air as Stroud tightened his grip.

Fournier tried to jab his elbows back into Stroud's torso, but Stroud pre-empted the response and pushed Fournier down to the ground. He kept his right arm around the man's throat, and used his left hand to force Fournier's face down to the carpet.

Fournier struggled, desperately pushing back against Stroud, using every ounce of his strength to somehow gain purchase and free himself.

It was no good. He didn't possess sufficient force or stamina to extricate himself from Stroud's hold, and Stroud – surprising himself – somehow managed to manoeuvre Fournier up against the wall while still on his knees, then forced his head against the skirting board.

'*Assistance!*' Fournier screamed. '*Assistance!*'

Stroud pulled Fournier's head back and got his forearm over the lower half of the man's face. The last thing he needed was for the concierge to call the police.

'Quiet!' he urged. 'Quiet now!'

Fournier struggled. Stroud held firm.

'I really don't want to do this,' Stroud said, out of breath, feeling his racing pulse, feeling the sheer physical stress of holding the man down. 'I don't want to fucking do this, but you people have fucked with me too much.'

Fournier moved his head suddenly. Stroud lost purchase for a moment.

'Enough!' Fournier cried out. 'Enough! This is complete madness! You don't understand—'

'Well you'd better start explaining it then, hadn't you?' Stroud said.

'Just let me go! Let me go! I will tell you!'

Stroud eased up a little. He loosened his grip on Fournier's neck, and shifted him back from the wall.

'My God, you are a crazy man!' Fournier said.

'Crazy? You call me crazy? What did you do to me, huh? What did you do to me in Germany?'

'That was nothing to do with me! I didn't do this to you!'

'But I saw you! I have photographs of you with him in that restaurant! Don't deny it, Fournier. You cannot deny what I saw with my own eyes. You and Ernst fucking Lügner in that restaurant. I saw you there. You were talking. You left together and I followed you.'

Fournier tried to manoeuvre himself out of Stroud's grip. He started up again, shouting at the top of his voice, '*Assistance! Assistance!*'

Stroud pushed his head against the floor, with some force.

'Shut the fuck up, for Christ's sake!'

'*Assistance!*' Fournier shouted, his voice even louder.

Stroud hit him on the side of the head.

Fournier pushed back with all his strength and caught Stroud off balance. Stroud didn't let go, however, and once again heaved forward with the full weight and force of his body. Fournier fell sideways, pulled his knees up towards his chest as a reflexive action, and then put his arms over his head, his elbows tight against his face to protect himself.

'Enough of this,' Stroud said. He felt his heart thundering out of his chest. He could hear the exhaustion in his own voice. He really didn't know how much longer he could keep this up.

'Let me go,' Fournier said, his voice a little calmer. 'Let me go and I will answer your questions.'

'I'm supposed to believe you?'

'You have no choice, Monsieur Stroud. I am the only one who can help you.'

'You were in that restaurant,' Stroud said. 'Yesterday. I saw you. You were there with Lügner—'

'Yes,' Fournier said, his voice strained. 'Yes, I was there, but his name is not Lügner.'

'I know that,' Stroud said. 'I doubt your name is Fournier either.'

'You learn quickly, Monsieur Stroud. I think you can be assured that everyone in this game is a liar.'

'What game? What do you mean?'

'You have to let me up,' Fournier said. 'You are hurting me. I have a bad heart, you know?'

He turned his head and looked back at Stroud. There was defiance in his eyes – defiance, fear, anger, even hatred – but there was also something that told Stroud he might well be telling the truth. If Fournier's heart gave out, Stroud understood that he alone would be held responsible for the man's death.

Stroud moved. Fournier didn't react immediately. Then he slowly raised his head and put his arms against the wall to support himself. Stroud was back on his haunches, and he let go of Fournier completely. Fournier didn't speak. He turned around and sat with his back against the wall.

'I am sorry if I hurt you,' Stroud said. 'I have been chasing the truth for nearly a month and I am frustrated and angry.'

Fournier shook his head and half smiled. 'Only a month? Try twenty years.'

'So what *is* the truth?' Stroud asked. 'What am I looking for here, and why does everyone I meet seem to want me to disappear?'

'Because you are trouble. You have put yourself right in the middle of a battlefield, and no one really knows who you are or what you want.'

'I just want to find out what happened to Vincent Raphael. He was my friend. I honestly believed he was dead, and now it seems that perhaps he isn't. Now it seems that he had another name and he's vanished yet again.'

'The Dutchman, yes?'

'Dekker. Hendrik Dekker.'

Fournier nodded as if it was all very obvious and straight-forward.

'So, is he still alive? If so, where is he, and why did he want everyone to believe he was dead?'

Fournier shook his head. 'This is a long and complicated story, Monsieur Stroud.' He put his hands down on the floor. 'I need to stand up. It's okay if I stand up?'

Stroud nodded and rose to his feet, paying attention to every move Fournier made. The door to the apartment was still wide open. The concierge, unless she was far away in some other part of the building, must have heard her tenant's pleas for help. However, there had been no sound from the hallway or down below.

Fournier stood for a little while. He looked pale and tired.

'What I said about my heart is true,' he said. 'I have some pills. I need to take a pill. I need some water, too. Do you want some water, Monsieur Stroud?'

'No,' Stroud said. 'Where are your pills?'

'In there,' Fournier said, indicating with a nod of his head. 'In my study.'

'Okay, let's go, but slowly. Any sudden move and I will—'

Fournier raised his hand. 'I am not a stupid man. I am sixty-three years old. I have a weak heart. I do not want to wrestle with you any more.'

Fournier walked, Stroud followed, and when they went through into the living room of the apartment, it seemed obvious to Stroud that this man couldn't have a family. If he did, they lived somewhere else. The room was spartan, minimal furniture, a complete absence of ornament or decoration. Stroud looked through to the small kitchen. Again, it seemed to be furnished with the irreducible minimum of essentials. Fournier's study was through a door to the right, and here Stroud saw a desk, a single chair, a typewriter, a stack of paper, and on the floor, small towers of books through which Fournier wended his way to reach the far side of the room.

He stopped near the desk and looked at Stroud. 'This has been difficult for you, no? This whole business has put a great burden on you, hasn't it?'

Stroud should have known. He should have seen it coming. The question was delivered in such a way as to sound compassionate, even empathetic.

Fournier smiled. 'You really are a journalist, aren't you? This is such a strange business, yes? To be involved with people who have been playing these games for most of their lives.'

It was almost textbook, the gun in Fournier's hand, the way he had so effortlessly directed Stroud's attention elsewhere as he slid the desk drawer open.

Stroud had seen such a gun before – a Walther PPK, perhaps the most easily recognised sidearm in the world.

'But it isn't a game, as you are now beginning to understand.'

Stroud's heart slowed down. He had been so predictably stupid. He was out of his depth, trying to make sense of things that made no sense, involving himself with people who seemed to know precisely what he was going to do days before he did it.

'Look,' Fournier said, and indicated past Stroud and towards the door.

Stroud looked. Two uniformed policemen stood there, each with his gun drawn.

'*Cet homme s'est introduit de force et m'attaqué,*' Fournier said. '*Il est Anglais, et il est fou.*'

'Your hands,' one of the policemen said. 'Put your hands behind your back.'

Stroud did as he was instructed. He had no other option. He was cornered by three armed men.

The handcuffs were tight, overly so, but he said nothing.

Fournier returned the gun to his desk and spoke rapidly to the police. Stroud understood none of it.

'You come with us now,' the second policeman said, and he was taken out of the apartment and down the stairs.

The concierge stood in the lobby. She watched Stroud without a word.

'*Merci, madame,*' the policeman said, and they took Stroud out into the street and put him in the back of a car.

50

Stroud didn't ask for assistance from the British embassy in Paris. He didn't ask to make a phone call. He was told that an advocate would be assigned and would be available to talk to him at the advocate's convenience. In all likelihood, that would not be until the following day. He didn't know whether his bag had been picked up from the hallway outside Fournier's apartment. He didn't know if his camera, notebooks, passport and money were now gone for good. He didn't know if the cryptic notes he'd made all the way through this nightmare were now being pored over, interpreted, misinterpreted perhaps, by an officer of the Police Nationale.

He thought of Daphne, Nina and Haig – the only people who might be concerned for where he was and what had happened to him.

He thought of Tegel, of Lügner, of Dekker's apartment in the Netherlands, of his unceremonious eviction from Istanbul. So many things unsaid, so many lies told, and now – in a Paris police station – he seemed to be no closer to the truth.

Fournier – whoever he was, and whatever purpose he served – had been right. Stroud was playing a game that he didn't understand, and for which – it seemed all too evident – he possessed no real faculty. Now he was the one who had been played, and thus his part in this had more than likely come to an end.

There was no real defence for what he had done. He had

committed a crime on French soil. Gaining access to Fournier's apartment under false pretences was tantamount to breaking and entering, and then there was assault, perhaps even actual bodily harm. Stroud had no doubt that Fournier would press charges. Fournier had already backed him off in Turkey, and now he had the perfect solution to ridding himself of Stroud completely. Whatever advocate assigned would present him with an option: plead guilty, be extradited, face the music with the British authorities at the other end. Fight this and we will drag you kicking and screaming through the French legal system and engineer a way to deliver the severest penalty possible. It would not be a negotiation. It would be straightforward. Stroud really didn't see how he could choose anything but the former of the two options.

The cell within which he was held was nothing more than four bare concrete walls, a metal bed bolted to the wall, a thin horsehair mattress – punctured in numerous places, stained in many more – and a narrow window close to the ceiling. Even standing on the bed and craning upwards, he couldn't reach it. The glass was rippled, and had he even been able to look through it, he would have seen nothing but distortions of whatever was beyond. His shoelaces and his belt had been taken, as had his watch. At one point the thin light that crept through that upper window became so weak that he could barely see the door, and then a single bulb – right above him in the centre of the ceiling – came on. He sat on the bed, back against the wall, knees pulled up to his chest, and tried not to think about what the next few hours held in store.

After some indeterminate time – two hours, perhaps three – there were sounds in the corridor. An oblong hatch was opened and a tray was passed through. Some sort of meat stew, flavourless and close to cold, a four- or five-inch crust of baguette, a beaker of water. The spoon he was given was something between plastic and rubber, impossible to snap or splinter. Stroud ate without thinking, without tasting, without feeling anything but a strange sense of disconnection.

Beyond and beneath everything, he knew he had changed. He was thinking differently, considering tomorrow, next week, next year. He was looking at what had happened with his life during the previous half-decade, all the emotions and aggression he had buried, the way his protest and frustration had manifested itself as apathy, alcoholism, a deep-seated resentment at the hand he'd been dealt. But it was all so much self-pitying bullshit. It had taken this – beatings, imprisonment, a real fear for his own survival – to wake him up to the fact that no one but himself was responsible for his condition.

Where he had been a victim, he had made the decision. Where he had given in, he had no one but himself to blame.

Raphael had been his mentor, his friend, his partner in crime. Crazy though he was, he had been the man to whom Stroud had looked for guidance. Raphael, as far as Stroud had been concerned, had embodied the very essence of what it was to be alive – flouting danger, a risk-taker, someone who jumped headlong, discovering only after the fact where he'd landed. But Raphael had never existed.

At some point during the handful of hours Stroud had spent with Daphne, she'd asked him a question. Had he ever known someone whose life he would rather have had? He had said no, but that was not true. Back then, in the thick of gunfire and war, as bombs exploded and people died, he used to watch Raphael and wish that Raphael's life was his own. That was who he wanted to be, and if he couldn't be that, then he wanted to be the very best imitation possible.

But what was he seeing – or rather, *who* was he seeing? Raphael, Dekker, or someone else entirely? Multiple names, but the same personality? There was no way to know. Perhaps, after all of this, there would be no way to find out.

Sounds beyond the door again. Stroud stood up and readied his tray. The hatch opened.

'Monsieur Stroud. Please walk to the far wall and sit on the floor.'

Stroud put his tray on the mattress and did as he was instructed.

The door opened. Two officers entered, one with a baton, the other with handcuffs.

The door was closed, and they stood there for just a moment before relaying the next instruction.

'Turn to the wall,' the officer with the cuffs said. 'Left hand in front of you, your right behind your back.'

The cuff was not so tight this time, but once it was secure, his left forearm was taken and the other cuff was applied.

'Turn,' the officer said.

'What's happening?'

'You see your advocate now.'

A sense of real foreboding gripped him. Where would they take him? Would he be bundled into the back of a police car, driven somewhere, perhaps shot, strangled, his body dropped into the Seine?

'Where are we going?' he asked, and he could hear the fear in his own voice.

'Do as you are told, *monsieur*. You come with us now. No more talking.'

51

Stroud willed himself to be quiet. His thoughts raged. He was torn between confusion and fear, the middle ground a no-man's-land of uncertainty and dismay.

Another featureless room. A plain table, two chairs, his hands still cuffed, but now a cable ran between them that was affixed to the floor beneath. He was going nowhere.

If he was responsible for his life, then he was also respons-ible for this moment, for all the moments that made up this catalogue of events. He and Raphael now shared a very different kind of history; in less than a month, he had found answers, but those answers had merely served to raise even more questions.

He was so tired. He was worn out, beaten down and broken. There had to be a point where the intimidation became intoler-able. And if he was pushed and pushed again beyond that limit, what then? Would he just crack? How much would it take to drive him over the edge?

That feeling of sensory overload was ramped up a thousand-fold when the door was opened and Ernst Lügner entered the interrogation room.

Reflexively, Stroud pulled back, his hands stopped dead by the cable that held his cuffs to the floor.

He started shouting then. He swore at Lügner. He had visions of blacking out, bright lights, the injections they'd given him.

Lügner just stood there, seemingly oblivious to the abuse

Stroud was levelling at him. His expression was implacable, and he waited until Stroud understood that what he was doing was serving no purpose at all.

Finally Stroud slammed his fists on the table.

'What are you people doing to me?' he asked. His throat was torn, his voice hoarse and weak.

Lügner took a step forward and smiled. 'Are we finished with this?'

'Fuck you, Lügner.'

'I think you know that that is not my name.'

'I don't care. Fuck you, whoever you are. What the hell is happening? Are you going to beat me again? Drug me?'

Lügner raised his hand.

'Just do it, you bastard. Just fucking do it. Kill me. Just kill me and get this over and done with.'

'Please,' Lügner said.

Stroud fell quiet. He knew that no matter what he asked, Lügner – or whatever the hell his name was – would only tell him what he wanted him to know. Once again, he was in a position where there was no room for manoeuvre, no leverage, no hope of negotiation.

Lügner withdrew the chair opposite and sat down.

'If I unlock this cable, do you give me your word that you will remain seated?'

'Fuck off.'

'Then we shall leave things as they are.'

'Okay. I give you my word. But what's to say I won't break it?'

Lügner smiled knowingly. 'You are a man of many frailties and flaws, Herr Stroud, but dishonesty is not one of them. In fact, I think it would be safe to say that your honesty is the only thing that has kept you from being killed.'

He withdrew a key from his jacket pocket and released the

padlock that secured the cable to the floor. He threaded it back through the hole in the table and let it lie there.

Stroud sat back, his hands in his lap, and looked at the man who had inflicted such torment and pain on him in Berlin.

Lügner returned the key to his pocket. 'You may call me Caleb.'

'What is that?' Stroud asked. 'A Hebrew name?'

Caleb didn't reply.

Stroud shook his head. 'You are insane.'

'Perhaps, but it is a necessary insanity.'

'What the hell are you talking about?'

'The things that are done sometimes need to be done. The harm inflicted is sometimes for the greater good.'

'What is that supposed to mean, for Christ's sake? You drugged me and damned near broke my fucking legs for my own benefit?'

'We had to be sure,' Caleb said. 'We had to be absolutely sure.'

'Sure? Sure of what?'

'Sure that you were who you said you were, that you were doing what you said you were doing.'

Stroud shook his head in disbelief. 'What's going on here? Lügner, Caleb, whoever the hell you are. What about the French guy? What about Fournier? You met with him in the restaurant, I saw you—'

'I know you saw us, and we knew you were there, Herr Stroud. Nothing you have done is unknown to us. Your attack on my friend was a little unexpected, however.'

'Your friend? What the fuck do you mean, your friend?'

Caleb smiled. There was a genuine sense of empathy in the expression. 'I want you to know that you will never receive an apology,' he said. 'No one will ever tell you they are sorry for what has happened to you. No one will ever try and make amends for the things you have suffered.'

'Well that's good to know,' Stroud said sarcastically.

'You are a man of some determination,' Caleb said. 'You have been through some difficult moments—'

'Difficult moments? Is that what you call them? Difficult fucking moments?'

'Please,' Caleb said. 'Just for a minute, would you listen? Just listen to what I have to say. I can help with some of the questions you have. Not all of them, you understand, but perhaps I can make sense of some of this.'

'That would be something,' Stroud said.

'First, would you perhaps like a cigarette, some coffee, something to eat?'

'You going to drug me again?'

'No, Herr Stroud, I am not going to drug you.'

'A cigarette, some coffee,' Stroud said. 'As you can probably appreciate, I don't have much of an appetite.'

Caleb rose and walked to the door. He knocked twice; the door was opened a couple of inches, and he gave instructions in French.

It was not long before a policeman returned with a tray. There was coffee for both of them, cigarettes and an ashtray. He set it down and left the room.

'You will understand if I do not release your handcuffs yet,' Caleb said. 'In a little while, perhaps.'

He put the cigarettes and coffee in front of Stroud.

'So who the hell are you?' Stroud asked. 'Who is Fournier? Who is … or *was* Hendrik Dekker, and what the hell does any of this have to do with Vincent Raphael?'

'Tell me what you think,' Caleb said. 'I will confirm or deny what I can.'

'Really? We're going to play childish games?'

'The games being played here are anything but childish,' Caleb said. 'I think you understand that.'

'Okay, if that's how we're going to do it,' Stroud said. 'First and foremost, Raphael was not his real name. He took the name of a child who died at four days old.'

'That is correct.'

'He was English.'

'He was not.'

'Dutch?'

'No, he was not Dutch.'

'Then what nationality was he?'

'Confirm or deny, Mr Stroud.'

'Well I'm not going to list every country in the world. So, Vincent, or whatever the hell his name was, died in Jordan in April of 1970.'

'He did not.'

Stroud felt his face drain of colour. Doubt had become suspicion, suspicion had become belief, but here was confirmation. Had he been asked to bet on Raphael having survived what happened in Jordan, he would have done so, but it had been academic, unrelated to fact, somehow disconnected from reality. To have someone tell him that Raphael hadn't died six years earlier was almost too much to comprehend.

'He didn't die,' he said, as if to hear it from his own lips would make it easier to absorb.

'No, Mr Stroud, he didn't die.'

'He became Hendrik Dekker.'

'Not at first, no.'

'He was someone else, and then he was Dekker.'

'He eventually became Hendrik Dekker, yes.'

'And he died in the explosion in Leiden.'

Caleb shook his head. 'No, he didn't die in Leiden.'

'He's a terrorist, though? All those things in the locker in Tegel were—'

'Were from somewhere else entirely,' Caleb said.

'So what was in the locker … and why tell me that if it wasn't the truth?'

Caleb didn't respond.

'Okay, okay. So Raphael, Dekker, not a terrorist.'

'That is correct.'

'He was not a photographer or a journalist.'

'He was a photographer and journalist.'

'But he was something else as well.'

'Yes,' Caleb said. 'He was something else as well.'

'Intelligence. A spy? A secret agent? What? What else was he?'

Caleb shook his head.

'So what? We're just going to sit here and do this until I run out of questions?'

'We do not have to sit here at all, Herr Stroud. I can release you now. I can put you on a plane and send you back to London or wherever you want to go, and you can continue to charge at this thing until you collapse from exhaustion or someone tires of you and kills you. It is your decision.'

Caleb took one of the cigarettes from the pack on the table and lit it. He smoked, he sipped his coffee. He remained utterly unperturbed.

'Is Raphael still alive?'

'That is a question you already know the answer to.'

'Is he here in Paris?'

'No.'

'In France?'

Caleb shook his head.

'The photograph I was originally shown, the one from Istanbul, was that Raphael?'

'Yes, it was.'

'My God,' Stroud said. 'I don't believe this.'

'You knew him,' Caleb said. 'Or you knew him as well as

anyone could have known him. It is not so difficult to believe, eh?'

Stroud's thoughts turned backwards and forwards, through everything he had ever known of the man, everything he'd thought he'd known. Above and beyond it all, the question remained: what was it that he'd had to escape from? What was Raphael so powerless to prevent that it required his own death to escape it?

'Does he know I'm looking for him?'

'Yes, he does.'

'Does he know where I am right now?'

'Yes.'

'Does he know you?'

Caleb nodded in the affirmative.

'And you and Fournier are working together?'

'Sometimes, sometimes not.'

'But you have a common agenda.'

Caleb smiled. 'Sometimes. And sometimes not.'

'Oh for Christ's sake! Will you just give me something, anything! Give me some kind of an idea of what the hell I've got myself into.'

'You didn't get yourself into anything, Herr Stroud. You were sent into it. Sent into the lion's den, if you will. It is true that you do not send a bird to spy on the cats, but sometimes, if the bird is small enough to go unnoticed, he defies expectation by being so unexpected.'

'This is just more cryptic nonsense,' Stroud said. 'Tell me something straight. Tell me one thing that is a straight fact, something that isn't a lie.'

Caleb slid the ashtray to one side and placed his hands flat on the table.

'Very well,' he said. 'I will tell you this much. What you have wandered into is a game of conspiracy and subterfuge that goes back more than thirty years. It is a game that has been played for centuries, of course, but I am speaking of this specific game. This is about nations at war, about murder and genocide. This is about a web of lies and deception that has seen kidnappings, bombings, assassinations, hijackings, the killing of innocent hostages, the murder of politicians, ministers, ambassadors, even ordinary people going about their day-to-day business in the streets of our cities.'

'Baader–Meinhof,' Stroud said. 'The kidnapping of Lorenz, the terrorists in Stockholm, the Munich Olympics. The things you were asking me about in Berlin.'

'For all their horror, these events are nothing but misdirection. They are the outward manifestation of a much grander, darker truth. Such incidents claim the lives of tens, sometimes hundreds of people. What we are talking about has claimed the lives of millions.'

'The war?'

'Which war, Herr Stroud? The Crusades? The Holocaust? The Arab–Israeli War that never seems to end? The Golan Heights? The Yom Kippur offensive? The air attacks on the Palestinian refugee camps in Lebanon, or perhaps the bombings in Jerusalem just twelve months ago? What about five thousand Syrian troops on the Damascus highway or the hostages in Entebbe? Are we not always at war? Is there ever a day when the fighting ceases?'

'So who are you? And who is Fournier? And what's your connection to Raphael?'

'Who am I?' Caleb shook his head. 'Perhaps that is the most difficult question of all to answer.'

'You must work for someone. You must have a nationality, an allegiance.'

'It is not that simple,' Caleb said. 'A nationality? That is the history of the Middle East. A war for nationality, a war for independence, a war for recognition. And as far as allegiance is concerned, I think you will find that allegiance and loyalty are merely items to barter and trade.'

'I am not talking about everyone else,' Stroud said. 'I am asking you.'

'I am loyal to no one and everyone,' Caleb replied. 'I am loyal to those I can trust, and disloyal to those I can't.'

'You trust Fournier?'

Caleb nodded.

'And Raphael? You trust Raphael?'

Again Caleb nodded.

Stroud opened his mouth to ask another question, but Caleb started to rise.

'I am sorry,' he said. 'The time has run away with me. There is a matter that needs attention. I will send someone to remove your handcuffs. We will get you some food, and then we will talk again after you have rested.'

'But—'

'Enough for now, Herr Stroud. I cannot stay any longer.'

Caleb reached the door and knocked.

'Just tell me why,' Stroud said.

'Why what, Herr Stroud?'

'Why Raphael had to disappear? Christ, that's not even his name. He isn't Hendrik Dekker either. I don't know what he's called. I don't think I know one true thing about him. I worked with him for fifteen years, and I think that everything he told me was a lie.'

'Not everything, no.'

'But a great deal of it. And now here I am, in the middle of God only knows what, and you're telling me that I should trust what you're telling me, and that you trust Raphael. Why do you trust him? Give me one good reason.'

'There are many reasons.'

'So tell me why he had to disappear, why he had to go to such lengths, why he hasn't made any contact with anyone for six years.'

Caleb looked down at the ground, and then sighed resignedly.

When he looked up, there was something quite different in his expression.

'You and Raphael are very much alike. Men of frailties and flaws. Perhaps he has a great deal more than you. He is also arrogant and headstrong, quick to lose his temper, and as ill-suited for this line of work as a man could be. But that does not mean he is not honourable.'

'Honourable? What are you talking about?'

'Sometimes we do harm for the greater good. The vaccine that kills ten but saves a thousand.'

'He has killed people?'

'Some. When he has had no choice.'

'No choice? There is always a choice.'

'Now you are being naïve, Herr Stroud.'

'So what is he doing, then? Tell me that much, at least. What the hell is he doing?'

'A good question, with no simple answer. But ultimately? Ultimately, perhaps, he is paying the price for the sins of his father.'

52

Stroud was woken abruptly, a hand on his shoulder, a voice saying his name repeatedly.

He opened his eyes and looked up. He had fallen asleep right there at the table, his head down on his arms, the exhaustion having finally taken him.

'It is time to leave, Monsieur Stroud,' the voice said.

Stroud focused, took in the uniformed man standing over him, another officer at the door. The man at the door had Stroud's jacket and holdall.

'What's happening?' he asked. 'What the hell is going on now?'

'It is time to go,' the policeman said. He unlocked Stroud's handcuffs. 'We take you to the airport. You go back to London now.'

Stroud sat up. 'What? London? What about Caleb? He said he was coming back to speak to me.'

'I know nothing of this,' the policeman said. 'You need to come now. We need to leave. You will miss the flight.'

'I don't want to take any flight,' Stroud said angrily. 'I want to see Caleb, Lügner, whatever his name is.'

The policeman at the door came forward. He put Stroud's bag and jacket on the table. 'Now,' he said. 'We go now. Stand up.'

Between them they manhandled him out of the chair and towards the door. Stroud resisted, but it was futile. They were intent on getting him out of the room. He stopped resisting and they let go of him. He kept on walking, one cop on each side, heading down the corridor towards a door at the end, the window of which indicated daylight beyond.

He put on his jacket and took his bag. Inside was his watch, his camera, his notebooks, his passport.

'This is insane,' he said. 'This is utterly fucking insane.'

He asked questions of his escorts as they drove. They gave no explanation. The car pulled up to departures, and he was directed through security and into the boarding lounge as the final call for the seven thirty flight to Gatwick was made.

His passport was given a cursory glance and he was marched down the stairs, out through the door and across to the plane. His arrival, flanked by two policemen, had everyone staring. The air hostesses didn't interfere, didn't ask questions, and Stroud was put in a seat right at the front.

The last irony, perhaps, and much the same as his extradition from Istanbul. Once again, he was being treated as a criminal but afforded a first-class seat.

One of the police officers spoke to a hostess out of earshot. All the while she watched Stroud. She smiled, she nodded, and then her expression took on a very different aspect altogether.

The officers left the plane, the door was secured, and Stroud looked out of the window and watched them grow smaller as the aircraft pulled away and headed for the runway.

He didn't ask the hostess what the policeman had said, nor did she give any indication of who she believed him to be, but for the entire flight he was treated with a definite sense of wariness.

Once they landed, he was instructed to wait as the remainder of the passengers disembarked.

He didn't ask for an explanation. He had heard altogether too many lies to now believe anything he was told.

The captain remained in the cockpit. The steward stood at the exit, the door to the aircraft now ajar, and the hostess to whom the policeman had spoken sat in a seat on the other side of the aisle.

They waited in silence. Stroud smoked. He asked for coffee. The hostess went back to the galley and returned with a cup.

Half an hour passed, perhaps more, and then there was the sound of someone coming up the metal steps.

Stroud didn't feel nervous. He didn't know why. If he was to believe Caleb, Raphael was alive. Raphael was Dekker, and before Dekker he had been somebody else. And now he was living under yet another name in some unknown location. As far as the manufacture of his apparent death was concerned, Stroud still knew nothing save some cryptic comment about the sins of his father. Raphael knew that Stroud was looking for him, and yet had chosen to make no contact.

Layers upon layers; a maze of rumours, suspicions and unanswered questions. Would it ever end? That was something Stroud would not know until the end arrived.

The aircraft door opened. A man appeared – heavy-set, dark hair, mid-fifties at a guess, an authoritarian air about him. He stepped forward as someone else came through.

'Marcus?' Stroud said. 'What the hell are you doing here?'

Haig shook his head. *Say nothing*, the gesture said.

'Mr Stroud,' the heavy-set man said. 'I am Detective Inspector Warren of Special Branch.'

'Special Branch? Christ almighty, what the hell is this? You think I'm a terrorist as well?'

'Don't say anything, Stroud,' Haig said.

Warren turned. 'Mr Haig, please.'

Stroud got up out of his seat. 'Tell me what the hell is going on.'

'Mr Stroud, please sit down,' Warren said.

'I will not.'

'Mr Stroud, you are travelling with a forged passport. From the information I have been given, the French security services have sent you back to London. You are now in my jurisdiction, and things do not look good for you. Now, we can either cooperate with a view to resolving this matter as rapidly as possible, or you can continue to be difficult. If you choose the latter course of action, I will have no option but to place you under arrest and take you into custody. That is something I wish to avoid.'

Warren's expression was businesslike and matter-of-fact. He was neither agitated nor unsettled. Just like Fournier, Lügner, the people in Turkey, he had done this before, perhaps many times, and nothing Stroud could do or say presented any threat to him.

Stroud sat down.

Warren nodded at the hostess. She and the steward made their way to the back of the plane. The captain closed the cockpit door, and Warren sat down beside Stroud.

Haig – still saying nothing – sat on the other side of the aisle.

'Your passport, please, Mr Stroud.'

Stroud took it from his holdall and handed it over.

Warren didn't look at it. He merely put it in his jacket pocket.

'Mr Haig here,' he went on, 'has agreed to stand as guarantor. He assures us that you are of good character, and that you have no connection to any known terrorist or subversive group, either in this country or any another. Let me assure you that we have investigated this matter, and though we have found no indication of affiliation to any organisation on our warning list, we will continue to be vigilant. You have broken the law, Mr Stroud. This is no light matter. The mere fact of having crossed international borders with false identification is sufficient to warrant a custodial sentence.'

Stroud knew better than to be defensive. He sat patiently and took the lecture.

'However, considering that this is a first offence, and with your reassurance that you will not break the law further, I have made a concession and will not be pressing charges. Let me be completely honest, Mr Stroud.' Warren leaned forward, his expression intense. 'I do not wish to hear your name again in connection with anything of this nature.'

'I understand,' Stroud said.

'Very well, then that shall be the end of it.'

Warren got up. He looked at Haig and extended his hand.

'Mr Haig.'

'Detective Inspector Warren.'

They shook. It was old-school. They had communicated only what was needed. Everything else was left unsaid.

Without a further word, without looking back at Stroud, Warren exited the aircraft and headed across the tarmac to the arrivals lounge.

Stroud looked at Haig.

Haig shook his head. 'Let's get out of here,' he said. 'We can talk at the office.'

53

Nina's reaction as Stroud walked into Haig's office took him by surprise.

'Oh my God,' she said, and threw her arms around him. 'I honestly thought you might not come back. I was really worried for you.'

'We both were,' Haig said. He walked around his desk and sat down. 'So tell me what the hell has been going on. Three days, now nearly four, and we haven't heard a word. I couldn't even track you as I had no idea what name was on your passport.'

'You could have asked the guy, Marcus. You sent me to him.'

Haig scowled and gave a momentary shake of his head. Evidently he didn't want Nina to hear how Stroud had obtained the counterfeit passport.

'Before I say anything,' Stroud said, 'I want to know how the hell you got me off that plane. Special Branch? Christ, Marcus, who the hell owed you to pull that off?'

'You're going to hate me,' Haig said. 'I really don't think I should tell you.'

'Tell me, for Christ's sake.'

'You and the Metropolitan Police Deputy Commissioner just happen to have someone in common.'

Stroud frowned.

'The only person in your former life who has enough money and clout to mix in those circles.'

'Oh no,' Stroud said. 'You didn't. Please tell me you didn't.'

'What does it matter? And what else was I supposed to do? You could be under arrest right now, stuck in some fucking police cell without any hope of bail.'

'What?' Nina said. 'What did he do?'

Stroud turned and looked at her. 'He asked my fucking father-in-law, Nina. Or rather, my ex-father-in-law. The one and only Donald Montgomery.'

He turned on Haig. 'For fuck's sake, Marcus. Do you have any idea what you've done?'

'Stop being so melodramatic. Who else was I going to ask?'

'Anyone but Donald fucking Montgomery. He is my only child's grandfather, and you have well and truly put the nail in the coffin as far as my reputation is concerned. You know, I have been thinking a great deal about how I can see my daughter again—'

'Stroud, it was either that or leave you to rot in a French bloody prison.'

'At least if I went to prison I'd be out again at some point.'

'What's done is done,' Haig said.

'And how did they even get hold of you?' Stroud asked.

'How the hell do I know? They probably tracked down your parents, and I was the only person they could think of who might want anything to do with you.'

Stroud shook his head in dismay. That would make sense. He could just hear his father bemoaning the fact that his son was once again in some dreadful scrape.

'So where are we?' Haig asked. 'What happened in Paris? Are we actually any closer to making any sense of this?'

'I assaulted a member of the French embassy in his own apartment,' Stroud said.

Haig looked at him, eyes wide. 'You did what?'

'Exactly what I said. I assaulted a member of the French

embassy in his own apartment. I wrestled him to the ground and then he tricked me into thinking he had a heart condition. He pulled a gun on me, the cops showed up and arrested me, and I was put in a cell in the commissariat. I was then told that I was going to be seen by an assigned advocate, and the man who showed up was Ernst Lügner.'

'The guy from Berlin?' Nina said.

'The very same. Except that his name is not Lügner, of course. He told me to call him Caleb.'

'And who was this French official?' Haig asked.

'His name, as far as I know, is Jean-Michel Fournier. He was the one in Istanbul. The one with the picture of Dekker.'

'He and Lügner work together?'

'Sometimes. Sometimes not. Apparently.'

'What the—'

'It gets better,' Stroud said. 'Raphael is alive, according to Caleb or Lügner or whoever he is. And his name is not Raphael. His name is not Hendrik Dekker either. He's not English and he's not Dutch. I don't know his nationality, and I don't know where he is now or what he's doing. Also according to Caleb, Raphael knows I am looking for him, and has decided to stay out of touch.'

Haig's face had lost all colour. He said nothing.

Nina didn't speak either.

Both of them looked at Stroud as if he'd just confirmed the date for the end of the world.

'Caleb,' Haig said eventually.

'That's what he said.'

'And this Lügner/Caleb guy is German.'

'That's what he said, but he could be anything. Right now, Marcus, I am so bloody confused, I'm not even sure of my own name and nationality.'

'But he came to see you as a French legal advocate in a French police station.'

'Yes, he did.'

'So he must be French security services or defence ministry or something. He has to come from somewhere that has greater authority than the national police.'

'One would assume so, yes.'

'And he told you that Raphael is definitely alive.'

'That's what he said, and I believed him. But once again, I could be completely wrong. Seems to me that these people are specialists in deception, misdirection, manipulation and outright lies. All I know is that my basic human rights have now been violated in three countries and all I have to show for it is a dossier with a label on it, probably fucking Interpol or something, and the definite feeling that I am still none the wiser about what the hell is really going on.'

Haig got up and walked to the window. He put his hands in his pockets and looked out across the city.

Stroud glanced at Nina.

You okay? she mouthed.

He nodded.

Haig turned back. 'To put it bluntly, I am fucking speechless.'

'Raphael is alive,' Stroud said. 'As unsure as I was, I am now equally sure. He is out there somewhere and he's involved in something that has driven him underground, so far underground that he has had to change his name at least twice and can't communicate with anyone he knew before Jordan. All I can conclude is that he's a spy, an agent of some sort, a double, triple, quadruple fucking agent. Who the fuck knows what he is or isn't? Nothing is certain in my mind except that he's not who either of us ever thought he was.'

Haig sat down heavily. 'So what now?'

Stroud looked at his watch. It was nearly ten. 'Right now, I

314

need a bath, a change of clothes, a decent meal, a few hours' sleep. After that, I'll try and get all this into perspective. Maybe I've missed something. Maybe there's something I've forgotten. I don't know, Marcus. I just feel like I need a few hours away from it before I start again.'

'Yes, yes.' Marcus nodded, still distracted. 'Tomorrow, then,' he said. 'Come and see me tomorrow.'

Outside Haig's office Nina asked if Stroud wanted to come over and stay at her flat.

'I can make you something to eat,' she said.

'Nina, really, I appreciate it, but I actually feel like I need to be alone. I'll get a hotel room. I need to go and buy clothes. I just want to be outside and look at the sky and I don't want to talk about this or think about it. I don't even want to feel like I'm making an effort not to talk about it. I'm sorry, but it's been a rough few days.'

She smiled, put her hand on his forearm.

'I understand completely,' she said. 'I'm just really pleased to see you. I was worried about you. I'm so relieved to know you're okay.'

'Thank you.'

Stroud watched her go.

He felt hollow inside, like there was nothing left of him.

54

Stroud lay on the hotel bed and stared at the ceiling. He was tired, but he knew he wouldn't sleep. Thoughts fired back and forth, in turn triggering other thoughts, and though it all seemed random, he knew that somewhere within the maze there was a way out.

Whatever name Ernst Lügner might use, he was German. Of that, Stroud was sure. His manner, his accent, his very presence possessed that Teutonic air. And yet in Paris he had used the Hebrew name Caleb. He had spoken of wars that went back decades. Yom Kippur, the Golan Heights, the Arab–Israeli conflict had all been mentioned; he'd told Stroud that he had wandered into *a game of conspiracy and subterfuge that goes back more than thirty years.* He'd spoken of murder and kidnappings, of hostages, but he'd also used the word genocide. That, more than anything he'd said, had stayed with Stroud. Why genocide, unless he was referring to the Holocaust? You couldn't consider the history of the Middle East without taking into account the murder of more than six million Jews.

Stroud was no expert regarding the situation in Palestine. He merely saw the conflict, the bloodshed, the loss of life, the acts of terrorism perpetrated all over the world in the name of whoever believed they had a better God. The Middle East had been where Raphael's life had ended, but out of that moment another life had begun.

Raphael was a journalist, but also a spy, a soldier, a mercenary perhaps, but for whom? Where did his loyalties lie? Where was he now, and what was it that had warranted such a long and unbroken silence?

All that Stroud had was the man he now knew to be Caleb, a connection to the Middle East, and a web of conspiracy and subterfuge that was three decades old. That time frame tied into the end of the Second World War, the creation of Israel, the Nuremberg trials, the revelations concerning the true horror of the Nazis' Final Solution. It had to have something to do with the geography of that region, all that had happened there, and the ramifications that had spread out across Europe. In Berlin, Caleb had asked him about Baader–Meinhof, the Red Army Faction, the 2 June Movement. He had wanted to know if Stroud knew any of the people he named, if he had any knowledge of what had happened at the Olympics in Munich. What else had he said? That he needed to be sure. Sure of what? He said he wanted to know if Stroud really was looking for Raphael. As opposed to what? It had to be motivation. What was Stroud's motivation? To find Raphael for his own reasons, or at the behest of someone or something else?

Did Caleb think that he was looking for Raphael in order to expose him, bring him to harm, turn him over to the authorities?

Had Caleb and Fournier been sent to ensure that he never found him?

If that was the case, then who were they, and who did they actually work for?

Caleb. The Middle East. Israel. Thirty years.

He needed someone who would have some clue as to how these things were connected, or perhaps could tell him that they were not connected at all. Where was this heading, or was he chasing the wrong thread entirely?

317

He got up and fetched the telephone directory from the desk near the window.

He needed a foreign correspondent, a newspaperman, a desk editor, someone for whom the Middle East was known and familiar territory. He didn't want to go to *The Times*. He didn't want to see Nina or anyone else. He merely wanted an opportunity to get his own thoughts organised and ordered. He needed to understand some of this himself before he tried to make sense of it for anyone else.

He looked through the list of newspaper offices in the phone book. Who did he know? Who might be able to help him? Of course, Haig would know people. More than likely he could give him a complete history of the subject from the dawn of time. Haig had been on that desk, had been foreign editor, and if he himself didn't know, then there would be a roster of people to whom Stroud could be directed. But he wanted to leave Haig out of this for now. The thing that Haig had asked him to do had now become something else entirely, and until Stroud understood its import, he wanted to address it alone.

And then it came to him. The Israeli embassy. He could approach them as a journalist, speak to a press agent. Not only would they be up to speed from the political perspective, but they'd also have a real understanding of the religious and ethnic aspects.

He called, asked if it would be possible to speak to someone on background for a story he was putting together.

'I can perhaps fit you in on Thursday afternoon,' the girl at the other end said.

'I really would like to see someone today, if there's any way it can be done. I don't need a lot of time, and I'm not going to be in the UK again for a while.'

'Can I ask what you specifically require, Mr Stroud?'

'It's general background on the current political climate. The piece I'm writing is really to acknowledge what was accomplished by the Israeli commandos at Entebbe, you know? The fact that they rescued the hostages from right under the noses of—'

'One moment, Mr Stroud, I just have another call.'

The line went dead, and for a moment Stroud believed he'd been cut off, but within a few seconds the girl returned.

'If you don't need a great deal of time, we may be able to accommodate you at a quarter past one. One of our diplomatic consultants has a window, but he has another appointment at two.'

'That would be more than adequate,' Stroud said.

'Please ensure you bring your passport and official credentials, Mr Stroud. Security measures for accessing the building are extremely rigorous, as I am sure you can appreciate.'

'Yes, of course. I understand completely.'

He hung up. He needed press credentials.

Nina was the only one who might be able to help him. He called her, told her what he needed.

'Why?'

'Better that you don't know, Nina.'

'For Christ's sake, Stroud, I broke my wrist climbing into someone's flat in Holland, and now you want me to get you a press card?'

'I need your help,' Stroud said. 'Marcus won't do it. I know that for a fact. He had to guarantee to Special Branch that I would behave myself. And I don't want him to know, okay? I'm doing my best to give him some hope of deniability.'

'But it's okay to hang me out to dry, is it?'

'Nina, seriously, if I didn't need you to do this, I wouldn't ask.'

'Then just tell me the truth, okay? Tell me that this is not serious. Tell me you're not going to use it to get into somewhere where you really shouldn't be.'

'I promise you,' Stroud said. 'I give you my word. I need to see someone, an official, but I can only see them with credentials. It's a completely legitimate meeting for some background, okay?'

Nina was silent for a few seconds. Stroud could hear her breathing.

'Okay,' she said, but there was reservation, even anxiety in her tone. 'Let me see what I can do. Call me in half an hour.'

'Thank you,' Stroud said, but the line went dead before the words had left his lips.

He went down to the hotel restaurant. It was late for lunch, but the kitchen made him a sandwich and a cup of coffee. The bar was open, but the last thing he needed was a drink. He took the sandwich back to his room and called Nina.

'You are now the *Times* deputy foreign affairs correspondent,' she said. 'But if this ever comes out and I get fired, you owe me a job.'

'Nina, you're a godsend. Meet me at the Crown and Sceptre at twelve thirty, okay?'

'I'm not going to meet you, Stroud. I'll have someone take it down there in an envelope and leave it behind the bar. This never happened. We never had this conversation, okay?'

Once again, she hung up before Stroud could respond.

55

'I am not quite sure how I can help you, Mr Stroud,' Yael Wexler said.

Wexler was younger than Stroud had expected, perhaps late twenties or early thirties, and yet he managed to present an air of seriousness that belied his youth.

He glanced once more at Stroud's press card. 'You are the London *Times* deputy foreign affairs correspondent, and yet you seem particularly uninformed as to the dynamics of the Middle Eastern situation.'

'I am really sorry,' Stroud said, 'and I have absolutely no intention of wasting your time. To be completely honest, I'm new to the job. I have been away for some time, Europe primarily, and I have only just taken on this role. I hoped to have some more time to get orientated, but here we have this international incident, the rescue of the hostages from Entebbe, the world's focus on your prime minister's policies concerning—'

Wexler raised his hand and smiled. 'I understand, Mr Stroud. However, in order for me to be of assistance to you, I need to know precisely what it is that you're asking.'

Stroud sat back. He had not prepared himself for this. Once again, in his rush to obtain more information, he had not clearly defined what he wanted to know. For better or worse, he decided that his only avenue was to be honest – at least to a point – about why he was there.

'I am looking into the death of a friend,' he said. 'He was killed in Jordan some years ago. He was a journalist, a good one, and an honourable man. He was interested in little but the truth, and he understood that the underlying irresolution of the situation in the Middle East was attributable to an absence of truth. There are vested interests. There are political agendas. Perhaps it may even be the case that those who say that the conflict will never end are those who *want* it to continue. For what reason? They each have their own reasons. Personally, I don't believe that honest men with honest interests are not capable of resolving such a thing, unless there are others who are feeding lies into the situation to keep the hostilities fuelled.'

'I could say I agree with you, Mr Stroud, but I would be agreeing with a great many people who have said the same thing for decades.'

'Yes. Yes, of course. Perhaps if we look at more recent events, then. The hostages taken, the kidnappings, the Munich Olympics, the Saudi Arabian embassy in Paris, Black September at Athens Airport—'

'And so it goes on,' Wexler said.

'Yes. Endlessly. So, looking at these situations, I guess I'm trying to make some sense…' Stroud shook his head. 'To be completely honest, I don't know *what* I'm trying to make sense of.'

'You don't actually want a comment regarding the Entebbe raid. You need a grounding in the overall political and geo-graphical nature of this situation. If that's the case, then a few hours in the library will give you a far better perspective than I ever could in half an hour.'

'Yes, of course. I'm sorry for having wasted your time.'

'And as for your friend, it sounds to me like you need help from the police, both here and in Jordan. I am a diplomat, and this is not a diplomatic matter. Nor does it seem to concern the Israeli embassy.'

'You're right,' Stroud said. 'I just have a whole handful of threads and none of them seem to have any connection to one another, and yet I'm tied up in the middle of it.'

'I am sorry for your loss, Mr Stroud. It seems that this relentless war is always measured in terms of the political and geographical, but the real cost is in the suffering of the homeless, the refugee camps, the innocent victims. It seems global, but it is always personal. Situations like this really bring it home. A good man is trying to do his job and is killed for no reason.'

'I don't think I could ever conceive of not having a true homeland, a recognised nationality. I don't think it's something we can really comprehend.'

'It has been this way forever,' Wexler said. 'That is how it seems. Ever since Caleb wandered in the wilderness.'

Stroud felt his heart skip a beat. 'Caleb?'

'The Twelve Spies of Moses,' Wexler said.

'What is that?'

'It's from the Book of Bamidbar. In Christianity it's called the Book of Numbers.'

'The Book of Numbers ... in the Bible?'

Wexler frowned. 'That's the only place I know where there is a Book of Numbers, Mr Stroud. Why?'

'What is this Twelve Spies thing?'

'It relates to the promise that God made to the Israelites that they would be delivered into the Promised Land. Moses sent twelve spies into Canaan with the instruction to spend forty days studying the land, the geography, the agriculture, you know? Ten of the twelve came back and misled him. They said that the land of Canaan was not fit for their purpose. Only

Caleb and Joshua told the truth. They said that Canaan could be their homeland. Because of this, the Israelites wandered in the desert for forty years. Of the original twelve, only Caleb and Joshua survived, and they were permitted passage to the Promised Land.'

'And does that name, Caleb, have any other significance?'

'Aside from the fact that both Caleb and Joshua are revered as true and faithful, the history itself is often considered symbolic of the endless struggle of the Jews to find a homeland. Most recently there is the persecution of the Jews in Europe, but this has been going on for centuries.'

'The Jews who left Germany ... where did they go?'

'Anywhere they were welcome. At first, neighbouring countries, but as war seemed ever more likely, they tried their best to get out of Europe altogether. America, Canada and here in Britain were the preferred destinations. A lot of Jews ended up in London, and I know there are second- and third-generation Jewish families in New York who consider themselves more American than anything else.' Wexler smiled. 'I say that because I am related to some of them.'

'And are there records?'

'Of Jews arriving in America?'

'No, arriving here. German Jews who came here.'

'I am sure there are, yes. How accurate they would be, I don't know. Ironically, the German records of who left Germany would possibly be far more accurate than the records of arrival in England. German administrative fastidiousness, you know?'

Stroud was lost in his own thoughts.

Wexler glanced at his watch. 'I am sorry, but I really must bring this conversation to a conclusion, Mr Stroud. I don't think I've been a great help to you...'

'Perhaps you have,' Stroud said. 'I am beginning to get the

idea that I may have been looking at this from entirely the wrong perspective.'

Wexler got up. 'Well, I trust that your investigation can now make some progress.' He walked to the door of the office. 'Let me show you the way out, Mr Stroud.'

56

Back in his hotel room, Stroud thought about the very first conversation with Marcus. The photograph that he'd been shown was supposedly of Raphael talking to someone from Mossad.

Had Lügner had a specific reason for using the name Caleb? Had he been trying to direct Stroud's attention towards something in particular by talking about the last thirty years, the Holocaust, the current situation in the Middle East? Was Stroud being given pieces of a jigsaw puzzle, apparently random, and yet when sequenced correctly, they would give him a recognisable picture?

Was he following the right thread when considering the possibility that Lügner was trying to help him? And if so, why?

German Jews coming into Britain. Where would records of these migrations be kept? Were they accessible?

Stroud called Nina at the paper. She wasn't at her desk. He went through the phone book and found an organisation called the Jewish Historical Society. He called them, persisted long enough until he found someone who could help him.

'All comes under the Home Office,' he was told. 'Public Records Office. I think it is called the Aliens Department, but I could be wrong on that point.'

Stroud called the Home Office, again persisted until he found someone who was neither too busy nor too self-important to talk to him.

'Yes, that's correct. Office of Public Records would have that kind of material. Aliens Department, Alien Personnel Files. Would you like the telephone number?'

'That would be much appreciated,' Stroud said.

He took the number, called them, verified that the Office of Public Records was actually open to the public, that there was indeed an Aliens Department. He asked if an appointment was necessary.

'What is it that you require, sir?'

'Records of German Jews migrating into Britain during the 1930s.'

'Let me check,' the girl at the other end said. She was back within a couple of minutes. 'It's coming up to quarter past three,' she said. 'We close at five thirty. If you can get here by four, we can have someone available to see you.'

'Thank you,' he said. 'I'll be there by four.'

He put down the phone and leaned back in his chair. He closed his eyes just for a moment. He was fighting fatigue, but his mind was going at a hundred knots. He hoped that this wasn't some other hiding to nowhere with even more questions than answers at the end.

He called Nina once more, just to keep her in the loop, but again found her absent.

The Public Records Office was on Chancery Lane. Stroud made it there by quarter to, and waited in the vast and imposing reception hall for someone called Christopher Yardley.

Yardley, a man in his mid-forties, balding and bespectacled, came down the steps from an upper landing. He was smiling, seemed pleased to have a visitor. Once an introduction had been made, he explained that he was not necessarily a specialist in this precise field of research, but he had been in the Aliens Department for over twenty years now and he knew his way around.

327

'It may be the proverbial needle in a haystack,' Stroud said, 'but I am looking for someone.'

Yardley nodded, indicated that Stroud should follow him, and they went back up the stairs and through a heavy door. Beyond was a corridor, doors to the left and right. They seemed to walk for a good five minutes before taking a left turn, threading their way through a maze of banked filing cabinets and down another flight of stairs. Through a further door, along a short corridor, and then into a high vaulted chamber.

'Here we are,' Yardley said, and with a sweep of his arm he took in the ornate balustrades and wrought-iron stairways, the narrow gantries and seemingly endless expanse of wooden drawers. 'Like I said, I've been here for twenty years and it still impresses me.'

'I think impressed is an understatement,' Stroud said. 'I had no idea.'

'Oh, this is just the Aliens Department, Mr Stroud. We have innumerable departments that cover an expanse far greater than this. This is a minor bureau within a unit within a division within a sub-department.'

Yardley smiled, seemingly proud to have created the effect he'd hoped to create.

'So, we should begin,' he said. 'What exactly is it that you need?'

Stroud explained as they made their way downstairs to a central index card hub.

'German Jews into Britain during the thirties,' Yardley said. 'Yes, well, that's a history all its own.'

They sat at a table, and he took a notepad and pencil.

'There were what's known as alien tribunals,' he explained. 'More than a hundred of these reviewed the status of all Germans, Austrians and Italians living in the British Isles. The vast majority of these people were considered friendly, and the vast majority of those were Jews. Anyone detained was done so under what was called Defence Regulation 18B. About two thousand were interned, and then it was decided that they should be shipped back overseas. That process was initiated, and it continued until a U-boat sunk a ship called the *Arondora Star*, I think in 1940. Something like eight hundred or a thousand lives were lost. As far as Jews coming into the country was concerned, that was managed by the Home Office. There was a strong Jewish community in Britain already, and they had to assure the Treasury that the Jews permitted entry would not place a financial burden on the state.'

Yardley shook his head resignedly. 'Of course, at the time, there was no way to know what would ultimately happen. There was, I'm sorry to say, a strong anti-Semitic fervour, the feeling that Jews coming into Britain would take British jobs, and that the British taxpayer would be saddled with the cost of supporting these refugees. Up until the actual outbreak of the war, something in the region of seventy thousand Jews were given permission to remain. However, more than half a million were denied. That seventy thousand included nearly eight thousand unaccompanied children who came in on something called the *Kindertransport*. Parents, certain that the situation could only get worse, gave over responsibility for the lives of their children to complete strangers in the hope that they might survive.'

He looked away and sighed. 'A truly awful plight. One can hardly imagine how they must have felt.'

'So what happened to those Jews, specifically the German Jews, who were allowed to stay?'

'They went to the Isle of Man,' Yardley said. 'I'll show you.'

He got up and walked to a bank of cabinets on Stroud's right, returning with a large black-bound ledger. Opening it, he showed Stroud lists of names – a hundred or more per page – and in the furthest column to the right, reference numbers. It seemed that each name had been assigned a number between one and twelve. It also seemed clear that where there was a group of individuals with the same family name, they had been allocated the same number.

'And this number is what?' Stroud asked.

Yardley closed the book, reopened it to the first page; there, listed in a column, were the names of the camps. Mooragh, Peveril, Onchan, Granville, Sefton and so on, each of them numbered.

'So if I was looking for a specific person?' Stroud asked.

'Their name?'

Stroud raised his eyebrows and shook his head. 'Caleb.'

'That's a forename, surely?'

'I think so, yes.'

'So this Caleb would have been an adult or a child?'

'A child,' Stroud said.

Yardley smiled, seemingly relieved. 'Then we have just saved ourselves a great deal of work.'

'How so?'

'Because there were only three camps that took females, families and unaccompanied children. Those children were, in essence, assigned a family, and were given a legal guardian within the community who was responsible for their welfare.'

'And the names of those camps?'

'Rushen, Port St Mary and Port Erin. Camps four, five and six respectively.'

'So I sit here and I go through these ledgers, noting each name that is given a four, five or six, and it will tell me if there was a child by the name of Caleb who was sent there.'

'In principle, yes.'

'In principle?'

Yardley leaned forward and smiled sympathetically. 'Names were changed for personal reasons, false names were sometimes given. It was a very difficult time, you understand. Sometimes it is obvious that the name given was an attempt to hide the Jewish origin. And at this end, there were spelling errors, misunderstandings, all manner of clerical omissions. The records, I have to say, may very well be inaccurate, and you may not find what you are looking for.'

'I get that,' Stroud said, 'but I need to go through these anyway. How many ledgers are there?'

'I'd say twenty or twenty-five in all. I will bring a couple more, and when you are done with those, we will bring the next ones.'

'Thank you,' Stroud said. He turned the first ledger around and started scanning the numbers in the final column.

57

A little after five, Yardley returned to see how Stroud was getting on.

Stroud's mind was crowded with names, dates, numbers, the endless cross-referencing back to other columns as soon as he found any record of the correct internment camp numbers.

'I am more than happy to help for the next half an hour,' Yardley said, 'but I really do have to close up at five thirty.'

'I understand completely,' Stroud said. 'If I don't find anything, I'll have to come back tomorrow,' he added, knowing all too well that he might trawl through every single ledger and find nothing.

But luck, fortune, whatever it might have been called, was on his side, and it was Christopher Yardley who found it.

'I perhaps have something of interest here, Mr Stroud,' he said, and turned the ledger around so Stroud could see it.

There, roughly halfway down the page, was the name *Liebenfeld*. A family entry for Port St Mary on 7 June 1940.

'This is right at the beginning,' Yardley said. 'The Isle of Man camps didn't really get going until the latter part of May. These must have been some of the first arrivals.'

Stroud went back across the ledger to the list of names. Rivka Liebenfeld, Eliana, Caleb and Joshua. Beneath it were their respective dates of birth, Rivka in March 1908, Eliana in

September of '29, the two boys in 1933, January and June respectively.

'That puts Rivka Liebenfeld at – what? – thirty-two years
old, the girl at ten, the two boys at seven,' Stroud said. 'But they
can't be brothers. Caleb is born in January, Joshua in June of the
same year.'

'I can only assume that this woman was assigned as guardian
to one of the boys,' Yardley said. 'The unaccompanied children
I mentioned.'

'Yes,' Stroud said. 'Yes, of course.'

It was the names of the two boys that held Stroud's attention.
Caleb and Joshua. The only ones of the Twelve Spies to tell the
truth, and the only ones to make it to the Promised Land. Had
Lügner used the name to direct Stroud toward this?

His second thought concerned the father. Why had the father
not arrived with his family? What had happened to prevent him
leaving Germany? Had he died, perhaps? When Stroud had
asked what Raphael was really doing, what was it Caleb had
said? *Paying the price for the sins of his father.*

Was this the first real thread of truth that would take him to
Raphael?

He looked up at Yardley. 'There is no way to know what happened to these people after the war, right? I mean, no records
here of when they were released, if they stayed in England, if
they went somewhere else?'

Yardley shook his head. 'Unfortunately not,' he said. 'This is
all we have.'

Stroud took a notepad from his bag and wrote down the
names and the dates of birth.

'I'm going to see if I get anywhere with this,' he told Yardley.
'If I don't, would it be okay if I came back tomorrow?'

'Yes, of course,' Yardley said. 'We're open at nine.'

'And I can bring someone to help me?'

'Most certainly, Mr Stroud. It is the Public Records Office, after all.'

Stroud thanked him, shook his hand, wished him a good evening.

Out on Chancery Lane, he stood and looked at the sheet of paper in his hand. The Liebenfeld family – a mother, a daughter and two sons. One was her own, it seemed, and the other was perhaps one of the many thousands who'd been sent overseas by their parents. Stroud thought of Eva. He couldn't even begin to comprehend what it must have been like for a mother or father to consign their child to a stranger, knowing that whatever lay in store for them would be better than their fate if they stayed behind. To them, despite the anguish, England – even those camps on the Isle of Man – must have seemed like a Promised Land.

This was what he had. Caleb and Joshua. This was *all* he had, and he prayed that the lead would take him somewhere significant.

Had he walked to the end of Chancery Lane, he would have been on Fleet Street. Here he could have used any number of archival departments to start looking for records of the Liebenfeld family, but he wanted to try the most obvious place first. He found a pub on the corner of Carey Street that had a public phone inside. He ordered a pint of Guinness and asked for the phone book.

There were seven Liebenfelds listed, two of them with the initial R. He didn't want to call from somewhere he could be overhead, so he wrote down all the numbers. Once he'd finished his drink, he left and made his way back to the hotel.

In his room, he sat and stared at the phone for a while. If Rivka Liebenfeld was on this list, then she had stayed in England after the war. She would now be sixty-eight years old. The daughter would be forty-six, and both Joshua and Caleb would be forty-three. Raphael was forty-three, and he'd been born in June. The name Vincent Raphael had been taken from a child born in the same month, the same year, who had died after four days.

He lifted the receiver and dialled the first number. It rang out. He dialled the second, and after a mere ten seconds the line connected and a woman said, 'Hello?'

'Hello. Is this Mrs Liebenfeld?'

'This is *Miss* Liebenfeld.'

'Oh, I might have the wrong number. I am trying to track down a Mrs Rivka Liebenfeld.'

There was a momentary hesitation, and then, 'Yes.'

'This is Rivka Liebenfeld?'

'No, this is her daughter, Eliana.'

For a moment Stroud was lost for words.

'Yes,' he said. 'Miss Liebenfeld. I was trying to get hold of your mother because I am looking for someone—'

'I know who you are,' Eliana Liebenfeld said, her voice calm and measured.

Stroud's heart missed a beat.

'I know who you are, Mr Stroud, and I know exactly who you are looking for. Do you have a pen?'

'A pen? Yes, I have a pen.'

'You need to come to this address.'

Stroud's handwriting was all over the place. He scrawled the address down as quickly as he could.

'Take the Underground. Get off two or three times. Change trains. Walk from one station to another. Do everything you can to ensure you are not being followed.'

'Not being followed?'

'This is what I have been told to tell you. Follow these instructions. It is important. I will see you when you get here.'

'But—'

The line went dead.

Stroud set down the receiver. He waited until his heart slowed, and then he got up, put on his jacket and left the room.

Stroud was heading east, out towards one of the monolithic and brutally ugly housing developments that had been put up after the war. He followed the instructions given by Eliana Liebenfeld. He changed trains three times, walked back the way he'd come, even crossed the street and went into a pub. Here he stayed for fifteen minutes, and then exited by climbing over the fence behind the building and making his way along a narrow alleyway and back into the street. The sense of paranoia was intense, almost overwhelming. He could hear the woman's voice. *I know who you are. I know exactly who you are looking for.*

Someone had known the truth of Vincent Raphael right from the start. Perhaps it was this woman. If Lügner was Caleb, then was Raphael actually Joshua Liebenfeld? A Jew spirited out of Nazi Germany, interned on the Isle of Man, and then hiding behind one name after another?

Stroud didn't arrive at the housing development until nearly nine. He threaded his way through a maze of underpasses and corridors, struck at once by the bleak sense of isolation that such an environment engendered. Here and there a resident had changed the colour of their front door, hung some bright curtains in the window, but the sense of repetition and uninterrupted sameness was soul-destroying. The Blitz had torn up the terraces and back-to-backs, and in its place a vast warren of box-like structures had been erected. Perhaps better than the devastated ruins and irreconcilable division that surviving Berliners now suffered, but it nevertheless didn't seem to be fitting recompense for those who had both given and lost everything during six years of terrible war.

At last Stroud was orientated. He made his way along a

shadow walkway with a single flickering fluorescent tube in the ceiling and stood for a moment outside the front door of the address he'd been given. He raised his hand to knock, but the door opened from within.

The woman who stood there was the right age, mid forties, her thick black hair shot through with veins of grey. Her eyes spoke of secrets and grief.

'Miss Liebenfeld?' Stroud asked.

'Come in,' she said, and opened the door wide.

58

Eliana Liebenfeld was not a well woman. Everything about her – the way she spoke, the way she moved – communicated a sense of exhaustion and deep physical pain.

She made tea, insisted on it, and Stroud sat patiently in a small sitting room while she busied herself in the kitchen. On the walls were clumsy reproductions of well-known landscapes, the furniture had seen better days, and Stroud noticed a marked absence of any personal items – framed pictures, trinkets, souvenirs from trips abroad.

When she returned, bearing a tray with a teapot, cups, a plate of plain biscuits, Stroud rose and helped her. She sat then, waited for the tea to brew, and poured. It was strong and black, no milk or sugar was offered, and Stroud knew he would struggle to drink it.

'The man you know is not my brother,' she said. 'Of course, he was treated as my brother, but he is not blood.'

Stroud didn't say anything. Eliana had started to talk without prompting, and he felt that questions would only serve to interrupt what she had already decided to say.

'My mother is here,' she went on. 'She is very ill. This is her flat. I do not live here. Not far away, however. I come every day. I have done so for the last few years while she has been getting sicker. I do not believe she will live much longer.'

'I am sorry to hear that,' Stroud said.

Eliana looked at him as if who he was and why he was there was of no importance. It was an odd sensation. As if to explain what he was feeling, she said, 'I don't know who you are. I suppose I don't need to know. My brother told me to speak to you, to tell you some things.'

Stroud put the cup and saucer on the low table and sat back.

'Of course, our name is not actually Liebenfeld, and Caleb's name is not Caleb. That is the name my mother gave him when she took him in. His father was murdered by a Brownshirt, and then his mother was killed in a road accident. He didn't have a good start to his life. He was five when he came to us, a wretched little creature with no family or hope of survival. Our family name is Lindenauer. We changed it to Liebenfeld because the Lindenauer name had been so terribly, terribly disgraced.'

Eliana looked up. Her eyes were brimming with tears, and Stroud perceived a well of grief deep enough to swallow someone and never let them go.

'My father,' she said, her voice a whisper. 'Shimon Lindenauer.' She smiled weakly. 'You will find him. He is here in your newspapers.'

'You came to England with your mother,' Stroud said. 'All of you. That's correct?'

'We all came. The whole family. My brother is Joshua. Caleb was named after the tribe of Judah. My brother, my little brother was Joshua of the tribe of Ephraim. My father was a devout man.'

Eliana turned away. 'He was a devout man, and then they came and he lost his faith ...' Her voice trailed away.

'Who came?'

'The Germans came, you know? Everywhere the Brownshirts with their clubs and their banners and their songs.'

She leaned forward, as if importing something that should remain only between herself and Stroud.

339

'They beat us. They took us away. They locked us up. They broke windows and burned shops. They kicked little children in the street and they pulled women by their hair and they laughed. They made us wear badges to say we were Jews. *Untermenschen.* Filth. They said we were not human. I was eight years old and they told me I was not a human being.'

She sat back again and sipped her tea. Stroud watched her eyes as she recalled horrors he couldn't even imagine.

'So we came here. My father, my mother, me and Joshua and Caleb. We escaped from Germany, but we couldn't run from what my father had done.' She shook her head slowly, as if she couldn't believe her own memories. 'Shimon Lindenauer. The merchant. The seller of souls.'

She looked back towards the window, and then to Stroud. 'Caleb told me to tell you. He said you were a good man, an honourable man. He said that you were not a liar like so many of the others who came.'

'The others?'

'The ones who were trying to find Joshua.'

'Do you have a picture of Joshua, Miss Lindenauer?'

'You cannot use that name. It is no longer our name, and it must never be spoken again, you understand?'

'Yes. I'm sorry,' Stroud said, taken aback by the force of her reaction. 'Miss Liebenfeld. Do you have a picture of Joshua?'

Eliana looked up at the wall to her right. 'There,' she said, pointing to one of the cheap landscapes.

Stroud frowned.

'Behind there,' she said, and waved at him as if directing him to bring it to her.

Stroud got up. He took the picture from the wall, expecting to see something behind it. There was nothing.

'On the back,' Eliana said, pointing to the picture in his hand.

Stroud turned the picture over. Covering the entire surface

of the backing were small black-and-white photos. He scanned them quickly, the faces blurring one into another, and then he stopped.

Raphael. Younger, his hair thick and dark, smiling, his arm around the shoulder of another young man who could only be Caleb. Stroud turned the picture towards Eliana and pointed to the snapshot.

Eliana smiled. Once again her eyes brimmed with tears.

'My boys,' she said. 'My little brothers. My Joshua and Caleb.'

Stroud stared at the photo. His heart was beating furiously, his pulse racing. He felt light-headed, found it difficult to focus, but there was no mistaking the evidence right there in front of him.

If what Eliana had told him was true – and based on the photograph he had no reason to disbelieve her – Vincent Raphael and Ernst Lügner had been raised together as Jewish refugees in England, bound by a common history, each of them haunted by something that Shimon Lindenauer had done. The merchant. The seller of souls.

It explained why Caleb had not said *our father*, for Shimon Lindenauer was not his father. Lindenauer was father to Joshua and Eliana, husband to Rivka, and had brought his family to England to escape the Nazis. But he never made it to Port St Mary, and there was no record of him alongside this family in the Public Records Office. What had happened to him, and more importantly, why was Joshua, the man who had been both Raphael and Hendrik Dekker, now paying for his sins?

Eliana had said that Shimon Lindenauer was *here in your newspapers*. He needed to know what she meant.

'Miss Liebenfeld. Is Joshua alive?'

She shook her head. 'Joshua is gone. Joshua is not here any more.'

'But is he alive, Miss Liebenfeld? Is he still alive?'

She didn't answer. She was gone, her mind wandering through layers of memory that she had spent decades trying to forget.

'And your father,' he said. 'What happened to your father?'

She smiled, but she was not smiling at Stroud. Perhaps she was remembering Joshua as he had been, perhaps a time when the ghost of their father had not haunted them. But why? What had he done, and why had he not stayed with them once they'd arrived?

'What happened to my father?' she echoed. 'They found him out and they tried him. A jury of his peers. The high council.' She looked at Stroud. 'They found him guilty, of course. He *was* guilty. Everyone knew what he had done.'

'And what happened, Eliana? What happened to your father?'

'They stoned him to death. They took him down into the darkness and they stoned him to death.'

What little communication then took place between Stroud and Eliana Liebenfeld was merely a repetition of what she had already divulged. He asked her once again if Joshua was alive, but she would not speak further. He asked her if he could take the picture of Joshua and Caleb. She responded as if his intent was to burn down the flat with both her and her mother inside.

By the time he left, it was past ten. The night was cold, the sky clear, and he retraced his steps through the endless maze of featureless hallways and narrow stairwells to the outside world.

Looking back at the sprawling geometric mass of concrete behind him, he wondered how many people's lives were marked by little more than loss and pain.

Vincent Raphael was Joshua Lindenauer. That was the name with which he had been born. June of 1933, somewhere in Germany, son of Shimon and Rivka, sister of Eliana, and soon to be joined by Caleb. All five of them had made it out of Germany and into England, but something – or someone – had followed Shimon, and he'd been punished for his sins. What sins? And stoned to death? Had she really meant that, or was it symbolic of something else?

According to Christopher Yardley, as soon as war broke out, immigration restrictions were implemented, visas were denied or cancelled, and thus very few Jews were subsequently permitted entry to the country. Eliana had spoken of the torments in Germany when she was eight years old. Her eighth birthday had been in September of 1937. Sometime after that, they had arrived in England as a family. Rivka and the children had been interned at Port St Mary in June 1940. That put Lindenauer's death somewhere between the two dates. If Stroud had understood Eliana correctly, her father had been killed here in England. Tried, found guilty and stoned to death.

Back at his hotel, the bar was still open, and the kitchen managed to rustle up a corned beef sandwich. He ate that and three bags of crisps, washed down with a pint of Guinness and a double Scotch, and then he sat in the corner of the bar, smoking one cigarette after another, doing his best to keep his eyes open and his mind focused on this new revelation.

His friend – a man he'd known, worked with, loved for more than fifteen years – was a Jewish refugee out of Nazi Germany. It beggared belief, but if his father had indeed perpetrated some unforgivable crime, then perhaps it went some way towards explaining why Raphael had spent his life on the run, living under assumed names, carrying false documents, never really divulging anything of his personal life. He'd spent his life escaping from a history that was not his own.

Stroud could only continue with the same blind faith he'd possessed before seeing Eliana. As far as he was concerned, Raphael was alive until proven otherwise. His mission to prove that he was dead had now become the opposite.

He went up to his room. He scanned through the notes he'd made, but his mind was already closing down.

He desperately needed some rest. He lay on the bed in his clothes. He wished he'd had another Scotch, and it was with that thought that his eyes closed and he feel into sleep, both deep and uninterrupted.

59

Stroud ate breakfast before he started work. His mind was calmer, a little less in disarray. From his room he called Nina's number; once again it rang out. He called the City desk directly. He was asked whether Miss Benson was one of the new temps.

'I have no idea,' Stroud said. 'I just know that she's one of the copy-editors. She has her wrist in a cast.'

'Oh yes, I know who you mean. Pretty girl. Dark hair. I remember her. I've seen her around, yes, but not today.'

'Okay, thanks. I'll try later.'

He had to make a decision to pursue the story of Shimon Lindenauer at the *Times* archives or go somewhere else. He decided to go elsewhere. The British Library Newspaper Archives in Colindale, north of central London. They stored both British and Irish newspapers dating back to the 1840s. Stroud had been there many times before. Sometimes it had been an utterly fruitless endeavour. The sheer volume of material – over six hundred thousand bound volumes and nearly four hundred thousand reels of microfilm – was daunting, and to embark upon the task of finding anything without a specific thread to follow was futile. But this time he had a specific thread – a name, a window of something like two and a half years between the Lindenauers' departure from Germany and Rivka arriving at Port St Mary with a different surname and three children in tow. Had Shimon Lindenauer been murdered, the likelihood of that appearing in one of the tabloids was high.

Stroud headed north-west out of Charing Cross. He didn't call ahead to make an appointment. He didn't want to be told that there was no one available, that his request couldn't be currently accommodated, that he would have to wait a week. He needed to keep going, to keep pushing on this thing. For the first time in almost a month, he truly believed that the reality of Vincent Raphael's life and death was just inches beyond his reach.

Luck – a commodity in which he rarely placed any trust – was on his side. He arrived just before ten, explained what he was after to a very helpful receptionist, and she directed him to the correct department.

Upon arriving, he was greeted by Reg Maynard, the departmental duty archivist. Maynard was middle-aged, a little overweight, sporting a three-piece suit despite the unrelenting heat of the summer. He listened to Stroud, at first nodding, then smiling.

'Oh, we do love a murder mystery,' he said. 'Let's see what we can find, eh?'

Stroud followed him along the endless rows of shelving to a central desk.

'Now, considering the potential unpleasantness of this, it really would have been grist to the mill for the tabloids,' Maynard said.

'I thought the same. The fact that he was a Jewish refugee, that he might actually have been stoned to death.'

'Yes, all very biblical, isn't it? So we'll go with the *Daily Mail*, shall we? The *Mail* is always good if you want to find something lurid and sensational.'

Maynard started to heave down the heavy ledgers.

'Let's begin with the first editions of 1937 and work through

346

from there,' he said. 'That'll be something close to nine hundred, perhaps a thousand newspapers all told.'

Having set down two of the large volumes on the desk, he opened a drawer and took out a pair of thin cotton gloves. 'Wear these, please,' he said. 'Not only do they help preserve the integrity of the paper, they also stop you getting thoroughly blackened fingers.'

Stroud took the gloves and put them on.

Maynard then showed him where to follow the sequence once he was done.

'Of course it goes without saying that returning them to the exact place you took them from would be most appreciated.'

'Absolutely,' Stroud said.

'Good. Then I shall leave you to it. Happy hunting.'

Maynard made his way back along the narrow corridor between the shelves, and Stroud got to work.

What began as a search for a killing in London soon became a history lesson.

Those final years that led to the invasion of Poland were populated with events that only now, in hindsight, really augured the horror to come. By June of 1938, German children were forbidden to talk to Jews. Any child found to be wearing clothes purchased from a Jewish outfitter was forced to stand in the corner of the classroom. The Star of David was daubed on Jewish shops.

At last Stroud found what he was looking for. The newspaper, dated Wednesday 10 January 1940, ran a story headlined *Highgate Murder Horror*.

The discovery of a body in a disused siding at Highgate Underground station has fuelled rumours of further conflicts between British nationals and refugees seeking settlement in

England. A Jewish man, identified as Shimon Lindenauer, was found dead on the evening of 9 January, having suffered a brutal attack on his person. According to police sources, Lindenauer appears to have been beaten to death, though further information from an uncorroborated source has revealed that the victim may have been subjected to stoning. Currently there are no suspects and no arrests have been made.

The alarming nature of the assault has highlighted tensions within the Jewish community in the capital. Spokesman for the Jewish Council of Great Britain, Rabbi Tuvia Zaslow, has categorically stated that rumours concerning the supposed High Court of Zion are entirely unsubstantiated. The self-styled court, composed of Jewish elders and community leaders, has long been a subject of interest; it apparently serves a judicial and punitive function for those refugees believed to have acted against the common good of the Jewish peoples in Germany and other European countries where fascist anti-Semitism has become prominent.

Stroud read the piece again. He sat back in his chair. The High Court of Zion. A judicial and punitive body that imposed sentences against those who had acted against the common good of the Jewish people.

He'd never heard of such a thing, and yet it didn't seem beyond the bounds of possibility. The Jews were being hounded out of their homes, their property and possessions 'consolidated', their lands stolen. They had been forced to flee their respective countries for sanctuary elsewhere. It was a time of war, a time of great danger, and no matter the promises a man made in peacetime, when faced with the ruin of his family, his loyalties would inevitably lie with his own blood. What had Lindenauer done? What had Eliana called him? *The merchant. The seller of souls.*

Stroud made all the notes he needed and returned the ledgers. He could spend a day trying to find out more about this alleged High Court of Zion, or he could go and ask someone who might know. If there was a Jewish Council of Great Britain in 1940, then it seemed very likely that such a thing would still exist.

He thanked Maynard for his time and care.

'And did you find what you were looking for?'

'I found *something*, Mr Maynard.'

Maynard smiled knowingly. 'God bless the *Daily Mail*, eh?'

60

The Jewish Council of Great Britain, disbanded in 1962, had been succeeded by the British branch of the International Jewish Congress, a global charitable organisation that upheld the Jewish faith and maintained records of all works and persons in its many and varied national offices. It was housed in a suitably impressive Georgian building close to High Holborn.

Stroud was greeted cordially. Yes, someone could see him, but it might be half an hour or so. He sat and waited in the elegantly furnished reception area. It was there, surrounded by opulent furnishings, oil paintings and ornaments, that he became aware of how ragged and scruffy he looked. He'd bought underwear and shirts on the go, worn them a couple of days and then thrown them away. His shoes were scuffed, he was unshaven, and his bag had long since passed the point of no return. He realised how he must have looked to those he'd asked for help. Most of the time people took you at face value, but if you were intent on being taken seriously, it really did make sense to present a somewhat professional appearance. Supposedly he was an experienced, well-respected photojournalist. From his dress, he looked more like someone in a Salvation Army soup queue.

'Mr Stroud?'

He looked up. An impeccably attired elderly man stood in a

doorway on the far right-hand side of the lobby. 'If you would care to follow me?'

Stroud got up, straightening his jacket as he did so. He felt awkward, out of place, and the first thing he said as he sat down was 'I have to apologise for my appearance. I have been travelling almost non-stop for a month. I'm working on an investigation, you see, and sometimes these things have a habit of taking over your life.'

'It's quite all right, Mr Stroud. Please don't concern yourself with that. I understand that you require some assistance with a certain matter.'

'Yes, if that's possible.'

'My name is Zerach Barsky. I am the registrar here. What is it you are trying to find out?'

Stroud set his bag down on the floor. From it he took his notepad. He opened it to a fresh page. 'Do you mind if I take notes?'

Barsky smiled and waved his hand.

'I am investigating a disappearance,' Stroud said, 'and this investigation has led me to an incident that occurred here in London in January 1940.'

'An incident?'

'It seems a man was murdered, his body left in a siding near Highgate Tube station.'

Barsky nodded, but his expression didn't change.

'There was a suspicion he might have been stoned to death.'

Barsky raised his eyebrows. 'Oh dear,' he said. 'How dreadful.'

'I want to ask you something,' Stroud said, 'but I want to assure you that I am not asking for research purposes. I am a journalist, yes, but more a photographer. I do not write journalistic pieces. I am not investigating this matter as such, but I need to know something about it as it may shed light on something else.'

'What is it you want to ask me, Mr Stroud?'

'Mr Barsky, I want to know if you have ever heard of the High Court of Zion.'

Barsky was close to inscrutable, but there was something in his eyes, a flash of recognition, a flash of hurt, perhaps. 'Yes,' he said. 'I know of this.'

'It existed?'

Barsky nodded. 'Yes, Mr Stroud, it existed.'

'And what was it?'

'As it sounds. It was a court.'

'And its purpose?'

'To review evidence put before it concerning the actions or omissions of those who came to Great Britain.'

'The Jewish refugees.'

'Yes, the Jewish refugees.'

'And—'

Barsky raised his hand. Stroud fell silent.

'Have you ever heard of a man called Chaim Weizmann, Mr Stroud?'

Stroud shook his head. 'No, I haven't.'

'He was the first president of Israel. He said that the world was divided into places where the Jews cannot live and places where they may not enter. That, I am sad to say, still rings true, even now.'

Barsky looked at his fingernails. He straightened the lower hem of his waistcoat. He looked back at Stroud.

'It is impossible to understand persecution until one has been persecuted, Mr Stroud. The Jews were banned from almost every aspect of society. Their homes and possessions were taken from them, and then their lives were taken, too. I don't believe there is a Jew alive who didn't lose a mother or father, a brother, sister, uncle, cousin, some blood relative. We suffered in a very terrible way, and throughout these past decades we have been fighting

352

to have that suffering acknowledged and recognised. Even now, we are working to retrieve those things that are rightfully ours. Land, homes, money, personal possessions. The stigma and discrimination levelled at us has coloured us for history, and even though the fascists have gone, the legacy with which they branded us still remains.'

Barsky looked at Stroud for a good fifteen seconds. Stroud met his gaze. He knew that Barsky was not looking at him, but at the potential consequences of what he was about to say.

'Throughout those years of exodus from Europe, there were those who sought to do all they could for others. And yes, there were those who sought to do all they could for themselves. Seemingly not content with ensuring that they retained their own wealth and position, they traded with the devil, Mr Stroud. They traded with the Nazis. They used the situation to give up their enemies, and in some cases they even gave up their friends. In return for their betrayal, they received the proceeds of companies, property, works of art, money. It has been said, and I have no reason to doubt it, that the High Court of Zion was created to address such matters. Those who committed such crimes ultimately found themselves hunted by the Nazis too. There was no amnesty, no matter what might have been done to help them. I suspect the man of whom you speak, this body that was found, was such a man.'

'Why do you say that?'

Barsky shrugged, almost as if what he was saying was obvious. 'Because of the stoning, Mr Stroud. Stoning was the punishment for those who had betrayed Jews to the Nazis for personal gain.'

'His name was Shimon Lindenauer. He came here from Germany with his wife, his son, his daughter, and a second boy that they had taken in.'

'The name means nothing to me.'

'His wife and children took a different name. They were interned on the Isle of Man.'

'As were so many.'

'Do you know if there would be any way to find out if what happened to him was actually as a result of this court?'

Barsky leaned forward. His expression was that of a patient man explaining something to someone struggling to understand the simplest of things.

'Mr Stroud, these are old wounds. Yes, there are people who would know what happened. I can imagine that some of the younger ones, perhaps even those who carried out such sentences, if that's what you could call them, are still alive. Maybe some of them stayed right here in London and made it their home after the war. London has no shortage of Jews, you know. But you would be asking them to admit to a crime, to admit to murder. You would be asking them, after many years of silence, to tell a journalist something that could see them exiled from their own communities. In times of war, the gravest crimes are forgiven. But once peace is gained, the forgiveness dries up.'

Barsky paused, looked down for a moment, and when he returned his gaze to Stroud, there was an intensity in his eyes that was unsettling.

'People were murdered. They themselves were murderers, yes, but that does not excuse the self-appointed executioner. To take the life of another is not for a man to decide. It is for the law, the judicial system, for God. Crimes were committed, crimes punishable by law, but as a Jew, as a survivor of the Holocaust, I would not divulge this information to you even if I knew. However, I will say this. If a Jewish man was found dead, a man who had been stoned to death, his body left in a public place for all to see, and his family disavowed him by taking a different name, then I can only imagine one such reason for this.'

'The High Court of Zion. The penalty for betraying his countrymen to the Nazis.'

Barsky smiled. He rose from the chair and extended his hand.

'It has been a pleasure to meet you, Mr Stroud, and I wish you success in your endeavour.'

61

By the time Stroud left, it was close to noon. He was hungry, and he stopped in a café for a bacon sandwich and a cup of coffee. Unsatisfied, he ordered a second sandwich, a second cup of coffee, and considered what course of action to take. Even now, and despite the meeting with Eliana Liebenfeld, he still didn't know where Raphael was, nor – factually – if he was alive.

He knew that he had become so engrossed in the details that he was failing to see the bigger picture. It had happened before. He needed to go through everything with someone. He needed to talk to Nina, not only because she would see this objectively, but because she had been involved in it from the beginning.

He left the café and called her from a phone box. No answer at her flat, no answer at her desk. He could take a route to the paper via her place. If she wasn't home, he could see if she'd shown up at work. He was not worried for her; he'd seen her only the morning before. True, he'd been somewhat taken aback by the enthusiasm of her greeting. It was almost as if she hadn't expected to see him again. Perhaps that was nothing but his own misinterpretation, influenced by fatigue, an element of paranoia, the underlying and relentless sense of frustration he was experiencing. That was why he needed to talk, if only to put everything out there in words. Perhaps she wouldn't have any better ideas than him, but at least it might serve to give him a little objectivity.

The block where she lived was much the same as the one they'd been to in Leiden. Two flats above, two below. He got into the foyer and buzzed her. No response. He buzzed another flat and asked whether they'd seen Miss Benson.

'Last saw her a week or so ago, mate,' the occupant said. 'Doesn't seem to be home a lot. But then the girl before her wasn't home a great deal either.'

'The girl before?'

'Sure. I don't know what the set-up is, maybe a flat-sharing thing. The girl before the current one was only here about three months, and then she moved on. Thought they might be air stewardesses or theatre people or something. You know, some kind of seasonal thing.'

'Okay. Much appreciated.'

Stroud went on to the paper. He checked if Haig was in. He wasn't. He took the stairs to the third floor. The City desk was at the far end of the floor. He made his way through a maze of corridors, desks hemmed in by partitions, stacks of newspapers and books, telephone directories, atlases, all manner of reference material that had accumulated around this hive of busy working journalists. The clatter of typewriters, the hubbub of thirty or forty simultaneous telephone conversations, snippets of which he caught as he passed.

'But did he actually say those words? That's what I need to know, Frank.'

'…and she came back later, didn't even offer an explanation as to where she'd been.'

'Not a snowball's chance in hell, Tom. You're dreaming, my friend.'

He knew that he missed it. The rush, the energy of chasing something, the way a story could sometimes burrow right under your skin; an itch that couldn't be scratched by anything other than the truth.

He felt it now. Raphael. Dekker. Joshua Lindenauer. Paying for the sins of the father. A man stoned to death by order of the High Court of Zion in January 1940. The shame that Rivka must have endured; the subsequent internment, the fact that her family name had to be consigned to an ignominious history.

Stroud believed it, but he still wanted Raphael to tell him it was true. And he wanted Raphael to tell him what he'd been doing to make amends. Why the cover, why the aliases, why the need to 'die'? What was it that he'd really been doing as he travelled back and forth across the world's conflict zones? Stroud now felt sure that Raphael was a spy, a political agent of some sort, a courier perhaps. He was employed in some hidden activity that had nothing to do with the journalistic front. He had spent his working life running towards what everyone else was running away from. He wanted to get closer, get involved, see it from within. And once he'd found out what he wanted, to whom did he report? Did Haig know? Had Haig known all along? Someone knew, that was for sure, and it sure as hell wasn't Stroud.

It was not so much a sense of betrayal that Stroud felt as a sense of exclusion. There was a cadre of individuals with a common language that only the initiated could understand. Raphael had belonged. Based on his personal experience, he had been right there in the middle of it. But Stroud had not. For all their closeness, their camaraderie, their shared experiences, Raphael had determined that Stroud didn't belong. That was the thing that stuck in Stroud's craw, and that was what he hoped he would one day understand.

City desk manager Val Whitman – indomitable, gruff, chain-smoking matriarch – smiled at Stroud.

'Oh my, oh my,' she said. 'Look what the cat dragged in. I thought you'd be dead by now.'

Stroud laughed. 'Always good to know folk are thinking of me.'

'So where the hell have you been?'

'Here, there, everywhere. I was in Amsterdam for a while, then Istanbul, back to the Netherlands, Germany, France.'

'Chasing news or chasing girls?'

'Who the hell do you think I am?' Stroud said.

'A thorn in the side. You forget too easily that you and Raphael and our mutual boss, the mighty Marcus Haig, were all scruffy good-for-nothings when I was on Foreign.'

Stroud sat down. 'That was a long time ago.'

'It was indeed. A dreadful catalogue of disasters that I wouldn't have missed for the world.' She lit a cigarette and sat back in her chair. 'So, my dear Stroud, what can I do for you?'

'I'm looking for Nina.'

'Give me a clue, sunshine. Nina who?'

'Nina. Copy-editor Nina. Nina Benson.'

Val raised her eyebrows, frowned. 'See,' she said. 'This face is registering nothing. I don't have a copy-editor called Nina Benson. You sure she's City?'

'She said she was. City, covered crime. Nina Benson. B-E-N-S-O-N.'

'She new?'

Stroud shrugged. 'I don't know. I thought she'd been here a while.'

'Well if she'd been here for more than two weeks, I'd definitely know who she was. You go off and check with Accounting, and I'll go on doing what I'm paid for. Stop by in another three or four years, okay?'

'You don't change, do you?'

Val frowned, utterly mystified. 'What's to change? How can you improve on this?'

Stroud headed back downstairs to Accounting on the second.

'Tracking down an employee,' he told one of the payroll clerks. 'I thought she was on City, but maybe I got it wrong or she moved department or something.'

'Her name?'

'Nina Benson. B-E-N-S-O-N.'

The clerk went to a long bank of filing drawers. Stroud waited.

'I have a Martin Benson at the print works. No Nina. N-I-N-A, right?'

'Guess so. Don't know of any other way to spell it.'

The clerk checked again. 'Nope. No Nina Benson on our payroll.'

'You're absolutely sure?'

Her expression said: *Really? You think I don't know how to read?*

'Sorry. Just surprised. There's no other record, no other files, maybe for temps, part-timers, something like that?'

'If someone has ever been paid by us, even if they're now in jail or dead, they're recorded here. This is for the entire group, every company, every department, every office, every individual. Whoever you're asking for has never been paid by *The Times*.'

Stroud didn't question it. It had to be an administrative error. Marcus would know what had happened.

'While I'm here, I'm running expenses and guess I need to turn in some receipts. Plane tickets, hotels, stuff like that.'

'Then you'll need Expenses, not Payroll. Three doors down.' The clerk pointed along the corridor to the left.

'Appreciated.'

In Expenses, he asked who took care of receipts. He was directed to a young woman called Felicity.

'So, what's this all about?' she asked.

'Flights, hotel bills, general running costs on a story I'm working on for Marcus.'

'Marcus?'

'Marcus Haig. Foreign department.'

'What's your reference number?'

Stroud shrugged.

'If you've got an expense tab, then you'll have a reference number.'

'Not a clue,' Stroud said.

'Okay. Can you ask him?'

'He's not in, as far as I understand.'

'Have you received any petty cash?'

'Yes. I had a couple of hundred about a month ago, and then two grand.'

Felicity seemed taken aback. 'Two grand? In cash?'

'I've been to Istanbul, Berlin, Paris ... living the high life, you know?'

'Well, even a tenner goes in the petty cash log, and that'll have to have your reference number with it.'

She wheeled her chair back and hauled down a heavy ledger. 'S-T-R-O-U-D.'

'Yes,' Stroud said, already beginning to feel a sense of unease.

Felicity ran down columns, went back to the start of July and ran through them again. Finally she looked up, and Stroud knew even before she spoke what she was going to say.

'Nothing, right?'

She shook her head. 'Not under your name, and nothing going out of Foreign that tallies with the kind of sums you're talking about.'

He got up from his chair. He was already asking himself questions, the answers to which he had some inkling of, and he didn't feel good.

He thanked Felicity for her help, then he left the room and headed upstairs.

He had to find Haig. For some reason – unknown, more than likely self-serving – Haig had lied to him. Of that there appeared to be no doubt. He had lied about Raphael, lied about Nina, lied about what he was sending Stroud to do.

Whatever this game was, it had put Stroud's life in danger. He felt sick and angry. He felt cheated and betrayed. And if Nina had been in on it all along, there was nothing that either of them could say that would temper his fury.

He took the stairs at a run.

62

Carole was helpful in the most unhelpful way.

'He's not here. He was in yesterday morning, as you know, but after you left he was gone. He called to say he'd be working from home.'

'You remember Nina, right?'

'Nina Benson.'

'Yes,' Stroud said. 'Nina Benson.'

'What about her?'

'She told me she worked on City. I went down and talked to Val, and Val has never heard of her.'

Carole blanched.

'Carole, what is going on?'

'As far as I understood it, she came up from City.'

Stroud held her gaze. Carole looked both awkward and defiant.

'There are certain employer–employee confidences, you know. Marcus is my boss, Stroud, as you're well aware.'

Stroud sighed deeply. He sat back in his chair and shook his head resignedly.

'Do you know what Marcus asked me to do?' he asked.

'Yes, of course.'

'You remember Vincent, don't you?'

'I don't think he was someone you could easily forget.'

'He's not dead, Carole. Not only is he not dead, his name isn't Vincent Raphael.'

Carole laughed nervously. 'What are you talking about?'

'After Vincent Raphael died – supposedly died – he showed up in the Netherlands as Hendrik Dekker.'

Carole put her hand to her mouth.

'What?' Stroud asked.

She shook her head, her eyes wide. She was caught in something and she saw no easy way out.

'What about Hendrik Dekker, Carole?'

'Nothing,' she said, but she said it far too quickly.

Stroud leaned forward. 'I need a friend here, Carole. You and I have known one another a long time. We knew each other ten years before you become Marcus's secretary. I need some help. I need to know what the fuck is going on here.'

'I don't know what's going on.'

'Listen to me, Carole. I am really fucking angry right now. I need someone to start telling me the fucking truth. You've heard that name before, haven't you? You've heard the name Hendrik Dekker.'

Carole hesitated, then nodded.

'So tell me, how the hell do you know that name?'

'I can't,' she said. 'Stroud, I can't.'

Stroud gritted his teeth. He could feel his knuckles whitening. 'I am not fucking around, Carole. Tell me how the fuck you know that name. '

'From the phone calls,' Carole blurted.

'Phone calls? What phone calls?'

'When he called here and spoke to Marcus.'

Stroud's mind seemed to collapse inwards. He opened his mouth to speak, but there was silence. He focused on Carole's face. He tried to orientate himself, tried to find some small anchor to hold onto that would prevent him spinning completely out of control.

'Hendrik Dekker called here? He called here and spoke to Marcus.'

'Y-yes. Yes, he did. That was what he said his name was, anyway. Marcus always closed the door. Sometimes he seemed to do nothing but shout.'

'Did you hear anything of what was discussed?'

'No. No, I didn't. I mean, I didn't listen in. I wouldn't do that.'

'Anything at all, Carole? I really need you to think.'

'I heard your name.'

'When Marcus was on the phone to this person, Marcus used my name?'

'Yes, yes. That's what I heard. I heard them talking about you, okay? Christ almighty, what do you want from me? This is none of my business. I shouldn't have said anything.'

'And what about Nina?'

'What about her?'

'Who is she, Carole? Who the fuck is Nina Benson?'

'Really, there's no need to talk to me like—'

Stroud slammed the flat of his hand on the desk. The sound was like a gunshot. Carole jumped, and then she glared at Stroud, her eyes brimming with tears.

'Who the fuck is Nina Benson?'

'Stop it! Stop it, for God's sake! Who the hell do you think you are? You can't just come in here and ask personal and private questions—'

Stroud got up. He towered over her, intimidating her, intending to do so, and he didn't feel the slightest degree of concern for what she might be experiencing.

'Carole, tell me who the fuck she is, or so help me God—'

'She's government, okay? She works for the government! That's all I know.'

'Marcus told you this?'

'No, he didn't. He just asked for someone who could help you and I was told to send Nina Benson.'

'Told by whom?'

'I don't know names, Stroud. I don't ask. I sit here all day. I take phone calls, I make phone calls. I am asked to get certain people in certain offices, and there is more than one phone line, and sometimes I am asked to make phone calls on a different line and I know that it goes somewhere that has nothing to do with the newspaper.'

'Where does it go? Whitehall? The Foreign Office?'

'I'm not saying anything.'

'Carole—'

'No, Stroud! No! Stop threatening me! That's enough now. That is really and truly enough. I am not saying another word. If you want to know what's going on, then you are going to have to ask Marcus yourself. I am not going to violate any agreements I have made.'

'Agreements to keep your mouth shut.'

'I think you could say that.'

'Official agreements?'

Carole stared back at him.

'What the hell? You're bound by the Official Secrets Act?'

She blinked. Just once. Had Stroud not been looking directly at her, he would never have noticed it.

'Oh my God,' he said. 'Marcus is a spook, isn't he? Raphael too. They're damned spies. And Nina Benson was assigned to keep an eye on me. They're after Raphael, aren't they?'

He sat down once more. Whatever threads of faith he might still have possessed in his friendships with Marcus Haig and Vincent Raphael had been cut away.

Carole retrieved a tissue from her bag and dabbed the tears from her cheeks.

'I'm sorry, Carole. I am truly sorry. I really didn't mean to upset you.'

She shook her head. 'I've said too much. That's it, you see? I've said things that I should never have said, and now I'll lose my job.'

'I don't think—'

'This is very serious,' she said. 'It's really very serious. This is not just the newspaper. This is government business. There are things that stay behind closed doors, and for very good reason.'

Stroud looked at her. She was visibly shaken; terrified, in fact.

He got up. He hesitated in the doorway, looked back at Carole. 'There's very little I hate more than people who say they're one thing when they're something else. When you learn that your oldest friends are not your friends at all ...'

He didn't finish the sentence. He just closed his eyes for a moment, shook his head, and left.

Stroud caught a two thirty out of St. Pancreas and arrived in St Albans a little before three. A taxi took him to the very outskirts of the town, and then he walked across two fields and down a narrow country lane to the perimeter of Haig's property. He stood for a moment at the lower gate, looking up towards the house where one of his oldest friends lived with his wife and children. Cathy. Justin. Emily. Here was the life that Marcus had created for himself. The renovated farmhouse, the adjoining barn, the security and stability and comfort of it all. But it was a lie, a facade, a pretence.

Did Cathy know? Did Marcus's own wife know who her husband was, who he worked for? Who the hell *did* he work for? MI6? It would make sense, after all. What better cover for a constantly travelling, constantly vigilant spook than to carry

press ID and a camera? Access all areas. An immediately cred-
ible and logical explanation for questions, invasion of privacy,
attempting to find people, to find information, to find things
that no one else was looking for. And Raphael, too. The two
of them in it together. Best friends in the world, all three of
them on equal terms, and yet in reality, Stroud had never even
belonged.

He didn't judge himself harshly for not having seen through
it. These people – whoever *these people* were – were trained to live
a life of lies, a life that demanded of them an appearance that
belied the truth. He didn't want to consider it. The ramifications were staggering. In one profound and almost unbelievable
moment – a simple change of expression, the way Carole didn't
answer a question – his perception of the last decade and a half
had been turned on its head. Sharpeville, the Congo, Cuba,
Cyprus, Biafra, Palestine – every place they'd been together,
Haig and Raphael in on the secret, Stroud tagging along, the
backward cousin, the stupid one, the one who always needed the
punchline explained.

He went through the gate and started up towards the house.
Cathy's car was in the drive, as was Marcus's. They were both
home, the kids too no doubt, and Stroud was going to walk
in there and challenge him. He didn't care. He was furious,
enraged. He had been lied to for a decade and a half, and he
was not going to be lied to any more. He wanted answers, real
answers to his questions, and if he didn't get them ... well, if he
didn't get them, he didn't know what he was going to do, but it
wouldn't be pleasant.

Cathy appeared at the French windows to the side of the
house and spotted him. She frowned, then smiled, and then she
waved to him.

Stroud opened the door and went inside.

'Stroud,' she said. She gave him a hug, kissed his cheek. 'What are you doing here?'

'I came to see Marcus. He's in, right?'

'Yes, he's in the study. He's been on the phone since yesterday lunchtime. I don't know what's going on. I had to tell him to stop barking at the kids. He came to bed at three this morning. I told him he works too hard, that he's going to wind up with a heart attack, but does he listen?'

Stroud wanted to get away from her. He couldn't face her, because he knew that if he stayed and listened, he would not be able to hold himself back from telling her the truth. *Do you know who your husband works for, Cathy? I mean really. Do you know what he really does, because I sure as hell don't. Do you know, or are you as clueless as me? Oh, and you remember Raphael, don't you? Of course you do. I bet you lost count of the number of times he got drunk and hit on you even when he knew you were going to marry Marcus. That's a laugh, isn't it? Well, here's the scoop, Cathy. He's not Vincent Raphael at all. He's a Jewish refugee with a dead father . . . a father who was stoned to death during the war because he was a Nazi fucking collaborator. How's that for a kicker, eh?*

He didn't say any of those things. Cathy was not in the firing line. He felt sure she was as much in the dark as he was.

'It's good to see you, Cathy. Kids okay, apart from their mean daddy?'

Cathy smiled, took his hand. 'They're fine, Stroud, just fine. However, I have to say that you don't look so good. You look like you really need a break. Are you okay?'

'I just need to see Marcus,' Stroud replied. 'It's been a tough case. We're working on it together. That's probably what he's been on the phone about.'

'Okay. Well, you know where to go. Come and talk to me after you're done. Catch me up on all that's new, okay?'

'Sure, Cathy, sure,' he replied, knowing that the likelihood of such a thing was pretty slim.

He stepped past her and walked through the kitchen to the study at the back of the house. He could hear Marcus's voice inside. He didn't knock. He just went right on in there, stepped up to the desk and put his hand on the phone cradle.

Haig looked up, the disconnected receiver in his hand.

'What the fuck, Stroud?'

'Put the phone down, Marcus.'

'What the hell are you talking about? What are you doing? I was in the middle of goddamned important fucking phone call.'

Stroud leaned forward and snatched the receiver from Haig's hand. He proceeded to smash it into the base unit. The base unit fell off the desk. Stroud let the receiver go.

Haig stood up.

'Sit down, Marcus. Sit the fuck down and tell me what the fuck is going on.'

'Are you insane, Stroud? What the hell are you talking about?

'You know exactly what I'm talking about. Vincent Raphael, Hendrik Dekker, Shimon Lindenauer, the Liebenfeld family, the Jews and the fucking Nazis and the High Court of fucking Zion, Marcus. What the fuck were you thinking? You sent me on a wild fucking goose chase across half of Europe. I got arrested, beaten up, locked in a fucking hotel, got my passport taken off me and burned, or so I fucking thought, and all the while this was some sort of stupid fucking game! And what about Nina, eh? Nina fucking Benson, the bright little copyeditor girl from the City desk. Oh, she can give you a hand, Stroud. She's really not doing very much right now and she can go through some registration cards with you. You fucking lying bastard son-of-a-fucking-bitch, Marcus. Now tell me what the living fuck is going on, or I'm going to take that phone and ram it down your lying fucking throat.'

Haig just stood there, unmoved and unmoving.

'Speak, Marcus, or I swear I will put you through the fucking window.'

'My wife and children are in the house, Stroud.'

'I don't give a single solitary fuck if Jesus Christ, Idi fucking Amin and the President of the United fucking States are in your house. Tell me. Tell me! Tell me right the fuck now!'

The door opened behind Haig. Cathy stood there, wide-eyed and white-faced.

'Cathy, I need to speak to Stroud,' Haig said.

'I heard shouting,' she said. 'What's happening? What are you boys arguing about?'

'Cathy,' Haig repeated, a harshness in his tone, a fierceness in his eyes. 'I need to talk to Stroud. Please leave us be.'

'Enough swearing, okay? You can keep your bloody voices down as well. If you upset the children...'

Haig looked over Stroud's shoulder. 'Cathy. Really. Will you please just shut the fucking door!'

Cathy glared at her husband, and then slammed the door hard.

'Bastard,' Stroud heard her say as she stormed back towards the kitchen.

'Now I've upset my wife,' Haig said. He sat down heavily, reached for a pack of cigarettes in his desk and lit one.

'Are you going to sit down too, or are you going to stand there and keep on shouting at me?'

Stroud didn't move.

'Will you just sit down, for Christ's sake?'

Stroud did so.

'Do you want a drink?' Haig asked. He got up and walked to the cabinet near the wall. 'I don't know about you, but I could bloody well use one.'

Stroud didn't reply. Haig brought two glasses and a bottle of

Scotch. He poured an inch or so into each, slid a glass towards Stroud and took his seat again.

'So what are we doing here?' he asked.

'I don't know what you're doing, Marcus, but I'm here to find out the truth.'

'Truth is a relative thing, Stroud.'

'Fuck off, Marcus. I don't want any bullshit. Are you MI6?'

Haig looked at him. A light had gone on somewhere.

'Of a kind,' he said.

'What does that mean?'

'MI6 is a beast with many faces.'

'Okay, if we're going to be pedantic, let me simplify it. Are you or are you not employed by some division or department that concerns British overseas intelligence?'

'I am, yes.'

'Since when?'

Haig smiled. He didn't seem perturbed. Stroud's outburst was perhaps anticipated, or Haig had been in this very situation before and knew precisely how to deal with it.

'Since whenever.'

'Not whenever, Marcus. Since when exactly?'

'Since Cambridge.'

'Before you knew me?'

'A year or two, I would think.'

'Raphael too?'

Haig laughed. 'Oh no. Raphael was a different thing altogether. Raphael started into this game long before I did.'

'Because of his father?'

'I knew you were the one. You have always been a great deal brighter than you give yourself credit for, you know that? I knew you'd figure it all out somehow.'

'He was MI6 too?'

'Like I said, MI6 isn't—'

'Okay, he was a fucking spy. A spy like you.'

'I don't think of myself as a spy, Stroud. I think of myself as a loyal subject of Her Majesty's government, determined to do what is needed to ensure the security of the state and her foreign interests.'

'You can lose the patriotic fucking epithets,' Stroud said. 'I want to know why you hired me, at your own expense as far as I can gather, to prove that Raphael was dead when you knew all along that he was alive.'

'Because I couldn't look for him myself.'

'But you have people. You must have endless fucking people, endless resources.'

'Not the kind of people I could use.'

'What does that even mean? If you wanted him found, why not just find him?'

'Because he didn't want to be found.'

'What, he dropped off your grid? He went rogue?'

'In simple terms, yes. Raphael went rogue.'

'After what? Jordan?'

Haig didn't reply.

'Was that what faking his own death was all about?'

'I can't tell you, Stroud.'

'Yes you can, and you fucking better.'

'Or what? If I don't tell you, what are you going to do? Kill me?'

Stroud looked at him. There was real defiance in his expression.

'So, you needed to find Raphael, and you couldn't use your own people. That's what we're saying, right?'

Haig stayed silent.

'So if you can't use your own people, there must be a very good reason why. If you went after Raphael officially, something else would come out. Is that what's going on here? Am I maybe getting warm, Marcus? I mean, hell, let's just set aside Istanbul and Berlin, okay? Let's forget about Ernst fucking Lügner and Caleb and Jean-Michel Fournier, and me getting locked up and drugged and kicked senseless. Let's just put that over on one side for a moment and ask ourselves a few basic questions.'

No response.

'Okay, Marcus?'

Haig nodded. 'As you wish.'

'Did Raphael betray someone? Did he do something that he shouldn't have done? Or does he know something about you?'

The eyes. Haig blinked. Again, almost unnoticeable, but Stroud saw it and caught it like bait on a line.

'He knew something about you, didn't he? Is that what this is all about? Are you the fucking traitor here? What are you, a double agent? A communist? I've heard quite a lot of those good old boys out of Cambridge had their communist sensibilities. I've been hearing a great deal about Black September and the Munich Olympics and Baader–Meinhof and the like. Are you in league with the devil, Marcus? Are you feeding information to someone who really shouldn't be getting it?'

'You're talking about something you can't even begin to comprehend,' Haig said. He drained his glass, reached for the bottle and poured another good double.

'Try me, Marcus. Apparently we've been friends for a long time. I always thought we pretty much saw eye to eye on most things. Try me out with your story. Who knows, I might even buy it.'

Haig laughed dismissively and drank his Scotch.

Stroud grabbed his own glass and hurled it at the bookshelf behind Haig's head. It shattered, fragments of lead crystal scattering across the carpet and ricocheting off the window.

Haig, stunned, started up out of his chair. Stroud got up and pushed him back into it. Stroud was taller, a little heavier, and for a split second there was a flash of fear in Haig's eyes.

'Don't look at me like that, Marcus. Don't treat me like a fool. You owe me more than that. Fifteen years I've been lied to, fifteen fucking years I've trusted you, relied on you, considered you a friend, and now you're talking to me like I'm a child who can't even tie his own shoelaces.'

Haig looked up. He was no longer surprised, no longer anxious. The implacable mien had returned and he waited patiently for Stroud to sit down again.

'Raphael was a liability,' he said. 'Yes, he is Joshua Lindenauer. Yes, he was a refugee. Yes, his father delivered wealthy Jews into the hands of the Nazis, and continued to be richly rewarded for his betrayals until he became just another Jew himself. As was so very predictable. As long as you served a purpose, you stayed alive; as soon as that purpose was no longer being fulfilled, you were gone. And so they came here, the whole family. They managed to get out of Germany by the skin of their teeth. It took a lot of money, of course, but Shimon Lindenauer had no shortage of money. They brought the other boy with them. Caleb. That was the name given to him by his new family. And then the Jews in London figured out who the father was. He was fucked before he even got off the boat. They hunted him down. They tried him. They held an actual trial, and they sentenced him to death. They stoned the greedy son-of-a-bitch to death and left him there by the side of a railway track.'

'I know this, Marcus. Right now you're not telling me anything I haven't already figured out.'

'What you don't know is that Raphael was recruited by Mossad.'

'Mossad?'

'He's a fucking Jew, Stroud. He speaks Hebrew, German, English, now Dutch and French and Lord only knows what

375

else. The names you've heard are not even half the names he's used.'

'But British military intelligence and Mossad are not opposed.'

'There are no enemies, Stroud. There are no allies. There are fair-weather friends. And when the weather turns, everyone hides out in their own back yard and looks over the fence with binoculars.'

'Raphael was a Mossad agent.'

'No, he wasn't. Or at least that was what was believed. He said he turned them down. He came back here and debriefed. He gave up some useful information he'd picked up along the way.'

'So he wasn't a double agent for Mossad?'

'We don't know.'

'We?'

Haig waved his hand. The gesture said that such a question was never going to be answered.

'So why send me on this fool's errand? Why pay me out of your own pocket to find someone you could very easily have found yourself?'

'Because I couldn't be seen to be looking,' Haig said. 'I knew you would find him. I knew that if you were face to face with him he would not kill you. You have too much history, and Raphael still possesses some romantic notion that loyalty and personal history count for something. I knew you could go on looking for as long as it took, and your life would not be in danger from Raphael.'

'Which means that it was in danger from someone else?'

Haig smiled. 'You're in danger every time you leave the house, cross the street, get on the Tube.'

Stroud didn't challenge the response, nor pursue the question. The answer didn't need to be spoken to be known.

'Ernst Lügner's real name is Caleb Liebenfeld,' Stroud said.

376

'It is. At least that's the name he was given. I don't think he knows what his original family name was.'

'And he was – *is* – Raphael's adoptive brother, or as near as can be.'

'I guess so, yes.'

'He seemed very intent on making sure I had no harmful intention towards Raphael.'

'As I said, there are those who consider that personal history and individual loyalty play some part in this game.'

'Is that what it is to you, Marcus? A game?'

'There is no other way to look at it, unless you want to lose your mind completely.'

Stroud was quiet. Something didn't make sense. What Haig was saying, divisiveness and inbuilt caution aside, didn't ring true.

'Raphael and Caleb are on the same side. You and Raphael are on the same side. You need to find Raphael.'

'Correct.'

'However, Caleb is very intent on making sure that I don't get to Raphael until he understands my motive. Yet he knows that I was sent to look for Raphael by you. And yet you're all supposed to be on the same team.'

Haig didn't challenge what Stroud was saying, nor did he make any attempt to clarify it.

'And if I was to take a punt on who might have Raphael's best interests at heart, you or Caleb, I think I would go for Caleb.'

Again, nothing from Haig.

'Which suggests that you do not have Raphael's best interests at heart.'

A sense of unease invaded Stroud's stomach. He felt on edge, yet did his best to appear calm and untroubled.

'And if you are looking for him off the books, so to speak, and he seems to want to remain hidden, then it must be because you mean him harm. Am I on track, Marcus? Is this going in the right direction? Did you send me to find Raphael because you need to get rid of him, not because he's an agent for some other national agency, but because he knows something about you? Did you actually think he was dead? Did you really believe that he'd died in Jordan, and whatever he knew about you was blown to kingdom come along with him? But then he showed up again, a photograph, a rumour, something that someone said that made you feel he was still out there?'

There was no indication that Stroud was even following the right thread. Haig could be saying nothing merely because nothing needed to be said. What could Stroud prove? And even if he was on the nail, who could he tell who would believe him?

'Are you done with your fantastic theory, Stroud?' Haig eventually asked.

'Who is Nina Benson? She doesn't work for the paper, and never has. She's not at City, not on the payroll—'

'Do you want the money, Stroud? Because if you want the money, you still have to find Raphael for me. That was the deal.'

'The deal, as you call it, Marcus, was for me to prove that he was dead.'

'And is he dead?'

'No, Marcus, he's not dead, and you know it. Christ, you've even spoken to him on the phone. Of course, at the time he was going by the name of Hendrik Dekker, but you still fucking spoke to him, didn't you?'

Haig smiled. 'And the only way you could know that is if Carole or Nina Benson told you.'

'Where is she, Marcus? Where is Nina?'

'Right now? I have no idea.'

'I'm not buying that for a second. Where the hell is she?'

Haig got up from the desk and walked to the window. He looked out across the expanse of the garden towards the trees down by the lane. When he turned back to face Stroud, he had his hands in his pockets. He seemed at ease, even relaxed, and when he spoke, there was none of the earlier tension or threat in his voice.

'Sometimes a thing is done because it was the best thing to do at the time,' he said. 'Only in hindsight, and with all the benefits of further information, do you see that perhaps it could have been different. Men have been at war as long as there have been men. The things we are dealing with here are the consequences of decisions made a long, long time ago. We do not have the benefit of understanding why those decisions were made, of course. We only see what is here in front of us, in this exact, precise moment, and we evaluate the information we have and take a course of action.'

'Marcus, if this is some kind of justification for some other bullshit thing that's going on, I really don't want to—'

'Raphael isn't dead, Stroud. Yes, I knew that all along. I still need you to help me find him. We need to bring him in. We need to find out what he knows. We need to understand some of the things that have been happening in Europe, in the Middle East, and right now it seems he is the only man who can help us.'

For a moment, Stroud's attention was distracted by the sound of voices elsewhere in the house.

Haig, his mind focused on what he was saying, seemed not to notice it.

Stroud heard Cathy. He was sure of it.

'And so I need you to make good on our deal. You need the money, and I need Raphael, you see? It's not complicated. It's a very simple premise. You keep on looking until you find him, and then you tell me—'

Now the voices were very audible. Haig stopped talking.

'For Christ's sake,' he said, and he started towards the study door even as it opened.

Cathy appeared.

'Cathy, what did I say? What did I ask you? Please, we're trying to have a—'

'There are people here, Marcus.'

'People? What people? What are you talking about?'

'They say they're from Special Branch. Someone called Armitage. He says he has a warrant for your arrest.'

Haig visibly paled. 'What is this?' he said. He pushed past Stroud towards the doorway, where his exit was suddenly blocked by a tall and imposing figure.

Haig turned back to Stroud. 'You brought people here? You fucking brought people here?'

'Marcus Haig?' the man said, stepping into the room.

'Who the fuck are you?'

'My name is Armitage. I am with Special Branch.'

'What do you want? What the hell are you doing in my house?'

'Please answer the question, sir. Are you Marcus Anthony Haig?'

'You know I am. Now tell me what the hell you're doing in my fucking house.'

'Marcus Anthony Haig, you are under arrest. You do not have to say anything, but it may harm your defence—'

'What the fuck is this?' Haig said.

Stroud looked at Cathy. Cathy, white as a ghost, was stunned. Tears filled her eyes. She kept opening her mouth as if to speak, but no words were forthcoming.

'You do not have to say anything, sir, but it may harm your defence if you do not mention when questioned something which you later rely on—'

Haig moved rapidly, far more rapidly than either Stroud or

Armitage could have anticipated. He ducked left towards the window, then back to the right, pushing past both Stroud and Armitage and darting through the office doorway.

'Marcus!' Cathy shouted after him, but Haig was already in the kitchen. Faced with a second officer, he sidestepped him, grabbed a set of car keys from the counter and charged out of the back door.

Armitage followed moments later, Stroud behind him, but by the time they reached the doorway, Haig was halfway across the lawn.

'Mr Haig!' Armitage shouted after him.

Cathy appeared behind Stroud. 'Marcus! Marcus!' she shouted, but Haig was already near the front drive.

Stroud took off across the grass, Armitage alongside him. It was only as Haig reached his car that another uniformed officer appeared from the side of the building and cut him off.

Haig backed up, charged once again. The uniformed officer turned sideways, lowered his shoulder, but Haig's speed and impetus were too great. The man careened off the side of the vehicle and Haig managed to wrench open the door.

He was inside the car by the time Armitage and Stroud arrived.

'Get out of the car!' Armitage commanded.

Haig attempted to close the door, at the same time trying desperately to get the key in the ignition.

Armitage took the force of the door against his upper arm as Stroud ran around to the passenger side. He tried to reach in to grab hold of Haig, but Haig lashed back at him. The side of his fist caught Stroud's jawline. Stroud fell back, but gathered himself rapidly.

Haig scrabbled to get the glove compartment open. Stroud's first thought was that he was going for a gun.

'Marcus, for Christ's sake, stop!'

Haig lashed out again as Stroud got into the passenger seat. He leaned his entire weight sideways, pinning Haig's arms, and from the other side, Armitage and the policeman managed to drag Haig bodily out of the car.

Haig, on his knees at first, fell sideways.

Cathy reached the car. 'Marcus! What's going on, Marcus! Tell me what's happening.'

Armitage held him down. The policeman produced handcuffs and applied them; all the while, Haig was struggling, kicking out.

'Get the fuck off me!' he screamed. 'Cathy, call David! Tell him a couple of ignorant fucking goons are trying to arrest me!'

'Mr Haig. Enough, sir,' the policeman said. 'Please do not resist.'

'You are under arrest, Mr Haig,' Armitage repeated. 'You do not have to say anything, but it may harm your defence if you do not mention when questioned something which you later rely on in court. Anything you say may be given in evidence.'

Haig, still protesting, was manhandled off the ground. Armitage instructed the officer to take him to the car.

Cathy was sobbing hysterically, repeatedly asking her husband what was going on. Marcus said nothing. He walked with his head down, seemingly oblivious to his wife's upset and confusion.

Armitage waved over a policewoman, told her to take Cathy to the house.

'We should go back to the study,' he said to Stroud, and with that he turned and started walking.

Stroud followed him, made eye contact with Haig one last time as Haig got into the car. He glared at Stroud defiantly.

Armitage entered the kitchen through the back door. Stroud

followed him. As they turned left and started towards the study, another figure appeared at the end of the hallway.

Stroud knew who it was immediately.

'Stroud,' she said.

'Nina,' Stroud replied. 'If that's even your fucking name.'

63

Yet another featureless room, a locked door, a table centred, two chairs, a mirrored window on the right of Stroud that he knew was one-way. He had no idea who was behind it, and he didn't care. Nina sat in front of him, and on the table was a dossier that bore his name.

'You have a file on me, and I don't even know who you are,' he said.

'My name is Angela,' Nina said. 'Angela Denton.'

'And who do you work for?'

'I work for Her Majesty's government.'

'I am aware of that,' Stroud said, 'but which department? Special Branch? MI5? MI6?'

Angela smiled. 'Let's just say that I police the policemen.'

'You're internal security?'

'I deal with the consequences of people not doing the things they agreed to do.'

'Okay. So this was all a stunt?'

She opened the dossier and withdrew a single sheet of paper. She turned it around and slid it towards Stroud.

'You know what this is?' she asked.

'It's the Official Secrets Act.'

She handed him a pen.

'Really?'

'Really.'

Stroud signed it, handed it back.

'So tell me,' he said. 'Tell me what this was all about.'

'Tell me what you know.'

'No,' Stroud said. 'I am worn out with explaining this. I really am. In fact I don't even understand what I'm explaining. I think you owe me this much, considering everything I've been through. And if you have to go and get permission from someone else to tell me, then bring that someone and they can tell me themselves.'

Angela paused, as if internally gauging how much she could say.

'Very simply, it was an attempt by Marcus Haig to find Joshua Lindenauer. Certainly from the viewpoint of what we wanted you to know, this is what this has all been about.'

'I'm sorry. What you *wanted* me to know?'

'That is correct, Mr Stroud.'

'So the little that I do understand is probably bullshit anyway?'

'Let me tell you what I can. We'll go from there, okay?'

'Knock yourself out, Angela Denton.'

'On the face of it, Marcus Haig just wanted to find out if Lindenauer was still alive. As you surmised, he couldn't use official lines. What I can tell you is that Lindenauer knew something about Haig, and Haig couldn't risk it being revealed.'

'I can't call him Lindenauer. He's Raphael. Can we just call him Raphael?'

'Of course we can.'

'So what you're telling me is that Raphael knows something about Haig. Haig doesn't want whatever this is known, but he thinks he's safe because Raphael is dead. But Raphael surfaces again and Haig panics.'

'In the simplest terms, yes, except that Haig knew that Raphael wasn't dead.'

'What?'

'They made an agreement.'

'An agreement?'

'Haig was ... Well, let's just say that Marcus Haig was actively serving a foreign interest, and has been since before 1970. We knew that. He was not aware that we knew. He believed that Raphael was the only one who was privy to his divided loyalty.'

'He was a double agent.'

'In a sense, yes. More accurately, he was an agent provocateur. He did what he could to keep things in a state of imbalance and conflict.'

'Between?'

'I cannot say. What I can say is that there have been a great many incidents of terrorism over the past decade. Primarily manifesting themselves in Europe, but originating in the Middle East.'

'Black September, Baader–Meinhof, all that stuff that Lügner was asking me about.'

'That kind of thing, yes. A great many people have made very strenuous efforts to resolve some of the issues that surround these political differences, and yet there has been no end to the conflict. And it's a generally accepted principle that where conflict continues despite all efforts to resolve it, there is someone or something that wishes for the conflict to continue.'

'So what? Haig was involved in keeping conflicts going in the Middle East?'

'Amongst other things, yes.'

'Why? Why the hell would he do that?'

Angela smiled knowingly. 'For the oldest reason in the world.'

'Money.'

'War is profitable, Mr Stroud, not only to warmongers, arms dealers and the like, but also to governments. And where you have countries that possess vast natural resources, you usually find that the religious and ideological motivations for the conflict are merely the window-dressing. Some of Marcus Haig's loyalties lay with groups that needed a continuing conflict.'

'So what was this agreement between Raphael and Haig?'

'Haig was using information he gathered from his British intelligence work. He passed it on to ... Well, let's just say he passed it on to certain parties that didn't have the same intentions as our government. Raphael found out what he was doing. Haig was cornered. In an effort to gain some leverage over Raphael, Haig had him investigated. He succeeded in finding out who Raphael really was and where he'd come from. He then turned the tables on Raphael, threatening to expose the fact that his father had collaborated with the Nazis. Raphael's family – his mother, his sister, even his adopted brother – would all have been disgraced. It would wind up in the newspapers, the family tried by the court of public opinion. It would have devastated his mother, perhaps even driven her to suicide. Raphael also knew that both his own career and that of his stepbrother, Caleb, would be over. And Caleb was pretty much the only person he could truly trust. Thus Raphael and Haig made an agreement. Haig would not expose Raphael's history, and Raphael would not expose Haig. And the only way Raphael felt he could honour that was by disappearing altogether. Hence his apparent death.'

'So why not stay dead? Why come back?'

'He was never not back,' Angela said. 'He made his agreement with Haig, and then he came to us. We protected him. We used what he knew to subvert some of Haig's subsequent operations. Not all of them, of course, as Haig's paymasters might then suspect that Haig was feeding them intentionally useless information. If that had happened, he would have been of no further use to us. We kept Raphael off the radar, of course. We did everything possible to keep his identity secret, but we knew that it was merely a matter of time before it became obvious that he was still alive. Hendrik Dekker was only one of several names he had during those six years. And so he continued to work for us, for the Dutch, for the French—'

'With Fournier?'

'Yes, with Fournier, and with many others whose activities aligned with our own. Haig didn't know where Raphael had gone, and he didn't go looking for him. If he suspected that Raphael was one of the reasons for the failure of his operations, he never said so. It was a closed chapter. There was never a word between them, and as far as Haig was concerned, that was the end of it. He knew he was taking a risk, of course. If it came to light that he'd known that Raphael was still alive and had covered it up, then he would have been compromised in the eyes of his controllers. However, he knew that the information he possessed about Raphael was sufficient leverage to keep him away.'

'And then?'

'And then the French, the Israelis, various agencies that were involved in trying to bring some sort of stability to the area, began to appreciate that there were other forces at work. An investigation was initiated. It spanned numerous countries, perhaps the largest collaboration of intelligence agencies since the Second World War. Everyone was being looked at. Everyone who'd ever had anything to do with these areas was scrutinised. Information was falling into the wrong hands at an alarming rate, and it was information of the most sensitive nature. Agencies initiated extensive programmes to find the leaks and deal with them. The fact that Raphael ended up having his photograph taken in Istanbul was something we could never have stopped. We anticipated that such issues might arise, not only with Raphael, but with anyone who had worked in the area.

Prevention was not possible in such situations. Only cure, and only after the fact.'

'And this picture of Raphael in Istanbul wound up with Haig.'

Angela paused, then nodded. 'Yes, the picture found its way to Haig.'

'And what? He thought Raphael might be brought in and questioned, and then he himself would be exposed?'

'We don't know what he thought. We'll find out now, of course, and who knows what other things we'll discover in the process. Haig will give us threads. We don't yet know who or what we will find at the end of those threads. The only thing we're sure of is that he was very intent on finding Raphael, presumably to have him removed from the equation altogether. For Haig, it was nothing but risk management. But as I said, he couldn't do it on official lines. To have made it official would have raised suspicion, and that suspicion would inevitably have been directed back towards Haig himself.'

'Which is where I came in.'

'Yes, you did, but we didn't know that until it happened.'

'I'm sorry?'

'To be completely frank, Mr Stroud, we didn't know if Haig would react to the Istanbul picture, and we certainly couldn't have predicted how. It's not the first time we have attempted to provoke a response from him. The photo proved insufficient for him to do anything too drastic, and yet enough of an alarm bell to set wheels in motion. That he contacted you was not something we could have known he would do. Once he did, and once we understood what he was asking of you, we could begin to anticipate and direct how it unfolded.'

Stroud leaned back in the chair. He didn't know what he was feeling, but it wasn't good.

'The picture of Raphael that Fournier had in Istanbul, the

one with Dekker's name on it. You set that up, right? You made sure I saw it.'

'We would have found a way for you to get that name at some point. The way you discovered it was not completely unexpected. It just removed the need for any further manipulation or contrivance.'

'And it was never possible to just lock Haig up somewhere, maybe? Don't they still throw traitors in the Tower?'

'Things are never quite as simple as they seem, Mr Stroud. An individual can be forwarding information to an enemy agency. We may be very aware of where it is going. A source that is trusted by our opposition can sometimes be employed to great advantage. Of course, there are times when a leak becomes too great a liability, and then we have to take them out of the chain. If that happens, we appreciate that whatever prior information may have reached the opposition from that source would then be considered dubious.'

Angela leaned forward. Her expression was serious and intense. If she had even existed in the first place, long gone was the girl who had got drunk with Stroud and followed him to the Netherlands.

'We can suspect without being able to prove. We can investigate, and yet still not find sufficient evidence to act. Sometimes we need to make someone believe that we will prosecute, and for that we need something of significance. What I said initially was true: we wanted you to believe that this was all about Haig finding Raphael. For us, however, it opened up another opportunity.'

'To bring Raphael home,' Stroud said.

Angela smiled. 'You are a quick learner, Mr Stroud.'

'So this whole thing was engineered simply to neutralise Haig and recover Raphael.'

'Not only to neutralise Haig, but to have sufficient evidence of his wrongdoings that he would be forced to make a choice.'

Stroud frowned.

'We needed Haig and Raphael to actually speak to one other. We needed to have it on record that Haig knew Raphael was alive, and had known he was alive all the way back to the original incident in Jordan. We needed him to actually detail the nature of their agreement all those years ago. That is what has facilitated the present result.'

'Raphael is back, and you get to keep Haig, too. You can go on using him to serve his controllers, but he's only giving them what you want.'

'We needed him not only impotent as far as Raphael was concerned, but back on our side with loyalties reaffirmed. We needed to make him think that we could and would prosecute. For that we require a confession. A confession precludes a case being heard in open court. To have used Raphael's testimony would have meant delivering Raphael in person. That was not an option. However, with the conversations that took place between Haig and Raphael now on record, we will use that to secure Haig's confession. He will never be charged, and there will be no prosecution. Unless he makes the very foolish decision to honour his agreements with someone else. That, as far as I can see, will never happen. Haig, whatever he might be, is not a fool. Most importantly, his cooperation will ensure that Raphael's name is never mentioned. We needed Raphael to be dead in 1970, Mr Stroud, and we need him to stay dead.'

'So now he returns to the fold, and Haig can be manoeuvred and manipulated any which way you want, right?'

'Bluntly and inelegantly phrased, but yes. We have them both.'

Stroud sat and looked at the woman he thought he had known.

'You play chess with people's lives, don't you?'

'That's one way of putting it.'

'And sometimes it's necessary to sacrifice a few pawns to save the kings, queens and bishops.'

'I assume so. I don't play chess.'

'You should. You'd be good at it.'

'Raphael knew, as a result of these many and varied investigations, that it was only a matter of time before someone got to him. We needed a catalyst, and it turned out that the catalyst was you. Had we believed you were in real danger, we would have taken steps to pre-empt that. And we couldn't tell you what was really going on, because however hard you might have tried, it would have been impossible not to inadvertently do something to alert Haig. As I said, Marcus Haig is no fool and he has been playing this game for a very long time. So, everything was in hand—'

'Except for Berlin.'

Angela raised her eyebrows.

'You let Lügner, Caleb, whoever he was, beat the crap out of me.'

'He is not one of us. He needed to know that you weren't one of us either. He had to satisfy himself that you weren't trying to find Raphael for some other interested party.'

'But Caleb is playing the same game as you. You are on the same side, right?'

Angela smiled. 'Sometimes. Sometimes not.'

'So ... what? Raphael works for you, and his brother, step-brother, whoever the hell he is, works for someone else?'

'Who they work for is not important, Mr Stroud, except to say that at this juncture we currently share a common interest and our purposes are coordinated.'

'And why did it end now? I never found Raphael. Did you need to stop me before I actually did?'

'It ended now because we had adequate information concerning Haig's activities to take action.'

'And now you want me to stop looking, right?'

'You are looking for a dead man, Mr Stroud. There is no one to find.'

Stroud was quiet for a few moments, then he looked up. 'Who is Detective Inspector Warren?'

Angela smiled. 'He is exactly who he said he was.'

'Marcus said he called my ex-father-in-law and got him to ask this DI Warren to help get me out of France.'

'That is correct. I understand that Donald Montgomery and DI Warren are members of the same golf club.'

'So that wasn't bullshit?'

'No, it wasn't. We were aware that Haig made that call.'

'Because you had his phone bugged.'

'When you work for the government, Mr Stroud, there is almost nothing in your life that isn't known. We just let that happen. It served Haig to get you out of France without a fuss, and it served us because we didn't need to be officially involved in your recovery.'

'And now my ex-father-in-law, pretty much the only man with enough influence over my ex-wife to let me see my daughter again, thinks I was thrown out of France for assaulting a foreign ambassador.'

Angela shook her head. 'I don't believe that is his opinion.'

Stroud frowned. 'You spoke to him?'

'We had to. After you came home, I met with him. I made it clear that what had happened was something that needed to remain completely confidential. I told him that you had been assisting us with a very significant matter of national security, and that without you, there would have been a diplomatic and political incident with truly unthinkable consequences.'

Stroud looked closely at Angela Denton. He saw the faintest smile on her lips. She hadn't needed to do that. All that would have been required of her was Montgomery's agreement to keep his mouth shut.

'You did that for me?' he asked.

'I never do anything unless I consider it is in the best interests of those who maintain their allegiance with us.' She smiled – it was businesslike, matter-of-fact. He knew that she'd fooled him completely.

He sighed heavily. 'Crazy, crazy fucking business.'

'Are there any further questions, Mr Stroud?'

'Is Haig in jail?' Stroud asked.

'He is being detained at Her Majesty's pleasure while we undertake the required investigation.'

'Charged with?'

'Officially, there will be no charges. As I said, he will never appear in open court. Nothing will ever be recorded in the public domain.'

'But just amongst us girls, eh? What do you have him for?'

Angela didn't reply.

'Okay, so answer me this, Miss Denton. You showed up as a copy-editor from the City desk. Haig asked you to help me. Later on, I asked about you and I was told that you didn't exist, had never existed and no one knew where you were. Someone said they knew *of* you, even mentioned the cast on your wrist, but there was no record of your employment. As you yourself said, Marcus isn't stupid. Wouldn't he have made sure that you were actually who you said you were before he let you go traipsing off into Europe with me?'

'Let us just say that Marcus Haig was not the only person within that organisation who was also in our employ—'

'Carole?' Haig asked. 'Is Carole one of yours? She knew you were government. Is she on your payroll?'

Angela didn't register Stroud's questions. 'Haig asked for someone who could assist you, and someone was sent. He was perhaps too concerned with the overall picture to look at minor details. He was told that I was available, that I was sufficiently competent, and that was that.'

'But then you fell through a window and had to come home.'

'That was unfortunate for us both. I had to come back, and you were left alone. Had you not been alone, the incident at Tegel would perhaps not have played out as it did.'

Stroud was silent for a few seconds. His mind struggled to navigate the convoluted chain of events. He tried to read something in Angela's eyes, something in her body language. There was nothing. Just nothing at all.

'What about Daphne?'

'The French girl? What about her?'

'Was that a set-up too?'

Angela laughed drily. 'We may possess an ability to direct certain events as they take place, but as for predicting the future…'

'She's not French intelligence or something, is she?'

'She is a Parisian photographer, Mr Stroud, and that, as far as I know, is all she is.'

Stroud closed his eyes for a moment. It was as if he was trying to let go of something that didn't want to leave.

Eventually he said, 'What's it like, Miss Denton?'

'What's what like, Mr Stroud?'

'Living like this. Wearing different faces, having different names, never knowing who's really working for whom and what their motives are. How does anyone live like that? I mean, is it even a life?'

Once again there was no direct response from Angela.

'Is there anything else, Mr Stroud?'

'Just so I am completely clear on this, Vincent Raphael *is* alive?'

'Correct.'

'So what name is he using now?'

'I cannot tell you.'

'What country is he in?'

Angela shook her head.

'Anything?' Stroud asked.

'I am sorry,' she said. 'I can't give you anything … aside from this.' She took an envelope from the dossier and put it on the table.

'What's that?'

'You were promised a certain sum of money if you proved that Raphael was dead.'

Stroud couldn't hide his surprise.

'In case anyone ever asks, which I very much doubt they will, you have proved beyond all doubt that Vincent Raphael was killed in an explosion in Jordan in September 1970.'

'I have?'

'Yes, Mr Stroud, you have.'

Stroud looked at the envelope. He picked it up and put it into his jacket pocket.

'I am taking this because you used me,' he said. 'On principle, I shouldn't, but I feel I have earned it.'

Angela rose from the chair. Stroud followed suit.

'Just on a personal note,' she said, 'I think you did a remarkable job. You have shown tremendous determination and initiative. If you were ever to consider a career in intelligence, it might be something you'd be well suited to.'

Stroud smiled. 'Thanks for the offer, but I have something entirely different in mind.'

She extended her hand.

'Goodbye, Mr Stroud.'

'Goodbye, Miss Denton. It was a pleasure not knowing you.'

64

Stroud stayed in England for a little more than two weeks. He tried his best to find out what was happening with Haig, but there was no source to whom he could appeal. Cathy had been told the irreducible minimum. Haig was simply 'helping the authorities with their enquiries'. He was housed in a suite of rooms at a country estate in Berkshire. She visited, she took the kids, and he went on assuring her that it would all be over soon and things would be back to normal.

Stroud knew that the truth he'd been told was the truth they wanted him to have. If there was one thing he'd learned, it was that much of his life had been spent in the company of liars. Maybe Haig would cooperate. Maybe he wouldn't. It was a game in which Stroud no longer wished to participate.

Finally, he'd had enough. He let it go – Haig, Raphael, Angela Denton, all of it. He wanted no more of it. He knew it would serve no purpose to go on looking for Raphael. Raphael was a ghost, just as he'd always been.

Ten days after his meeting with Angela Denton, Stroud telephoned Cathy Haig. She told him that Julia had called three days earlier. She'd left a number, wanted Stroud to call her.

'I would have contacted you earlier, but I didn't know how to,' Cathy said. 'I think Julia has been trying to find you too. You don't make it easy, Stroud.'

His heart thudding, pulse racing, desperate to get off the phone and call his ex-wife, Stroud said, 'I just wanted to disappear for a little while, Cathy. Things have been tough. I know they're really tough for you too—'

'Call Julia, okay? We'll be fine. You take care, Stroud.'

She hung up. It was self-defence. Stroud could hear the grief and despair in her voice.

Seated on the edge of the bed in his hotel room, he looked at the number he'd scribbled on the notepad. His hand was shaking.

He lifted the receiver and dialled it. It rang three times, and then a voice said, 'Hello?'

Stroud's heart stopped.

'Hello? Who's that?' the voice asked.

'Eva?'

A moment's silence, then, 'Yes, who's this?'

Stroud couldn't speak. His eyes stung with tears and he closed them.

'Dad?'

He gasped suddenly, started to say something, anything, but then Julia was on the line.

'Stroud? Is that you?'

'J-Julia?'

'You got my message.'

'I did.'

'Good. My father spoke to me. You and I have to talk. Eva wants to see you, but there are going to be conditions and agreements, okay?'

'Okay. Okay. Yes, of course. Agreements, yes.'

'Are you drunk, Stroud?'

'No, Julia. Far from it. Just surprised, shocked. I never expected—'

'Well don't go expecting too much, all right? Eva is doing

really well at school, and I am not having you drive a train through her life. Do you understand?'

'Yes, absolutely. I wouldn't dream of it.'

She was quiet for a moment, and then she said, 'Are you all right?'

Stroud laughed suddenly, reflexively. 'Yes, I'm good, Julia. And you?'

'It doesn't matter. This isn't about us. You have my number. Let's wait a few weeks for things to settle down. Eva has some exams at school, and I want her to focus on those. After that, we can speak, discuss things, see what we can work out.'

'Yes. Thank you, Julia. Thank you for this.'

'I don't know how it came about, Stroud, and I don't know that I want to know. My father never liked you. I think that comes as no surprise. But he was the one who suggested this. It's not a custody thing. It's not a matter for lawyers and courts and the like. This is between me and you, okay? We're the ones who will talk about it and work out how you might spend some time with your daughter.'

'And Eva? What does she want? Does she want to see me?'

'Believe me, if there had been any hope of finding you before now, she'd have probably run away from home. Let's just say that this has been a bone of contention between me and her for a very long time. But now it's over. I'm sure we can work something out, and as long as you keep your side of whatever arrangement we make, I see no reason why you can't spend some time with her on a regular basis.'

'Okay,' Stroud said, disbelieving, almost stunned, wondering even as he hung up the receiver if he would suddenly wake and learn that he'd been subjected to the cruellest dream imaginable. But it was no dream. The paper was still in his hand, with it the certainty that before too long he would actually be able to speak to Eva.

He stood up and walked to the window. He could still hear her voice in his head.

Dad?

He started to cry, and it was some considerable time before he stopped.

65

Summer would run all the way to Christmas. That was how it felt. The air was redolent with the scent of flowers, and from where he sat, Stroud could see the artists setting up their easels along the banks of the river. He'd been here over a month, yet each day brought a reminder of how much there was to love about this city.

The money had given him a new lease of life. He had rented an apartment close to Daphne's studio, and while she maintained the small flat above it, the pair of them sometimes staying over as if to relive the memory of their first night together, she was now spending most of her time at Stroud's place.

He was not working; he didn't need to work for some time, and would not consider it. He and Daphne seemed to have settled easily into a routine. It was as if they had been together for years.

He had spoken to Eva three times before he left England. At first she'd seemed unsure, withdrawn, so unlike the girl he'd imagined her to be. He'd said little, merely asked about her interests, about school, about anything that seemed relevant. Towards the end of their second conversation, she became more willing to share her thoughts and feelings. By the third, she had found the confidence and self-assurance to ask him questions in return.

He told her everything he could. He only held back those things he felt should be communicated face to face, or never at all. He told her about his work, his time with her mother. He explained that if anyone was truly responsible for the failure of the marriage, it had been him.

In response to that, she was quiet, and then she said, 'I don't believe that's possible.'

'How so?' he asked.

'Because something like a marriage succeeds or fails because of both people. It can't always be just one person's fault, can it? My best friend's mum and dad got divorced. She cheated on him. You can say it was all her fault, but maybe there was something that happened that made her feel she needed to be with someone else to get what she wanted out of a relationship. There are always two sides to everything, aren't there?'

'Yes,' Stroud said. 'There are always two sides.'

'Grandad has said some pretty horrible stuff about you in the past. I didn't pay much attention, to be honest. I kind of knew he was just being mean.'

It was then that he realised that the resentment and ill-feeling he'd anticipated was just not there.

'For a long time I didn't understand what had happened,' she said. 'I just knew you were there, and then you were gone. I thought I must have done something to make you go away.'

'No,' Stroud said. 'It was nothing to do with you. Quite the contrary, Eva. Your mum and I just didn't work together, that was all. It was a great marriage, though, if only because you came out of it.'

'You don't need to say that, Dad. I don't feel guilty about it.'

'I feel guilty,' Stroud said. 'And I'm sorry that I've missed so many years of your life.'

'Not so many years,' Eva said, 'and to be honest, they were pretty boring anyway.'

Stroud laughed. He felt emotions he'd believed would be unknown forever.

He told her that he was really looking forward to seeing her.

'Mum says that you're living in Paris.'

'I am, yes. At least for the meantime. But it's only a couple of hours away, and I'll be in London for work on a regular basis. Finding time to see you won't be a problem.'

'Mum says I need to get through my exams first, though. Sometimes she's such a bloody pain.'

'Take care, Eva. Do well in your exams.'

'Thanks, Dad. I'll do my best.'

Stroud knew that he and Julia would never be close. Not in the way they'd once been. He didn't see them sharing anything other than friendly, yet somehow distant exchanges. Neither one of them was the person they had once been, and neither one of them wished to be that person again.

It didn't matter. Knowing that he would forever be the kind of man to shun routine and defy expectation, he could nevertheless see himself settling in Paris for the foreseeable future. Daphne was so different from anyone else he'd known – less complex, seeming to expect nothing of him except what was already there – and he still didn't understand how fortune or chance had brought them together. He didn't question it. He didn't need an answer.

He glanced at his watch. She was due any moment. He caught the waiter's attention, ordered another *café allongé*, and lit a cigarette.

As he turned back, he saw her walking towards him from the other side of the bridge. He raised his hand and waved. She waved back.

The moment itself was so simple and yet so very special. Here he had found something for which he had been looking for a long time, and yet in some strange way, he'd not even been aware that it was missing.

The waiter appeared to his left.

'*Monsieur?*' he said. He set the coffee down on the table.

'*Merci,*' Stroud replied.

'*Monsieur* ... telephone.'

Stroud looked at him. '*Pardon?*'

'Inside,' the waiter said. 'For you, *monsieur*. There is a tele-phone inside.'

'For me?'

'Come,' the waiter said.

Stroud waited for Daphne to reach him. He kissed her, told her that there was a phone call for him. He'd be back in just a moment.

'Here?' she asked.

'I think it's a mistake,' he said. 'This coffee's for you. I'll just be a minute.'

He followed the waiter into the building. There was a phone at the far end of the bar, the receiver off the hook. He picked it up.

'Hello?' he said. 'I think perhaps there's been a mistake ...'

The voice at the end was one he would never forget.

'No mistake, my friend,' Raphael said. 'I'm going to give you an address. Make excuses. Get a taxi and come alone. Forget everything you've been told. Things are moving very fast, and I need your help ...'

Credits

R.J. Ellory and Orion Fiction would like to thank everyone at Orion who worked on the publication of *Proof of Life* in the UK.

Editorial
Emad Akhtar
Tom Witcomb
Celia Killen

Copy editor
Jane Selley

Proof reader
Clare Wallis

Contracts
Anne Goddard
Paul Bulos
Jake Alderson

Design
Debbie Holmes
Joanna Ridley
Nick May

Editorial Management
Charlie Panayiotou
Jane Hughes
Alice Davis

Finance
Jasdip Nandra
Afeera Ahmed
Elizabeth Beaumont
Sue Baker

Audio
Paul Stark
Amber Bates

Production
Ruth Sharvell

Marketing
Lucy Cameron

Publicity
Patricia Deveer

Sales
Jen Wilson
Esther Waters
Victoria Laws
Rachael Hum
Ellie Kyrke-Smith
Frances Doyle
Georgina Cutler

Rights
Susan Howe
Krystyna Kujawinska
Jessica Purdue
Richard King
Louise Henderson

Operations
Jo Jacobs
Sharon Willis
Lisa Pryde
Lucy Brem